BOOKS BY MILDRED D. TAYLOR

ROLL OF THUNDER, HEAR MY CRY

MILDRED D. TAYLOR

FRONTISPIECE BY JERRY PINKNEY

PUFFIN BOOKS

PUFFIN BOOKS

Published by Penguin Group

Penguin Young Readers Group,

345 Hudson Street, New York, New York 10014, U.S.A.

Penguin Books Ltd, 80 Strand, London WC2R ORL, England

Penguin Books Australia Ltd, 250 Camberwell Road,

Camberwell, Victoria 3124, Australia

Penguin Books Canada Ltd, 10 Alcorn Avenue, Toronto, Ontario, Canada M4V 3B2

Penguin Books (N.Z.) Ltd, 182-190 Wairau Road, Auckland 10, New Zealand

First published in the United States of America by Dial Books, 1976
Published by Puffin Books, 1991
This Puffin Modern Classics edition published by Puffin Books,
a division of Penguin Young Readers Group, 2004

40 39

Library of Congress Catalog Card Number: 91-53031

This edition ISBN 0-14-240112-9

Printed in the United States of America

To the memory of my beloved father,
who lived many adventures of the boy Stacey
and who was in essence the man David

Author's Note

My father was a master storyteller. He could tell a fine old story that made me hold my sides with rolling laughter and sent happy tears down my cheeks, or a story of stark reality that made me shiver and be grateful for my own warm, secure surroundings. He could tell stories of beauty and grace, stories of gentle dreams, and paint them as vividly as any picture with splashes of character and dialogue. His memory detailed every event of ten or forty years or more before, just as if it had happened yesterday.

By the fireside in our northern home or in the South where I was born, I learned a history not then written in books but one passed from generation to generation on the steps of moonlit porches and beside dying fires in one-room houses, a history of great-grandparents and of slavery and of the days following slavery; of those who lived still not free, yet who would not let their spirits be enslaved. From my father the storyteller I learned to respect the past, to respect my own heritage and myself. From my father the man I learned even more, for he was endowed with a special grace that made him tower above other men. He was warm and steadfast, a man whose principles would not bend, and he had within him a rare strength that sustained not only my sister and me and all the family, but all those who sought his advice and leaned upon his wisdom.

He was a complex person, yet he taught me many simple things, things important for a child to know: how to ride a horse and how to skate; how to blow soap bubbles and how to tie a kite knot that met the challenge of the March winds; how to bathe a huge faithful mongrel dog named Tiny. In time, he taught me the complex things too. He taught me of myself, of life. He taught me of hopes and dreams. And he taught me the love of words. Without his teachings, without his words, my words would not have been.

My father died last week. The stories as only he could tell them died with him. But his voice of joy and laughter, his enduring strength, his principles and constant wisdom remain, a part of all those who knew and loved him well. They remain also within the pages of this book, its guiding spirit and total power.

Mildred D. Taylor
April 1976

ROLL OF THUNDER, HEAR MY CRY

1

"Little Man, would you come on? You keep it up and you're gonna make us late."

My youngest brother paid no attention to me. Grasping more firmly his newspaper-wrapped notebook and his tin-can lunch of cornbread and oil sausages, he continued to concentrate on the dusty road. He lagged several feet behind my other brothers, Stacey and Christopher-John, and me, attempting to keep the rusty Mississippi dust from swelling with each step and drifting back upon his shiny black shoes and the cuffs of his corduroy pants by lifting each foot high before setting it gently down again. Always meticulously neat, six-year-old Little Man never allowed dirt or tears or stains to mar anything he owned. Today was no exception.

"You keep it up and make us late for school, Mama's gonna wear you out," I threatened, pulling with exasperation at the high collar of the Sunday dress Mama had made me wear for the first day of school—as if that event were something special. It seemed to me that showing up at school at all on a bright August-like October morning made for running the cool forest trails and wading barefoot in the forest pond was concession enough; Sunday clothing was asking too much. Christopher-John and Stacey were not too pleased about the clothing or school either. Only Little Man, just beginning his school career, found the prospects of both intriguing.

"Y'all go ahead and get dirty if y'all wanna," he replied without even looking up from his studied steps. "Me, I'm gonna stay clean."

"I betcha Mama's gonna 'clean' you, you keep it up," I grumbled.

"Ah, Cassie, leave him be," Stacey admonished, frowning and kicking testily at the road.

"I ain't said nothing but—"

Stacey cut me a wicked look and I grew silent. His disposition had been irritatingly sour lately. If I hadn't known the cause of it, I could have forgotten very easily that he was, at twelve, bigger than I, and that I had promised Mama to arrive at school looking clean and ladylike. "Shoot," I mumbled finally, unable to restrain myself from further comment, "it ain't my fault you gotta be in Mama's class this year."

Stacey's frown deepened and he jammed his fists into his pockets, but said nothing.

Christopher-John, walking between Stacey and me, glanced uneasily at both of us but did not interfere. A short, round boy of seven, he took little interest in troublesome things, preferring to remain on good terms with everyone. Yet he was always sensitive to others and now, shifting the handle of his lunch can from his right hand to his right wrist and his smudged notebook from his left hand to his left armpit, he stuffed his free hands into his pockets and attempted to make his face as moody as Stacey's and as cranky as mine. But after a few moments he seemed to forget that he was supposed to be grouchy and began whistling cheerfully. There was little that could make Christopher-John unhappy for very long, not even the thought of school.

I tugged again at my collar and dragged my feet in the dust, allowing it to sift back onto my socks and shoes like gritty red snow. I hated the dress. And the shoes. There was little I could do in a dress, and as for shoes, they imprisoned freedom-loving feet accustomed to the feel of the warm earth.

"Cassie, stop that," Stacey snapped as the dust billowed in swirling clouds around my feet. I looked up sharply, ready to protest. Christopher-John's whistling increased to a raucous, nervous shrill, and grudgingly I let the matter drop and trudged along in moody silence, my brothers growing as pensively quiet as I.

Before us the narrow, sun-splotched road wound like a lazy red serpent dividing the high forest bank of quiet, old trees on the left from the cotton field, forested by giant green-and purple stalks, on the right. A barbed-wire fence ran the length of the deep field, stretching eastward for over a quarter of a mile until it met the sloping green pasture that signaled the end of our family's four hundred acres. An ancient oak tree on the slope, visible even now, was the official dividing mark between Logan land and the beginning of a dense forest. Beyond the protective fencing of the forest, vast farming fields, worked by a multitude of share-cropping families, covered two thirds of a ten-square-mile plantation. That was Harlan Granger land.

Once our land had been Granger land too, but the Grangers had sold it during Reconstruction to a Yankee for tax money. In 1887, when the land was up for sell again, Grandpa had bought two hundred acres of it, and in 1918, after the first two hundred acres had been paid off, he had bought another two hundred. It was good rich land, much of it still virgin forest, and there was no debt on half of it. But there was a mortgage on the two hundred acres bought in 1918 and there were taxes on the full four hundred, and for the past three years there had not been enough money from the cotton to pay both and live on too.

That was why Papa had gone to work on the railroad.

In 1930 the price of cotton dropped. And so, in the spring of 1931, Papa set out looking for work, going as far north as Memphis and as far south as the Delta country. He had gone west too, into Louisiana. It was there he found work laying track for the railroad. He worked the remainder of the year away from us, not returning until the deep winter when the ground was cold and barren. The following spring after the planting was finished, he did the same. Now it was 1933, and Papa was again in Louisiana laying track.

I asked him once why he had to go away, why the land was so important. He took my hand and said in his quiet way: "Look out there, Cassie girl. All that belongs to you. You ain't never had to live on nobody's place but your own and long as I live and the family survives, you'll never have to. That's important. You may not understand that now, but one day you will. Then you'll see."

I looked at Papa strangely when he said that, for I knew that all the land did not belong to me. Some of it belonged to Stacey, Christopher-John, and Little Man, not to mention the part that belonged to Big Ma, Mama, and Uncle Hammer, Papa's older brother who lived in Chicago. But Papa never divided the land in his mind; it was simply Logan land. For it he would work the long, hot summer pounding steel; Mama would teach and run the farm; Big Ma, in her sixties, would work like a woman of twenty in the fields and keep the house; and the boys and I would wear threadbare clothing washed to dishwater color; but always, the taxes and the mortgage would be paid. Papa said that one day I would understand.

I wondered.

When the fields ended and the Granger forest fanned both sides of the road with long overhanging branches, a tall, emaciated-looking boy popped suddenly from a forest trail and swung a thin arm around Stacey. It was T.J. Avery. His younger brother Claude emerged a moment later, smiling weakly as if it pained him to do so. Neither boy had on shoes, and their Sunday clothing, patched and worn, hung loosely upon their frail frames. The Avery family share-cropped on Granger land.

"Well," said T.J., jauntily swinging into step with Stacey, "here we go again startin' another school year."

"Yeah," sighed Stacey.

"Ah, man, don't look so down," T.J. said cheerfully. "Your mama's really one great teacher. I should know." He certainly should. He had failed Mama's class last year and was now returning for a second try.

"Shoot! You can say that," exclaimed Stacey. "You don't have to spend all day in a classroom with your mama."

"Look on the bright side," said T.J. "Jus' think of the advantage you've got. You'll be learnin' all sorts of stuff 'fore the rest of us. . . ." He smiled slyly. "Like what's on all them tests."

Stacey thrust T.J.'s arm from his shoulders. "If that's what you think, you don't know Mama."

"Ain't no need gettin' mad," T.J. replied undaunted.

· 8 ·

"Jus' an idea." He was quiet for a moment, then announced, "I betcha I could give y'all an earful 'bout that burnin' last night."

"Burning? What burning?" asked Stacey.

"Man, don't y'all know nothin'? The Berrys' burnin'. I thought y'all's grandmother went over there last night to see 'bout 'em."

Of course we knew that Big Ma had gone to a sick house last night. She was good at medicines and people often called her instead of a doctor when they were sick. But we didn't know anything about any burnings, and I certainly didn't know anything about any Berrys either.

"What Berrys he talking 'bout, Stacey?" I asked. "I don't know no Berrys."

"They live way over on the other side of Smellings Creek. They come up to church sometimes," said Stacey absently. Then he turned back to T.J. "Mr. Lanier come by real late and got Big Ma. Said Mr. Berry was low sick and needed her to help nurse him, but he ain't said nothing 'bout no burning."

"He's low sick all right—'cause he got burnt near to death. Him and his two nephews. And you know who done it?"

"Who?" Stacey and I asked together.

"Well, since y'all don't seem to know nothin'," said T.J., in his usual sickening way of nursing a tidbit of information to death, "maybe I ought not tell y'all. It might hurt y'all's little ears."

"Ah, boy," I said, "don't start that mess again." I didn't like T.J. very much and his stalling around didn't help.

"Come on, T.J.," said Stacey, "out with it."

"Well . . ." T.J. murmured, then grew silent as if considering whether or not he should talk.

We reached the first of two crossroads and turned north; another mile and we would approach the second crossroads and turn east again.

Finally T.J. said, "Okay. See, them Berrys' burnin' wasn't no accident. Some white men took a match to 'em."

"Y-you mean just lit 'em up like a piece of wood?" stammered Christopher-John, his eyes growing big with disbelief.

"But why?" asked Stacey.

T.J. shrugged. "Don't know why. Jus' know they done it, that's all."

"How you know?" I questioned suspiciously.

He smiled smugly. " 'Cause your mama come down on her way to school and talked to my mama 'bout it."

"She did?"

"Yeah, and you should've seen the way she look when she come outa that house."

"How'd she look?" inquired Little Man, interested enough to glance up from the road for the first time.

T.J. looked around grimly and whispered, "Like . . . death." He waited a moment for his words to be appropriately shocking, but the effect was spoiled by Little Man, who asked lightly, "What does death look like?"

T.J. turned in annoyance. "Don't he know nothin'?"

"Well, what does it look like?" Little Man demanded to know. He didn't like T.J. either.

"Like my grandfather looked jus' 'fore they buried him," T.J. described all-knowingly.

"Oh," replied Little Man, losing interest and concentrating on the road again.

"I tell ya, Stacey, man," said T.J. morosely, shaking his head, "sometimes I jus' don't know 'bout that family of yours."

Stacey pulled back, considering whether or not T.J.'s words were offensive, but T.J. immediately erased the question by continuing amiably. "Don't get me wrong, Stacey. They some real swell kids, but that Cassie 'bout got me whipped this mornin'."

"Good!" I said.

"Now how'd she do that?" Stacey laughed.

"You wouldn't be laughin' if it'd've happened to you. She up and told your mama 'bout me goin' up to that Wallace store dancin' room and Miz Logan told Mama." He eyed me disdainfully then went on. "But don't worry, I got out of it though. When Mama asked me 'bout it, I jus' said ole Claude was always sneakin' up there to get some of that free candy Mr. Kaleb give out sometimes and I had to go and get him 'cause I knowed good and well she didn't want us up there. Boy, did he get it!" T.J. laughed. "Mama 'bout wore him out."

I stared at quiet Claude. "You let him do that?" I exclaimed. But Claude only smiled in that sickly way of his and I knew that he had. He was more afraid of T.J. than of his mother.

Again Little Man glanced up and I could see his dislike for T.J. growing. Friendly Christopher-John glared at T.J., and putting his short arm around Claude's shoulder said, "Come on, Claude, let's go on ahead." Then he and Claude hurried up the road, away from T.J.

Stacey, who generally overlooked T.J.'s underhanded stunts, shook his head. "That was dirty."

"Well, what'd ya expect me to do? I couldn't let her think I was goin' up there 'cause I like to, could I? She'd've killed me!"

"And good riddance," I thought, promising myself that if he ever pulled anything like that on me, I'd knock his block off.

We were nearing the second crossroads, where deep gullies lined both sides of the road and the dense forest crept to the very edges of high, jagged, clay-walled banks. Suddenly, Stacey turned. "Quick!" he cried. "Off the road!" Without another word, all of us but Little Man scrambled up the steep right bank into the forest.

"Get up here, Man," Stacey ordered, but Little Man only gazed at the ragged red bank sparsely covered with scraggly brown briars and kept on walking. "Come on, do like I say."

"But I'll get my clothes dirty!" protested Little Man.

"You're gonna get them a whole lot dirtier you stay down there. Look!"

Little Man turned around and watched saucer-eyed as a bus bore down on him spewing clouds of red dust like a huge yellow dragon breathing fire. Little Man headed toward the bank, but it was too steep. He ran frantically along the road looking for a foothold and, finding one, hopped onto the bank, but not before the bus had sped past enveloping him in a scarlet haze while laughing white faces pressed against the bus windows.

Little Man shook a threatening fist into the thick air, then looked dismally down at himself.

"Well, ole Little Man done got his Sunday clothes dirty," T.J. laughed as we jumped down from the bank. Angry tears welled in Little Man's eyes but he quickly brushed them away before T.J. could see them.

"Ah, shut up, T.J.," Stacey snapped.

"Yeah, shut up, T.J.," I echoed.

"Come on, Man," Stacey said, "and next time do like I tell ya."

Little Man hopped down from the bank. "How's come they did that, Stacey, huh?" he asked, dusting himself off. "How's come they didn't even stop for us?"

"'Cause they like to see us run and it ain't our bus," Stacey said, balling his fists and jamming them tightly into his pockets.

"Well, where's our bus?" demanded Little Man.

"We ain't got one."

"Well, why not?"

"Ask Mama," Stacey replied as a towheaded boy, bare-footed and pale, came running down a forest path toward us. The boy quickly caught up and fell in stride with Stacey and T.J.

"Hey, Stacey," he said shyly.

"Hey, Jeremy," Stacey said.

There was an awkward silence.

"Y'all jus' startin' school today?"

"Yeah," replied Stacey.

"I wishin' ours was jus' startin'," sighed Jeremy. "Ours been goin' since the end of August." Jeremy's eyes were a whitewashed blue and they seemed to weep when he spoke.

"Yeah," said Stacey again.

Jeremy kicked the dust briskly and looked toward the north. He was a strange boy. Ever since I had begun school, he had walked with us as far as the crossroads in the morning, and met us there in the afternoon. He was often ridiculed by the other children at his school and had shown up more than once with wide red welts on his arms which Lillian Jean, his older sister, had revealed with satisfaction were the result of his associating with us. Still, Jeremy continued to meet us.

When we reached the crossroads, three more children, a girl of twelve or thirteen and two boys, all looking very much like Jeremy, rushed past. The girl was Lillian Jean.

"Jeremy, come on," she said without a backward glance, and Jeremy, smiling sheepishly, waved a timid good-bye and slowly followed her.

We stood in the crossing gazing after them. Jeremy looked back once but then Lillian Jean yelled shrilly at him and he did not look back again. They were headed for the Jefferson Davis County School, a long white wooden building looming in the distance. Behind the building was a wide sports field around which were scattered rows of tiered gray-looking benches. In front of it were two yellow buses, our own tormentor and one that brought students from the other direction, and loitering students awaiting the knell of the morning bell. In the very center of the expansive front lawn, waving red, white, and blue with the emblem of the Confederacy emblazoned in its upper left-hand corner, was the Mississippi flag. Directly below it was the American flag. As Jeremy and his sister and brothers hurried toward those transposed flags, we turned eastward toward our own school.

The Great Faith Elementary and Secondary School, one of the largest black schools in the county, was a dismal end to an hour's journey. Consisting of four weather-beaten wooden houses on stilts of brick, 320 students, seven teachers, a principal, a caretaker, and the caretaker's cow, which kept the wide crabgrass lawn sufficiently clipped in spring and summer, the school was located near three plantations, the largest and closest by far being the Granger plantation. Most of the students were from families that sharecropped on Granger land, and the others mainly from Montier and Harrison plantation families. Because the students were needed in the fields from early spring when the cotton was planted until after most of the cotton had been picked in the fall, the school adjusted its terms accordingly, beginning in October and dismissing in March. But even so, after today a number of the older students would not be seen again for a month or two, not until the last puff of cotton had been gleaned from the fields, and eventually most would drop out of school altogether. Because of this the classes in the higher grades grew smaller with each passing year.

The class buildings, with their backs practically against the forest wall, formed a semicircle facing a small one-room church at the opposite edge of the compound. It was to this church that many of the school's students and their parents belonged. As we arrived, the enormous iron bell in the church belfry was ringing vigorously, warning the milling students that only five minutes of freedom remained.

Little Man immediately pushed his way across the lawn to the well. Stacey and T.J., ignoring the rest of us now that they were on the school grounds, wandered off to be with the other seventh-grade boys, and Christopher-John and Claude rushed to reunite with their classmates of last year. Left alone, I dragged slowly to the building that held the first four grades and sat on the bottom step. Plopping my pencils and notebook into the dirt, I propped my elbows on my knees and rested my chin in the palms of my hands.

"Hey, Cassie," said Mary Lou Wellever, the principal's daughter, as she flounced by in a new yellow dress.

"Hey, yourself," I said, scowling so ferociously that she kept on walking. I stared after her a moment noting that she *would* have on a new dress. Certainly no one else did. Patches on faded pants and dresses abounded on boys and girls come so recently from the heat of the cotton fields. Girls stood awkwardly, afraid to sit, and boys pulled restlessly at starched, high-buttoned collars. Those students fortunate enough to have shoes hopped from one pinched foot to the other. Tonight the Sunday clothes would be wrapped in newspaper and hung for Sunday and the shoes would be packed away to be brought out again only when the weather turned so cold that bare feet could no longer traverse the frozen roads; but for today we all suffered.

On the far side of the lawn I spied Moe Turner speeding toward the seventh-grade-class building, and wondered at his energy. Moe was one of Stacey's friends. He lived on the Montier plantation, a three-and-a-half-hour walk from the school. Because of the distance, many children from the Montier plantation did not come to Great Faith after they had finished the four-year school near Smellings Creek. But there were some girls and boys like Moe who made the trek daily, leaving their homes while the sky was black and not returning until all was blackness again. I for one was certainly glad that I didn't live that far away. I don't think my feet would have wanted that badly for me to be educated.

The chiming of the second bell began. I stood up dusting my bottom as the first, second, third, and fourth graders crowded up the stairs into the hallway. Little Man flashed proudly past, his face and hands clean and his black shoes shining again. I glanced down at my own shoes powdered red and, raising my right foot, rubbed it against the back of my left leg, then reversed the procedure. As the last gong of the bell reverberated across the compound, I swooped up my pencils and notebook and ran inside.

A hallway extended from the front to the back door of the building. On either side of the hallway were two doorways, both leading into the same large room which was divided into two classrooms by a heavy canvas curtain. The second and third grades were on the left, the first and fourth grades on the right. I hurried to the rear of the building, turned to the right, and slid into a third-row bench occupied by Gracey Pearson and Alma Scott.

"You can't sit here," objected Gracey. "I'm saving it for Mary Lou."

I glanced back at Mary Lou Wellever depositing her lunch pail on a shelf in the back of the room and said, "Not any more you ain't."

Miss Daisy Crocker, yellow and buckeyed, glared down at me from the middle of the room with a look that said, "Sooooooo, it's you, Cassie Logan." Then she pursed her lips and drew the curtain along the rusted iron rod and tucked it into a wide loop in the back wall. With the curtain drawn back, the first graders gazed quizzically at us. Little Man sat by a window, his hands folded, patiently waiting for Miss Crocker to speak.

Mary Lou nudged me. "That's my seat, Cassie Logan."

"Mary Lou Wellever," Miss Crocker called primly, "have a seat."

"Yes, ma'am," said Mary Lou, eyeing me with a look of pure hate before turning away.

Miss Crocker walked stiffly to her desk, which was set on a tiny platform and piled high with bulky objects covered by a tarpaulin. She rapped the desk with a ruler, although the room was perfectly still, and said, "Welcome, children, to Great Faith Elementary School." Turning slightly so that she stared squarely at the left side of the room, she continued, "To all of you fourth graders, it's good to have you in my class. I'll be expecting many good and wonderful things from you." Then addressing the right side of the room, she said, "And to all our little first grade friends only today starting on the road to knowledge and education, may your tiny feet find the pathways of learning steady and forever before you."

Already bored, I stretched my right arm on the desk and rested my head in my upraised hand.

Miss Crocker smiled mechanically, then rapped on her desk again. "Now, little ones," she said, still talking to the first grade, "your teacher, Miss Davis, has been held up in

Jackson for a few days so I'll have the pleasure of sprinkling your little minds with the first rays of knowledge." She beamed down upon them as if she expected to be applauded for this bit of news, then with a swoop of her large eyes to include the fourth graders, she went on.

"Now since there's only one of me, we shall have to sacrifice for the next few days. We shall work, work, work, but we shall have to work like little Christian boys and girls and share, share, share. Now are we willing to do that?"

"YES'M, MIZ CROCKER," the children chorused.

But I remained silent. I never did approve of group responses. Adjusting my head in my hand, I sighed heavily, my mind on the burning of the Berrys.

"Cassie Logan?"

I looked up, startled.

"Cassie Logan!"

"Yes, ma'am?" I jumped up quickly to face Miss Crocker.

"Aren't you willing to work and share?"

"Yes'm."

"Then say so!"

"Yes'm," I murmured, sliding back into my seat as Mary Lou, Gracey, and Alma giggled. Here it was only five minutes into the new school year and already I was in trouble.

By ten o'clock, Miss Crocker had rearranged our seating and written our names on her seating chart. I was still sitting beside Gracey and Alma but we had been moved from the third to the first row in front of a small potbellied stove. Although being eyeball to eyeball with Miss Crocker was nothing to look forward to, the prospect of being warm once the cold weather set in was nothing to be sneezed at either, so I resolved to make the best of my rather dubious position.

Now Miss Crocker made a startling announcement: This year we would all have books.

Everyone gasped, for most of the students had never handled a book at all besides the family Bible. I admit that even I was somewhat excited. Although Mama had several books, I had never had one of my very own.

"Now we're very fortunate to get these readers," Miss Crocker explained while we eagerly awaited the unveiling. "The county superintendent of schools himself brought these books down here for our use and we must take extra-good care of them." She moved toward her desk. "So let's all promise that we'll take the best care possible of these new books." She stared down, expecting our response. "All right, all together, let's repeat, 'We promise to take good care of our new books.'" She looked sharply at me as she spoke.

"WE PROMISE TO TAKE GOOD CARE OF OUR NEW BOOKS!"

"Fine," Miss Crocker beamed, then proudly threw back the tarpaulin.

Sitting so close to the desk, I could see that the covers of the books, a motley red, were badly worn and that the gray edges of the pages had been marred by pencils, crayons, and ink. My anticipation at having my own book ebbed to a sinking disappointment. But Miss Crocker continued to beam as she called each fourth grader to her desk and, recording a number in her roll book, handed him or her a book.

As I returned from my trip to her desk, I noticed the first graders anxiously watching the disappearing pile. Miss Crocker must have noticed them too, for as I sat down she said, "Don't worry, little ones, there are plenty of readers for you too. See there on Miss Davis's desk." Wide eyes turned to the covered teacher's platform directly in front of them and an audible sigh of relief swelled in the room.

I glanced across at Little Man, his face lit in eager excitement. I knew that he could not see the soiled covers or the marred pages from where he sat, and even though his penchant for cleanliness was often annoying, I did not like to think of his disappointment when he saw the books as they really were. But there was nothing that I could do about it, so I opened my book to its center and began browsing through the spotted pages. Girls with blond braids and boys with blue eyes stared up at me. I found a story about a boy and his dog lost in a cave and began reading while Miss Crocker's voice droned on monotonously.

Suddenly I grew conscious of a break in that monotonous tone and I looked up. Miss Crocker was sitting at Miss Davis's desk with the first-grade books stacked before her, staring fiercely down at Little Man, who was pushing a book back upon the desk.

"What's that you said, Clayton Chester Logan?" she asked.

The room became gravely silent. Everyone knew that Little Man was in big trouble for no one, but no one, ever called Little Man "Clayton Chester" unless she or he meant serious business.

Little Man knew this too. His lips parted slightly as he took his hands from the book. He quivered, but he did not take his eyes from Miss Crocker. "I—I said may I have another book please, ma'am," he squeaked. "That one's dirty."

"Dirty!" Miss Crocker echoed, appalled by such temerity. She stood up, gazing down upon Little Man like a bony giant, but Little Man raised his head and continued to look into her eyes. "Dirty! And just who do you think you are, Clayton Chester? Here the county is giving us these wonderful books during these hard times and you're going to stand there and tell me that the book's too dirty? Now you take that book or get nothing at all!"

Little Man lowered his eyes and said nothing as he stared at the book. For several moments he stood there, his face barely visible above the desk, then he turned and looked at the few remaining books and, seeming to realize that they were as badly soiled as the one Miss Crocker had given him, he looked across the room at me. I nodded and Little Man, glancing up again at Miss Crocker, slid the book from the edge of the desk, and with his back straight and his head up returned to his seat.

Miss Crocker sat down again. "Some people around here seem to be giving themselves airs. I'll tolerate no more of that," she scowled. "Sharon Lake, come get your book."

I watched Little Man as he scooted into his seat beside two other little boys. He sat for a while with a stony face looking out the window; then, evidently accepting the fact that the book in front of him was the best that he could expect, he turned and opened it. But as he stared at the book's inside cover, his face clouded, changing from sulky acceptance to puzzlement. His brows furrowed. Then his eyes grew wide, and suddenly he sucked in his breath and sprang from his chair like a wounded animal, flinging the book onto the floor and stomping madly upon it.

Miss Crocker rushed to Little Man and grabbed him up in powerful hands. She shook him vigorously, then set him on the floor again. "Now, just what's gotten into you, Clayton Chester?"

But Little Man said nothing. He just stood staring down at the open book, shivering with indignant anger.

"Pick it up," she ordered.

"No!" defied Little Man.

"No? I'll give you ten seconds to pick up that book, boy, or I'm going to get my switch."

Little Man bit his lower lip, and I knew that he was not going to pick up the book. Rapidly, I turned to the inside cover of my own book and saw immediately what had made Little Man so furious. Stamped on the inside cover was a chart which read:

PROPERTY OF THE BOARD OF EDUCATION
Spokane County, Mississippi
September, 1922

CHRONOLOGICAL ISSUANCE	DATE OF ISSUANCE	CONDITION OF BOOK	RACE OF STUDENT
1	September 1922	New	White
2	September 1923	Excellent	White
3	September 1924	Excellent	White
4	September 1925	Very Good	White
5	September 1926	Good	White
6	September 1927	Good	White
7	September 1928	Average	White
8	September 1929	Average	White
9	September 1930	Average	White
10	September 1931	Poor	White
11	September 1932	Poor	White
12	September 1933	Very Poor	nigra
13			
14			
15			

The blank lines continued down to line 20 and I knew that they had all been reserved for black students. A knot of anger swelled in my throat and held there. But as Miss Crocker directed Little Man to bend over the "whipping" chair, I put aside my anger and jumped up.

"Miz Crocker, don't, please!" I cried. Miss Crocker's dark eyes warned me not to say another word. "I know why he done it!"

"You want part of this switch, Cassie?"

"No'm," I said hastily. "I just wanna tell you how come Little Man done what he done."

"Sit down!" she ordered as I hurried toward her with the open book in my hand.

Holding the book up to her, I said, "See, Miz Crocker, see what it says. They give us these ole books when they didn't want 'em no more."

She regarded me impatiently, but did not look at the book. "Now how could he know what it says? He can't read."

"Yes'm, he can. He been reading since he was four. He can't read all them big words, but he can read them columns. See what's in the last row. Please look, Miz Crocker."

This time Miss Crocker did look, but her face did not change. Then, holding up her head, she gazed unblinkingly down at me.

"S-see what they called us," I said, afraid she had not seen.

"That's what you are," she said coldly. "Now go sit down."

I shook my head, realizing now that Miss Crocker did not even know what I was talking about. She had looked at the page and had understood nothing.

"I said sit down, Cassie!"

I started slowly toward my desk, but as the hickory stick sliced the tense air, I turned back around. "Miz Crocker," I said, "I don't want my book neither."

The switch landed hard upon Little Man's upturned bottom. Miss Crocker looked questioningly at me as I reached up to her desk and placed the book upon it. Then she swung the switch five more times and, discovering that Little Man had no intention of crying, ordered him up.

"All right, Cassie," she sighed, turning to me, "come on and get yours."

By the end of the school day I had decided that I would tell Mama everything before Miss Crocker had a chance to do so. From nine years of trial and error, I had learned that punishment was always less severe when I poured out the whole truth to Mama on my own before she had heard anything from anyone else. I knew that Miss Crocker had not spoken to Mama during the lunch period, for she had spent the whole hour in the classroom preparing for the afternoon session.

As soon as class was dismissed I sped from the room, weaving a path through throngs of students happy to be free. But before I could reach the seventh-grade-class building, I had the misfortune to collide with Mary Lou's father.

Mr. Wellever looked down on me with surprise that I would actually bump into him, then proceeded to lecture me on the virtues of watching where one was going. Meanwhile Miss Crocker briskly crossed the lawn to Mama's class building. By the time I escaped Mr. Wellever, she had already disappeared into the darkness of the hallway.

Mama's classroom was in the back. I crept silently along the quiet hall and peeped cautiously into the open doorway. Mama, pushing a strand of her long, crinkly hair back into the chignon at the base of her slender neck, was seated at her desk watching Miss Crocker thrust a book before her. "Just look at that, Mary," Miss Crocker said, thumping the book twice with her forefinger. "A perfectly good book ruined. Look at that broken binding and those foot marks all over it."

Mama did not speak as she studied the book.

"And here's the one Cassie wouldn't take," she said, placing a second book on Mama's desk with an outraged slam. "At least she didn't have a tantrum and stomp all over hers. I tell you, Mary, I just don't know what got into those children today. I always knew Cassie was rather high-strung, but Little Man! He's always such a perfect little gentleman."

Mama glanced at the book I had rejected and opened the front cover so that the offensive pages of both books faced her. "You say Cassie said it was because of this front page that she and Little Man didn't want the books?" Mama asked quietly.

"Yes, ain't that something?" Miss Crocker said, forgetting

her teacher-training-school diction in her indignation. "The very idea! That's on all the books, and why they got so upset about it I'll never know."

"You punish them?" asked Mama, glancing up at Miss Crocker.

"Well, I certainly did! Whipped both of them good with my hickory stick. Wouldn't you have?" When Mama did not reply, she added defensively, "I had a perfect right to."

"Of course you did, Daisy," Mama said, turning back to the books again. "They disobeyed you." But her tone was so quiet and noncommittal that I knew Miss Crocker was not satisfied with her reaction.

"Well, I thought you would've wanted to know, Mary, in case you wanted to give them a piece of your mind also."

Mama smiled up at Miss Crocker and said rather absently, "Yes, of course, Daisy. Thank you." Then she opened her desk drawer and pulled out some paper, a pair of scissors, and a small brown bottle.

Miss Crocker, dismayed by Mama's seeming unconcern for the seriousness of the matter, thrust her shoulders back and began moving away from the desk. "You understand that if they don't have those books to study from, I'll have to fail them in both reading and composition, since I plan to base all my lessons around—" She stopped abruptly and stared in amazement at Mama. "Mary, what in the world are you doing?"

Mama did not answer. She had trimmed the paper to the size of the books and was now dipping a gray-looking glue from the brown bottle onto the inside cover of one of the books. Then she took the paper and placed it over the glue.

"Mary Logan, do you know what you're doing? That book belongs to the county. If somebody from the superintendent's office ever comes down here and sees that book, you'll be in real trouble."

Mama laughed and picked up the other book. "In the first place no one cares enough to come down here, and in the second place if anyone should come, maybe he could see all the things we need—current books for all of our subjects, not just somebody's old throwaways, desks, paper, blackboards, erasers, maps, chalk . . ." Her voice trailed off as she glued the second book.

"Biting the hand that feeds you. That's what you're doing, Mary Logan, biting the hand that feeds you."

Again, Mama laughed. "If that's the case, Daisy, I don't think I need that little bit of food." With the second book finished, she stared at a small pile of seventh-grade books on her desk.

"Well, I just think you're spoiling those children, Mary. They've got to learn how things are sometime."

"Maybe so," said Mama, "but that doesn't mean they have to accept them . . . and maybe we don't either."

Miss Crocker gazed suspiciously at Mama. Although Mama had been a teacher at Great Faith for fourteen years, ever since she had graduated from the Crandon Teacher Training School at nineteen, she was still considered by many of the other teachers as a disrupting maverick. Her ideas were always a bit too radical and her statements a bit too pointed. The fact that she had not grown up in Spokane County but in the Delta made her even more suspect, and the more traditional thinkers like Miss Crocker were wary of her. "Well, if anyone ever does come from the county and sees Cassie's and Little Man's books messed up like that," she said, "I certainly won't accept the responsibility for them."

"It will be easy enough for anyone to see whose responsibility it is, Daisy, by opening any seventh-grade book. Because tomorrow I'm going to 'mess them up' too."

Miss Crocker, finding nothing else to say, turned imperiously and headed for the door. I dashed across the hall and awaited her exit, then crept back.

Mama remained at her desk, sitting very still. For a long time she did not move. When she did, she picked up one of the seventh-grade books and began to glue again. I wanted to go and help her, but something warned me that now was not the time to make my presence known, and I left.

I would wait until the evening to talk to her; there was no rush now. She understood.

2

"Cassie, you better watch yourself, girl," Big Ma cautioned, putting one rough, large hand against my back to make sure I didn't fall.

I looked down at my grandmother from midway up one of the wooden poles Papa had set out to mark the length of the cotton field. Big Ma was Papa's mother, and like him she was tall and strongly built. Her clear, smooth skin was the color of a pecan shell. "Ah, Big Ma, I ain't gonna fall," I scoffed, then climbed onto the next strong spike and reached for a fibrous puff at the top of a tall cotton stalk.

"You sho' better not fall, girl," grumbled Big Ma. "Some-times I wish we had more low cotton like down 'round Vicksburg. I don't like y'all children climbin' them things." She looked around, her hand on her hip. Christopher-John and Little Man farther down the field balanced skillfully on lower spikes of their own poles plucking the last of the cotton, but Stacey, too heavy now to climb the poles, was forced to remain on the ground. Big Ma eyed us all again, then with a burlap bag slung across her right shoulder and dangling at the left side of her waist she moved down the row toward Mama. "Mary, child, I think with what we picked today we oughta have ourselves another bale."

Mama was stooped over a low cotton branch. She stuffed one last puff into her bag and straightened. She was tawny-colored, thin and sinewy, with delicate features in a strong-jawed face, and though almost as tall as Big Ma, she seemed somewhat dwarfed beside her. "I expect you're right, Mama," she said. "Come Monday, we'd better haul it up to the Granger place and have it ginned. Then we can—Cassie, what's the matter?"

I didn't answer Mama. I had moved to the very top of my pole and could now see above the field to the road where two figures, one much taller than the other, were walking briskly. As the men rounded a curve in the road, they became more distinct. There was in the easy fluid gait of the shorter man a familiarity that made me gasp. I squinted, shadowing my eyes from the sun, then slipped like lightning down the pole.

"Cassie?"

"It's Papa!"

"David?" Mama questioned unbelievingly as Christopher-John and Little Man descended eagerly and dashed after Stacey and me toward the barbed-wire fence.

"Don't y'all go through that fence!" Big Ma called after us. But we pretended not to hear. We held the second and third rows of the prickly wire wide for each other to climb through: then all four of us sped down the road toward Papa.

When Papa saw us, he began running swiftly, easily, like the wind. Little Man, the first to reach him, was swept lightly upward in Papa's strong hands as Christopher-John, Stacey, and I crowded around.

"Papa, what you doing home?" asked Little Man.

Putting Little Man down, Papa said, "Just had to come home and see 'bout my babies." He hugged and kissed each of us, then stood back. "Just look at y'all," he said proudly. "Ain't y'all something? Can't hardly call y'all babies no more." He turned. "Mr. Morrison, what you think 'bout these children of mine?"

In our excitement, we had taken no notice of the other man standing quietly at the side of the road. But now, gazing upward at the most formidable-looking being we had ever encountered, we huddled closer to Papa.

The man was a human tree in height, towering high above Papa's six feet two inches. The long trunk of his massive body bulged with muscles, and his skin, of the deepest ebony, was partially scarred upon his face and neck, as if by fire. Deep lifelines were cut into his face and his hair was splotched with gray, but his eyes were clear and penetrating. I glanced at the boys and it was obvious to me that they were wondering the same thing as I: Where had such a being come from?

"Children," said Papa, "meet Mr. L.T. Morrison."

Each of us whispered a faint hello to the giant, then the six of us started up the road toward home. Before we reached the house, Mama and Big Ma met us. When Papa saw Mama, his square, high-cheekboned face opened to a wide smile and, lifting Mama with spirited gusto, he swung her around twice before setting her down and kissing her.

"David, is something the matter?" she asked.

Papa laughed. "Something gotta be wrong, woman, for me to come see 'bout you?"

"You got my letter?"

He nodded, then hugged and kissed Big Ma before introducing them both to Mr. Morrison.

When we reached the house we climbed the long, sloping lawn to the porch and went into Mama and Papa's room, which also served as the living area. Mama offered Mr. Morrison Grandpa Logan's chair, a cushioned oak rocker skillfully crafted by Grandpa himself; but Mr. Morrison did not sit down immediately. Instead, he stood gazing at the room.

It was a warm, comfortable room of doors and wood and pictures. From it a person could reach the front or the side porch, the kitchen, and the two other bedrooms. Its walls were made of smooth oak, and on them hung gigantic photographs of Grandpa and Big Ma, Papa and Uncle Hammer when they were boys, Papa's two eldest brothers, who were now dead, and pictures of Mama's family. The furniture, a mixture of Logan-crafted walnut and oak, included a walnut bed whose ornate headboard rose halfway up the wall toward the high ceiling, a grand chiffonier with a floor-length mirror, a large rolltop desk which had once been Grandpa's but now belonged to Mama, and the four oak chairs, two of them rockers, which Grandpa had made for Big Ma as a wedding present.

Mr. Morrison nodded when he had taken it all in, as if he approved, then sat across from Papa in front of the unlit fireplace. The boys and I pulled up straight-backed chairs near Papa as Big Ma asked, "How long you gonna be home, son?"

Papa looked across at her. "Till Sunday evening," he said quietly.

"Sunday?" Mama exclaimed. "Why, today's already Saturday."

"I know, baby," Papa said, taking her hand, "but I gotta get that night train out of Vicksburg so I can get back to work by Monday morning."

Christopher-John, Little Man, and I groaned loudly, and Papa turned to us. "Papa, can't you stay no longer than that? Last time you come home, you stayed a week," I said.

Papa gently pulled one of my pigtails. "Sorry, Cassie girl, but I stay any longer, I might lose my job."

"But, Papa—"

"Listen, all of y'all," he said, looking from me to the boys to Mama and Big Ma, "I come home special so I could bring Mr. Morrison. He's gonna stay with us awhile."

If Mama and Big Ma were surprised by Papa's words, they did not show it, but the boys and I looked with wide eyes at each other, then at the giant.

"Mr. Morrison lost his job on the railroad a while back," Papa continued, "and he ain't been able to find anything else. When I asked him if he wanted to come work here as a hired hand, he said he would. I told him we couldn't afford much—food and shelter and a few dollars in cash when I come home in the winter."

Mama turned to Mr. Morrison, studied him for a moment, and said, "Welcome to our home, Mr. Morrison."

"Miz Logan," said Mr. Morrison in a deep, quiet voice like the roll of low thunder, "I think you oughta know I got fired off my job. Got in a fight with some men . . . beat 'em up pretty bad."

Mama stared into Mr. Morrison's deep eyes. "Whose fault was it?"

Mr. Morrison stared back. "I'd say theirs."

"Did the other men get fired?"

"No, ma'am," answered Mr. Morrison. "They was white."

Mama nodded and stood. "Thank you for telling me, Mr. Morrison. You're lucky no worse happened and we're glad to have you here . . . especially now." Then she turned and went into the kitchen with Big Ma to prepare supper, leaving the boys and me to wonder about her last words.

"Stacey, what you think?" I asked as we milked the cows in the evening. "How come Papa come home and brung Mr. Morrison?"

Stacey shrugged. "Like he said, I guess."

I thought on that a moment. "Papa ain't never brung nobody here before."

Stacey did not reply.

"You think . . . Stacey, you think it's cause of them burnings T.J. was talking 'bout?"

"Burnings?" piped Little Man, who had interrupted his feeding of the chickens to visit with Lady, our golden mare. "What's burnings gotta do with anything?"

"That happened way over by Smellings Creek," said Stacey slowly, ignoring Little Man. "Papa got no need to think . . ." His voice trailed off and he stopped milking.

"Think what?" I asked.

"Nothin'," he muttered, turning back to the cow. "Don't worry 'bout it."

I glared at him. "I ain't worrying. I just wanna know, that's all, and I betcha anything Mr. Morrison come here to do more'n work. Sure wish I knew for sure."

Stacey made no reply, but Christopher-John, his pudgy hands filled with dried corn for the chickens and his lower lip quivering, said, "I—I know what I wish. I wish P-Papa didn't never have to go 'way no more. I wish he could just stay . . . and stay. . . ."

At church the next morning, Mrs. Silas Lanier leaned across me and whispered to Big Ma, "John Henry Berry died last night." When the announcement was made to the congregation, the deacons prayed for the soul of John Henry Berry and the recovery of his brother, Beacon, and his uncle, Mr. Samuel Berry. But after church, when some of the members stopped by the house to visit, angry hopeless words were spoken.

"The way I hears it," said Mr. Lanier, "they been after John Henry ever since he come back from the war and settled on his daddy's place up by Smellings Creek. Had a nice little place up there too, and was doing pretty well. Left a wife and six children."

Big Ma shook her head. "Just in the wrong place at the wrong time."

The boys and I sat at our study table pretending not to listen, but listening still.

"Henrietta Toggins," said Mrs. Lanier, "you know, Clara Davis's sister that live up there in Strawberry? Well, she's kin to the Berrys and she was with John Henry and Beacon when the trouble got started. They was gonna drop her off at home—you know John Henry had him one of them old Model-T pickups—but they needed some gas so they stopped by that fillin' station up there in Strawberry. They was waitin' there for they gas when some white men come up messin' with them—been drinkin', you know. And Henrietta heard 'em say, 'That's the nigger Sallie Ann said was flirtin' with her.' And when she heard that, she said to

· 39 ·

John Henry, 'Let's get on outa here.' He wanted to wait for the gas, but she made him and Beacon get in that car, and them men jus' watched them drive off and didn't mess with 'em right then.

"John Henry, he took her on home then headed back for his own place, but evidently them men caught up with him and Beacon again and starts rammin' the back of they car—least that's what Beacon and John Henry told they aunt and uncle when they seed 'em. John Henry knowed he was runnin' outa gas and he was 'fraid he couldn't make it to his own place, so he stopped at his uncle's. But them men dragged him and Beacon both outa that house, and when old man Berry tried to stop it, they lit him afire with them boys."

"It's sho' a shame, all right," said T.J.'s father, a frail, sickly man with a hacking cough. "These folks gettin' so bad in here. Heard tell they lynched a boy a few days ago at Crosston."

"And ain't a thing gonna be done 'bout it," said Mr. Lanier. "That's what's so terrible! When Henrietta went to the sheriff and told him what she'd seed, he called her a liar and sent her on home. Now I hear tells that some of them men that done it been 'round braggin' 'bout it. Sayin' they'd do it again if some other uppity nigger get out of line."

Mrs. Avery tisked, "Lord have mercy!"

Papa sat very quietly while the Laniers and the Averys talked, studying them with serious eyes. Finally, he took the pipe from his mouth and made a statement that seemed to the boys and me to be totally disconnected with the conversation. "In this family, we don't shop at the Wallace store."

The room became silent. The boys and I stared at the adults wondering why. The Laniers and the Averys looked uneasily about them and when the silence was broken, the subject had changed to the sermon of the day.

After the Laniers and the Averys had left, Papa called us to him. "Your mama tells me that a lot of the older children been going up to that Wallace store after school to dance and buy their bootleg liquor and smoke cigarettes. Now she said she's already told y'all this, but I'm gonna tell y'all again, so listen good. We don't want y'all going to that place. Children going there are gonna get themselves in a whole lot of trouble one day. There's drinking up there and I don't like it—and I don't like them Wallaces either. If I ever find out y'all been up there, for any reason, I'm gonna wear y'all out. Y'all hear me?"

"Yessir, Papa," piped Christopher-John readily. "I ain't never going up there."

The rest of us agreed; Papa always meant what he said—and he swung a mean switch.

3

By the end of October the rain had come, falling heavily upon the six-inch layer of dust which had had its own way for more than two months. At first the rain had merely splotched the dust, which seemed to be rejoicing in its own resiliency and laughing at the heavy drops thudding against it; but eventually the dust was forced to surrender to the mastery of the rain and it churned into a fine red mud that oozed between our toes and slopped against our ankles as we marched miserably to and from school.

To shield us from the rain, Mama issued us dried calf-skins which we flung over our heads and shoulders like stiff cloaks. We were not very fond of the skins, for once they were wet they emitted a musty odor which seeped into our clothing and clung to our skins. We preferred to do without them; unfortunately, Mama cared very little about what we preferred.

Since we usually left for school after Mama, we solved this problem by dutifully cloaking ourselves with the skins before leaving home. As soon as we were beyond Big Ma's eagle eyes, we threw off the cloaks and depended upon the overhanging limbs of the forest trees to keep us dry. Once at school, we donned the cloaks again and marched into our respective classrooms properly attired.

If we had been faced only with the prospect of the rain soaking through our clothing each morning and evening, we could have more easily endured the journey between home and school. But as it was, we also had to worry about the Jefferson Davis school bus zooming from behind and splashing us with the murky waters of the road. Knowing that the bus driver liked to entertain his passengers by sending us slipping along the road to the almost inaccessible forest banks washed to a smooth baldness by the constant rains, we continuously looked over our shoulders when we were between the two crossroads so that we could reach the bank before the bus was upon us. But sometimes the rain pounded so heavily that it was all we could do to stay upright, and we did not look back as often nor listen as carefully as we should; we consequently found ourselves comical objects to cruel eyes that gave no thought to our misery.

No one was more angered by this humiliation than Little Man. Although he had asked Mama after the first day of school why Jefferson Davis had two buses and Great Faith had none, he had never been totally satisfied by her answer. She had explained to him, as she had explained to Christopher-John the year before and to me two years before that, that the county did not provide buses for its black students. In fact, she said, the county provided very little and much of the money which supported the black schools came from the black churches. Great Faith Church just could not afford a bus, so therefore we had to walk.

This information cut deeply into Little Man's brain, and each day when he found his clean clothes splashed red by the school bus, he became more and more embittered until finally one day he stomped angrily into the kitchen and exploded, "They done it again, Big Ma! Just look at my clothes!"

Big Ma clucked her tongue as she surveyed us. "Well, go on and get out of 'em, honey, and wash 'em out. All of y'all, get out of them clothes and dry yo'selves," she said, turning back to the huge iron-bellied stove to stir her stew.

"But, Big Ma, it ain't fair!" wailed Little Man. "It just ain't fair."

Stacey and Christopher-John left to change into their work clothes, but Little Man sat on the side bench looking totally dejected as he gazed at his pale-blue pants crusted with mud from the knees down. Although each night Big Ma prepared a pot of hot soapy water for him to wash out his clothing, each day he arrived home looking as if his pants had not been washed in more than a month.

Big Ma was not one for coddling any of us, but now she turned from the stove and, wiping her hands on her long white apron, sat down on the bench and put her arm around Little Man. "Now, look here, baby, it ain't the end of the world. Lord, child, don't you know one day the sun'll shine again and you won't get muddy no more?"

"But, Big Ma," Little Man protested, "ifn that ole bus driver would slow down, I wouldn't get muddy!" Then he frowned deeply and added, "Or ifn we had a bus like theirs."

"Well, he don't and you don't," Big Ma said, getting up. "So ain't no use frettin' 'bout it. One day you'll have a plenty of clothes and maybe even a car of yo' own to ride 'round in, so don't you pay no mind to them ignorant white folks. You jus' keep on studyin' and get yo'self a good education and you'll be all right. Now, go on and wash out yo' clothes and hang 'em by the fire so's I can iron 'em 'fore I go to bed."

Turning, she spied me. "Cassie, what you want, girl? Go change into yo' pants and hurry on back here so's you can help me get this supper on the table time yo' mama get home."

That night when I was snug in the deep feathery bed beside Big Ma, the tat-tat of the rain against the tin roof changed to a deafening roar that sounded as if thousands of giant rocks were being hurled against the earth. By morning the heavy rain had become a drizzle, but the earth was badly sodden from the night's downpour. High rivers of muddy water flowed in the deep gullies, and wide lakes shimmered on the roads.

As we set out for school the whiteness of the sun attempted to penetrate the storm clouds, but by the time we had turned north toward the second crossing it had given up, slinking meekly behind the blackening clouds. Soon the thunder rolled across the sky, and the rain fell like hail upon our bent heads.

"Ah, shoot! I sure am gettin' tired of this mess," complained T.J.

But no one else said a word. We were listening for the bus. Although we had left home earlier than usual to cover the northern road before the bus came, we were not overly confident that we would miss it, for we had tried this strategy before. Sometimes it worked; most times it didn't. It was as if the bus were a living thing, plaguing and defeating us at every turn. We could not outwit it.

We plodded along feeling the cold mud against our feet, walking faster and faster to reach the crossroads. Then Christopher-John stopped. "Hey, y'all, I think I hear it," he warned.

We looked around, but saw nothing.

"Ain't nothin' yet," I said.

We walked on.

"Wait a minute," said Christopher-John, stopping a second time. "There it is again."

We turned but still there was nothing.

"Why don't you clean out your ears?" T.J. exclaimed.

"Wait," said Stacey, "I think I hear it too."

We hastened up the road to where the gully was narrower and we could easily swing up the bank into the forest.

Soon the purr of a motor came closer and Mr. Granger's sleek silver Packard eased into view. It was a grand car with chrome shining even in the rain, and the only one like it in the county, so it was said.

We groaned. "Jus' ole Harlan," said T.J. flippantly as the expensive car rounded a curve and disappeared, then he and Claude started down the bank.

Stacey stopped them. "Long as we're already up here, why don't we wait awhile," he suggested. "The bus oughta be here soon and it'll be harder to get up on the bank further down the road."

"Ah, man, that bus ain't comin' for a while yet," said T.J. "We left early this mornin', remember?"

Stacey looked to the south, thinking. Little Man, Christopher-John and I waited for his decision.

"Come on, man," T.J. persuaded. "Why stay up here waitin' for that devilish bus when we could be at school outa this mess?"

"Well . . ."

T.J. and Claude jumped from the bank. Then Stacey, frowning as if he were doing this against his better judgment, jumped down too. Little Man, Christopher-John, and I followed.

Five minutes later we were skidding like frightened pup-pies toward the bank again as the bus accelerated and bar-reled down the narrow rain-soaked road; but there was no place to which we could run, for Stacey had been right. Here the gullies were too wide, filled almost to overflowing, and there were no briars or bushes by which we could swing up onto the bank.

Finally, when the bus was less than fifty feet behind us, it veered dangerously close to the right edge of the road where we were running, forcing us to attempt the jump to the bank; but all of us fell short and landed in the slime of the gully.

Little Man, chest-deep in water, scooped up a handful of mud and in an uncontrollable rage scrambled up to the road and ran after the retreating bus. As moronic rolls of laughter and cries of "Nigger! Nigger! Mud eater!" wafted from the open windows, Little Man threw his mudball, missing the wheels by several feet. Then, totally dismayed by what had happened, he buried his face in his hands and cried.

T.J. climbed from the gully grinning at Little Man, but Stacey, his face burning red beneath his dark skin, glared so fiercely at T.J. that he fell back. "Just one word outa you, T.J.," he said tightly. "Just one word."

Christopher-John and I looked at each other. We had never seen Stacey look like this, and neither had T.J.

"Hey, man, I ain't said nothin'! I'm jus' as burnt as you are."

Stacey glowered at T.J. a moment longer, then walked

swiftly to Little Man and put his long arm around his shoulders, saying softly, "Come on, Man. It ain't gonna happen no more, least not for a long while. I promise you that."

Again, Christopher-John and I looked questioningly at each other, wondering how Stacey could make such a rash promise. Then, shrugging, we hurried after him.

When Jeremy Simms spied us from his high perch on the forest path, he ran hastily down and joined us.

"Hey," he said, his face lighting into a friendly grin. But no one spoke to him.

The smile faded and, noticing our mud-covered clothing, he asked, "Hey, St-Stacey, wh-what happened?"

Stacey turned, stared into his blue eyes and said coldly, "Why don't you leave us alone? How come you always hanging 'round us anyway?"

Jeremy grew even more pale. "C-cause I just likes y'all," he stammered. Then he whispered, "W-was it the bus again?"

No one answered him and he said no more. When we reached the crossroads, he looked hopefully at us as if we might relent and say good-bye. But we did not relent and as I glanced back at him standing alone in the middle of the crossing, he looked as if the world itself was slung around his neck. It was only then that I realized that Jeremy never rode the bus, no matter how bad the weather.

As we crossed the school lawn, Stacey beckoned Christopher-John, Little Man, and me aside. "Look," he whispered, "meet me at the toolshed right at noon."

"Why?" we asked.

He eyed us conspiratorily. "I'll show y'all how we're gonna stop that bus from splashing us."

"How?" asked Little Man, eager for revenge.

"Don't have time to explain now. Just meet me. And be on time. It's gonna take us all lunch hour."

"Y-you mean we ain't gonna eat no lunch!" Christopher-John cried in dismay.

"You can miss lunch for one day," said Stacey, moving away. But Christopher-John looked sourly after him as if he greatly questioned the wisdom of a plan so drastic that it could exclude lunch.

"You gonna tell T.J. and Claude?" I asked.

Stacey shook his head. "T.J.'s my best friend, but he's got no stomach for this kinda thing. He talks too much, and we couldn't include Claude without T.J."

"Good," said Little Man.

At noon, we met as planned and ducked into the unlocked toolshed where all the church and school garden tools were kept. Stacey studied the tools available while the rest of us watched. Then, grabbing the only shovels, he handed one to me, holding on to the other himself, and directed Little Man and Christopher-John to each take two buckets.

Stealthily emerging from the toolshed into the drizzle, we eased along the forest edge behind the class buildings to avoid being seen. Once on the road, Stacey began to run. "Come on, hurry," he ordered. "We ain't got much time."

"Where we going?" asked Christopher-John, still not

quite adjusted to the prospect of missing lunch.

"Up to where that bus forced us off the road. Be careful now," he said to Christopher-John, already puffing to keep up.

When we reached the place where we had fallen into the gully, Stacey halted. "All right," he said, "start digging." Without another word, he put his bare foot upon the top edge of the shovel and sank it deep into the soft road. "Come on, come on," he ordered, glancing up at Christopher-John, Little Man and me, who were wondering whether he had finally gone mad.

"Cassie, you start digging over there on that side of the road right across from me. That's right, don't get too near the edge. It's gotta look like it's been washed out. Christopher-John, you and Little Man start scooping out mud from the middle of the road. Quick now," he said, still digging as we began to carry out his commands. "We only got 'bout thirty minutes so's we can get back to school on time."

We asked no more questions. While Stacey and I shoveled ragged holes almost a yard wide and a foot deep toward each other, dumping the excess mud into the water-filled gullies, Little Man and Christopher-John scooped bucketfuls of the red earth from the road's center. And for once in his life, Little Man was happily oblivious to the mud spattering upon him.

When Stacey's and my holes merged into one big hole with Little Man's and Christopher-John's, Stacey and I threw down our shovels and grabbed the extra buckets. Then the four of us ran back and forth to the gullies, hastily filling the buckets with the murky water and dumping it into the hole.

Now understanding Stacey's plan, we worked wordlessly until the water lay at the same level as the road. Then Stacey waded into the gully water and pulled himself up onto the forest bank. Finding three rocks, he stacked them to identify the spot.

"It might look different this afternoon," he explained, jumping down again.

Christopher-John looked up at the sky. "Looks like it's gonna rain real hard some more."

"Let's hope so," said Stacey. "The more rain, the better. That'll make it seem more likely that the road could've been washed away like that. It'll also keep cars and wagons away." He looked around, surveying the road. "And let's hope don't nothin' come along 'fore that bus. Let's go."

Quickly we gathered our buckets and shovels and hurried back to school. After returning the tools to the toolshed, we stopped at the well to wash the mud from our arms and feet, then rushed into our classes, hoping that the mud caked on our clothes would go unnoticed. As I slipped into my seat Miss Crocker looked at me oddly and shook her head, but when she did the same thing as Mary Lou and Alma sat down, I decided that my mud was no more noticeable than anyone else's.

Soon after I had settled down to the boredom of Miss Crocker, the rain began to pound down again, hammering with great intensity upon the tin roof. After school it was still raining as the boys and I, avoiding T.J. and Claude, rushed along the slippery road recklessly bypassing more cautious students.

"You think we'll get there in time to see, Stacey?" I asked.

"We should. They stay in school fifteen minutes longer than we do and it always takes them a few minutes to load up."

When we reached the crossing, we glanced toward Jefferson Davis. The buses were there but the students had not been dismissed. We hastened on.

Expecting to see the yard-wide ditch we had dug at noon, we were not prepared for the twelve-foot lake which glimmered up at us.

"Holy smokes! What happened?" I exclaimed.

"The rain," said Stacey. "Quick, up on the bank." Eagerly, we settled onto the muddy forest floor and waited.

"Hey, Stacey," I said, "won't that big a puddle make that ole driver cautious?"

Stacey frowned, then said uncertainly, "I don't know. Hope not. There's big puddles down the road that ain't deep, just water heavy."

"If I was to be walking out there when the bus comes, that ole bus driver would be sure to speed up so's he could splash me," I suggested.

"Or maybe me," Little Man volunteered, ready to do anything for his revenge.

Stacey thought a moment, but decided against it. "Naw. It's better none of us be on the road when it happens. It might give 'em ideas."

"Stacey, what if they find out we done it?" asked Christopher-John nervously.

"Don't worry, they won't," assured Stacey.

"Hey, I think it's coming," whispered Little Man.

We flattened ourselves completely and peered through the low bushes.

The bus rattled up the road, though not as quickly as we had hoped. It rolled cautiously through a wide puddle some twenty feet ahead; then, seeming to grow bolder as it approached our man-made lake, it speeded up, spraying the water in high sheets of backward waterfalls into the forest. We could hear the students squealing with delight. But instead of the graceful glide through the puddle that its occupants were expecting, the bus emitted a tremendous crack and careened drunkenly into our trap. For a moment it swayed and we held our breath, afraid that it would topple over. Then it sputtered a last murmuring protest and died, its left front wheel in our ditch, its right wheel in the gully, like a lopsided billy goat on its knees.

We covered our mouths and shook with silent laughter.

As the dismayed driver opened the rear emergency exit, the rain poured down upon him in sharp-needled darts. He stood in the doorway looking down with disbelief at his sunken charge; then, holding on to the bus, he poked one foot into the water until it was on solid ground before gingerly stepping down. He looked under the bus. He looked at the steaming hood. He looked at the water. Then he scratched his head and cursed.

"How bad is it, Mr. Grimes?" a large, freckle-faced boy asked, pushing up one of the cracked windows and sticking out his head. "Can we push it out and fix it?"

"Push it out? Fix it?" the bus driver echoed angrily. "I got me a broken axle here an' a water-logged engine no doubt and no tellin' what-all else and you talkin' 'bout fixin' it! Y'all come on, get outa there! Y'all gonna have to walk home."

"Mister Grimes," a girl ventured, stepping hesitantly from the rear of the bus, "you gonna be able to pick us up in the mornin'?"

The bus driver stared at her in total disbelief. "Girl, all y'all gonna be walkin' for at least two weeks by the time we get this thing hauled outa here and up to Strawberry to get fixed. Now y'all get on home." He kicked a back tire, and added, "And get y'all's daddies to come on up here and give me a hand with this thing."

The students turned dismally from the bus. They didn't know how wide the hole actually was. Some of them took a wild guess and tried to jump it; but most of them miscalculated and fell in, to our everlasting delight. Others attempted to hop over the gullies to the forest to bypass the hole; however, we knew from much experience that they would not make it.

By the time most of the students managed to get to the

other side of the ditch, their clothes were dripping with the weight of the muddy water. No longer laughing, they moved spiritlessly toward their homes while a disgruntled Mr. Grimes leaned moodily against the raised rear end of the bus.

Oh, how sweet was well-maneuvered revenge!

With that thought in mind, we quietly eased away and picked our way through the dense forest toward home.

At supper Mama told Big Ma of the Jefferson Davis bus being stuck in the ditch. "It's funny, you know, such a wide ditch in one day. I didn't even notice the beginning of it this morning—did you, children?"

"No'm," we chorused.

"You didn't fall in, did you?"

"We jumped onto the bank when we thought the bus would be coming," said Stacey truthfully.

"Well, good for you," approved Mama. "If that bus hadn't been there when I came along, I'd probably have fallen in myself."

The boys and I looked at each other. We hadn't thought about that.

"How'd you get across, Mama?" Stacey asked.

"Somebody decided to put a board across the washout."

"They gonna haul that bus outa there tonight?" Big Ma inquired.

"No, ma'am," said Mama. "I heard Mr. Granger telling Ted Grimes—the bus driver—that they won't be able to get it out until after the rain stops and it dries up a bit. It's just too muddy now."

We put our hands to our mouths to hide happy grins. I even made a secret wish that it would rain until Christmas.

Mama smiled. "You know I'm glad no one was hurt—could've been too with such a deep ditch—but I'm also rather glad it happened."

"Mary!" Big Ma exclaimed.

"Well, I am," Mama said defiantly, smiling smugly to herself and looking very much like a young girl. "I really am."

Big Ma began to grin. "You know somethin'? I am too."

Then all of us began to laugh and were deliciously happy.

Later that evening the boys and I sat at the study table in Mama and Papa's room attempting to concentrate on our lessons; but none of us could succeed for more than a few minutes without letting out a triumphant giggle. More than once Mama scolded us, telling us to get down to business. Each time she did, we set our faces into looks of great seriousness, resolved that we would be adult about the matter and not gloat in our hour of victory. Yet just one glance at each other and we were lost, slumping on the table in helpless, contagious laughter.

"All right," Mama said finally. "I don't know what's going on here, but I suppose I'd better do something about it or you'll never get any work done."

It occurred to us that Mama might be preparing to whip

us and we shot each other warning glances. But even that thought couldn't dampen our laughter, now uncontrollable, welling up from the pits of our stomachs and forcing streams of laughter tears down our faces. Stacey, holding his sides, turned to the wall in an attempt to bring himself under control. Little Man put his head under the table. But Christopher-John and I just doubled up and fell upon the floor.

Mama took my arm and pulled me up. "Over here, Cassie," she said, directing me to a chair next to the fireplace and behind Big Ma, who was ironing our clothes for the next day.

I peeped around Big Ma's long skirts and saw Mama guiding Stacey to her own desk. Then back she went for Little Man and, picking him up bodily, set him in the chair beside her rocker. Christopher-John she left alone at the study table. Then she gathered all our study materials and brought them to us along with a look that said she would tolerate no more of this foolishness.

With Big Ma before me, I could see nothing else and I grew serious enough to complete my arithmetic assignment. When that was finished, I lingered before opening my reader, watching Big Ma as she hung up my ironed dress, then placed her heavy iron on a small pile of embers burning in a corner of the fireplace and picked up a second iron already warming there. She tested the iron with a tap of her finger and put it back again.

While Big Ma waited for the iron to get hot, I could see

Mama bending over outspread newspapers scraping the dried mud off the old field shoes of Papa's which she wore daily, stuffed with wads of newspaper, over her own shoes to protect them from the mud and rain. Little Man beside her was deep into his first-grade reader, his eyebrows furrowed in concentration. Ever since Mama had brought the reader home with the offensive inside cover no longer visible, Little Man had accepted the book as a necessary tool for passing the first grade. But he took no pride in it. Looking up, he noticed that Big Ma was now preparing to iron his clothes, and he smiled happily. Then his eyes met mine and silent laughter creased his face. I muffled a giggle and Mama looked up.

"Cassie, you start up again and I'm sending you to the kitchen to study," she warned.

"Yes'm," I said, settling back in my chair and beginning to read. I certainly did not want to go to the kitchen. Now that the fire no longer burned in the stove, it was cold in there.

The room grew quiet again, except for the earthy humming of Big Ma's rich alto voice, the crackle of the hickory fire, and the patter of rain on the roof. Engrossed in a mystery, I was startled when the comfortable sounds were shattered by three rapid knocks on the side door.

Rising quickly, Mama went to the door and called, "Who is it?"

"It's me, ma'am," came a man's gravelly voice. "Joe Avery."

Mama opened the door and Mr. Avery stepped dripping into the room.

"Why, Brother Avery," Mama said, "what are you doing out on a night like this? Come on in. Take off your coat and sit by the fire. Stacey, get Mr. Avery a chair."

"No'm," said Mr. Avery, looking rather nervously over his shoulder into the night. "I ain't got but a minute." He stepped far enough into the room so that he could close the door, then nodded to the rest of us. "Evenin', Miz Caroline, how you t'night?"

"Oh, I'll do, I reckon," said Big Ma, still ironing. "How's Miz Fannie?"

"She's fine," he said without dwelling on his wife. "Miz Logan . . . uh, I come to tell you somethin' . . . somethin' important—Mr. Morrison here?"

Mama stiffened. "David. You heard something about David?"

"Oh, no'm," replied Mr. Avery hastily. "Ain't heard nothin' 'bout yo' husband, ma'am."

Mama regarded him quizzically.

"It's . . . it's them again. They's ridin' t'night."

Mama, her face pale and frightened, glanced back at Big Ma; Big Ma held her iron in midair.

"Uh . . . children," Mama said, "I think it's your bedtime."

"But, Mama—" we chorused in protest, wanting to stay and hear who was riding.

"Hush," Mama said sternly. "I said it was time to go to bed. Now go!"

Groaning loudly enough to voice our displeasure, but not loudly enough to arouse Mama's anger, we stacked our books upon the study table and started toward the boys' room.

"Cassie, I said go to bed. That's not your room."

"But, Mama, it's cold in there," I pouted. Usually, we were allowed to build small fires in the other rooms an hour before bedtime to warm them up.

"You'll be warm once you're under the covers. Stacey, take the flashlight with you and light the lantern in your room. Cassie, take the lamp from the desk with you."

I went back and got the kerosene lamp, then entered my bedroom, leaving the door slightly ajar.

"Close that door, Cassie!"

Immediately, the door was closed.

I put the lamp on the dresser, then silently slid the latch off the outside door and slipped onto the wet front porch. I crossed to the boys' room. Tapping lightly, I whispered, "Hey, let me in."

The door creaked open and I darted in. The room was bathed in darkness.

"What they say?" I asked.

"Shhhhh!" came the answer.

I crept to the door leading into Mama's room and huddled beside the boys.

The rain softened upon the roof and we could hear Mama asking, "But why? Why are they riding? What's happened?"

"I don't rightly know," said Mr. Avery. "But y'all knows how they is. Anytime they thinks we steppin' outa our *place*, they feels like they gotta stop us. You know what some of 'em done to the Berrys." He paused, then went on bitterly, "It don't take but a little of nothin' to set them devilish night men off."

"But somethin' musta happened," Big Ma said. "How you know 'bout it?"

"All's I can tell ya, Miz Caroline, is what Fannie heard when she was leavin' the Grangers' this evenin'. She'd just finished cleanin' up the supper dishes when Mr. Granger come home with Mr. Grimes—ya know, that white school's bus driver—and two other mens. . . ."

A clap of deafening thunder drowned Mr. Avery's words, then the rain quickened and the conversation was lost.

I grabbed Stacey's arm. "Stacey, they're coming after *us*!"

"What!" squeaked Christopher-John.

"Hush," Stacey said harshly. "And Cassie, let go. That hurts."

"Stacey, somebody musta seen and told on us," I persisted.

"No . . ." Stacey replied unconvincingly. "It couldn't be."

"Couldn't be?" cried Christopher-John in a panic. "Whaddaya mean it couldn't be?"

"Stacey," said Little Man excitedly, "whaddaya think they gonna do to us? Burn us up?"

"Nothin'!" Stacey exclaimed, standing up suddenly. "Now why don't y'all go to bed like y'all s'pose to?"

We were stunned by his attitude. He sounded like Mama and I told him so.

He collapsed in silence by the door, breathing hard, and although I could not see him, I knew that his face was drawn and that his eyes had taken on a haggard look. I touched his arm lightly. "Ain't no call to go blaming yourself," I said. "We all done it."

"But I got us into it," he said listlessly.

"But we all wanted to do it," I comforted.

"Not me!" denied Christopher-John. "All I wanted to do was eat my lunch!"

"Shhhhh," hissed Little Man. "I can hear 'em again."

"I'd better go tell Mr. Morrison," Mr. Avery was saying. "He out back?"

"I'll tell him," said Mama.

We could hear the side door open and we scrambled up.

"Cassie, get back to your room quick," Stacey whispered. "They'll probably come check on us now."

"But what'll we do?"

"Nothin' now, Cassie. Them men probably won't even come near here."

"Ya really believe that?" asked Christopher-John hopefully.

"But shouldn't we tell Mama?" I asked.

"No! We can't ever tell nobody!" declared Stacey adamantly. "Now go on, hurry!"

Footsteps neared the door. I dashed onto the porch and hastened back to my own room, where I jumped under the bedcovers with my clothes still on. Shivering, I pulled the heavy patchwork quilts up to my chin.

A few moments later Big Ma came in, leaving the door to Mama's room open. Knowing that she would be suspicious of such an early surrender to sleep, I sighed softly and, making sleepy little sounds, turned onto my stomach, careful not to expose my shirt sleeves. Obviously satisfied by my performance, Big Ma tucked the covers more closely around me and smoothed my hair gently. Then she stooped and started fishing for something under our bed.

I opened my eyes. Now what the devil was she looking for down there? While she was searching, I heard Mama approaching and I closed my eyes again.

"Mama?"

"Stacey, what're you doing up?"

"Let me help."

"Help with what?"

"With . . . with whatever's the matter."

Mama was silent a moment, then said softly, "Thank you, Stacey, but Big Ma and I can handle it."

"But Papa told me to help you!"

"And you do, more than you know. But right now you could help me most by going back to bed. It's a school day tomorrow, remember?"

"But, Mama—"

"If I need you, I'll call you. I promise."

I heard Stacey walk slowly away, then Mama whispering in the doorway, "Cassie asleep?"

"Yeah, honey," Big Ma said. "Go on and sit back down. I'll be out in a minute."

Then Big Ma stood up and turned down the wick of the kerosene lamp. As she left the room, my eyes popped open again and I saw her outlined in the doorway, a rifle in her hands. Then she closed the door and I was left to the darkness.

For long minutes I waited, wide awake, wondering what my next move should be. Finally deciding that I should again consult with the boys, I swung my legs over the edge of the bed, but immediately had to swing them back again as Big Ma reentered the room. She passed the bed and pulled a straight-backed chair up to the window. Parting the curtains so that the blackness of the night mixed with the blackness of the room, she sat down without a sound.

I heard the door to the boys' room open and close and I knew that Mama had gone in. I waited for the sound of the door opening again, but it did not come. Soon the chill of the cotton sheets beneath me began to fade and as Big Ma's presence lulled me into a security I did not really feel, I fell asleep.

When I awoke, it was still nightly dark. "Big Ma?" I called. "Big Ma, you there?" But there was no reply from the chair by the window. Thinking that Big Ma had fallen asleep, I climbed from the bed and felt my way to her chair.

She wasn't there.

Outside, an owl hooted into the night, quiet now except for the drip-drap of water falling from the roof. I stood transfixed by the chair, afraid to move.

Then I heard a noise on the porch. I could not control my trembling. Again the noise, this time close to the door, and it occurred to me that it was probably the boys coming to confer with me. No doubt Mama had left them alone too.

Laughing silently at myself, I hurried onto the porch. "Stacey," I whispered. "Christopher-John?" There was a sudden movement near the end of the porch and I headed toward it, feeling along the wall of the house. "Little Man? Hey, y'all, stop fooling 'round and answer me."

I crept precariously near the edge of the high porch, my eyes attempting to penetrate the blackness of the night. From below, a scratchy bristlyness sprang upon me, and I lost my balance and tumbled with a thud into the muddy flower bed. I lay paralyzed with fear. Then a long wet tongue licked my face.

"Jason? Jason, that you?"

Our hound dog whined his reply.

I hugged him, then instantly let him go. "Was that you all the time? Look what you gone and done," I fussed, thinking of the mess I was in with mud all over me.

Jason whined again and I got up.

I started to climb back up onto the porch but froze as a caravan of headlights appeared suddenly in the east, coming fast along the rain-soaked road like cat eyes in the night. Jason whined loudly, growing skittish as the lights approached, and when they slowed and braked before the house he slunk beneath the porch. I wanted to follow, but I couldn't. My legs would not move.

The lead car swung into the muddy driveway and a shadowy figure outlined by the headlights of the car behind him stepped out. The man walked slowly up the drive.

I stopped breathing.

The driver of the next car got out, waiting. The first man stopped and stared at the house for several long moments as if uncertain whether it was the correct destination. Then he shook his head, and without a word returned to his car. With a wave of his hand he sent the other driver back inside, and in less than a minute the lead car had backed into the road, its headlights facing the other cars. Each of the cars used the driveway to turn around, then the caravan sped away as swiftly as it had come, its seven pairs of rear lights glowing like distant red embers until they were swallowed from view by the Granger forest.

Jason began barking now that the danger had passed, but he did not come out. As I reached for the porch to steady myself, there was a sense of quiet movement in the darkness. The moon slid from its dark covers, cloaking the earth in a shadowy white light, and I could see Mr. Morrison clearly, moving silently, like a jungle cat, from the side of the house to the road, a shotgun in his hand. Feeling sick, I crawled onto the porch and crept trembling toward the door.

Once inside the house, I leaned against the latch while waves of sick terror swept over me. Realizing that I must get into bed before Mama or Big Ma came from the other room, I pulled off my muddy clothes, turning them inside out to wipe the mud from my body, and put on my night clothes. Then I climbed into the softness of the bed. I lay very still for a while, not allowing myself to think. But soon, against my will, the vision of ghostly headlights soaked into my mind and an uncontrollable trembling racked my body. And it remained until the dawn, when I fell into a restless sleep.

4

"Cassie, what's the matter with you, girl?" Big Ma asked as she thrust three sticks of dried pine into the stove to rekindle the dying morning fire. "You sure are takin' a sorrowful long time to churn that butter."

"Nothin'," I muttered.

"Nothin'?" Big Ma turned and looked directly at me. "You been mopin' 'round here for the past week like you got the whoopin' cough, flu, and measles all put together."

I sighed deeply and continued to churn.

Big Ma reached out and felt my forehead, then my cheeks. Frowning, she pulled her hand away as Mama entered the kitchen. "Mary, feel this child's face," she said. "She seem warm to you?"

Mama cupped my face in her thin hands. "You feel sick, Cassie?"

"No'm."

"How do you feel?"

"All right," I said, still churning.

Mama studied me with the same disturbed look Big Ma wore and a tiny frown line appeared on her brow. "Cassie," she said softly, fixing her dark eyes upon me, "is there something you want to tell me?"

I was on the verge of blurting out the awful truth about the bus and the men in the night, but then I remembered the pact Stacey had made us all swear to when I had told him, Christopher-John, and Little Man about the caravan and I said instead, "No, ma'am," and began to churn again. Abruptly, Mama took hold of the churning stick, her eyes searching mine. As she studied me, she seemed about to ask me something, then the question faded and she pulled away, lifting the lid of the churn. "It looks ready now," she said with a sigh. "Dip out the butter like I showed you and wash it down. I'll take care of the milk."

I scooped the butter from the churning lid onto a plate and went through the curtain to the small pantry off the kitchen to get the molding dish. It had been placed on a high shelf under several other dishes and I had to stand on a stool to get it. As I eased it out, Mama and Big Ma spoke softly in worried tones on the other side of the curtain.

"Somethin' the matter with that child, Mary."

"She's not sick, Mama."

"There's all sorts of sickness. She ain't ate right for goin' on over a week. She ain't sleepin' right neither. Restless and murmurin' in her sleep all night long. And she won't hardly even go out and play, rather be in here helpin' us. Now you know that ain't like that child."

There was a moment's pause, then Mama whispered so I could hardly hear her. "You think . . . Mama, you think she could've seen—"

"Oh, Lord, no, child," Big Ma exclaimed hastily. "I checked in there right after they passed and she was sound asleep. She couldn't't've seen them ole devils. The boys neither."

Mama sighed. "The boys, they're not themselves either. All of them, too quiet. Here it is Saturday morning and they're quiet as church mice. I don't like it, and I can't shake the feeling it's got something to do with— Cassie!"

Without warning, I had lost my balance and with an absurd topple from the knee-high stool crashed upon the floor with the molding dish. "Cassie, you hurt?" Mama asked, stooping beside me.

"No'm," I mumbled, feeling very clumsy and close to tears. I knew that if I let the tears fall, Mama's suspicion that something was wrong would be confirmed for I never cried about such a silly thing as a fall; in fact, I seldom ever cried. So instead of crying, I jumped up quickly and began to pick up the broken pieces of the dish.

"I'm sorry, Mama," I said.

"That's all right," she said, helping me. When we had swept the chips away with the long field-straw broom, she told me, "Leave the butter, Cassie, and go on in with the boys."

"But, Mama—"

"I'll do the butter. Now go on, do like I say."

I stared up at Mama, wondering if she would ever know what we had done, then joined the boys who were sitting listlessly around the fire absently listening to T.J.

"See, fellows, there's a system to getting out of work," T.J. was expounding as I sat down. "Jus' don't be 'round when it's got to be done. Only thing is, you can't let your folks know that's what you're doin'. See, you should do like me. Like this mornin' when Mama wanted to bring back them scissors she borrowed from Miz Logan, I ups and volunteers so she don't have to make this long trip down here, she bein' so busy and all. And naturally when I got here, y'all wanted me to stay awhile and talk to y'all, so what could I do? I couldn't be impolite, could I? And by the time I finally convince y'all I gotta go, all the work'll be done at home." T.J. chuckled with satisfaction. "Yeah, you just have to use the old brain, that's all."

He was quiet a moment, expecting some comment on his discourse, but no one said a word.

T.J.'s eyes roamed the length of the room, then he admonished, "See, if you was smart like me, Stacey, you'd use the old brain to get the questions on that big test comin' up. Just think, they probably jus' sittin' right here in this very room waitin' to be discovered."

Stacey cast T.J. an annoyed look, but did not speak.

"Y'all sure are a sorry lot this mornin'," T.J. observed. "A fellow's just wastin' his know-how talkin' to y'all."

"Ain't nobody asked you to give it," said Stacey.

"Well, you don't have to get snippety about it," replied T.J. haughtily. Again, silence prevailed; but that would not do for T.J. "Say, how 'bout we sneak down to that ole Wallace store and learn how to do them new dances?"

"Mama told us not to go down there," Stacey said.

"You some mama's boy or somethin' you gotta do everything your mama tells—"

"You go on if you wanna," said Stacey quietly, not rising to T.J.'s bait, "but we staying here."

Again, silence.

Then T.J. said: "Say, y'all hear the latest 'bout them night men?" Suddenly, all eyes turned from the fire and riveted themselves upon him. Our faces were eager question marks; we were totally in T.J.'s power.

"What 'bout them?" Stacey asked, almost evenly.

T.J., of course, intended to nurse the moment for as long as he could. "You see when a fellow's as smart as me, he gets to know things that other folks don't. Now, this kind of information ain't for the ears of little kids so I really shouldn't even tell y'all—"

"Then don't!" said Stacey with smooth finality, turning back toward the fire as if he cared not at all about the night men. Taking his cue, I nudged Christopher-John and Christopher-John nudged Little Man, and the three of us forced ourselves to stare into the fire in feigned disinterest.

Without a captive audience, T.J. had to reinterest us by getting to the point. "Well, 'bout a week ago, they rode down to Mr. Sam Tatum's place—you know, down the Jackson Road toward Strawberry—and you know what they done?"

Stacey, Little Man, and I kept our eyes upon the fire, but Christopher-John piped eagerly, "What?"

I poked Christopher-John and he turned guiltily around, but T.J., triumphant with an assured audience of one, settled back in his chair ready to prolong the suspense. "You know Mama'd kill me if she knowed I was tellin' this. I heard her and Miz Claire Thompson talkin' 'bout it. They was real scared. Don't know why though. Them ole night men sure wouldn't scare me none. Like I told Claude—"

"Hey, y'all," Stacey said, standing and motioning us up. "Mama said she wanted us to take some milk and butter down to Miz Jackson before noon. We'd better get started."

I nodded, and Christopher-John, Little Man, and I got up.

"Tarred and feathered him!" T.J. announced hastily. "Poured the blackest tar they could find all over him, then plastered him with chicken feathers." T.J. laughed. "Can you imagine that?"

"But why?" asked Little Man, forgetting our ploy.

This time T.J. did not slow down. "I dunno if y'all's little ears should hear this, but it seems he called Mr. Jim

Lee Barnett a liar—he's the man who runs the Mercantile down in Strawberry. Mr. Tatum's s'pose to done told him that he ain't ordered up all them things Mr. Barnett done charged him for. Mr. Barnett said he had all them things Mr. Tatum ordered writ down and when Mr. Tatum asked to see that list of his, Mr. Barnett says, 'You callin' me a liar, boy?' And Mr. Tatum says, 'Yessuh, I guess I is!' That done it!"

"Then it wasn't 'cause of the bus?" Christopher-John blurted out.

"Bus? What's a bus got to do with it?"

"Nothin'," said Stacey quickly. "Nothin' at all."

"Well, if anybody said them night men was down in here 'cause of some stupid bus, they crazy," said T.J. authoritatively. " 'Cause my information come direct from Miz Claire Thompson who seen Mr. Tatum herself."

"You sure?" Stacey asked.

"Sure? Sure, I'm sure. When do I ever say anythin' when I ain't sure?"

Stacey smiled with relief. "Come on, let's get the milk."

All of us went into the kitchen, then to the bedrooms to get our coats. When we got outside, T.J. remembered that he had left his cap by the fire and ran back to retrieve it. As soon as we were alone, Little Man asked, "Stacey, you really think them night men put tar and feathers all over Mr. Tatum?"

"I s'pose so," said Stacey.

Little Man frowned, but it was Christopher-John who

spoke, whispering shrilly as if a stray morning ghost might overhear. "If they ever find out 'bout the bus, you think they gonna put tar and feathers all over us?"

Little Man's frown deepened and he observed gravely, "If they did, we'd never get clean again."

"Cassie," said Christopher-John, his eyes wide, "w-was you real s-scared when you seen 'em?"

Little Man shivered with excitement. "I wish I could've seen 'em."

"Well, I don't," declared Christopher-John. "In fact, I wish I'd never heard of no night men or buses or secrets or holes in the road!" And with that outburst, he stuffed his pudgy hands into his thin jacket, pressed his lips firmly together, and refused to say another word.

After a few moments, Stacey said, "What's keeping T.J.?" The rest of us shrugged, then followed Stacey back up the porch into Mama's room. As we entered, T.J. jumped. He was standing at the desk with Mama's W.E.B. Du Bois's *The Negro* in his hands.

"That don't look like your cap," said Stacey.

"Aw, man, I ain't done nothin'. Jus' lookin' at Miz Logan's history book, that's all. I'm mighty interested in that place called Egypt she been tellin' us 'bout and them black kings that was rulin' back then." Still talking, he casually put down the book and picked up his cap.

All four of us looked accusingly at T.J. and he halted. "Say, what is this? What's the meanin' of sneakin' up on me like that anyway? Y'all think I was lookin' for them test questions or somethin'? Shoot, a fellow'd think you didn't trust him." Then, thrusting his arm around Stacey's shoulders, he chided, "Friends gotta trust each other, Stacey, 'cause ain't nothin' like a true friend." And with those words of wisdom he left the room, leaving us to wonder how he had managed to slink out of this one.

The Monday after his arrival Mr. Morrison had moved into the deserted tenant shack that stood in the south pasture. It was a sorry mess, that house. Its door hung sadly from a broken hinge; its porch floorboards were rotted; and its one-room interior was densely occupied by rats, spiders, and other field creatures. But Mr. Morrison was a quiet man, almost shy, and although Mama had offered him lodging in our house, he preferred the old shack. Mama sensed that Mr. Morrison was a private person and she did not object to the move, but she did send the boys and me to the house to help clean it.

Little Man, Christopher-John, and I took to Mr. Morrison immediately and had no objections to the cleaning. Anybody who was a friend of Papa's was all right in our book; besides, when he was near, night men and burnings and midnight tarrings faded into a hazy distance. But Stacey remained aloof and had little to do with him.

After the cleaning I asked Mama if Christopher-John, Little Man, and I could go visit Mr. Morrison, but she said no.

"But, Mama, I wanna know more 'bout him," I explained.

"I just wanna know how come he's so big."

"You know about as much as you need to know," she decided. "And long as Mr. Morrison stays here, that's his house. If he wants you down there, he'll ask you."

"Don't know how come y'all wanna go down there noway," Stacey said moodily when Mama was out of hearing.

"'Cause we like him, that's why," I answered, tired of his distant attitude toward Mr. Morrison. Then, as discreetly as I could, I said, "What's the matter with you, boy, not liking Mr. Morrison?"

Stacey shrugged. "I like him all right."

"Don't act that way."

Stacey looked away from me. "Don't need him here. All that work he doing, I could've done it myself."

"Ah, you couldn't've done no such thing. Besides"—I looked around to be certain that Big Ma and Mama were not near—"besides, Papa didn't just bring him here to do no work. You know how come he really here."

Stacey turned toward me haughtily. "I could've taken care of that too."

I rolled my eyes at him, but held my peace. I didn't feel like a fight, and as long as Mr. Morrison was within hollering distance of the back porch, it made little difference to me what Stacey *thought* he could do.

"I sure wouldn't want that big ole man stayin' at my place," said T.J. on the way to school. "I betcha he get mad one time, he'd take ole Little Man and swing him over that tree yonder like he wasn't nothin' but a twig." He laughed then as Little Man set his lips and stared angrily up. "Course, I could probably 'bout do that myself."

"Couldn't neither!" denied Little Man.

"Hush, Man," said Stacey. "T.J., leave Man alone."

"Aw, I ain't botherin' him. Little Man's my buddy, ain't ya, Man?" Little Man scowled, but didn't reply. T.J. turned back to Stacey. "You ready for that history test?"

"Hope so," said Stacey. "But I keep forgetting them dates."

"Betcha I could help ya, if you be nice."

"How? You worse than I am 'bout dates."

T.J. grinned, then slyly pulled a folded sheet of paper from his pocket and handed it to Stacey. Stacey unfolded it, looked at it curiously, then frowned. "You planning on cheating?"

"Well, naw, I ain't plannin' on it," said T.J. seriously. "Jus' if I gotta."

"Well, you ain't gonna," said Stacey, tearing the paper in two.

"Hey, what's the matter with you, man!" cried T.J. grabbing for the paper. But Stacey turned his back to him and tore the paper into bits, then deposited them in the gully. "Man, that sho' ain't right! I wouldn't do you that way!"

"Maybe not," replied Stacey. "But at least this way you won't get into no trouble."

T.J. mumbled, "If failin' ain't trouble, I don't know what is."

Little Man, Christopher-John, Claude, and I were sitting on the bottom step of the seventh-grade-class building after school waiting for Stacey and T.J. when the front door banged open and T.J. shot out and tore across the yard. "What's the matter with him?" asked Christopher-John. "Ain't he gonna wait for Stacey?"

The rest of the seventh grade, led by Little Willie Wiggins and Moe Turner, spilled from the building. "There he go!" cried Little Willie as T.J. disappeared on the forest road. Moe Turner yelled, "Let's see where he goin'!" Then he and three other boys dashed away in pursuit of T.J. But the others stood restlessly near the steps as if school had not yet ended.

"Hey, what's going on?" I asked Little Willie. "What's everybody waiting 'round for?"

"And where's Stacey?" demanded Little Man.

Little Willie smiled. "Stacey inside with Miz Logan. He got whipped today."

"Whipped!" I cried. "Why, can't nobody whip Stacey. Who done it?"

"Your mama," laughed Little Willie.

"Mama!" Christopher-John, Little Man, and I exclaimed.

Little Willie nodded. "Yep. In front of everybody."

I swallowed hard, feeling very sorry for my older brother. It was bad enough to be whipped in front of thirty others by a teacher, but to get it by one's own mother—now that was downright embarrassing.

"Why'd Mama do that?" asked Christopher-John.

"She caught him with cheat notes during the history examination."

"Mama knows Stacey wouldn't cheat!" I declared.

Little Willie shrugged. "Well, whether she knowed it or not, she sho' 'nough whipped him. . . . Course, now, she give him a chance to get out of it when he said he wasn't cheatin' and she asked him how he got them cheat notes. But Stacey wouldn't tell on ole T.J., and you know good and well ole T.J. wasn't 'bout to say them notes was his."

"Cheat notes! But how'd T.J. get cheat notes? Stacey got rid of them things this morning!"

"Come noontime though," replied Little Willie, "T.J. was in them woods busy writing himself another set. Me and Moe seen him."

"Well, what the devil was Stacey doing with 'em?"

"Well, we was in the middle of the examination and ole T.J. slips out these cheat notes—me and Clarence here was sittin' right behind him and T.J. and seen the whole thing. Stacey was sittin' right side of T.J. and when he seen them notes, he motioned T.J. to put 'em away. At first T.J. wouldn't do it, but then he seen Miz Logan startin' toward 'em and he slipped Stacey the notes. Well, Stacey didn't see Miz Logan comin' when he took them notes, and by the time he saw her it was too late to get rid of 'em.

Wasn't nothin' Miz Logan could do but whip him. Failed him too."

"And ole T.J. just sat there and ain't said a word," interjected Clarence, laughing.

"But knowin' Stacey, I betcha ole T.J. ain't gonna get away with it," chuckled Little Willie. "And T.J. know it too. That's why he lit outa here like he done, and I betcha — Hey, Stacey!"

Everyone turned as Stacey bounded down the steps. His square face was unsmiling, but there was no anger in his voice when he asked quietly, "Anybody seen T.J.?" All the students answered at once, indicating that T.J. had headed west toward home, then surrounded Stacey as he started across the lawn. Christopher-John, Little Man, Claude, and I followed.

When we reached the crossroads, Moe Turner was waiting. "T.J. went down to the Wallace store," he announced.

Stacey stopped and so did everyone else. Stacey stared past Jefferson Davis, then back down the road toward Great Faith. Looking over his shoulder, he found me and ordered, "Cassie, you and Christopher-John and Man go on home."

"You come too," I said, afraid of where he was going.

"Got something to take care of first," he said, walking away.

"Mama gonna take care of you, too!" I hollered after him. "You know she said we wasn't to go down there, and she find out, she gonna wear you out again! Papa too!" But Stacey did not come back. For a moment, Little Man,

Christopher-John, Claude, and I stood watching Stacey and the others heading swiftly northward. Then Little Man said, "I wanna see what he gonna do."

"I don't," declared Christopher-John.

"Come on," I said, starting after Stacey with Little Man and Claude beside me.

"I don't want no whipping!" objected Christopher-John, standing alone in the crossroads. But when he saw that we were not coming back, he puffed to join us, grumbling all the while.

The Wallace store stood almost a half mile beyond Jefferson Davis, on a triangular lot that faced the Soldiers Bridge crossroads. Once the Granger plantation store, it had been run by the Wallaces for as long as I could remember, and most of the people within the forty-mile stretch between Smellings Creek and Strawberry shopped there. The other three corners of the crossroads were forest land, black and dense. The store consisted of a small building with a gas pump in front and a storage house in back. Beyond the store, against the forest edge, were two gray clapboard houses and a small garden. But there were no fields; the Wallaces did not farm.

Stacey and the other students were standing in the doorway of the store when Little Man, Christopher-John, Claude, and I ran up. We squeezed through so we could see inside. A man we all knew was Kaleb Wallace stood behind the counter. A few other men sat around a stove playing checkers, and Jeremy's older brothers, R.W. and Melvin, who had dropped out of school long ago, leaned sleepy-eyed against the counter staring at us.

"Y'all go on to the back," said Kaleb Wallace, "lessn y'all wanna buy something. Mr. Dewberry got the music goin' already."

As we turned away from the entrance, Melvin Simms said, "Just look at all the little niggers come to dance," and the laughter of the men filled the room.

Christopher-John tugged at my arm. "I don't like this place, Cassie. Let's go on home."

"We can't leave without Stacey," I said.

Music beckoned from the storage room where Dewberry Wallace was placing round brown bottles on a small table as we crowded in. Aside from the table, there was no furniture in the room. Boxes lined the walls and the center floor had been cleared for dancing—several older couples from Great Faith were already engaged in movements I had never seen before.

"What they doing?" asked Little Man.

I shrugged. "I guess that's what they call dancing."

"There he go!" someone shouted as the back door of the storeroom slammed shut. Stacey turned quickly and sped to the back of the building. T.J. was fleeing straight toward Soldiers Road. Stacey tore across the Wallace yard and, leaping high like a forest fox, fell upon T.J., knocking him down. The two boys rolled toward the road, each trying to keep the other's back pinned to the ground, but then Stacey, who was stronger, gained the advantage and T.J., finding that he could not budge him, cried, "Hey, wait a minute, man, let me explain—"

Stacey did not let him finish. Jumping up, he pulled T.J. up too and hit him squarely in the face. T.J. staggered back holding his eyes as if he were badly hurt, and Stacey momentarily let down his guard. At that moment, T.J. rammed into Stacey, forcing the fight to the ground again.

Little Man, Christopher-John, and I, with the others, circled the fighters, chanting loudly as they rolled back and forth punching at each other. All of us were so engrossed in the battle that no one saw a mule wagon halt on the road and a giant man step out. It wasn't until I realized that the shouting had stopped behind us and that the girls and boys beside me were falling back that I looked up.

Mr. Morrison towered above us.

He did not look at me or Christopher-John or Little Man, although I knew he had seen us, but walked straight to the fighters and lifted a still-swinging Stacey off T.J. After a long, tense moment, he said to Stacey, "You and your sister and brothers get on in the wagon."

We walked through the now-silent crowd. Kaleb and Dewberry Wallace, standing on the front porch of the store with the Simmses, stared at Mr. Morrison as we passed, but Mr. Morrison looked through them as if they were not there. Stacey sat in front of the wagon with Mr. Morrison; the rest of us climbed into the back. "Now we gonna get it," shuddered Christopher-John. "I told y'all we shoulda gone on home."

Before Mr. Morrison took the reins, he handed Stacey a handkerchief in which to wrap his bruised right hand, but he did not say a word and it wasn't until we had passed the crossroads leading to Great Faith that the silence was broken.

"Mr. Morrison . . . you gonna tell Mama?" Stacey asked huskily.

Mr. Morrison was very quiet as Jack the mule clopped noisily along the dry road. "Seems I heard your mama tell y'all not to go up to that Wallace store," he said at last.

"Y-yessir," said Stacey, glancing nervously at Mr. Morrison. Then he blurted out, "But I had good reason!"

"Ain't never no reason good enough to go disobey your mama."

The boys and I looked woefully at each other and my bottom stung from the awful thought of Mama's leather strap against it. "But Mr. Morrison," I cried anxiously, "T.J. was hiding there 'cause he thought Stacey wouldn't never come down there to get him. But Stacey had to go down there cause T.J. was cheating and—"

"Hush, Cassie," Stacey ordered, turning sharply around.

I faltered for only a moment before deciding that my bottom was more important than Stacey's code of honor "—and Stacey had to take the blame for it and Mama whipped him right in front of God and everybody!" Once the truth had been disclosed, I waited with dry throat and nauseous stomach for Mr. Morrison to say something. When he did, all of us strained tensely forward.

"I ain't gonna tell her," he said quietly.

Christopher-John sighed with relief. "Ain't going down there no more neither," he promised. Little Man and I agreed. But Stacey stared long and hard at Mr. Morrison.

"How come, Mr. Morrison?" he asked. "How come you ain't gonna tell Mama?"

Mr. Morrison slowed Jack as we turned into the road leading home. " 'Cause I'm leaving it up to you to tell her."

"What!" we exclaimed together.

"Sometimes a person's gotta fight," he said slowly. "But that store ain't the place to be doing it. From what I hear, folks like them Wallaces got no respect at all for colored folks and they just think it's funny when we fight each other. Your mama knowed them Wallaces ain't good folks, that's why she don't want y'all down there, and y'all owe it to her and y'allselves to tell her. But I'm gonna leave it up to y'all to decide."

Stacey nodded thoughtfully and wound the handkerchief tighter around his wounded hand. His face was not scarred, so if he could just figure out a way to explain the bruises on his hand to Mama without lying he was in the clear, for Mr. Morrison had not said that he *had* to tell her. But for some reason I could not understand he said, "All right, Mr. Morrison, I'll tell her."

"Boy, you crazy!" I cried as Christopher-John and Little Man speedily came to the same conclusion. If he did not care about his own skin, he could at least consider ours.

But he seemed not to hear us as his eyes met Mr. Morrison's and the two of them smiled in subtle understanding, the distance between them fading.

As we neared the house, Mr. Granger's Packard rolled from the dusty driveway. Mr. Morrison directed Jack to the side of the road until the big car had passed, then swung the wagon back into the road's center and up the drive. Big Ma was standing by the yard gate that led onto the drive, gazing across the road at the forest.

"Big Ma, what was Mr. Granger doing here?" Stacey asked, jumping from the wagon and going to her. Little Man, Christopher-John, and I hopped down and followed him.

"Nothin'," Big Ma replied absently, her eyes still on the forest. "Just worryin' me 'bout this land again."

"Oh," said Stacey, his tone indicating that he considered the visit of no importance. Mr. Granger had always wanted the land. He turned and went to help Mr. Morrison. Little Man and Christopher-John went with him, but I remained by the gate with Big Ma.

"Big Ma," I said, "what Mr. Granger need more land for?"

"Don't need it," Big Ma said flatly. "Got more land now than he know what to do with."

"Well, what he want with ours then?"

"Just like to have it, that's all."

"Well, seems to me he's just being greedy. You ain't gonna sell it to him, are you?"

Big Ma did not answer me. Instead, she pushed open the gate and walked down the drive and across the road into the forest. I ran after her. We walked in silence down the narrow cow path which wound through the old forest to the pond. As we neared the pond, the forest gapped open into a wide, brown glade, man-made by the felling of many trees, some of them still on the ground. They had been cut during the summer after Mr. Andersen came from Strawberry with an offer to buy the trees. The offer was backed with a threat, and Big Ma was afraid. So Andersen's lumbermen came, chopping and sawing, destroying the fine old trees. Papa was away on the railroad then but Mama sent Stacey for him. He returned and stopped the cutting, but not before many of the trees had already fallen.

Big Ma surveyed the clearing without a word, then, stepping around the rotting trees, she made her way to the pond and sat down on one of them. I sat close beside her and waited for her to speak. After a while she shook her head and said: "I'm sho' glad your grandpa never had to see none of this. He dearly loved these here old trees. Him and me, we used to come down here early mornin's or just 'fore the sun was 'bout to set and just sit and talk. He used to call this place his thinkin' spot and he called that old pond there Caroline, after me."

She smiled vaguely, but not at me.

"You know, I . . . I wasn't hardly eighteen when Paul

Edward married me and brung me here. He was older than me by 'bout eight years and he was smart. Ow-ow, my Lord, that was one smart man! He had himself a mind like a steel trap. Anything he seen done, he could do it. He had done learned carpentry back up there near Macon, Georgia, where he was born. Born into slavery he was, two years 'fore freedom come, and him and his mama stayed on at that plantation after the fightin' was finished. But then when he got to be fourteen and his mama died, he left that place and worked his way 'cross here up to Vicksburg."

"That's where he met you, ain't it, Big Ma?" I asked, already knowing the answer.

Big Ma nodded, smiling. "Sho' was. He was carpenterin' up there and my papa took me in with him to Vicksburg—we was tenant farmin' 'bout thirty miles from there—to see 'bout gettin' a store-bought rocker for my mama, and there was ole Paul Edward workin' in that furniture shop just as big. Had himself a good job, but that ole job wasn't what he wanted. He wanted himself some land. Kept on and kept on talkin' 'bout land, and then this place come up for sell."

"And he bought himself two hundred acres from that Yankee, didn't he?"

Big Ma chuckled. "That man went right on over to see Mr. Hollenbeck and said, 'Mr. Hollenbeck, I understand you got land to sell and I'd be interested in buyin' me 'bout two hundred acres if yo' price is right.' Ole Mr. Hollenbeck questioned him good 'bout where he was gonna get the money to pay him, but Paul Edward just said, 'Don't seem to me it's your worry 'bout how I'm gonna get the money just long as you get paid your price.' Didn't nothin' scare that man!" She beamed proudly. "And Mr. Hollenbeck went on and let him have it. Course now, he was just 'bout as eager to sell this land as Paul Edward was to buy. He'd had it for goin' on nigh twenty years—bought it during Reconstruction from the Grangers—"

" 'Cause they didn't have no money to pay their taxes—"

"Not only didn't have tax money, didn't have no money at all! That war left them plumb broke. Their ole Confederate money wasn't worth nothin' and both Northern and Southern soldiers had done ransacked their place. Them Grangers didn't have nothin' but they land left and they had to sell two thousand acres of it to get money to pay them taxes and rebuild the rest of it, and that Yankee bought the whole two thousand—"

"Then he turned 'round and tried to sell it back to 'em, huh, Big Ma?"

"Sho' did . . . but not till eighty-seven, when your grandpa bought himself that two hundred acres. As I hears it, that Yankee offered to sell all two thousand acres back to Harlan Granger's daddy for less'n the land was worth, but that old Filmore Granger was just 'bout as tight with a penny as anybody ever lived and he wouldn't buy it back. So Mr. Hollenbeck just let other folks know he was sellin', and it didn't take long 'fore he sold all of it 'cause it was some mighty fine land. Besides your grandpa, a bunch of other small farmers bought up eight hundred acres and Mr. Jamison bought the rest."

"But that wasn't *our* Mr. Jamison," I supplied knowingly. "That was his daddy."

"Charles Jamison was his name," Big Ma said. "A fine old gentleman, too. He was a good neighbor and he always treated us fair . . . just like his son. The Jamisons was what folks call 'Old South' from up in Vicksburg, and as I understands it, before the war they had as much money as anybody and even after the war they managed better than some other folks 'cause they had made themselves some Northern money. Anyways, old Mr. Jamison got it into his mind that he wanted to farm and he moved his family from Vicksburg down in here. Mr. Wade Jamison wasn't but 'bout eight years old then."

"But he didn't like to farm," I said.

"Oh, he liked it all right. Just wasn't never much hand at it though, and after he went up North to law school and all he just felt he oughta practice his law."

"Is that how come he sold Grandpa them other two hundred acres?"

"Sho' is . . . and it was mighty good of him to do it, too. My Paul Edward had been eyein' that two hundred acres ever since 1910 when he done paid off the bank for them first two hundred, but ole Mr. Jamison didn't wanna sell. 'Bout that same time, Harlan Granger 'come head of the Granger plantation—you know, him and Wade Jamison 'bout the same year's children—and he wanted to buy back every inch of land that used to belong to the Grangers. That man crazy 'bout anythin' that was before that war and he wantin' his land to be every bit like it was then. Already had more'n four thousand acres, but he just itchin' to have back them other two thousand his granddaddy sold. Got back eight hundred of 'em, too, from them other farmers that bought from Mr. Hollenbeck—"

"But Grandpa and old Mr. Jamison wasn't interested in selling, period, was they, Big Ma? They didn't care how much money Mr. Granger offered 'em!" I declared with an emphatic nod.

"That's the truth of it all right," agreed Big Ma. "But when Mr. Jamison died in 1918 and Wade 'come head of the family, he sold them two hundred acres to Paul Edward and the rest of his land to Harlan Granger, and moved his family into Strawberry. He could've just as easy sold the full thousand acres to the Grangers and gotten more money, but he didn't . . . and till this day Harlan Granger still hold it 'gainst him 'cause he didn't. . . ."

The soft swish of falling leaves made Big Ma look up from the pond and at the trees again. Her lips curved into a tender smile as she looked around thoughtfully. "You know," she said, "I can still see my Paul Edward's face the day Mr. Jamison sold him them two hundred acres. He put his arms 'round me and looked out at his new piece of land, then he said 'zactly the same thing he said when he grabbed himself that first two hundred acres. Said, 'Pretty Caroline,

how you like to work this fine piece of earth with me?' Sho'
did . . . said the 'zact same thing."

She grew quiet then and rubbed the wrinkles down one
hand as if to smooth them away. I gazed at the pond, glassy
gray and calm, until she was ready to go on. I had learned
that at times like these it was better to just sit and wait than
to go asking disrupting questions which might vex her.

"So long ago now," she said eventually, in a voice that was
almost a whisper. "We worked real hard gettin' them crops
sown, gettin' 'em reaped. We had us a time. . . . But there
was good times too. We was young and strong when we
started out and we liked to work. Neither one of us, I'm
proud to say, never was lazy and we didn't raise us no lazy
children neither. Had ourselves six fine children. Lost our
girls when they was babies, though. . . . I s'pose that's one
of the reasons I love your sweet mama so much. . . . But
them boys grew strong and all of 'em loved this place as
much as Paul Edward and me. They go away, they always
come back to it. Couldn't leave it."

She shook her head and sighed. "Then Mitchell, he got
killed in the war and Kevin got drowned. . . ." Her voice
faded completely, but when she spoke again it had hardened
and there was a determined glint in her eyes. "Now all the
boys I got is my baby boys, your papa and your Uncle
Hammer, and this they place as much as it is mine. They
blood's in this land, and here that Harlan Granger always
talkin' 'bout buyin' it. He pestered Paul Edward to death
'bout buyin' it, now he pesterin' me. Humph!" she grumped

angrily. "He don't know nothin' 'bout me or this land, he think I'm gonna sell!"

She became silent again.

A cold wind rose, biting through my jacket, and I shivered. Big Ma looked down at me for the first time. "You cold?"

"N-no, ma'am," I stuttered, not ready to leave the forest.

"Don't you be lyin' to me girl!" she snapped, putting out her hand. "It's time we was goin' back to the house anyways. Your mama'll be home soon."

I took her hand, and together we left the Caroline.

Despite our every effort to persuade Stacey otherwise, when Mama came home he confessed that he had been fighting T.J. at the Wallace store and that Mr. Morrison had stopped it. He stood awkwardly before her, disclosing only those things which he could honorably mention. He said nothing of T.J.'s cheating or that Christopher-John, Little Man, and I had been with him, and when Mama asked him a question he could not answer honestly, he simply looked at his feet and refused to speak. The rest of us sat fidgeting nervously throughout the interview and when Mama looked our way, we swiftly found somewhere else to rest our eyes.

Finally, seeing that she had gotten all the information she was going to get from Stacey, Mama turned to us. "I suppose you three went to the store too, huh?" But before any of us could squeak an answer, she exclaimed, "That does it!"

and began to pace the floor, her arms folded, her face cross.

Although she scolded us severely, she did not whip us. We were sent to bed early but we didn't consider that a punishment, and we doubted that Mama did either. How we had managed to escape a whipping we couldn't fathom until Saturday, when Mama woke us before dawn and piled us into the wagon. Taking us southwest toward Smellings Creek, she said, "Where we're going the man is very sick and he doesn't look like other people. But I don't want you to be afraid or uncomfortable when you see him. Just be yourselves."

We rode for almost two hours before turning onto a backwoods trail. We were jarred and bounced over the rough road until we entered a clearing where a small weather-grayed house stood and fields stretched barren beyond it. As Mama pulled up on the reins and ordered us down, the front door cracked warily open, but no one appeared. Then Mama said, "Good morning, Mrs. Berry. It's Mary Logan, David's wife."

The door swung wide then and an elderly woman, frail and toothless, stepped out. Her left arm hung crazily at her side as if it had been broken long ago but had not mended properly, and she walked with a limp; yet she smiled widely, throwing her good arm around Mama and hugging her. "Land sakes, child, ain't you somethin'!" she exclaimed. "Comin' to see 'bout these old bones. I jus' sez to Sam, I sez, 'Who you reckon comin' to see old folks like us?' These yo' babies, ain't they? Lord a'mighty, ain't they fine! Sho' is!" She hugged each of us and ushered us into the house.

The interior was dark, lit only by the narrow slat of gray daylight allowed in by the open door. Stacey and I carried cans of milk and butter, and Christopher-John and Little Man each had a jar of beef and a jar of crowder peas which Mama and Big Ma had canned. Mrs. Berry took the food, her thanks intermingled with questions about Big Ma, Papa, and others. When she had put the food away, she pulled stools from the darkness and motioned us to sit down, then she went to the blackest corner and said, "Daddy, who you s'pose done come to see 'bout us?"

There was no recognizable answer, only an inhuman guttural wheezing. But Mrs. Berry seemed to accept it and went on. "Miz Logan and her babies. Ain't that somethin'?" She took a sheet from a nearby table. "Gots to cover him," she explained. "He can't hardly stand to have nothin' touch him." When she was visible again, she picked up a candle stump and felt around a table for matches. "He can't speak no more. The fire burned him too bad. But he understands all right." Finding the matches, she lit the candle and turned once more to the corner.

A still form lay there staring at us with glittering eyes. The face had no nose, and the head no hair; the skin was scarred, burned, and the lips were wizened black, like charcoal. As the wheezing sound echoed from the opening that was a mouth, Mama said, "Say good morning to Mrs. Berry's husband, children."

The boys and I stammered a greeting, then sat silently

trying not to stare at Mr. Berry during the hour that we remained in the small house. But Mama talked softly to both Mr. and Mrs. Berry, telling them news of the community as if Mr. Berry were as normal as anyone else.

After we were on the main road again, having ridden in thoughtful silence over the wooded trail, Mama said quietly, "The Wallaces did that, children. They poured kerosene over Mr. Berry and his nephews and lit them afire. One of the nephews died, the other one is just like Mr. Berry." She allowed this information to penetrate the silence, then went on. "Everyone knows they did it, and the Wallaces even laugh about it, but nothing was ever done. They're bad people, the Wallaces. That's why I don't want you to ever go to their store again—for any reason. You understand?"

We nodded, unable to speak as we thought of the disfigured man lying in the darkness.

On the way home we stopped at the homes of some of Mama's students, where families poured out of tenant shacks to greet us. At each farm Mama spoke of the bad influence of the Wallaces, of the smoking and drinking permitted at their store, and asked that the family's children not be allowed to go there.

The people nodded and said she was right.

She also spoke of finding another store to patronize, one where the proprietors were more concerned about the welfare of the community. But she did not speak directly of what the Wallaces had done to the Berrys for, as she explained later, that was something that wavered between the known and the unknown and to mention it outright to any-one outside of those with whom you were closest was not wise. There were too many ears that listened for others be-sides themselves, and too many tongues that wagged to those they shouldn't.

The people only nodded, and Mama left.

When we reached the Turner farm, Moe's widowed fa-ther rubbed his stubbled chin and squinted across the room at Mama. "Miz Logan," he said, "you know I feels the same way you do 'bout them low-down Wallaces, but it ain't easy to jus' stop shoppin' there. They overcharges me and I has to pay them high interest, but I gots credit there 'cause Mr. Montier signs for me. Now you know most folks 'round here sharecroppin' on Montier, Granger, or Harrison land and most of them jus' 'bout got to shop at that Wallace store or up at the mercantile in Strawberry, which is jus' 'bout as bad. Can't go no place else."

Mama nodded solemnly, showing she understood, then she said, "For the past year now, our family's been shopping down at Vicksburg. There are a number of stores down there and we've found several that treat us well."

"Vicksburg?" Mr. Turner echoed, shaking his head. "Lord, Miz Logan, you ain't expectin' me to go all the way to Vicksburg? That's an overnight journey in a wagon down there and back."

Mama thought on that a moment. "What if someone would be willing to make the trip for you? Go all the way to Vicksburg and bring back what you need?"

"Won't do no good," retorted Mr. Turner. "I got no cash money. Mr. Montier signs for me up at that Wallace store so's I can get my tools, my mule, my seed, my fertilizer, my food, and what few clothes I needs to keep my children from runnin' plumb naked. When cotton-pickin' time comes, he sells my cotton, takes half of it, pays my debt up at that store and my interest for they credit, then charges me ten to fifteen percent more as 'risk' money for signin' for me in the first place. This year I earned me near two hundred dollars after Mr. Montier took his half of the crop money, but I ain't seen a penny of it. In fact, if I manages to come out even without owin' that man nothin', I figures I've had a good year. Now, who way down in Vicksburg gonna give a man like me credit?"

Mama was very quiet and did not answer.

"I sho' sorry, Miz Logan. I'm gonna keep my younguns from up at that store, but I gots to live. Y'all got it better'n most the folks 'round here 'cause y'all gots your own place and y'all ain't gotta cowtail to a lot of this stuff. But you gotta understand it ain't easy for sharecroppin' folks to do what you askin'."

"Mr. Turner," Mama said in a whisper, "what if someone backed your signature? Would you shop up in Vicksburg then?"

Mr. Turner looked at Mama strangely. "Now, who'd sign for me?"

"If someone would, would you do it?"

Mr. Turner gazed into the fire, burning to a low ash, then

got up and put another log on it, taking his time as he watched the fire shoot upward and suck in the log. Without turning around he said, "When I was a wee little boy, I got burnt real bad. It healed over but I ain't never forgot the pain of it. . . . It's an awful way to die." Then, turning, he faced Mama. "Miz Logan, you find someone to sign my credit, and I'll consider it deeply."

After we left the Turners', Stacey asked, "Mama, who you gonna get to sign?" But Mama, her brow furrowed, did not reply. I started to repeat the question, but Stacey shook his head and I settled back wondering, then fell asleep.

5

The blue-black shine that had so nicely encircled T.J.'s left eye for over a week had almost completely faded by the morning T.J. hopped into the back of the wagon beside Stacey and snuggled in a corner not occupied by the butter, milk, and eggs Big Ma was taking to sell at the market in Strawberry. I sat up front beside Big Ma, still sandy-eyed and not believing that I was actually going.

The second Saturday of every month was market day in Strawberry, and for as far back as I could remember the boys and I had been begging Big Ma to take us to it. Stacey had actually gone once, but Christopher-John, Little Man, and I had always been flatly denied the experience. We had, in fact, been denied so often that our pestering now occurred more out of habit than from any real belief that we would be allowed to go. But this morning, while the world lay black, Big Ma called: "Cassie, get up, child, if you gonna go to town with me, and be quiet 'bout it. You wake up Christopher-John or Little Man and I'll leave you here. I don't want them cryin' all over the place 'cause they can't go."

As Jack swept the wagon into the gray road, Big Ma pulled tightly on the reins and grumbled, "Hold on! You, Jack, hold on! I ain't got no time to be putting up with both you and T.J.'s foolishness."

"T.J!" Stacey and I exclaimed together. "He going?"

Big Ma didn't answer immediately; she was occupied in a test of wills with Jack. When hers had prevailed and Jack had settled into a moderate trot, she replied moodily, "Mr. Avery come by after y'all was asleep last night wanting T.J. to go to Strawberry to do some shopping for a few things he couldn't get at the Wallace store. Lord, that's all I need with all the trouble about is for that child to talk me to death for twenty-two miles."

Big Ma didn't need to say any more and she didn't. T.J. was far from her favorite person and it was quite obvious that Stacey and I owed our good fortune entirely to T.J.'s obnoxious personality.

T.J., however, was surprisingly subdued when he settled into the wagon; I suppose that at three-thirty in the morning even T.J.'s mouth was tired. But by dawn, when the December sun was creeping warily upward shooting pale streams of buff-colored light through the forest, he was fully awake and chattering like a cockatoo. His endless talk made me wish that he had not managed to wheedle his way so speedily back into Stacey's good graces, but Big Ma, her face furrowed in distant thoughts, did not hush him. He talked the rest of the way into Strawberry, announcing as we arrived, "Well, children, open your eyes and take in Strawberry, Mississippi!"

"Is this it?" I cried, a gutting disappointment enveloping me as we entered the town. Strawberry was nothing like the tough, sprawling bigness I had envisioned. It was instead a sad, red place. As far as I could see, the only things modern about it were a paved road which cut through its center and fled northward, away from it, and a spindly row of electrical lines. Lining the road were strips of red dirt splotched with patches of brown grass and drying mud puddles, and beyond the dirt and the mud puddles, gloomy store buildings set behind raised wooden sidewalks and sagging verandas.

"Shoot!" I grumbled. "It sure ain't nothing to shout about."

"Hush up, Cassie," Big Ma said. "You, too, T.J. Y'all in town now and I expects y'all to act like it. In another hour this place'll be teeming up with folks from all over the county and I don't want no trouble."

As the stores gave way to houses still sleeping, we turned onto a dirt road which led past more shops and beyond to a wide field dotted with wooden stalls. Near the field entrance several farm wagons and pickups were already parked, but Big Ma drove to the other side of the field where only two wagons were stationed. Climbing from the wagon, she said, "Don't seem like too many folks ahead of us. In the summer, I'd've had to come on Friday and spend the night to get a spot like this." She headed toward the back of the wagon. "Stacey, you and T.J. stay up there a minute and push them milk cans over here so's I can reach 'em."

"Big Ma," I said, following her, "all them folks up there selling milk and eggs too?"

"Not all, I reckon. Some of 'em gots meats and vegetables, quilts and sewing and such. But I guess a good piece of 'em sellin' the same as us."

I studied the wagons parked at the field entrance, then exclaimed, "Well, what the devil we doing way back here then! Can't nobody see us."

"You watch your mouth, girl," warned Big Ma. Then, arranging the milk cans and baskets of eggs near the wagon's edge, she softened her voice and promised, "We'll do all right. I got me some regular customers and they'll check to see if I'm here 'fore they buy."

"Not back here they won't," I grumbled. Maybe Big Ma knew what she was doing, but it made absolutely no sense to me to be so far from the entrance. Most of the other farmers seemed to have the right idea, and I couldn't help but try to make her see the business sense in moving the wagon forward. "Why don't we move our wagon up there with them other wagons, Big Ma? There's plenty of room, and we could sell more."

"Them's white folks' wagons, Cassie," Big Ma said gruffly, as if that explained everything. "Now, hush up and help me get this food out."

"Shoot," I mumbled, taking one of the buckets from Stacey, "by the time a body walk way back here, they'll have bunions on their soles and corns on their toes."

By noon the crowd which had covered the field during the early morning had thinned noticeably, and wagons and trucks began to pack up and head for town. After we had eaten our cold lunch of oil sausages and cornbread washed down with clabber milk, we did the same.

On the main street of Strawberry once more, Big Ma parked the wagon in front of a building where four shingles hung from a rusted post. One of the shingles read: "Wade W. Jamison, Attorney-at-Law."

"Mr. Jamison live here?" I cried, scrambling down. "I wanna see him."

"He don't live here," said Big Ma, opening her large purse. She pulled out a long manila envelope, checked inside, then gingerly put it back again. "This here's his office and I got some business with him. You get on back in the wagon." Big Ma climbed down, but I didn't get back in. "Can't I just go up and say 'Hey'?" I persisted.

"I'm gonna 'Hey' you," Big Ma said, "you keep pesterin' me." She glanced over at Stacey and T.J. "Y'all wait here for me and soon's I get back, we'll go do that shoppin' so's we can get on home 'fore it gets dark."

When she had gone inside, T.J. said, "What you wanna see that ole white man for anyway, Cassie? What you and him got to talk 'bout?"

"I just wanted to see him, that's all," I said, going to the raised sidewalk and taking a seat. I liked Mr. Jamison and I didn't mind admitting it. He came to see us several times a year, mainly on business, and although the boys and I were somewhat shy of him, we were always glad to see him. He was the only white man I had ever heard address Mama and Big Ma as "Missus," and I liked him for it. Besides that, in his way he was like Papa: Ask him a question and he would give it to you straight with none of this pussyfooting-around business. I liked that.

After several minutes of watching farmers in faded overalls and their women in flour-sack-cut dresses promenading under the verandas, T.J. said, "Why don't we go on down to the mercantile and look around?"

Stacey hesitated. "I don't know. I think Big Ma wanted to go with us."

"Ah, shoot, man, we'll be doin' her a favor. We go on down to the mercantile now and order up our stuff, we'll save her some time so when she come from seein' that lawyer, we can jus' go on home. Besides, I got somethin' to show ya."

Stacey pondered the suggestion for a long moment. "Well, I guess it'll be all right," he said finally.

"Big Ma said stay here!" I objected, hoping that Mr. Jamison would come out with Big Ma.

"Stay here then," Stacey called over his shoulder as he crossed the street with T.J.

I dashed after them. I wasn't about to stay on that sidewalk by myself.

The Barnett Mercantile had everything. Its shelves, counters, and floor space boasted items from ladies' ribbons to burlap bags of seeds; from babies' bottles to brand-new pot-bellied stoves. T.J., who had been to the store several times before, wove his way among the farmers and led us to a counter at the far corner of the room. The counter had a glass top, and beneath the glass were handguns artfully displayed on a bolt of red velvet.

"Jus' look at it," T.J. said dreamily. "Ain't she somethin'?"

"What?" I said.

"That pearl-handled one. Stacey, man, you ever seen a gun like that before in your whole life? I'd sell my life for that gun. One of these days I'm gonna have it, too."

"I reckon I ain't," said Stacey politely. "It's a nice-looking gun all right."

I stared down at the gun. A price tag of $35.95 stared back at me. "Thirty-five dollars and ninety-five cents!" I almost screamed. "Just for an ole gun? What the devil you gonna use it for? Can't hunt with it."

T.J. looked at me with disgust. "Ain't s'pose to hunt with it. It's for protection."

"Protection of what?" I asked, thinking of Papa's sturdy shotgun that hung over his and Mama's bed, and the sleek Winchester rifle which Big Ma kept locked in the trunk beneath our own bed. "That thing couldn't hardly kill a rattlesnake."

"There's other things a body needs protectin' from more than a rattlesnake," he said haughtily. "I get me that gun and ain't nobody gonna mess with me. I wouldn't need nobody."

Stacey backed away from the counter. He seemed nervous being in the store. "We better get those things you need and get on outa here 'fore Big Ma comes looking for us."

"Ah, man, there's plenty of time," said T.J., looking longingly at the gun. "Sure wish I could jus' hold it, jus' once."

"Come on, T.J.," ordered Stacey, "or me and Cassie's gonna go on back outside."

"Oh, all right." T.J. turned reluctantly away and went to a counter where a man was measuring nails onto a scale. We stood patiently waiting behind the people in front of us and when our turn came, T.J. handed his list to the man. "Mr. Barnett, sir," he said, "I got me this here list of things my mama want."

The storekeeper studied the list and without looking up asked, "You one of Mr. Granger's people?"

"Yessir," answered T.J.

Mr. Barnett walked to another counter and began filling the order, but before he finished a white woman called,

"Mr. Barnett, you waiting on anybody just now?"

Mr. Barnett turned around. "Just them," he said, indicating us with a wave of his hand. "What can I do for you, Miz Emmaline?" The woman handed him a list twice as long as T.J.'s and the storekeeper, without a word of apology to us, proceeded to fill it.

"What's he doing?" I objected.

"Hush, Cassie," said Stacey, looking very embarrassed and uncomfortable. T.J.'s face was totally bland, as if nothing at all had happened.

When the woman's order was finally filled, Mr. Barnett again picked up T.J.'s list, but before he had gotten the next item his wife called, "Jim Lee, these folks needing help over here and I got my hands full." And as if we were not even there, he walked away.

"Where's he going?" I cried.

"He'll be back," said T.J., wandering away.

After waiting several minutes for Mr. Barnett's return, Stacey said, "Come on, Cassie, let's go." He started toward the door and I followed. But as we passed one of the counters, I spied Mr. Barnett wrapping an order of pork chops for a white girl. Adults were one thing; I could almost understand that. They ruled things and there was nothing that could be done about them. But some kid who was no bigger than me was something else again. Certainly Mr. Barnett had simply forgotten about T.J.'s order. I decided to remind him and, without saying anything to Stacey, I turned around and marched over to Mr. Barnett.

"Uh . . . 'scuse me, Mr. Barnett," I said as politely as I could, waiting a moment for him to look up from his wrapping. "I think you forgot, but you was waiting on us 'fore you was waiting on this girl here, and we been waiting a good while now for you to get back."

The girl gazed at me strangely, but Mr. Barnett did not look up. I assumed that he had not heard me. I was near the end of the counter so I merely went to the other side of it and tugged on his shirt sleeve to get his attention.

He recoiled as if I had struck him.

"Y-you was helping us," I said, backing to the front of the counter again.

"Well, you just get your little black self back over there and wait some more," he said in a low, tight voice.

I was hot. I had been as nice as I could be to him and here he was talking like this. "We been waiting on you for near an hour," I hissed, "while you 'round here waiting on everybody else. And it ain't fair. You got no right—"

"Whose little nigger is this!" bellowed Mr. Barnett.

Everyone in the store turned and stared at me. "I ain't nobody's little nigger!" I screamed, angry and humiliated. "And you ought not be waiting on everybody 'fore you wait on us."

"Hush up, child, hush up," someone whispered behind me. I looked around. A woman who had occupied the wagon next to ours at the market looked down upon me. Mr. Barnett, his face red and eyes bulging, immediately pounced on her.

"This gal yourn, Hazel?"

"No, suh," answered the woman meekly, stepping hastily away to show she had nothing to do with me. As I watched her turn her back on me, Stacey emerged and took my hand.

"Come on, Cassie, let's get out of here."

"Stacey!" I exclaimed, relieved to see him by my side. "Tell him! You know he ain't fair making us wait—"

"She your sister, boy?" Mr. Barnett spat across the counter.

Stacey bit his lower lip and gazed into Mr. Barnett's eyes. "Yessir."

"Then you get her out of here," he said with hateful force. "And make sure she don't come back till yo' mammy teach her what she is."

"I already know what I am!" I retaliated. "But I betcha you don't know what you are! And I could sure tell you, too, you ole—"

Stacey jerked me forward, crushing my hand in the effort, and whispered angrily, "Shut up, Cassie!" His dark eyes flashed malevolently as he pushed me in front of him through the crowd.

As soon as we were outside, I whipped my hand from his. "What's the matter with you? You know he was wrong!"

Stacey swallowed to flush his anger, then said gruffly, "I know it and you know it, but he don't know it, and that's where the trouble is. Now come on 'fore you get us into a real mess. I'm going up to Mr. Jamison's to see what's keeping Big Ma."

"What 'bout T.J.?" I called as he stepped into the street.

Stacey laughed wryly. "Don't worry 'bout T.J. He knows exactly how to act." He crossed the street sullenly then, his hands jammed in his pockets.

I watched him go, but did not follow. Instead, I ambled along the sidewalk trying to understand why Mr. Barnett had acted the way he had. More than once I stopped and gazed over my shoulder at the mercantile. I had a good mind to go back in and find out what had made Mr. Barnett so mad. I actually turned once and headed toward the store, then remembering what Mr. Barnett had said about my returning, I swung back around, kicking at the sidewalk, my head bowed.

It was then that I bumped into Lillian Jean Simms.

"Why don't you look where you're going?" she asked huffily. Jeremy and her two younger brothers were with her. "Hey, Cassie," said Jeremy.

"Hey, Jeremy," I said solemnly, keeping my eyes on Lillian Jean.

"Well, apologize," she ordered.

"What?"

"You bumped into me. Now you apologize."

I did not feel like messing with Lillian Jean. I had other things on my mind. "Okay," I said, starting past, "I'm sorry."

Lillian Jean sidestepped in front of me. "That ain't enough. Get down in the road."

I looked up at her. "You crazy?"

"You can't watch where you going, get in the road. Maybe that way you won't be bumping into decent white folks with your little nasty self."

This second insult of the day was almost more than I could bear. Only the thought of Big Ma up in Mr. Jamison's office saved Lillian Jean's lip. "I ain't nasty," I said, properly holding my temper in check, "and if you're so afraid of getting bumped, walk down there yourself."

I started past her again, and again she got in my way. "Ah, let her pass, Lillian Jean," said Jeremy. "She ain't done nothin' to you."

"She done something to me just standing in front of me." With that, she reached for my arm and attempted to push me off the sidewalk. I braced myself and swept my arm backward, out of Lillian Jean's reach. But someone caught it from behind, painfully twisting it, and shoved me off the sidewalk into the road. I landed bottom first on the ground.

Mr. Simms glared down at me. "When my gal Lillian Jean says for you to get yo'self off the sidewalk, you get, you hear?"

Behind him were his sons R.W. and Melvin. People from the store began to ring the Simmses. "Ain't that the same little nigger was cuttin' up back there at Jim Lee's?" someone asked.

"Yeah, she the one," answered Mr. Simms. "You hear me talkin' to you, gal? You 'pologize to Miz Lillian Jean this minute."

I stared up at Mr. Simms, frightened. Jeremy appeared frightened too. "I—I apologized already."

Jeremy seemed relieved that I had spoken. "She d-did, Pa. R-right now, 'fore y'all come, she did—"

Mr. Simms turned an angry gaze upon his son and Jeremy faltered, looked at me, and hung his head.

Then Mr. Simms jumped into the street. I moved away from him, trying to get up. He was a mean-looking man, red in the face and bearded. I was afraid he was going to hit me before I could get to my feet, but he didn't. I scrambled up and ran blindly for the wagon. Someone grabbed me and I fought wildly, attempting to pull loose. "Stop, Cassie!" Big Ma said. "Stop, it's me. We're going home now."

"Not 'fore she 'pologizes to my gal, y'all ain't," said Mr. Simms.

Big Ma gazed down at me, fear in her eyes, then back at the growing crowd. "She jus' a child—"

"Tell her, Aunty—"

Big Ma looked at me again, her voice cracking as she spoke. "Go on, child . . . apologize."

"But, Big Ma—"

Her voice hardened. "Do like I say."

I swallowed hard.

"Go on!"

"I'm sorry," I mumbled.

"I'm sorry, *Miz* Lillian Jean," demanded Mr. Simms.

"Big Ma!" I balked.

"Say it, child."

A painful tear slid down my cheek and my lips trembled. "I'm sorry . . . M-Miz . . . Lillian Jean."

When the words had been spoken, I turned and fled crying into the back of the wagon. No day in all my life had ever been as cruel as this one.

6

The ride home was long and silent. None of us felt like talking, not even T.J. Big Ma had informed him shortly after leaving Strawberry that she did not want to hear another word out of him before we reached home. He sulked for a while with a few audible grumbles which no one paid any attention to, but finally he fell asleep and did not awaken until we had driven up the Granger road and stopped in front of the Avery house.

By the time Jack pulled into our own yard, the night was a thick blackness and smelled of a coming rain. Big Ma climbed wearily down from the wagon and went into the house without a word. I stayed with Stacey to help him put the wagon inside the barn and unhitch and feed Jack. While I held the flashlight on the barn doors, Stacey slowly slid aside the plank of wood that held the doors fastened. "Cassie," he said, in a quiet, thoughtful voice, "don't go blaming Big Ma for what she done."

"Why not?" I asked angrily. "She made me apologize to that ole ugly Lillian Jean 'bout something wasn't even my fault. She took them ole Simmses' side without even hearing mine."

"Well, maybe she couldn't help it, Cassie. Maybe she had to do it."

"Had to do it!" I practically screamed. "She didn't have to do nothin'! She's grown just like that Mr. Simms and she should've stood up for me. I wouldn't've done her that way."

Stacey put the plank on the ground and leaned against the barn. "There's things you don't understand, Cassie—"

"And I s'pose you do, huh? Ever since you went down into Louisiana to get Papa last summer you think you know so doggone much! Well, I betcha I know one thing. If that had been Papa, he wouldn't've made me apologize! He would've listened to me!"

Stacey sighed and swung open the barn doors. "Well, Papa . . . that's different. But Big Ma ain't Papa and you can't expect . . ." His voice trailed off as he peered into the barn. Suddenly he cried, "Cassie, give me that flashlight!" Then, before I could object, he tore the flashlight from my hand and shone it into the barn.

"What's Mr. Granger's car doing in our barn?" I exclaimed as the silver Packard was unveiled by the light. Without answering me, Stacey swiftly turned and ran toward the house. I followed closely behind. Throwing open the door to Mama's room, we stood dumbfounded in the doorway. Instead of Mr. Granger, a tall, handsome man, nattily dressed in a gray pin-striped suit and vest, stood by the fire with his arm around Big Ma. For a moment we swayed with excitement, then as if by signal we both cried, "Uncle Hammer!" and dashed into his arms.

Uncle Hammer was two years older than Papa and, unmarried, he came every winter to spend the Christmas season with us. Like Papa, he had dark, red-brown skin, a square-jawed face, and high cheekbones; yet there was a great difference between them somehow. His eyes, which showed a great warmth as he hugged and kissed us now, often had a cold, distant glaze, and there was an aloofness in him which the boys and I could never quite bridge.

When he let us go, Stacey and I both grew consciously shy, and we backed away. I sat down beside Christopher-John and Little Man, who were silently gazing up at Uncle Hammer, but Stacey stammered, "Wh-what's Mr. Granger's car doing in our barn?"

"That's your Uncle Hammer's car," Mama said. "Did you unhitch Jack?"

"Uncle Hammer's!" Stacey exclaimed, exchanging shocked glances with me. "No kidding?"

Big Ma stammered, "Hammer, you—you went and got a car like Harlan Granger's?"

Uncle Hammer smiled a strange, wry smile. "Well, not exactly like it, Mama. Mine's a few months newer. Last year when I come down here, I was right impressed with that big ole Packard of Mr. Harlan Filmore Granger's and I thought I'd like to own one myself. It seems that me and Harlan Granger just got the same taste." He winked slyly at Stacey. "Don't it, Stacey?"

Stacey grinned.

"You like, maybe we'll all go riding in it one day. If it's all right with your mama."

"Oh, boy!" cried Little Man.

"You mean it, Uncle Hammer?" I asked. "Mama, can we?"

"We'll see," Mama said. "But in any case, not tonight. Stacey, go take care of Jack and draw up a bucket of water for the kitchen. We've done the other chores."

Since no one told me to help Stacey, I forgot all about Jack and settled back to listen to Uncle Hammer. Christopher-John and Little Man, who Big Ma had feared would be moping because they had not been allowed to go to town, seemed not at all concerned that Stacey and I had gone. They were awestruck by Uncle Hammer, and compared to his arrival a day in Strawberry was a minor matter.

For a while Uncle Hammer talked only to Mama and Big Ma, laughing from deep down inside himself like Papa, but then to my surprise he turned from them and addressed me. "I understand you had your first trip to Strawberry today, Cassie," he said. "What did you think?"

Big Ma stiffened, but I was pleased to have this opportunity to air my side of the Strawberry affair. "I didn't like it," I said. "Them ole Simmses—"

"Mary, I feel a bit hungry," Big Ma interrupted abruptly. "Supper still warm?"

"Yes, ma'am," said Mama standing. "I'll set it on the table for you."

As Mama stood up, I started again. "Them ole Simmses—"

"Let Cassie get it, Mary," said Big Ma nervously. "You must be tired."

I looked strangely at Big Ma, then up at Mama.

"Oh, I don't mind," said Mama, heading for the kitchen. "Go ahead, Cassie, and tell your uncle about Strawberry."

"That ole Lillian Jean Simms made me so mad I could just spit. I admit that I bumped into her, but that was 'cause I was thinking 'bout that ole Mr. Barnett waiting on everybody else in his ole store 'fore he waited on us—"

"Jim Lee Barnett?" asked Uncle Hammer, turning toward Big Ma. "That ole devil still living?"

Big Ma nodded mutely, and I went on. "But I told him he shouldn't've been 'round there waiting on everybody else 'fore he got to us—"

"Cassie!" Big Ma exclaimed, hearing this bit of news for the first time.

Uncle Hammer laughed. "You told him that!"

"Yessir," I said softly, wondering why he was laughing.

"Oh, that's great! Then what happened?"

"Stacey made me leave and Mr. Barnett told me I couldn't come back no more and then I bumped into that confounded Lillian Jean and she tried to make me get off the sidewalk and then her daddy come along and he—"

Big Ma's eyes grew large and she whispered hoarsely, "Cassie, I don't think—"

"—and he twisted my arm and knocked me off the sidewalk!" I exclaimed, unwilling to muffle what Mr. Simms had done. I glanced triumphantly at Big Ma, but she wasn't looking at me. Her eyes, frightened and nervous, were on Uncle Hammer. I turned and looked at him too.

His dark eyes had narrowed to thin, angry slits. He said: "He knocked you off the sidewalk, Cassie? A grown man knocked you off the sidewalk?"

"Y-yessir."

"This Lillian Jean Simms, her daddy wouldn't be Charlie Simms, would it?"

"Y-yessir."

Uncle Hammer grasped my shoulders. "What else he do to you?"

"N-nothin'," I said, frightened by his eyes. " 'Cepting he wanted me to apologize to Lillian Jean 'cause I wouldn't get in the road when she told me to."

"And you did?"

"Big Ma said I had to."

Uncle Hammer released me and sat very still. No one

said a word. Then he stood slowly, his eyes icing into that cold distant way they could, and he started toward the door, limping slightly on his left leg. Christopher-John, Little Man, and I stared after him wonderingly, but Big Ma jumped up from her chair, knocking it over in her haste, and dashed after him. She grabbed his arm. "Let it be, son!" she cried. "That child ain't hurt!"

"Not hurt! You look into her eyes and tell me she ain't hurt!"

Mama came back from the kitchen with Stacey behind her. "What is it?" she asked, looking from Big Ma to Uncle Hammer.

"Charlie Simms knocked Cassie off the sidewalk in Strawberry and the child just told Hammer," said Big Ma in one breath, still holding on to Uncle Hammer's arm.

"Oh, Lord," Mama groaned. "Stacey, get Mr. Morrison. Quick, now!" As Stacey sped from the room, Mama's eyes darted to the shotgun over the bed, and she edged between it and Uncle Hammer. Uncle Hammer was watching her and he said quietly, "Don't worry. I ain't gotta use David's gun. . . . I got my own."

Suddenly Mama lunged to the side door, blocking it with her slender body. "Hammer, now you listen to me—"

But Uncle Hammer gently but firmly pushed her to one side and, brushing Big Ma from his arm, opened the door and bounded down the steps into the light rain.

Little Man, Christopher-John, and I dashed to the door as Big Ma and Mama ran after him. "Get back inside,"

Mama called over her shoulder, but she was too busy trying to grab Uncle Hammer to see to it that we obeyed, and we did not move. "Hammer, Cassie's all right," she cried. "Don't go making unnecessary trouble!"

"Unnecessary trouble! You think my brother died and I got my leg half blown off in their German war to have some red-neck knock Cassie around anytime it suits him? If I'd've knocked his girl down, you know what'd've happened to me? Yeah, you know all right. Right now I'd be hanging from that oak over yonder. Let go of me, Mary."

Mama and Big Ma could not keep him from reaching the car. But just as the Packard roared to life, a huge figure loomed from the darkness and jumped into the other side, and the car zoomed angrily down the drive into the blackness of the Mississippi night.

"Where'd he go?" I asked as Mama slowly climbed the steps. Her face under the glow of the lamp was tired, drained. "He went up to the Simmses', didn't he? Didn't he, Mama?"

"He's not going anywhere," Mama said, stepping aside and waiting until both Big Ma and Stacey were inside; then she locked the door.

"Mr. Morrison'll bring him back," said Christopher-John confidently, although he looked somewhat bewildered by all that had happened.

"If he don't," said Little Man ominously, "I betcha Uncle Hammer'll teach that ole Mr. Simms a thing or two. 'Round here hitting on Cassie."

"I hope he knocks his block off," I said.

Mama's gaze blazed down upon us. "I think little mouths that have so much to say must be very tired."

"No, ma'am, Mama, we ain't—"

"Go to bed."

"Mama, it ain't but—" Mama's face hardened, and I knew that it would not be in my best interest to argue further; I turned and did as I was told. Christopher-John and Little Man did the same. When I got to my door, I asked, "Ain't Stacey coming?"

Mama glanced down at Stacey sitting by the fire. "I don't recall his mouth working so hard, do you?"

"No'm," I muttered and went into my room. After a few minutes Mama came in. Without a word of reprimand, she picked up my clothes from where I had tossed them at the foot of the bed, and absently draping them over the back of a chair, she said, "Stacey tells me you blame Big Ma for what happened today. Is that right?"

I thought over her question and answered, "Not for all of it. Just for making me apologize to that ole dumb Lillian Jean Simms. She oughtn't've done that, Mama. Papa wouldn't've—"

"I don't want to hear what Papa wouldn't have done!" Mama snapped. "Or what Mr. Morrison wouldn't have done or Uncle Hammer! You were with Big Ma and she did what she had to do and believe me, young lady, she didn't like doing it one bit more than you did."

"Well," I muttered, "maybe so, but—"

"There's no maybe to it."

"Yes'm," I said softly, deciding that it was better to study the patchwork pattern on the quilt until the anger left Mama's eyes and I could talk to her again. After a moment she sat beside me on the bed and raised my chin with the tip of her forefinger. "Big Ma didn't want you to be hurt," she said. "That was the only thing on her mind . . . making sure Mr. Simms didn't hurt you."

"Yes'm," I murmured, then flared, "But, Mama, that Lillian Jean ain't got the brains of a flea! How come I gotta go 'round calling her 'Miz' like she grown or something?"

Mama's voice grew hard. "Because that's the way of things, Cassie."

"The way of what things?" I asked warily.

"Baby, you had to grow up a little today. I wish . . . well, no matter what I wish. It happened and you have to accept the fact that in the world outside this house, things are not always as we would have them to be."

"But, Mama, it ain't fair. I didn't do nothin' to that confounded Lillian Jean. How come Mr. Simms went and pushed me like he did?"

Mama's eyes looked deeply into mine, locked into them, and she said in a tight, clear voice, "Because he thinks Lillian Jean is better than you are, Cassie, and when you—"

"That ole scrawny, chicken-legged, snaggle-toothed, cross—"

"Cassie." Mama did not raise her voice, but the quiet force of my name silenced me. "Now," she said, folding my hand in hers, "I didn't say that Lillian Jean *is* better than you. I said Mr. Simms only *thinks* she is. In fact, he thinks she's better than Stacey or Little Man or Christopher-John—"

"Just 'cause she's his daughter?" I asked, beginning to think Mr. Simms was a bit touched in the head.

"No, baby, because she's white."

Mama's hold tightened on mine, but I exclaimed, "Ah, shoot! White ain't nothin'!"

Mama's grip did not lessen. "It is something, Cassie. White is something just like black is something. Everybody born on this earth is something and nobody, no matter what color, is better than anybody else."

"Then how come Mr. Simms don't know that?"

"Because he's one of those people who has to believe that white people are better than black people to make himself feel big." I stared questioningly at Mama, not really understanding. Mama squeezed my hand and explained further. "You see, Cassie, many years ago when our people were first brought from Africa in chains to work as slaves in this country—"

"Like Big Ma's papa and mama?"

Mama nodded. "Yes, baby, like Papa Luke and Mama Rachel, except they were born right here in Mississippi. But their grandparents were born in Africa, and when they came there were some white people who thought that it was wrong for any people to be slaves; so the people who needed slaves to work in their fields and the people who were making money bringing slaves from Africa preached that black people weren't really people like white people were, so slavery was all right.

"They also said that slavery was good for us because it taught us to be good Christians—like the white people." She sighed deeply, her voice fading into a distant whisper. "But they didn't teach us Christianity to save our souls, but to teach us obedience. They were afraid of slave revolts and they wanted us to learn the Bible's teachings about slaves being loyal to their masters. But even teaching us Christianity didn't make us stop wanting to be free, and many slaves ran away—"

"Papa Luke ran away," I reminded her, thinking of the story of how Great-Grandpa had run away three times. He had been caught and punished for his disobedience, but his owners had not tried to break him, for he had had a knowledge of herbs and cures. He had tended both the slaves and the animals of the plantation, and it was from him that Big Ma had learned medicines.

Mama nodded again. "That's right, honey. He was hiding in a cave when freedom came, so I understand." She was silent a moment, then went on. "Well, after a while, slavery became so profitable to people who had slaves and even to those who didn't that most folks decided to believe that black people really weren't people like everybody else. And when the Civil War was fought and Mama Rachel and Papa Luke and all the other slaves were freed, people continued to think that way. Even the Northerners who fought the war didn't really see us equal to white people. So now, even though seventy years have passed since slavery, most white people still think of us as they did then—that we're not as good as they are—and people like Mr. Simms hold on to that belief harder than some other folks because they have little else to hold on to. For him to believe that he is better than we are makes him think that he's important, simply because he's white."

Mama relaxed her grip. I knew that she was waiting for me to speak. There was a sinking feeling in my stomach and I felt as if the world had turned itself upside down with me in it. Then I thought of Lillian Jean and a surging anger gurgled upward and I retaliated, "Well, they ain't!" But I leaned closer to Mama, anxiously hoping that she would agree with me.

"Of course they aren't," Mama said. "White people may demand our respect, but what we give them is not respect but fear. What we give to our own people is far more important because it's given freely. Now you may have to call Lillian Jean 'Miss' because the white people say so, but you'll also call our own young ladies at church 'Miss' because you really do respect them.

"Baby, we have no choice of what color we're born or who our parents are or whether we're rich or poor. What we do have is some choice over what we make of our lives once we're here." Mama cupped my face in her hands. "And I pray to God you'll make the best of yours." She hugged me warmly then and motioned me under the covers.

As she turned the lamp down low, I asked, "Mama, Uncle Hammer. If Mr. Morrison can't stop him, what'll happen?"

"Mr. Morrison will bring him back."

"But just what if he can't and Uncle Hammer gets to Mr. Simms?"

A shadowy fear fleeted across her face, but disappeared with the dimming light. "I think . . . I think you've done enough growing up for one day, Cassie," she said without answering my question. "Uncle Hammer'll be all right. Now go to sleep."

Mama had been right about Uncle Hammer. When I awoke the next morning and followed the smell of frying ham and baking biscuits into the kitchen, there he sat at the table drinking coffee with Mr. Morrison. He was unshaven and looked a bit bleary-eyed, but he was all right; I wondered if Mr. Simms looked so good. I didn't get a chance to ask, because as soon as I had said good morning Mama called me into her room, where a tub of hot water was waiting by the fireplace.

"Hurry up," she said. "Uncle Hammer's going to take us to church."

"In his car?"

Mama's brow furrowed. "Well, I just don't know. He did say something about hitching up Jack . . ."

My smile faded, but then I caught the teasing glint in her eyes, and she began to laugh. "Ah, Mama!" I laughed, and splashed into the water.

After my bath I went into my room to dress. When I rejoined Mama she was combing her hair, which fanned her head like an enormous black halo. As I watched, she shaped the long thickness into a large chignon at the nape of her neck and stuck six sturdy hairpins into it. Then, giving the chignon a pat, she reached for her pale-blue cotton dress sprinkled with tiny yellow-and-white flowers and polished white buttons running from top to bottom along its front. She glanced down at me. "You didn't comb your hair."

"No'm. I want you to fix me my grown-up hairdo."

Mama began buttoning the top of her dress with long, flying fingers as I slowly fastened the lower buttons. I loved to help Mama dress. She always smelled of sunshine and soap. When the last button had slipped into place, she buckled a dark-blue patent-leather belt around her tiny waist and stood ready except for her shoes. She looked very pretty.

"Where's your brush?"

"Right here," I said, picking up the brush from where I had laid it on the chair.

Mama sat down in Papa's rocker and I sat on the deerskin rug in front of her. Mama divided my hair from ear to ear into two sections and braided the front section to one side and the back section right in the center. Then she wound each braid into a flat chignon against my head. My hair was too thick and long for me to do it well myself, but Mama could do it perfectly. I figured I looked my very best that way.

When Mama finished, I ran to the mirror, then turned, facing her with a grin. She grinned back and shook her head at my vanity.

"One day, Mama, you gonna fix my hair like yours?"

"That'll be a few years yet," she answered, readjusting the cardboard lining she had placed in her shoes to protect her feet from the dirt and gravel which could easily seep through the large holes in the soles. She set the shoes on the floor and stepped into them. Now, with the soles facing downward and Mama's feet in them, no one could tell what the shiny exteriors hid; yet I felt uncomfortable for Mama and wished that we had enough money for her to have her shoes fixed or, better still, buy new ones.

After breakfast Stacey, Christopher-John, Little Man, and I sat impatiently by the dying morning fire waiting for Mama, Big Ma, and Uncle Hammer. Uncle Hammer was dressing in the boys' room and Mama was in with Big Ma. I checked to make sure none of them was about to appear, then leaned toward Stacey and whispered, "You think Uncle Hammer whipped Mr. Simms?"

"No," said Stacey quietly.

"No!" cried Little Man.

"Y-you don't mean Mr. Simms whipped Uncle Hammer?" stammered an unbelieving Christopher-John.

"Nothin' happened," said Stacey in explanation as he tugged irritably at his collar.

"Nothin'?" I repeated, disappointed.

"Nothin'."

"How you know?" asked Little Man suspiciously.

"Mama said so. I asked her straight out this morning."

"Oh," replied Little Man, resigned.

"But something must've happened," I said. "I mean Uncle Hammer and Mr. Morrison look like they haven't even been to bed. How come they look like that if nothin' happened?"

"Mama said Mr. Morrison talked all night to Uncle Hammer. Talked him tired and wouldn't let him go up to the Simmses'."

"Ah, shoot!" I exclaimed, my dream of revenge against the Simmses vanishing as Stacey talked. I propped my elbows on my knees, then settled my head in my upraised hands and stared into the glowing embers. A burning knot formed in my throat and I felt as if my body was not large enough to hold the frustration I felt, nor deep enough to drown the rising anger.

"It ain't fair," Christopher-John sympathized, patting me lightly with his pudgy hand.

"Sho' ain't," agreed Little Man.

"Cassie," Stacey said softly. At first I didn't look at him, thinking he would go ahead and say what he had to say. But when he didn't, I turned toward him. He leaned forward secretively and automatically Christopher-John and Little Man did the same. "Y'all better be glad nothin' happened," he said in a whisper. " 'Cause I heard Big Ma tell Mama last night that if Mr. Morrison didn't stop Uncle Hammer, Uncle Hammer might get killed."

"Killed?" we echoed as the fire sputtered and died. "Who'd do that?" I cried. "Not one of them puny Simmses?"

Stacey started to speak, but then Mama and Big Ma entered, and he cautioned us into silence.

When Uncle Hammer joined us, freshly shaven and in another suit, the boys and I put on our coats and headed for the door; Uncle Hammer stopped us. "Stacey, that the only coat you got, son?" he asked.

Stacey looked down at his faded cotton jacket. Everyone else did too. The jacket was too small for him, that was obvious, and compared to Little Man's and Christopher-John's and mine, it was admittedly in sadder shape. Yet we were all surprised that Uncle Hammer would ask about it, for he knew as well as anyone that Mama had to buy our clothes in shifts, which meant that we each had to wait our turn for new clothes. Stacey looked up at Mama, then back at Uncle Hammer. "Y-yessir," he answered.

Uncle Hammer stared at him, then waving his hand ordered, "Take it off." Before Stacey could question why, Uncle Hammer disappeared into the boys' room.

Again Stacey looked at Mama. "You'd better do like he says," she said.

Uncle Hammer returned with a long box, store wrapped in shiny red Christmas paper and a fancy green ribbon. He handed the package to Stacey. "It was supposed to be your Christmas present, but I think I'd better give it to you now. It's cold out there."

Gingerly, Stacey took the box and opened it.

"A coat!" cried Little Man joyously, clapping his hands.

"Wool," Mama said reverently. "Go ahead, Stacey. Try it on."

Stacey eagerly slipped on the coat; it was much too big for him, but Mama said that she could take up the sleeves and that he would grow into it in another year. Stacey beamed down at the coat, then up at Uncle Hammer. A year ago he would have shot into Uncle Hammer's arms and hugged his thanks, but now at the manly age of twelve he held out his hand, and Uncle Hammer shook it.

"Come on, we'd better go," said Mama.

The morning was gray as we stepped outside, but the rain had stopped. We followed the path of bedded rocks that led to the barn, careful not to slip into the mud, and got into the Packard, shining clean and bright from the washing Uncle Hammer and Mr. Morrison had given it after breakfast. Inside the Packard, the world was a wine-colored luxury. The boys and I, in the back, ran our hands over the rich felt seats, tenderly fingered the fancy door handles and window knobs, and peered down amazed at the plush carpet peeping out on either side of the rubber mats. Mr. Morrison, who was not a churchgoing man, waved good-bye from the barn and we sped away.

As we drove onto the school grounds and parked, the people milling in front of the church turned, staring at the Packard. Then Uncle Hammer stepped from the car and someone cried, "Well, I'll be doggone! It's our Hammer!

Hammer Logan!" And in a body, the crowd engulfed us.

T.J. ran up with Moe Turner and Little Willie Wiggins to admire the car. "It's Uncle Hammer's," said Stacey proudly. But before the boys could sufficiently admire the car, Mama and Big Ma shooed us toward the church for the service. It was then that T.J. noticed Stacey's new coat.

"Uncle Hammer gave it to him," I said. "Ain't it something?"

T.J. ran his long fingers over the lapels, and shrugged. "It's all right, I guess, if you like that sort of thing."

"All right!" I cried, indignant at his casual reaction to the coat. "Boy, that's the finest coat you ever did lay eyes on and you know it!"

T.J. sighed. "Like I said, it's all right . . . if you like lookin' like a fat preacher." Then he and Little Willie and Moe laughed, and went on ahead.

Stacey looked down at the coat with its long sleeves and wide shoulders. His smile faded. "He don't know what he's talking 'bout," I said. "He's just jealous, that's all."

"I know it," snapped Stacey sourly.

As we slid into the pew in front of T.J., T.J. whispered, "Here comes the preacher," then leaned forward and said snidely, "How do you do, Reverend Logan?"

Stacey turned on T.J., but I poked him hard. "Mama's looking," I whispered, and he turned back around.

After church, as T.J. and the others looked longingly at the car, Mama said, "Stacey, maybe T.J. wants to ride."

Before Stacey could reply, I spoke up hurriedly. "No,

ma'am, Mama, he got something else he gotta do." Then under my breath so that I would not be guilty of a lie, I added, "He gotta walk home like he always do."

"That'll teach him," whispered Little Man.

"Yeah," agreed Christopher-John, but Stacey sulked by the window and said nothing.

The sun was out now and Uncle Hammer suggested that we take a real ride before going home. He drove us the full twenty-two miles up to Strawberry by way of the Jackson Road, one of two roads leading to the town. But Mama and Big Ma objected so much to going through Strawberry that he turned the big car around and headed back toward home, taking the old Soldiers Road. Supposedly, Rebel soldiers had once marched up the road and across Soldiers Bridge to keep the town from falling into the hands of the Yankee Army, but I had my doubts about that. After all, who in his right mind would want to capture Strawberry . . . or defend it either for that matter?

The road was hilly and curving, and as we sped over it scattered road stones hit sharply against the car's underbelly and the dust swelled up in rolls of billowing clouds behind us. Little Man, Christopher-John, and I shrieked with delight each time the car climbed a hill and dropped suddenly downward, fluttering our stomachs. Eventually, the road intersected with the Jefferson Davis School Road. Uncle Hammer stopped the car at the intersection and, leaning his right arm heavily over the steering wheel, motioned languidly at the Wallace store. "Got me a good mind to burn that place out," he said.

"Hammer, hush that kind of talk!" ordered Big Ma, her eyes growing wide.

"Me and John Henry and David grew up together. And John Henry and me even fought in their war together. What good was it? A black man's life ain't worth the life of a cowfly down here."

"I know that, son, but that kinda talk get you hung and you know it."

Mama touched Uncle Hammer's arm. "There might be another way, Hammer . . . like I told you. Now don't go do something foolish. Wait for David—talk to him."

Uncle Hammer looked glassy-eyed at the store, then sighed and eased the Packard across the road toward Soldiers Bridge. We were taking the long way home.

Soldiers Bridge was built before the Civil War. It was spindly and wooden, and each time I had to cross it I held my breath until I was safely on the other side. Only one vehicle could cross at a time, and whoever was on the bridge first was supposed to have the right of way, although it didn't always work that way. More than once when I had been in the wagon with Mama or Big Ma, we had had to back off the bridge when a white family started across after we were already on it.

As the bridge came into view the other side of the river was clearly visible, and it was obvious to everyone that an old Model-T truck, overflowing with redheaded children, had reached the bridge first and was about to cross, but suddenly Uncle Hammer gassed the Packard and sped onto the creaking structure. The driver of the truck stopped, and for no more than a second hesitated on the bridge, then without a single honk of protest backed off so that we could pass.

"Hammer!" Big Ma cried. "They think you're Mr. Granger."

"Well, now, won't they be surprised when we reach the other side," said Uncle Hammer.

As we came off the bridge, we could see the Wallaces, all three of them—Dewberry, Thurston, and Kaleb—touch their hats respectfully, then immediately freeze as they saw who we were. Uncle Hammer, straight-faced and totally calm, touched the brim of his own hat in polite response and without a backward glance sped away, leaving the Wallaces gaping silently after us.

Stacey, Christopher-John, Little Man, and I laughed, but Mama's cold glance made us stop. "You shouldn't have done that, Hammer," she said quietly.

"The opportunity, dear sister, was too much to resist."

"But one day we'll have to pay for it. Believe me," she said, "one day we'll pay."

7

"Stacey, go bring me your coat," Mama said a few days later as we gathered around the fire after supper. "I've got time to take up the sleeves now."

"Uh-oh!" exclaimed Christopher-John, then immediately opened his reader as Mama looked down at him.

Little Man cupped his hand and whispered to me, "Boy, now he's gonna get it!"

"Uh . . . th-that's all right, Mama," stuttered Stacey. "The c-coat's all right like it is."

Mama opened her sewing box. "It's not all right. Now go get it for me."

Stacey stood up and started slowly toward his room. Little Man, Christopher-John, and I watched him closely, wondering what he was going to do. He actually went into the room, but was gone only a moment before he reappeared and nervously clutched the back of his chair. "I ain't got the coat, Mama," he said.

"Not got the coat!" cried Big Ma. Uncle Hammer looked up sharply from his paper, but remained silent.

"Stacey," Mama said irritably, "bring me that coat, boy."

"But, Mama, I really ain't got it! I gave it to T.J."

"T.J.!" Mama exclaimed.

"Yes, ma'am, Mama," Stacey answered, then went on hurriedly as Mama's eyes glittered with rising anger. "The coat was too big for me and . . . and T.J. said it made me look like . . . like a preacher . . . and he said since it fit him just right, he'd . . . he'd take it off my hands till I grow into it, then thataway all the guys would stop laughing at me and calling me preacher." He paused, waiting for someone to speak; but the only sound was a heavy breathing and the crackle of burning hickory. Then, seeming more afraid of the silence than putting his neck further into the noose, he added, "But I didn't give it to him for good, Mama—just lent it to him till I get big enough for it and then . . ."

Stacey's voice faded into an inaudible whisper as Mama slowly put the sewing box on the table behind her. I thought she was headed for the wide leather strap hanging in the kitchen, but she did not rise. In quiet anger she glared at Stacey and admonished, "In this house we do not give away what loved ones give to us. Now go bring me that coat."

Backing away from her anger, Stacey turned to leave, but Uncle Hammer stopped him. "No," he said, "leave the coat where it is."

Mama turned bewildered toward Uncle Hammer. "Hammer, what're you saying? That's the best coat Stacey's ever had and probably ever will have as long as he lives in this house. David and I can't afford a coat like that."

Uncle Hammer leaned back in his chair, his eyes cold on Stacey. "Seems to me if Stacey's not smart enough to hold on to a good coat, he don't deserve it. As far as I'm concerned, T.J. can just keep that coat permanently. At least he knows a good thing when he sees it."

"Hammer," Big Ma said, "let the boy go get the coat. That T.J. probably done told him all sorts—"

"Well, ain't Stacey got a brain? What the devil should he care what T.J. thinks or T.J. says? Who is this T.J. anyway? Does he put clothes on Stacey's back or food in front of him?" Uncle Hammer stood and walked over to Stacey as Little Man, Christopher-John, and I followed him fearfully with our eyes. "I suppose if T.J. told you it was summertime out there and you should run buck naked down the road because everybody else was doing it, you'd do that too, huh?"

"N-no sir," Stacey replied, looking at the floor.

"Now you hear me good on this—look at me when I talk to you, boy!" Immediately Stacey raised his head and looked at Uncle Hammer. "If you ain't got the brains of a flea to see that this T.J. fellow made a fool of you, then you'll never get anywhere in this world. It's tough out there, boy, and as long as there are people, there's gonna be somebody trying to take what you got and trying to drag you down. It's up to you whether you let them or not. Now it seems to me you wanted that coat when I gave it to you, ain't that right?"

Stacey managed a shaky "Yessir."

"And anybody with any sense would know it's a good thing, ain't that right?"

This time Stacey could only nod.

"Then if you want something and it's a good thing and you got it in the right way, you better hang on to it and don't let nobody talk you out of it. You care what a lot of useless people say 'bout you you'll never get anywhere, 'cause there's a lotta folks don't want you to make it. You understand what I'm telling you?"

"Y-yessir, Uncle Hammer," Stacey stammered. Uncle Hammer turned then and went back to his paper without having laid a hand on Stacey, but Stacey shook visibly from the encounter.

Christopher-John, Little Man, and I exchanged apprehensive glances. I don't know what they were thinking, but I for one was deciding right then and there not to do anything to rub Uncle Hammer the wrong way; I had no intention of ever facing a tongue-lashing like that. Papa's bottom-warming whippings were quite enough for me, thank you.

The last days of school before Christmas seemed interminable. Each night I fell asleep with the hope that the morning would bring Papa, and each morning when he wasn't there I trudged to school consoling myself that he would be home when I returned. But the days passed, prickly cold and windy, and he did not come.

Added to the misery of the waiting and the cold was Lillian Jean, who managed to flounce past me with a superior smirk twice that week. I had already decided that she had had two flounces too many, but since I hadn't yet decided how to handle the matter, I postponed doing anything until after I had had a chance to talk with Papa about the whole Strawberry business. I knew perfectly well that he would not tear out of the house after Mr. Simms as Uncle Hammer had done, for he always took time to think through any move he made, but he would certainly advise me on how to handle Lillian Jean.

Then too there was T.J., who, although not really my problem, was so obnoxiously flaunting Stacey's wool coat during these cold days that I had just about decided to deflate him at the same time I took care of Lillian Jean. Ever since the night Mr. Avery had brought him to the house to return the coat and he had been told by Uncle Hammer and a faltering Stacey that the coat was his, T.J. had been more unbearable than usual. He now praised the coat from the wide tips of its lapels to the very edges of its deep hem. No one had ever had a finer coat; no one had ever looked better in such a coat; no one could ever hope to have such a coat again.

Stacey was restrained from plugging T.J.'s mouth by Uncle Hammer's principle that a man did not blame others for his own stupidity; he learned from his mistake and became stronger for it. I, however, was not so restrained and as far as I was concerned, if T.J. kept up with this coat business, he could just hit the dirt at the same time as "Miss" Lillian Jean.

The day before Christmas I awoke to the soft murmuring of quiet voices gathered in the midnight blackness of morning. Big Ma was not beside me, and without a moment's doubt I knew why she was gone. Jumping from the bed, my feet barely hitting the deerskin rug, I rushed into Mama's room.

"Oh, Papa!" I cried. "I knew it was you!"

"Ah, there's my Cassie girl!" Papa laughed, standing to catch me as I leapt into his arms.

By the dawn, the house smelled of Sunday: chicken frying, bacon sizzling, and smoke sausages baking. By evening, it reeked of Christmas. In the kitchen sweet-potato pies, egg-custard pies, and rich butter pound cakes cooled; a gigantic coon which Mr. Morrison, Uncle Hammer, and Stacey had secured in a night's hunt baked in a sea of onions, garlic, and fat orange-yellow yams; and a choice sugar-cured ham brought from the smokehouse awaited its turn in the oven. In the heart of the house, where we had gathered after supper, freshly cut branches of long-needled pines lay over the fireplace mantle adorned by winding vines of winter holly and bright red Christmas berries. And in the fireplace itself, in a black pan set on a high wire rack, peanuts roasted over the hickory fire as the waning light of day swiftly deepened into a fine velvet night speckled with white forerunners of a coming snow, and the warm sound of husky voices and rising laughter mingled in tales of sorrow and happiness of days past but not forgotten.

". . . Them watermelons of old man Ellis' seemed like they just naturally tasted better than anybody else's," said Papa, "and ole Hammer and me, we used to sneak up there whenever it'd get so hot you couldn't hardly move and take a couple of them melons on down to the pond and let them get real chilled. Then, talking 'bout eating! We did some kind of good eating."

"Papa, you was stealing?" asked an astonished Little Man. Although he usually strongly disapproved of being held, he was now reclining comfortably in Papa's lap.

"Well . . ." Papa said, "not exactly. What we'd do was exchange one of the melons from our patch for his. Course it was still wrong for us to do it, but at the time it seemed all right—"

"Problem was, though," laughed Uncle Hammer, "old man Ellis grew them ole fat green round watermelons and ours was long and striped—"

"And Mr. Ellis was always right particular 'bout his melons," interjected Papa. "He took the longest time to figure out what we was up to, but, Lord, Lord, when he did—"

"—You should've seen us run," Uncle Hammer said, standing. He shot one hand against and past the other. "Ma—an! We was gone! And that ole man was right behind us with a hickory stick hitting us up side the head—"

"Ow—weee! That ole man could run!" cried Papa. "I didn't know nobody's legs could move that fast."

Big Ma chuckled. "And as I recalls, your Papa 'bout wore y'all out when Mr. Ellis told him what y'all'd been up to. Course, you know all them Ellises was natural-born runners. Y'all remember Mr. Ellis' brother, Tom Lee? Well, one time he . . ."

Through the evening Papa and Uncle Hammer and Big Ma and Mr. Morrison and Mama lent us their memories, acting out their tales with stageworthy skills, imitating the characters in voice, manner, and action so well that the listeners held their sides with laughter. It was a good warm time. But as the night deepened and the peanuts in the pan grew shallow, the voices grew hushed, and Mr. Morrison said:

". . . They come down like ghosts that Christmas of seventy-six. Them was hard times like now and my family was living in a shantytown right outside Shreveport. Reconstruction was just 'bout over then, and them Northern soldiers was tired of being in the South and they didn't hardly care 'bout no black folks in shantytown. And them Southern whites, they was tired of the Northern soldiers and free Negroes, and they was trying to turn things back 'round to how they used to be. And the colored folks . . . well, we was just tired. Warn't hardly no work, and during them years I s'pose it was jus' 'bout as hard being free as it was being a slave. . . .

"That night they come—I can remember just as good—it was cold, so cold we had to huddle all 'gainst each other just trying to keep warm, and two boys—'bout eighteen or nineteen, I reckon—come knocking on my daddy's door. They was scairt, clean out of their heads with fright. They'd just come back from Shreveport. Some white woman done accused them of molestin' her and they didn't know nowhere to run so they come up to my daddy's 'cause he had a good head and he was big, bigger than me. He was strong too. So strong he could break a man's leg easy as if he was snapping a twig—I seen him do it that night. And the white folks was scairt of him. But my daddy didn't hardly have time to finish hearing them boys' story when them devilish night men swept down—"

"Night men!" I echoed in a shrill, dry whisper. Stacey sitting beside me on the floor stiffened; Christopher-John nudged me knowingly; Little Man leaned forward on Papa's lap.

"David . . ." Mama started, but Papa enfolded her slender hand in his and said quietly, "These are things they need to hear, baby. It's their history."

Mama sat back, her hand still in Papa's, her eyes wary. But Mr. Morrison seemed not to notice. ". . . swept down like locusts," he continued in a faraway voice. "Burst in on us with their Rebel sabers, hacking and killing, burning us out. Didn't care who they kilt. We warn't nothing to them. No better than dogs. Kilt babies and old women. Didn't matter."

He gazed into the fire.

"My sisters got kilt in they fire, but my Mama got me out. . . ." His voice faded and he touched the scars on his neck. "She tried to get back into the house to save the girls, but she couldn't. Them night men was all over her and she threw me—just threw me like I was a ball—hard as she could, trying to get me away from them. Then she fought. Fought like a wild thing right 'side my daddy. They was both of them from breeded stock and they was strong like bulls—"

"Breeded stock?" I said. "What's that?"

"Cassie, don't interrupt Mr. Morrison," said Mama, but Mr. Morrison turned from the fire and explained. "Well, Cassie, during slavery there was some farms that mated folks like animals to produce more slaves. Breeding slaves brought a lot of money for them slave owners, 'specially after the government said they couldn't bring no more slaves from Africa, and they produced all kinds of slaves to sell on the block. And folks with enough money, white men and even free black men, could buy 'zactly what they wanted. My folks was bred for strength like they folks and they grandfolks 'fore 'em. Didn't matter none what they thought 'bout the idea. Didn't nobody care.

"But my mama and daddy they loved each other and they

loved us children, and that Christmas they fought them demons out of hell like avenging angels of the Lord." He turned back toward the fire and grew very quiet; then he raised his head and looked at us. "They died that night. Them night men kilt 'em. Some folks tell me I can't remember what happened that Christmas—I warn't hardly six years old—but I remembers all right. I makes myself remember."

He grew silent again and no one spoke. Big Ma poked absently at the red-eyed logs with the poker, but no one else stirred. Finally Mr. Morrison stood, wished us a good night, and left.

Uncle Hammer stood also. "Guess I'll turn in too. It's near one o'clock."

"Wait awhile, Hammer," said Big Ma. "Now you and David both home, I gotta talk to y'all—'bout the land. . . ."

Visions of night men and fire mixed in a caldron of fear awakened me long before dawn. Automatically, I rolled toward the comforting presence of Big Ma, but she was not beside me.

A soft light still crept under the door from Mama and Papa's room and I immediately hurried toward it. As I opened the door and stepped into the shadowy room, lit now only by the flickering yellow of the low fire, Big Ma was saying, ". . . y'all start messin' with these folks down in here, no telling what'll happen."

"Is it better to just sit back and complain about how they do us?" Mama snapped, her voice rising. "Everybody from Smellings Creek to Strawberry knows it was them but what do we do about it? We line their pockets with our few pennies and send our children up to their store to learn things they've got no business learning. The older children are drinking regularly there now, even though they don't have any money to pay, and the Wallaces are simply adding the liquor charges to the family bill . . . just more money for them as they ruin our young people. As I see it the least we can do is stop shopping there. It may not be real justice, but it'll hurt them and we'll have done something. Mr. Turner and the Averys and the Laniers and over two dozen other families, and perhaps even more, say they'll think about not shopping there if they can get credit somewhere else. We owe it to the Berrys—"

"Frankly," interrupted Uncle Hammer, "I'd rather burn them out myself."

"Hammer, you go to burning and we'll have nothing," Mama retorted.

"Ain't gonna have nothing noway," replied Uncle Hammer. "You think by shopping up at Vicksburg you gonna drive them Wallaces out, then you got no idea of how things work down here. You forgetting Harlan Granger backs that store?"

"Mary, child, Hammer's right," Big Ma said. "I'm doing what I told y'all 'bout this land 'cause I don't want some legal thing to come up after I'm gone that let that Harlan

Granger get this place. But we go backing folks' credit with our land, we'd lose it sure; and we do that, I couldn't face Paul Edward—"

"I didn't say we should back it," Mama said, "but we're just about the only family with any collateral at all."

Papa looked up from the fire. "That may be, honey, but we put up this land to back this thing and it'll be just like giving it away. Times like they are, it ain't likely that any of these people can pay the bills they make—as much as they might mean to—and if they can't pay, where would we be? We've got no cash money to pay other folks' debts." He shook his head. "No . . . we'll have to find another way. . . . Go to Vicksburg maybe and see what we can arrange—" His eyes fell upon me in the shadows and he leaned forward. "Cassie? What is it, sugar?"

"Nothin', Papa," I mumbled. "I just woke up, that's all."

Mama started to rise but Papa motioned her down and got up himself. Escorting me back to bed, he said gently, "Got no cause for bad dreams, Cassie girl. Not tonight anyway."

"Papa," I said, snuggling under the warm quilts as he tucked them around me, "we gonna lose our land?"

Papa reached out and softly touched my face in the darkness. "If you remember nothing else in your whole life, Cassie girl, remember this: We ain't never gonna lose this land. You believe that?"

"Yessir, Papa."

"Then go to sleep. Christmas is coming."

"Books!" cried Little Man on Christmas morning.

For Stacey there was *The Count of Monte Cristo*; for me, *The Three Musketeers*; and for Christopher-John and Little Man, two different volumes of *Aesop's Fables*. On the inside cover of each book in Mama's fine hand was written the name of the owner. Mine read: "This book is the property of Miss Cassie Deborah Logan. Christmas, 1933."

"Man sold me them books told me these two was written by a black man," Papa said, opening my book and pointing to a picture of a man in a long, fancy coat and a wigful of curly hair that fell to his shoulders. "Name of Alexander Du—mas, a French fellow. His daddy was a mulatto and his grandmama was a slave down on one of them islands—Mar-ti-nique, it says here. Man said to me, they right hard reading for children, but I told him he didn't know my babies. They can't read 'em now, I said, they'll grow into 'em."

In addition to the books there was a sockful of once-a-year store-bought licorice, oranges, and bananas for each of us and from Uncle Hammer a dress and a sweater for me, and a sweater and a pair of pants each for Christopher-John and Little Man. But nothing compared to the books. Little Man, who treasured clothes above all else, carefully laid his new pants and sweater aside and dashed for a clean sheet of brown paper to make a cover for his book, and throughout the day as he lay upon the deerskin rug looking at the bright, shining pictures of faraway places, turning each page as if it were gold, he would suddenly squint down at his hands, glance at the page he had just turned, then dash into the kitchen to wash again—just to make sure.

After the church services, the Averys returned home with us for Christmas dinner. All eight of the Avery children, including the four pre-schoolers, crowded into the kitchen with the boys and me, smelling the delicious aromas and awaiting the call to eat. But only the eldest girls, who were helping Mama, Big Ma, and Mrs. Avery prepare the finishing touches to the meal, were allowed to remain. The rest of us were continuously being shooed out by Big Ma. Finally, the announcement we were all waiting for was made and we were allowed to begin the Christmas feast.

The meal lasted for over two hours through firsts, seconds, and thirds, talk and laughter, and finally dessert. When we were finished the boys and I, with Claude and T.J., went outside, but the half-inch layer of snow made everything sloppy, so we soon went back in and joined the adults by the fire. Shortly afterward, there was a timid knock on the front door. Stacey opened the door and found Jeremy Simms standing there looking frozen and very frightened as he peered into the bright room. Everyone turned to stare at him. Stacey glanced around at Papa, then back at Jeremy. "You—you wanna come in?" he asked awkwardly.

Jeremy nodded and stepped hesitantly inside. As Stacey

motioned him toward the fire, Uncle Hammer's eyes narrowed, and he said to Papa, "He looks like a Simms."

"I believe he is," agreed Papa.

"Then what the devil—"

"Let me handle it," Papa said.

Jeremy, who had heard, flushed a deep red and quickly handed Mama a small burlap bag. "I—I brung them for y'all." Mama took the bag. As she opened it, I peeped over her shoulder; the bag was full of nuts.

"Nuts?" I questioned. "Nuts! Why we got more nuts now than we know what—"

"Cassie!" Mama scowled. "What have I told you about that mouth of yours?" Then she turned to Jeremy. "This is very thoughtful of you, Jeremy, and we appreciate them. Thank you."

Jeremy nodded slightly as if he did not know how to accept her thanks, and stiffly handed a slender, paper-wrapped object to Stacey. "Made this for ya," he said.

Stacey looked at Papa to see if he should take it. For a long moment Papa studied Jeremy, then he nodded. "It—it ain't much," stammered Jeremy as Stacey tore off the wrapping. "M-made it myself." Stacey slid his fingers down the smooth, sanded back of a wooden flute. "Go 'head and try it," said a pleased Jeremy. "It blows real nice."

Again Stacey looked at Papa, but this time Papa gave him no indication what he should do. "Thanks, Jeremy, it's real nice," he said finally. Then, flute in hand, he stood uncomfortably by the door waiting for Jeremy to leave.

When Jeremy did not move, Papa asked, "You Charlie Simms's boy?"

Jeremy nodded. "Y-yessir."

"Your daddy know you here?"

Jeremy bit his lower lip, and looked at his feet. "N-no sir, I reckon not."

"Then I expect you'd better be getting on home, son, 'fore he come looking for you."

"Yessir," said Jeremy, backing away.

As he reached the door, I cried after him, "Merry Christmas, Jeremy!" Jeremy looked back and smiled shyly. "Merry Christmas to y'all too."

T.J. made no comment on Jeremy's visit until both Papa and Uncle Hammer had left the room. He was afraid of Papa and downright terrified of Uncle Hammer, so he never had much to say when either was around, but now that they had gone outside with Mr. Avery, he said, "You ain't gonna keep that thing, are you?"

Stacey looked malevolently at T.J. and I knew that he was thinking of the coat. "Yeah, I'm gonna keep it. Why?"

T.J. shrugged. "Nothin'. 'Ceptin' I sure wouldn't want no whistle some ole white boy been blowin' on."

I watched Stacey closely to see if he was going to allow himself to be goaded by T.J.; he was not. "Ah, stuff it, T.J.," he ordered.

"Ah, man, don't get me wrong," said T.J. quickly. "You wanna keep the ole thing, it's up to you. But for me, somebody give me something, I want it to be something fine—

like that pretty little pearl-handled pistol. . . ."

When the Averys had left, Stacey asked, "Papa, how come Jeremy give me this flute? I mean, I didn't give him nothin'."

"Maybe you did give him something," said Papa, lighting his pipe.

"No sir, Papa. I ain't never give him nothin'!"

"Not even your friendship?"

"Well . . . not really. I mean . . . he's a crazy kid and he likes to walk to school with us, but—"

"You like him?"

Stacey frowned, thinking. "I told him I didn't want him walking with us, but he keeps on anyway and the white kids laugh at him 'cause he do. But he don't seem to let it bother him none. . . . I s'pose I like him all right. Is that wrong?"

"No," Papa said carefully. "That ain't wrong."

"Actually, he's much easier to get along with than T.J.," Stacey went on. "And I s'pose if I let him, he could be a better friend than T.J."

Papa took the pipe from his mouth, rubbed his moustache and spoke quietly. "Far as I'm concerned, friendship between black and white don't mean that much 'cause it usually ain't on a equal basis. Right now you and Jeremy might get along fine, but in a few years he'll think of himself as a man but you'll probably still be a boy to him. And if he feels that way, he'll turn on you in a minute."

"But Papa, I don't think Jeremy'd be that way."

Papa's eyes narrowed and his resemblance to Uncle Hammer increased. "We Logans don't have much to do with white folks. You know why? 'Cause white folks mean trouble. You see blacks hanging 'round with whites, they're headed for trouble. Maybe one day whites and blacks can be real friends, but right now the country ain't built that way. Now you could be right 'bout Jeremy making a much finer friend than T.J. ever will be. The trouble is, down here in Mississippi, it costs too much to find out. . . . So I think you'd better not try."

Stacey looked full into Papa's face and read his meaning.

On my way to bed, I stopped by the boys' room to retrieve an orange Christopher-John had swiped from my stocking and spied Stacey fingering the flute. As I stood in the doorway, he lingered over it, then, carefully rewrapping it, placed it in his box of treasured things. I never saw the flute again.

The day after Christmas Papa summoned Stacey, Christopher-John, Little Man, and me into the barn. We had hoped against hope that Mama would not tell him about our trip to the Wallace store or, if she did, that he would forget what he had promised. We should have known better. Mama always told Papa everything, and Papa never forgot anything.

After we had received our punishment, we emerged sore and teary-eyed and watched Papa, Uncle Hammer, and Mr. Morrison climb into the Packard and speed away. Mama said they were going to Vicksburg.

"Why Vicksburg, Mama?" asked Stacey.

"They've got some business to attend to," she said shortly. "Come on now, get busy. We've got chores to do."

In the late afternoon, shortly after the men had returned, Mr. Jamison arrived. He brought with him a fruit cake sent by Mrs. Jamison and a bag of lemon drops for each of the boys and me. Mama allowed us to say our thanks, then sent us outside. We played for a while in the patches of snow that remained, but when that grew tiresome, I popped into the house to see what was happening; Mama ordered me to pop back out again.

"What they doing?" asked Little Man.

"Looking at a whole bunch of papers," I said. "And Uncle Hammer was signing something."

"What kind of papers?" asked Stacey.

I shrugged. "I dunno. But Mr. Jamison was saying something 'bout selling the land."

"Selling the land?" questioned Stacey. "You sure?"

I nodded. "He said: 'Y'all sign them papers and Miz Caroline got no more legal right to this land. Can't sell it, can't sign on it. It'll be in y'all's name and it'll take both of y'all to do anything with it.' "

"Both of who?"

I shrugged again. "Papa and Uncle Hammer, I guess."

After a while it grew chilly and we went inside. Mr. Jamison, sitting next to Big Ma, was putting some papers into his briefcase. "I hope you feel better now that that's done, Miz Caroline," he said, his voice a soft mixture of Southern aristocracy and Northern schooling.

"Hammer and David, they been takin' care of things a long time now," Big Ma said. "Them and Mary works hard to pay the taxes and mortgage on this here place and I been wantin' to make sure while I'm still breathin' that they gets title to this place under the law without no trouble. I ain't wantin' a whole lot of problems after I'm gone 'bout who gots rights to this land." She paused a moment, then added, "That happens sometimes, you know."

Mr. Jamison nodded. He was a long, thin man in his mid-fifties with a perfect lawyer face, so placid that it was difficult to guess what thoughts lay behind it.

The boys and I sat down silently at the study table, and the silence allowed us to stay. I figured that Mr. Jamison would be leaving now. His business was evidently finished and despite the fact that the family thought well of him, he was not considered a friend in the usual sense, and there seemed no reason for him to stay longer. But now Mr. Jamison put his briefcase back on the floor, indicating that he was not leaving, and looked first at Big Ma and Mama, then across at Papa and Uncle Hammer.

"There's talk that some of the people around here are looking to shop in Vicksburg," he said.

Big Ma looked around at Papa and Uncle Hammer, but neither of them acknowledged her glance; their eyes were pinned on Mr. Jamison.

"There's talk too why folks are looking to shop there." He paused, met Papa's eyes, then Uncle Hammer's, and went on. "As you know, my family has roots in Vicksburg—we've a number of friends there still. I got a call from one of them this morning. Said you were looking to find credit for about thirty families."

Papa and Uncle Hammer neither affirmed nor denied this. "You know as well as I do that credit doesn't come easy these days," continued Mr. Jamison. "You expect to get any, you'll need something to back it."

"I reckon we know that," said Uncle Hammer.

Mr. Jamison glanced at Uncle Hammer and nodded. "I reckoned you did. But as far as I can see, the only thing any of you got to back that credit with is this land . . . and I'd hate to see you put it up."

"Why's that?" asked Uncle Hammer, wary of his interest.

"Because you'd lose it."

The fire popped and the room grew silent. Then Papa said, "What you getting at?"

"I'll back the credit."

Again, silence. Mr. Jamison allowed Papa and Uncle Hammer several moments to search for a motive behind his masklike face. "I'm a Southerner, born and bred, but that doesn't mean I approve of all that goes on here, and there are a lot of other white people who feel the same."

"If you and so many others feel that way," said Uncle Hammer with a wry sneer, "then how come them Wallaces ain't in jail?"

"Hammer—" Big Ma started.

"Because," answered Mr. Jamison candidly, "there aren't

enough of those same white people who would admit how they feel, or even if they did, would hang a white man for killing a black one. It's as simple as that."

Uncle Hammer smiled slightly and shook his head, but his eyes showed a grudging respect for Mr. Jamison.

"Backing the loan will be strictly a business matter. In the fall when the crops are in, those people who've bought the goods in Vicksburg will have to pay for them. If they don't, then I'll have to. Of course, as a businessman, I'm hoping that I won't have to put out a penny—my own cash box isn't exactly overflowing—so there'll have to be a credit limit. Still, it would lend me a great deal of satisfaction to know that I was a part of all this." He looked around. "What do you think?"

"You know it ain't hardly likely," Papa said, "that after accounts are figured, there'll be any money to pay any debts at all, except those up at that Wallace store."

Mr. Jamison nodded knowingly. "But the offer still stands."

Papa inhaled deeply. "Well, then, I'd say it's up to those people who'd be buying on your signature. They want to do it, then we got no say in it. We always pay cash."

"You know if you sign that credit," said Uncle Hammer, "you won't be the most popular man down in here. You thought about that?"

"Yes," said Mr. Jamison thoughtfully, "my wife and I discussed it fully. We realize what could happen. . . . But I'm just wondering if you do. Besides the fact that a number of white folks around here resent this land you've got and your independent attitude, there's Harlan Granger. Now I've known Harlan all my life, and he's not going to like this."

I wanted to ask what Mr. Granger had to do with anything, but common sense told me that I would only earn eviction by asking. But then Mr. Jamison went on and explained without any prodding from me.

"Ever since we were boys, Harlan's lived in the past. His grandmother filled him with all kinds of tales about the glory of the South before the war. You know, back then the Grangers had one of the biggest plantations in the state and Spokane County practically belonged to them . . . and they thought it did too. They were consulted about everything concerning this area and they felt it was up to them to see that things worked smoothly, according to the law—a law basically for whites. Well, Harlan feels the same now as his grandmother did back then. He also feels strongly about this land and he resents the fact that you won't sell it back to him. You back the credit with it now and he'll seize this opportunity to take it away from you. You can count on it."

He paused, and when he spoke again his voice had grown so quiet I had to lean forward to hear his next words. "And if you continue to encourage people not to shop at the Wallace store, you could still lose it. Don't forget that Harlan leases that store land to the Wallaces and gets a hefty percentage of its revenue. Before he let the Wallaces set up storekeeping, he was only getting his sharecroppers' money. Now he gets a nice bit of Montier's and Harrison's sharecroppers' money too since both of those plantations are too small to have a store, and he's not hardly going to stand for your interfering with it.

"But even more important than all that, you're pointing a finger right at the Wallaces with this boycott business. You're not only accusing them of murder, which in this case would be only a minor consideration because the man killed was black, but you're saying they should be punished for it. That they should be punished just as if they had killed a white man, and punishment of a white man for a wrong done to a black man would denote equality. Now *that* is what Harlan Granger absolutely will not permit."

Mr. Jamison was silent, waiting; no one else spoke and he went on again.

"What John Henry Berry and his brother were accused of—making advances to a white woman—goes against the grain of Harlan Granger and most other white folks in this community more than anything else, you know that. Harlan may not believe in the methods of the Wallaces, but he'll definitely support them. Believe me on that."

Mr. Jamison picked up his briefcase, ran his fingers through his graying hair, and met Papa's eyes. "The sad thing is, you know in the end you can't beat him or the Wallaces."

Papa looked down at the boys and me awaiting his reply, then nodded slightly, as if he agreed. "Still," he said, "I want these children to know we tried, and what we can't do now, maybe one day they will."

"I do hope that's so, David," murmured Mr. Jamison going to the door. "I truly hope that's so."

In the days that followed Mr. Jamison's visit, Papa, Mama, and Uncle Hammer went to the houses of those families who were considering shopping in Vicksburg. On the fourth day Papa and Uncle Hammer again went to Vicksburg, but this time in the wagon with Mr. Morrison. Their journey took two days and when they returned, the wagon was loaded with store-bought goods.

"What's all that?" I asked Papa as he jumped from the wagon. "That for us?"

"No, Cassie girl. It's things folks ordered from Vicksburg."

I wanted to ask more questions about the trip, but Papa seemed in a hurry to be off again and my questions went unanswered until the following day, when Mr. Granger arrived. Christopher-John and I were drawing water from the well when the silver Packard glided to a smooth stop in the drive and Mr. Granger stepped out. He stared sour-faced at Uncle Hammer's Packard in the barn, then opened the gate to the front yard and stepped briskly across the lawn to the house.

Hastily Christopher-John and I tugged on the well rope, pulled up the water tube, and poured the water into the bucket. Each of us gripping a side of the heavy bucket, we hurried to the back porch where we deposited it, then tip-toed silently through the empty kitchen to the door leading to Mama and Papa's room. Little Man and Stacey, just leaving the room under Mama's orders, allowed the door to remain slightly cracked, and all four of us huddled against it stepladder fashion.

"You sure giving folks something to talk 'bout with that car of yours, Hammer," Mr. Granger said in his folksy dialect as he sat down with a grunt across from Papa. In spite of his college education he always spoke this way. "What they got you doing up North? Bootlegging whiskey?" He laughed dryly, indicating that the question was to be taken lightly, but his eyes tight on Uncle Hammer showed that he intended to have an answer.

Uncle Hammer, leaning against the fireplace mantel, did not laugh. "Don't need to bootleg," he said sullenly. "Up there I got me a man's job and they pay me a man's wages for it."

Mr. Granger studied Uncle Hammer. Uncle Hammer wore, as he had every day since he had arrived, sharply creased pants, a vest over a snow-white shirt, and shoes that shone like midnight. "You right citified, ain't you? Course you always did think you was too good to work in the fields like other folks."

"Naw, that ain't it," said Uncle Hammer. "I just ain't never figured fifty cents a day was worth a child's time, let alone a man's wages." Uncle Hammer said nothing else; he didn't need to. Everyone knew that fifty cents was the top price paid to any day laborer, man, woman, or child, hired to work in the Granger fields.

Mr. Granger ran his tongue around his teeth, making his lips protrude in odd half circles, then he turned from Uncle Hammer to Papa. "Some folks tell me y'all running a regular traveling store up here. Hear tell a fellow can get just 'bout anything he wants from up at Tate's in Vicksburg if he just lets y'all know."

Papa met Mr. Granger's eyes, but did not speak.

Mr. Granger shook his head. "Seems to me you folks are just stirring up something. Y'all got roots in this community. Even got yourselves that loan Paul Edward made from the First National Bank up in Strawberry for that eastern two hundred acres. Course now with times like they are, that mortgage could come due anytime . . . and if it comes due and y'all ain't got the money to pay it, y'all could lose this place."

"Ain't gonna lose it," said Uncle Hammer flatly.

Mr. Granger glanced up at Uncle Hammer, then back to Papa. He took a cigar from his pocket, then a knife to cut off the tip. After he had thrown the tip into the fire, he settled back in his chair and lit the cigar while Papa, Mama, Uncle Hammer, and Big Ma waited for him to get on. Then he said: "This is a fine community. Got fine folks in it—both white and colored. Whatever's bothering you people, y'all just tell me. We'll get it straightened out without all this big to-do."

Uncle Hammer laughed outright. Mr. Granger looked

up sharply, but Uncle Hammer eyed him insolently, a smile still on his lips. Mr. Granger, watching him, cautioned sternly, "I don't like trouble here. This is a quiet and peaceful place. . . . I aim to see it stays that way." Turning back to Papa, he continued. "Whatever problems we have, we can work them out. I ain't gonna hide that I think y'all making a big mistake, both for the community and for yourselves, going all the way down to Vicksburg to do your shopping. That don't seem very neighborly—"

"Neither does burning," said Uncle Hammer.

Mr. Granger puffed deeply on his cigar and did not look at Uncle Hammer. When he spoke again it was to Big Ma. His voice was harsh, but he made no comment on what Uncle Hammer had said. "I don't think your Paul Edward would've condoned something like this and risked losing this place. How come you let your boys go do it?"

Big Ma smoothed the lap of her dress with her hands. "They grown and it's they land. I got no more say in it."

Mr. Granger's eyes showed no surprise, but he pursed his lips again and ran his tongue around his teeth. "The price of cotton's mighty low, y'all know that," he said finally. "Could be that I'll have to charge my people more of their crops next summer just to make ends meet. . . . I'd hate to do it, 'cause if I did my people wouldn't hardly have enough to buy winter stores, let alone be able to pay their debts. . . ."

There was a tense, waiting silence before his glance slid to Papa again.

"Mr. Joe Higgins up at First National told me that he couldn't hardly honor a loan to folks who go around stirring up a lot of bad feelings in the community—"

"And especially stirring the colored folks out of their place," interjected Uncle Hammer calmly.

Mr. Granger paled, but did not turn to Uncle Hammer. "Money's too scarce," he continued as if he had not heard, "and folks like that are a poor risk. You ready to lose your land, David, because of this thing?"

Papa was lighting his pipe. He did not look up until the flame had caught in the tobacco and held there. Then he turned to Mr. Granger. "Two hundred acres of this place been Logan land for almost fifty years now, the other two hundred for fifteen. We've been through bad times and good times but we ain't never lost none of it. Ain't gonna start now."

Mr. Granger said quietly, "It was Granger land before it was Logan."

"Slave land," said Papa.

Mr. Granger nodded. "Wouldn't have lost this section if it hadn't been stolen by your Yankee carpetbaggers after the war. But y'all keep on playing Santa Claus and I'm gonna get it back—real easy. I want you to know that I plan to do whatever I need to, to keep peace down in here."

Papa took the pipe from his mouth and stared into the fire. When he faced Mr. Granger again his voice was very quiet, very distinct, very sure. "You being white, you can just 'bout plan on anything you want. But I tell you this one thing: You plan on getting this land, you're planning on the wrong thing."

Mama's hand crossed almost unseen to Papa's arm.

Mr. Granger looked up slyly. "There's lots of ways of stopping you, David."

Papa impaled Mr. Granger with an icy stare. "Then you'd better make them good," he said.

Mr. Granger stood to go, a smile creeping smugly over his lips as if he knew a secret but refused to tell. He glanced at Uncle Hammer, then turned and left, leaving the silence behind him.

8

"Uh . . . Miz Lillian Jean, wouldja wait up a minute, please?"

"Cassie, you cracked?" cried Stacey. "Cassie, where you . . . get back here! Cassie!"

Stacey's words faded into the gray stillness of the January morning as I turned deaf ears to him and hurried after Lillian Jean. "Thanks for waiting up," I said when I caught up with her.

She stared down at me irritably. "What you want?"

"Well," I said, walking beside her, "I been thinking 'bout what happened in Strawberry back last month."

"Yeah?" commented Lillian Jean suspiciously.

"Well, to tell you the truth, I was real upset for a while there. But my papa told me it don't do no good sitting around being mad. Then I seen how things was. I mean, I should've seen it all along. After all, I'm who I am and you're who you are."

Lillian Jean looked at me with astonishment that I could see the matter so clearly. "Well, I'm glad you finally learned the way of things."

"Oh, I did," I piped readily. "The way I see it—here, let me take them books for you, Miz Lillian Jean—the way I see it, we all gotta do what we gotta do. And that's what I'm gonna do from now on. Just what I gotta."

"Good for you, Cassie," replied Lillian Jean enthusiastically. "God'll bless you for it."

"You think so?"

"Why, of course!" she exclaimed. "God wants all his children to do what's right."

"I'm glad you think so . . . Miz Lillian Jean."

When we reached the crossroads, I waved good-bye to Lillian Jean and waited for the others. Before they reached me, Little Man exclaimed, "Owwww, I'm gonna tell Mama! Carrying that ole dumb Lillian Jean's books!"

"Cassie, whatja do that for?" questioned Christopher-John, his round face pained.

"Ah, shoot," laughed T.J. "Ole Cassie jus' learned she better do what's good for her if she don't want no more of Mr. Simms's back hand."

I clinched my fists behind me, and narrowed my eyes in the Logan gaze, but managed to hold my tongue.

Stacey stared at me strangely, then turned and said, "We'd better get on to school."

As I followed, Jeremy touched my arm timidly. "C-Cassie, you didn't have to do that. That—that ole Lillian Jean, she ain't worth it."

I stared at Jeremy, trying to understand him. But he shied away from me and ran down the road after his sister.

"Mama gonna whip you good, too," said prideful Little Man, still fuming as we approached the school. "'Cause I'm gonna sure tell it."

"Naw you ain't," said Stacey. There was a shocked silence as all heads turned to him. "This here thing's between Cassie and Lillian Jean and ain't nobody telling nobody nothin' 'bout this." He stared directly at T.J., caught his eye, and repeated, "Nobody."

"Ah, man!" cried T.J. "It ain't none of my business." Then, after a moment's silence, he added, "I got too many worries of my own to worry 'bout Cassie Uncle Tomming Lillian Jean."

My temper almost flew out of my mouth, but I pressed my lips tightly together, forcing it to stay inside.

"Them final examinations comin' up in two weeks, man, and ain't no way I can afford to fail them things again," T.J. continued.

"Then you won't," said Stacey.

"Shoot, that's what I thought last year. But your mama

makes up the hardest examinations she know how." He paused, sighed, and ventured, "Bet though if you kinda asked her 'bout what kind of questions—"

"T.J., don't you come talking to me 'bout no more cheating!" cried Stacey angrily. "After all that trouble I got in the last time 'count of you. You got questions, you ask Mama yourself, but you say one more word to me 'bout them tests, I'm gonna—"

"All right, all right." T.J. smiled in feigned apology. "It's just that I'm gonna have to figure out somethin'."

"I got a solution," I said, unable to resist just one bit of friendly advice.

"What's that?"

"Try studying."

After Uncle Hammer left on New Year's Day, Papa and I had gone into the forest, down the cow path, and to the misty hollow where the trees lay fallen. For a while we stood looking again at the destruction, then, sitting on one of our fallen friends, we talked in quiet, respectful tones, observing the soft mourning of the forest.

When I had explained the whole Strawberry business to Papa, he said slowly, "You know the Bible says you're s'pose to forgive these things."

"Yessir," I agreed, waiting.

"S'pose to turn the other cheek."

"Yessir."

Papa rubbed his moustache and looked up at the trees

standing like sentinels on the edge of the hollow, listening. "But the way I see it, the Bible didn't mean for you to be no fool. Now one day, maybe I can forgive John Andersen for what he done to these trees, but I ain't gonna forget it. I figure forgiving is not letting something nag at you—rotting you out. Now if I hadn't done what I done, then I couldn't've forgiven myself, and that's the truth of it."

I nodded gravely and he looked down at me. "You're a lot like me, Cassie girl, but you got yourself a bad temper like your Uncle Hammer. That temper can get you in trouble."

"Yessir."

"Now this thing between you and Lillian Jean, most folks would think you should go around doing what she tell you . . . and maybe you should—"

"Papa!"

"Cassie, there'll be a whole lot of things you ain't gonna wanna do but you'll have to do in this life just so you can survive. Now I don't like the idea of what Charlie Simms did to you no more than your Uncle Hammer, but I had to weigh the hurt of what happened to you to what could've happened if I went after him. If I'd've gone after Charlie Simms and given him a good thrashing like I felt like doing, the hurt to all of us would've been a whole lot more than the hurt you received, so I let it be. I don't like letting it be, but I can live with that decision.

"But there are other things, Cassie, that if I'd let be, they'd eat away at me and destroy me in the end. And it's the same with you, baby. There are things you can't back down on, things you gotta take a stand on. But it's up to you to decide what them things are. You have to demand respect in this world, ain't nobody just gonna hand it to you. How you carry yourself, what you stand for—that's how you gain respect. But, little one, ain't nobody's respect worth more than your own. You understand that?"

"Yessir."

"Now, there ain't no sense in going around being mad. You clear your head so you can think sensibly. Then I want you to think real hard on whether or not Lillian Jean's worth taking a stand about, but keep in mind that Lillian Jean probably won't be the last white person to treat you this way." He turned toward me so that he looked me full in the face, and the seriousness of his eyes startled me. He held my chin up with the wide flat of his hard hand. "This here's an important decision, Cassie, very important—I want you to understand that—but I think you can handle it. Now, you listen to me, and you listen good. This thing, if you make the wrong decision and Charlie Simms gets involved, then I get involved and there'll be trouble.

"B-big trouble?" I whispered. "Like the trees?"

"Don't know," said Papa. "But it could be bad."

I pondered his words, then I promised, "Mr. Simms ain't never gonna hear 'bout it, Papa."

Papa studied me. "I'll count on that, Cassie girl. I'll count real hard on that."

For the month of January I was Lillian Jean's slave and she thoroughly enjoyed it. She even took to waiting for me in the morning with Jeremy so that I could carry her books. When friends of hers walked with us, she bragged about her little colored friend and almost hugged herself with pleasure when I called her "Miz" Lillian Jean. When we were alone, she confided her secrets to me: the boy she had passionately loved for the past year and the things she had done to attract his attention (with no success, I might add); the secrets of the girls she couldn't stand as well as those she could; and even a tidbit or two about her elder brothers' romantic adventures. All I had to do to prime the gossip pump was smile nicely and whisper a "Miz Lillian Jean" every now and then. I *almost* hated to see the source dry up.

At the end of examination day, I shot out of Miss Crocker's class and hurried into the yard. I was eager to get to the crossroads to meet Lillian Jean; I had promised myself to first take care of the examinations and then . . .

"Little Man! Claude! Christopher-John! Come on, y'all!" I cried. "There's Stacey!" The four of us dashed across the yard trailing Stacey and T.J. to the road. When we caught up with them, it was obvious that the jovial mask T.J. always wore had been stripped away.

"She did it on purpose!" T.J. accused, a nasty scowl twisting his face.

"Man, you was cheating!" Stacey pointed out. "What you 'spect for her to do?"

"She could've give me a break. Warn't nothin' but a couple bits of ole paper. Didn't need 'em nohow."

"Well, whatja have them for?"

"Ah, man, leave me be! All y'all Logans think y'all so doggone much with y'all's new coats and books and shiny new Packards!" He swirled around, glaring down at Christopher-John, Little Man, and me. "I'm sick of all y'all. Your mama and your papa, too!" Then he turned and fled angrily up the road.

"T.J.! Hey, man, where you going?" Stacey yelled after him. T.J. did not answer. The road swelled into a small hill and he disappeared on the other side of it. When we reached the crossroads and saw no sign of him on the southern road leading home, Stacey asked Claude, "Where he go?"

Claude looked shame-faced and rubbed one badly worn shoe against the other. "Down to that ole store, I reckon."

Stacey sighed. "Come on then, we'd better get on home. He'll be all right by tomorrow."

"Y'all go on," I said. "I gotta wait for Lillian Jean."

"Cassie—"

"I'll catch up with ya," I said before Stacey could lecture me. "Here, take my books, will ya?" He looked at me as if he should say something else, but deciding not to, he pushed the younger boys on and followed them.

When Lillian Jean appeared, I sighed thankfully that only Jeremy was with her; it could be today for sure. Jeremy, who seemed to be as disappointed in me as Little

Man, hurried on to catch Stacey. That was fine, too; I knew he would. I took Lillian Jean's books, and as we sauntered down the road, I only half listened to her; I was sweeping the road, looking for the deep wooded trail I had selected earlier in the week. When I saw it, I interrupted Lillian Jean apologetically. "'Scuse me, Miz Lillian Jean, but I got a real nice surprise for you . . . found it just the other day down in the woods."

"For me?" questioned Lillian Jean. "Ah, you is a sweet thing, Cassie. Where you say it is?"

"Come on. I'll show you."

I stepped into the dry gully and scrambled onto the bank. Lillian Jean hung back. "It's all right," I assured her. "It ain't far. You just gotta see it, Miz Lillian Jean."

That did it. Grinning like a Cheshire cat, she crossed the gully and hopped onto the bank. Following me up the overgrown trail into the deep forest, she asked, "You sure this is the way, little Cassie?"

"Just a bit further . . . up ahead there. Ah, here it is."

We entered a small dark clearing with hanging forest vines, totally hidden from the road.

"Well? Where's the surprise?"

"Right here," I said, smashing Lillian Jean's books on the ground.

"Why, what you do that for?" Lillian Jean asked, more startled than angry.

"I got tired of carrying 'em," I said.

"This what you brought me all the way down here for!

Well, you just best get untired and pick 'em up again."
Then, expecting that her will would be done with no more
than that from her, she turned to leave the glade.

"Make me," I said quietly.

"What?" The shock on her face was almost comical.

"Said make me."

Her face paled. Then, red with anger, she stepped daintily
across the clearing and struck me hard across the face. For
the record, she had hit me first; I didn't plan on her hitting
me again.

I flailed into her, tackling her with such force that we
both fell. After the first shock of my actually laying hands
on her, she fought as best she could, but she was no match
for me. I was calm and knew just where to strike. I punched
her in the stomach and buttocks, and twisted her hair, but not
once did I touch her face; she, expending her energy in
angry, nasty name-calling, clawed at mine, managing to
scratch twice. She tried to pull my hair but couldn't, for I
had purposely asked Big Ma to braid it into flat braids
against my head.

When I had pinned Lillian Jean securely beneath me, I
yanked unmercifully on her long, loose hair and demanded
an apology for all the names she had called me, and for the
incident in Strawberry. At first she tried to be cute—"Ain't
gonna 'pologize to no nigger!" she sassed.

"You wanna be bald, girl?"

And she apologized. For herself and for her father. For
her brothers and her mother. For Strawberry and Missis-

sippi, and by the time I finished jerking at her head, I think she would have apologized for the world being round had I demanded it. But when I let her go and she had sped safely to the other side of the clearing with the trail in front of her, she threatened to tell her father.

"You do that, Lillian Jean. You just do that and I'm gonna make sure all your fancy friends know how you keeps a secret. Bet you won't be learning no more secrets after that."

"Cassie! You wouldn't do that. Not after I trusted you—"

"You mutter one word of this to anybody, Lillian Jean," I said, attempting to narrow my eyes like Papa's, "just one person and everybody at Jefferson Davis is gonna know who you crazy 'bout and all your other business . . . and you know I know. Besides, if anybody ever did find out 'bout this fight, you'd be laughed clear up to Jackson. You here going on thirteen, getting beat up by a nine-year-old."

I was starting up the trail, feeling good about myself, when Lillian Jean asked, bewildered, "But, Cassie, why? You was such a nice little girl. . . ."

I stared at her astonished. Then I turned and left the forest, not wanting to believe that Lillian Jean didn't even realize it had all been just a game.

"Cassie Logan!"

"Yes'm, Miz Crocker?"

"That's the third time I've caught you daydreaming this morning. Just because you managed to come in first on the examinations last week doesn't mean a thing this week. We're in a new quarter and everyone's slate is clean. You'll make no A's by daydreaming. You understand that?"

"Yes'm," I said, not bothering to add that she repeated herself so much that all a body had to do was listen to the first few minutes of her lesson to be free to daydream to her heart's content.

"I think you'd just better sit in the back where you're not so comfortable," she said. "Then maybe you'll pay more attention."

"But—"

Miss Crocker raised her hand, indicating that she did not want to hear another word, and banished me to the very last row in front of the window. I slid onto the cold seat after its former occupant had eagerly left it for my warm quarters by the stove. As soon as Miss Crocker turned away, I mumbled a few indignant phrases, then hugged my Christmas sweater to me. I tried to pay attention to Miss Crocker but the cold creeping under the windowsill made it impossible. Unable to bear the draft, I decided to line the sill with paper from my notebook. I ripped out the paper, then turned to the window. As I did, a man passed under it and disappeared.

The man was Kaleb Wallace.

I raised my hand. "Uh, Miz Crocker, may I be excused please, ma'am? I gotta . . . well, you know. . . ."

As soon as I had escaped Miss Crocker, I dashed to the front of the building. Kaleb Wallace was standing in front of the seventh-grade-class building talking to Mr. Wellever and two white men whom I couldn't make out from where I stood. When the men entered the building, I turned and sped to the rear and carefully climbed onto the woodpile stacked behind it. I peeked cautiously through a broken window into Mama's classroom. The men were just entering, Kaleb Wallace first, followed by a man I didn't know and Mr. Harlan Granger.

Mama seemed startled to see the men, but when Mr. Granger said, "Been hearing 'bout your teaching, Mary, so as members of the school board we thought we'd come by and learn something," she merely nodded and went on with her lesson. Mr. Wellever left the room, returning shortly with three folding chairs for the visitors; he him-self remained standing.

Mama was in the middle of history and I knew that was bad. I could tell Stacey knew it too; he sat tense near the back of the room, his lips very tight, his eyes on the men. But Mama did not flinch; she always started her history class the first thing in the morning when the students were most alert, and I knew that the hour was not yet up. To make matters worse, her lesson for the day was slavery. She spoke on the cruelty of it; of the rich economic cycle it generated as slaves produced the raw products for the fac-tories of the North and Europe; how the country profited and grew from the free labor of a people still not free.

Before she had finished, Mr. Granger picked up a stu-dent's book, flipped it open to the pasted-over front cover, and pursed his lips. "Thought these books belonged to the county," he said, interrupting her. Mama glanced over at him, but did not reply. Mr. Granger turned the pages, stopped, and read something. "I don't see all them things you're teaching in here."

"That's because they're not in there," Mama said.

"Well, if it ain't in here, then you got no right teaching it. This book's approved by the Board of Education and you're expected to teach what's in it."

"I can't do that."

"And why not?"

Mama, her back straight and her eyes fixed on the men, answered, "Because all that's in that book isn't true."

Mr. Granger stood. He laid the book back on the student's desk and headed for the door. The other board member and Kaleb Wallace followed. At the door Mr. Granger stopped and pointed at Mama. "You must be some kind of smart, Mary, to know more than the fellow who wrote that book. Smarter than the school board, too, I reckon."

Mama remained silent, and Mr. Wellever gave her no support.

"In fact," Mr. Granger continued, putting on his hat, "you so smart I expect you'd best just forget about teaching altogether . . . then thataway you'll have plenty of time to write your own book." With that he turned his back on her, glanced at Mr. Wellever to make sure his meaning was clear, and left with the others behind him.

We waited for Mama after school was out. Stacey had sent T.J. and Claude on, and the four of us, silent and patient, were sitting on the steps when Mama emerged. She smiled down at us, seemingly not surprised that we were there.

I looked up at her, but I couldn't speak. I had never really thought much about Mama's teaching before; that was just a part of her being Mama. But now that she could not teach, I felt resentful and angry, and I hated Mr. Granger.

"You all know?" she asked. We nodded as she slowly descended the stairs. Stacey took one handle of her heavy black satchel and I took the other. Christopher-John and Little Man each took one of her hands, and we started across the lawn.

"M-Mama," said Christopher-John when we reached the road, "can't you ever teach no more?"

Mama did not answer immediately. When she did, her voice was muffled. "Somewhere else maybe, but not here—at least not for a while."

"But how's come, Mama?" demanded Little Man. "How's come?"

Mama bit into her lower lip and gazed at the road. "Because, baby," she said finally, "I taught things some folks just didn't want to hear."

When we reached home, Papa and Mr. Morrison were both in the kitchen with Big Ma drinking coffee. As we entered, Papa searched our faces. His eyes settled on Mama; the pain was in her face. "What's wrong?" he asked.

Mama sat down beside him. She pushed back a strand of hair that had worked its way free of the chignon, but it fell back into her face again and she left it there. "I got fired."

Big Ma put down her cup weakly without a word.

Papa reached out and touched Mama. She said, "Harlan Granger came to the school with Kaleb Wallace and one of the school-board members. Somebody had told them about those books I'd pasted over . . . but that was only an excuse. They're just getting at us any way they can because of shopping in Vicksburg." Her voice cracked. "What'll we do, David? We needed that job."

Papa gently pushed the stray hair back over her ear. "We'll get by. . . . Plant more cotton maybe. But we'll get by." There was quiet reassurance in his voice.

Mama nodded and stood.

"Where you goin', child?" Big Ma asked.

"Outside. I want to walk for a bit."

Christopher-John, Little Man, and I turned to follow her, but Papa called us back. "Leave your mama be," he said.

As we watched her slowly cross the backyard to the barren garden and head toward the south pasture, Mr. Morrison said, "You know with you here, Mr. Logan, you got no need of me. Maybe there's work to be had around here. . . . Maybe I could get something . . . help you out."

Papa stared across at Mr. Morrison. "There's no call for

you to do that," he said. "I'm not paying you anything as it is."

Mr. Morrison said softly, "I got me a nice house to live in, the best cooking a man could want, and for the first time in a long time I got me a family. That's right good pay, I'd say."

Papa nodded. "You're a good man, Mr. Morrison, and I thank you for the offer, but I'll be leaving in a few weeks and I'd rather you was here." His eyes focused on Mama again, a tiny figure in the distance now.

"Papa," rasped Christopher-John, moving close to him, "M-Mama gonna be all right?"

Papa turned and, putting his arms around Christopher-John, drew him even nearer. "Son, your mama . . . she's born to teaching like the sun is born to shine. And it's gonna be hard on her not teaching anymore. It's gonna be real hard 'cause ever since she was a wee bitty girl down in the Delta she wanted to be a teacher."

"And Grandpa wanted her to be one, too, didn't he, Papa?" said Christopher-John.

Papa nodded. "Your mama was his baby child and every penny he'd get his hands on he'd put it aside for her schooling . . . and that wasn't easy for him either cause he was a tenant farmer and he didn't see much cash money. But he'd promised your grandmama 'fore she died to see that your mama got an education, and when your mama 'come high-school age, he sent her up to Jackson to school, then on to teacher training school. It was just 'cause he died her last year of schooling that she come on up here to teach 'stead of going back to the Delta."

"And y'all got married and she ain't gone back down there no more," interjected Little Man.

Papa smiled faintly at Little Man and stood up. "That's right, son. She was too smart and pretty to let get away." He stooped and looked out the window again, then back at us. "She's a strong, fine woman, your mama, and this thing won't keep her down . . . but it's hurt her bad. So I want y'all to be extra thoughtful for the next few days—and remember what I told you, you hear?"

"Yessir, Papa," we answered.

Papa left us then and went onto the back porch. There he leaned against the porch pillar for several minutes staring out toward the pasture; but after a while he stepped into the yard and crossed the garden to join Mama.

"T.J.? You sure?" Stacey asked Little Willie Wiggins at recess the next day. Little Willie nodded morosely and answered, "Heard it myself. Clarence, too. Was standin' right up 'side him at the store when he told Mr. Kaleb. Come talkin' 'bout how Miz Logan failed him on purpose and then said she wasn't a good teacher and that she the one stopped everybody from comin' up to they store. Said she even was destroyin' school property—talkin' 'bout them books, you know."

"Who's gonna take him?" I cried.

"Hush, Cassie," said Stacey. "How come you just telling this now, Little Willie?"

Little Willie shrugged. "Guess I got fooled by ole T.J. Clarence and me, we told him we was gonna tell it soon as we left the store, but T.J. asked us not to do it. Said he was goin' right back and tell them it wasn't nothin' but a joke, what he said. And he went back too, and I thought nothin' was gonna come of it." He hesitated, then confessed, "Didn't say nothin' 'bout it before 'cause me and Clarence wasn't s'pose to be up there ourselves . . . but then here come Mr. Granger yesterday and fires Miz Logan. I figure that's T.J.'s doin'."

"He probably figured it too," I said. "That's why he ain't in school today."

"Talking 'bout he sick," said Christopher-John.

"If he ain't now, he gonna be," prophesied Little Man, his tiny fists balled for action. "'Round here telling on Mama."

After school when Claude turned up the forest trail leading to the Avery house, we went with him. As we emerged from the forest into the Avery yard, the house appeared deserted, but then we spied T.J., lazily swinging straddle-legged atop an inner tube hanging from an old oak in the front yard. Stacey immediately charged toward him, and when T.J. saw him coming he tried to swing his long right leg over the tube to escape. He didn't make it. Stacey jumped up on the inner tube, giving them both a jerky ride before they landed hard on Mrs. Avery's azalea bush.

"Man, what's the matter with you?" T.J. cried as he rolled from under Stacey to glance back at the flattened bush. "My mama gonna kill me when she see that bush."

Stacey jumped up and jerked at T.J.'s collar. "Was you the one? Did you do it?"

T.J. looked completely bewildered. "Do what? What you talkin' 'bout?"

"Didja tell it? You tell them Wallaces 'bout Mama?"

"Me?" asked T.J. "Me? Why, man, you oughta know me better'n that."

"He do know you," I said. "How come you think we up here?"

"Hey, now, wait a minute," objected T.J. "I don't know what somebody been tellin' y'all, but I ain't told them Wallaces nothin'."

"You was down there," Stacey accused. "The day Mama caught you cheating, you went down to them Wallaces."

"Well, that don't mean nothin'," said T. J., jerking away from Stacey's grip and hopping to his feet. "My daddy says I can go down there if I wanna. Don't mean I told them ole folks nothin' though."

"Heard you told them all sorts of things . . . like Mama didn't know nothin' and she wasn't even teaching what she s'pose to—"

"Didn't neither!" denied T.J. "Ain't never said that! All I said was that it was her that . . ." His voice trailed off as he realized he had said too much, and he began to laugh uneasily. "Hey, look, y'all, I don't know how come Miz Logan got fired, but I ain't said nothin' to make nobody fire her. All I said was that she failed me again. A fellow got a right to be mad 'bout somethin' like that, ain't he?"

Stacey's eyes narrowed upon T.J. "Maybe," he said. "But he ain't got no right to go running his mouth off 'bout things that ain't s'pose to be told."

T.J. stepped backward and looked nervously over his shoulder to the south, where the fields lay fallow. The rutted wagon trail which cut through the fields leading from the distant Granger mansion revealed a thin woman stepping briskly toward us. T.J. seemed to take heart from the figure and grew cocky again. "Don't know who's been tellin', but it ain't been me."

A moment's silence passed, and then Stacey, his eyes cold and condemning, said quietly, "It was you all right, T.J. It was you." Then, turning, he motioned us back toward the forest.

"Ain't you gonna beat him up?" cried a disappointed Little Man.

"What he got coming to him is worse than a beating," replied Stacey.

"What could be worse than that?" asked Christopher-John.

"You'll see," said Stacey. "And so will T.J."

T.J.'s first day back at school after almost a week's absence was less than successful. Avoiding us in the morning, he arrived late, only to be shunned by the other students. At first he pretended that the students' attitude didn't matter, but by the afternoon when school was out, he hurried after us, attempting to convince us that he was merely a victim of circumstances.

"Hey, y'all ain't gonna hold what Little Willie said against me, are you?" he asked.

"You still saying what Little Willie said ain't true?" questioned Stacey.

"Why, shoot, yeah!" he exclaimed. "When I catch up with that little rascal, I'm gonna beat him to a pulp, 'round here tellin' everybody I got Miz Logan fired. Ain't nobody even speakin' to me no more. Little Willie probably told them Wallaces that hisself, so he figures to get out of it by tellin' everybody it was—"

"Ah, stop lying, T.J.," I said testily. "Don't nobody believe you."

"Well, I should've known you wouldn't, Cassie. You never liked me noway."

"Well, anyway, that's the truth," I agreed.

"But," said T.J., grinning again and turning toward Little Man and Christopher-John, "my little buddy Christopher-John believes me, don't you, fellow? And you still my pal, ain't you, Little Man?"

An indignant Little Man looked up at T.J., but before he could speak, easygoing Christopher-John said, "You told on Mama, T.J. Now she all unhappy 'cause she can't teach school no more and it's all your fault, and we don't like you no more!"

"Yeah!" added Little Man in agreement.

T.J. stared down at Christopher-John, not believing that he had said that. Then he laughed uneasily. "I don't know what's got into folks. Everybody's gone crazy—"

"Look," Stacey said, stopping, "first you run off with the mouth to them Wallaces and now you blaming Little Willie for what you done. Why don't you just admit it was you?"

"Hey, man!" T.J. exclaimed, grinning his easy grin. But then, finding that the grin and the smooth words no longer worked, his face dropped. "Oh, all right. All right. So maybe what if I did say somethin' 'bout Miz Logan? I can't even remember saying nothin' 'bout it, but if both Little Willie and Clarence said I did then maybe I did. Anyways, I'm real sorry 'bout your mama losin' her job and—"

All of us, including Claude, stared distastefully at T.J. and walked away from him.

"Hey, wait. . . . I said I was sorry, didn't I?" he asked, following us. "Look, what's a fellow got to do anyway? Hey, y'all, look, this here is still ole T.J.! I ain't changed. Y'all can't turn on me just 'cause—"

"You the one turned, T.J.," Stacey called over his shoulder. "Now leave us alone. We don't want no more to do with you."

T.J., for the first time comprehending that we were no

longer his friends, stopped. Then, standing alone in the middle of the road, he screamed after us, "Who needs y'all anyway? I been tired of y'all always hangin' 'round for a long while now, but I been too nice to tell ya. . . . I should've known better. What I look like, havin' a bunch of little kids 'round all the time and me here fourteen, near grown. . . ."

We walked on, not stopping.

"Got me better friends than y'all! They give me things and treat me like I'm a man and . . . and they white too. . . ."

His voice faded into the wind as we left him and we heard no more.

9

Spring. It seeped unseen into the waiting red earth in early March, softening the hard ground for the coming plow and awakening life that had lain gently sleeping through the cold winter. But by the end of March it was evident everywhere: in the barn where three new calves bellowed and chicks the color of soft pale sunlight chirped; in the yard where the wisteria and English dogwood bushes readied themselves for their annual Easter bloom, and the fig tree budded producing the forerunners of juicy, brown fruit for which the boys and I would have to do battle with fig-loving Jack; and in the smell of the earth itself. Rain-drenched, fresh, vital, full of life, spring enveloped all of us.

I was eager to be in the fields again, to feel the furrowed rows of damp, soft earth beneath my feet; eager to walk barefooted through the cool forest, hug the trees, and sit under their protective shadow. But although every living thing knew it was spring, Miss Crocker and the other teachers evidently did not, for school lingered on indefinitely. In the last week of March when Papa and Mr. Morrison began to plow the east field, I volunteered to sacrifice school and help them. My offer was refused and I trudged wearily to school for another week.

"I guess I won't be seein' much of y'all after next Friday," said Jeremy one evening as we neared his forest trail.

"Guess not," said Stacey.

"Be nice if our schools ended at the same time."

"You crazy!" I cried, remembering that Jefferson Davis didn't dismiss until mid-May.

Jeremy stammered an apology. "I—I just meant we could still see each other." He was silent a moment, then brightened. "Maybe I can come over to see y'all sometime."

Stacey shook his head. "Don't think Papa would like that."

"Well . . . I just thought . . ." He shrugged. "It'll sure be lonely without y'all."

"Lonely?" I asked. "With all them brothers and sisters you got?"

Jeremy frowned. "The little ones, they too young to play with, and the older ones . . . Lillian Jean and R.W.

and Melvin, I guess I don't like them very much."

"What you saying?" asked Stacey. "You can't not like your own sister and brothers."

"Well, I can understand that," I said soberly. "I sure don't like them."

"But they're his kin. A fellow's gotta like his own kin."

Jeremy thought about that. "Well, Lillian Jean's all right, I guess. She ain't so persnickety since Cassie stopped bein' her friend." He smiled a secret smile to himself. "But that R.W. and Melvin, they ain't very nice. You oughta see how they treat T.J. . . ." He halted, looked up embarrassed, and was quiet.

Stacey stopped. "How they treat him?"

Jeremy stopped too. "I don't know," he said as if he was sorry he had mentioned it. "They just don't do him right."

"How?" asked Stacey.

"Thought you didn't like him no more."

"Well . . . I don't," replied Stacey defensively. "But I heard he was running 'round with R.W. and Melvin. I wondered why. Them brothers of yours must be eighteen or nineteen."

Jeremy looked up at the sun, squinted, then glanced up his forest trail a few feet ahead. "They brung T.J. by the house a couple of times when Pa wasn't home. They treated him almost friendly like, but when he left they laughed and talked 'bout him—called him names." He squinted again at the trail and said hurriedly, "I better go. . . . See y'all tomorrow."

"Mama, how come you suppose R.W. and Melvin putting in time with T.J.?" I asked as I measured out two heaping tablespoons of flour for the cornbread.

Mama frowned down into the flour barrel. "Only one tablespoon, Cassie, and not so heaping."

"But, Mama, we always use two."

"That barrel will have to last us until Papa goes back to the railroad. Now put it back."

As I returned one tablespoon of flour to the barrel, I again asked, "What you think, Mama? How come them Simmses running 'round with T.J.?"

Mama measured out the baking powder and gave it to me. It was a teaspoon less than we had been using, but I didn't ask her about it. It was running low too.

"I don't really know, Cassie," she said, turning to the stove to stir milk into the butter beans. "They may just want him around because it makes them feel good."

"When T.J.'s around me, he don't make me feel good."

"Well, you told me Jeremy said they were laughing at T.J. behind his back. Some folks just like to keep other folks around to laugh at them . . . use them."

"I wonder how come T.J. don't know they laughing at him? You s'pose he's that dumb?"

"T.J.'s not 'dumb,' Cassie. He just wants attention, but he's going after it the wrong way."

I was going to ask what use T.J. could possibly be to anyone, but I was interrupted by Little Man running into the kitchen. "Mama!" he cried. "Mr. Jamison just drove up!" He had been in the barn cleaning the chicken coop with Christopher-John and stubby particles of straw still clung to his head. I grinned at his mussed appearance but didn't have time to tease him before he was gone again.

Mama looked at Big Ma, a question in her eyes, then followed Little Man outside. I decided that the cornbread could wait and dashed after them.

"Girl, get back in here and finish mixin' this cornbread!" ordered Big Ma.

"Yes'm," I said. "I'll be right back." Before Big Ma could reach me, I was out the back door running across the yard to the drive.

Mr. Jamison touched his hat as Mama approached. "How you doing, Miz Logan?" he asked.

"Just fine, Mr. Jamison," Mama answered. "And yourself?"

"Fine. Fine," he said absently. "Is David here?"

"He's over in the east field." Mama studied Mr. Jamison. "Anything wrong?"

"Oh, no . . . no. Just wanted to speak to him."

"Little Man," Mama said, turning, "go get Papa."

"Oh, no—don't do that. I'll just walk on over there if that's all right. I need the exercise." Mama nodded, and after he had spoken to me Mr. Jamison crossed the yard to the field. Little Man and I started to follow after him but Mama called us back and returned us to our jobs.

Mr. Jamison did not stay long. A few minutes later he

emerged from the field alone, got into his car, and left.

When supper was ready, I eagerly grabbed the iron bell before Christopher-John or Little Man could claim it, and ran onto the back porch to summon Papa, Mr. Morrison, and Stacey from the fields. As the three of them washed up on the back porch, Mama went to the end of the porch where Papa stood alone. "What did Mr. Jamison want?" she asked, her voice barely audible.

Papa took the towel Mama handed him, but did not reply immediately. I was just inside the kitchen dipping out the butter beans. I moved closer to the window so that I could hear his answer.

"Don't keep anything from me, David. If there's trouble, I want to know."

Papa looked down at her. "Nothing to worry 'bout, honey. . . . Just seems that Thurston Wallace been in town talking 'bout how he's not gonna let a few smart colored folks ruin his business. Says he's gonna put a stop to this shopping in Vicksburg. That's all."

Mama sighed and stared out across the plowed field to the sloping pasture land. "I'm feeling scared, David," she said.

Papa put down the towel. "Not yet, Mary. It's not time to be scared yet. They're just talking."

Mama turned and faced him. "And when they stop talking?"

"Then . . . then maybe it'll be time. But right now, pretty lady," he said, leading her by the hand toward the kitchen door, "right now I've got better things to think about."

Quickly I poured the rest of the butter beans into the bowl and hurried across the kitchen to the table. As Mama and Papa entered, I slid onto the bench beside Little Man and Christopher-John. Papa beamed down at the table.

"Well, look-a-here!" he exclaimed. "Good ole butter beans and cornbread! You better come on, Mr. Morrison! You too, son!" he called. "These womenfolks done gone and fixed us a feast."

After school was out, spring drooped quickly toward summer; yet Papa had not left for the railroad. He seemed to be waiting for something, and I secretly hoped that whatever that something was, it would never come so that he would not leave. But one evening as he, Mama, Big Ma, Mr. Morrison, and Stacey sat on the front porch while Christopher-John, Little Man, and I dashed around the yard chasing fireflies, I overheard him say, "Sunday I'm gonna have to go. Don't want to though. I got this gut feeling it ain't over yet. It's too easy."

I released the firefly imprisoned in my hand and sat beside Papa and Stacey on the steps. "Papa, please," I said, leaning against his leg, "don't go this year." Stacey looked out into the falling night, his face resigned, and said nothing.

Papa put out his large hand and caressed my face. "Got to, Cassie girl," he said softly. "Baby, there's bills to pay and ain't no money coming in. Your mama's got no job come fall and there's the mortgage and next year's taxes to think of."

"But, Papa, we planted more cotton this year. Won't that pay the taxes?"

Papa shook his head. "With Mr. Morrison here we was able to plant more, but that cotton is for living on; the railroad money is for the taxes and the mortgage."

I looked back at Mama wanting her to speak, to persuade him to stay, but when I saw her face I knew that she would not. She had known he would leave, just as we all had known.

"Papa, just another week or two, couldn't you—"

"I can't, baby. May have lost my job already."

"But Papa—"

"Cassie, that's enough now," Mama said from the deepening shadows.

I grew quiet and Papa put his arms around Stacey and me, his hands falling casually over our shoulders. From the edge of the lawn where Little Man and Christopher-John had ventured after lightning bugs, Little Man called, "Somebody's coming!" A few minutes later Mr. Avery and Mr. Lanier emerged from the dusk and walked up the sloping lawn. Mama sent Stacey and me to get more chairs for the porch, then we settled back beside Papa still sitting on the steps, his back propped against a pillar facing the visitors.

"You goin' up to the store tomorrow, David?" Mr. Avery

asked after all the amenities had been said. Since the first trip in January, Mr. Morrison had made one other trip to Vicksburg, but Papa had not gone with him.

Papa motioned to Mr. Morrison. "Mr. Morrison and me going the day after tomorrow. Your wife brought down that list of things you need yesterday."

Mr. Avery cleared his throat nervously. "It's—it's that list I come 'bout, David. . . . I don't want them things no more."

The porch grew silent.

When no one said anything, Mr. Avery glanced at Mr. Lanier, and Mr. Lanier shook his head and continued. "Mr. Granger making it hard on us, David. Said we gonna have to give him sixty percent of the cotton, 'stead of fifty . . . now that the cotton's planted and it's too late to plant more. . . . Don't s'pose though that it makes much difference. The way cotton sells these days, seems the more we plant, the less money we gets anyways—"

Mr. Avery's coughing interrupted him and he waited patiently until the coughing had stopped before he went on. "I'm gonna be hard put to pay that debt in Vicksburg, David, but I'm gonna. . . . I want you to know that."

Papa nodded, looking toward the road. "I suppose Montier and Harrison raised their percentages too," he said.

"Montier did," replied Mr. Avery, "but far as I know Mr. Harrison ain't. He's a decent man."

"That does it," Mama sighed wearily.

Papa kept looking out into the darkness. "Forty percent. I expect a man used to living on fifty could live on forty . . . if he wanted to hard enough."

Mr. Avery shook his head. "Times too hard."

"Times are hard for everybody," Papa said.

Mr. Avery cleared his throat. "I know. I—I feel real bad 'bout what T.J. done—"

"I wasn't talking 'bout that," said Papa flatly.

Mr. Avery nodded self-consciously, then leaned forward in his chair and looked out into the forest. "But—but that ain't all Mr. Granger said. Said, too, we don't give up this shoppin' in Vicksburg, we can jus' get off his land. Says he tired of us stirrin' up trouble 'gainst decent white folks. Then them Wallaces, they come by my place, Brother Lanier's, and everybody's on this thing that owes them money. Said we can't pay our debts, they gonna have the sheriff out to get us . . . put us on the chain gang to work it off."

"Oh, good Lord!" exclaimed Big Ma.

Mr. Lanier nodded and added, "Gotta go up to that store by tomorrow to show good faith."

Mr. Avery's coughing started again and for a while there was only the coughing and the silence. But when the coughing ceased, Mr. Lanier said, "I pray to God there was a way we could stay in this thing, but we can't go on no chain gang, David."

Papa nodded. "Don't expect you to, Silas."

Mr. Avery laughed softly. "We sure had 'em goin' for a time though, didn't we?"

"Yes," agreed Papa quietly, "we sure did."

When the men had left, Stacey snapped, "They got no right pulling out! Just 'cause them Wallaces threaten them one time they go jumping all over themselves to get out like a bunch of scared jackrabbits—"

Papa stood suddenly and grabbed Stacey upward. "You, boy, don't you get so grown you go to talking 'bout more than you know. Them men, they doing what they've gotta do. You got any idea what a risk they took just to go shopping in Vicksburg in the first place? They go on that chain gang and their families got nothing. They'll get kicked off that plot of land they tend and there'll be no place for them to go. You understand that?"

"Y-yessir," said Stacey. Papa released him and stared moodily into the night. "You were born blessed, boy, with land of your own. If you hadn't been, you'd cry out for it while you try to survive . . . like Mr. Lanier and Mr. Avery. Maybe even do what they doing now. It's hard on a man to give up, but sometimes it seems there just ain't nothing else he can do."

"I . . . I'm sorry, Papa," Stacey muttered.

After a moment, Papa reached out and draped his arm over Stacey's shoulder.

"Papa," I said, standing to join them, "we giving up too?"

Papa looked down at me and brought me closer, then waved his hand toward the drive. "You see that fig tree over yonder, Cassie? Them other trees all around . . . that oak and walnut, they're a lot bigger and they take up more room and give so much shade they almost overshadow that little ole fig. But that fig tree's got roots that run deep, and it belongs in that yard as much as that oak and walnut. It keeps on blooming, bearing good fruit year after year, knowing all the time it'll never get as big as them other trees. Just keeps on growing and doing what it gotta do. It don't give up. It give up, it'll die. There's a lesson to be learned from that little tree, Cassie girl, 'cause we're like it. We keep doing what we gotta, and we don't give up. We can't."

After Mr. Morrison had retired to his own house and Big Ma, the boys, and I had gone to bed, Papa and Mama remained on the porch, talking in hushed whispers. It was comforting listening to them, Mama's voice a warm, lilting murmur, Papa's a quiet, easy-flowing hum. After a few minutes they left the porch and their voices grew faint. I climbed from the bed, careful not to awaken Big Ma, and went to the window. They were walking slowly across the moon-soaked grass, their arms around each other.

"First thing tomorrow, I'm gonna go 'round and see how many folks are still in this thing," Papa said, stopping under the oak near the house. "I wanna know before we make that trip to Vicksburg."

Mama was quiet a moment. "I don't think you and Mr. Morrison should go to Vicksburg right now, David. Not with the Wallaces threatening people like they are. Wait awhile."

Papa reached into the tree and broke off a twig. "We can't just stop taking care of business 'cause of them Wallaces, Mary. You know that."

Mama did not reply.

Papa leaned against the tree. "I think I'll take Stacey with me."

"Now, David, no—"

"He'll be thirteen next month, honey, and he needs to be with me more. I can't take him with me on the railroad, but I can take him with me where I go 'round here. And I want him to know business . . . how to take care of it, how to take care of things when I ain't around."

"David, he's just a boy."

"Baby, a boy get as big as Stacey down here and he's near a man. He's gotta know a man's things. He gotta know how to handle himself."

"I know, but—"

"Mary, I want him strong . . . not a fool like T.J."

"He's got more brains and learning than that," Mama snapped.

"I know," Papa said quietly. "Still it worries me, seeing T.J. turning like he is."

"Seems to me it isn't bothering Joe Avery much. He doesn't seem to be doing anything about it."

Papa allowed the silence to seep between them before he said, "It's not like you, honey, to be bitter."

"I'm not bitter," said Mama, folding her arms across her chest. "It's just that the boy's gotten out of hand, and doesn't seem like anybody's doing anything about it."

"The other day Joe told me he couldn't do nothing with T.J. anymore. That's a hard thing for a man to admit."

"He can still put a good strip of leather against his bottom, can't he?" It was clear that Mama was unsympathetic to Mr. Avery's problem.

"Said he tried, but his health's so poor, he ended up with a bad coughing spell. Got so sick from it, he had to go to bed. Said after that Fannie tried to whip the boy, but T.J.'s stronger than her, and it didn't do no good." Papa paused, then added, "He's gotten pretty sassy, too, I understand."

"Well, sassy or not," Mama grumbled, "they'd better figure out some way of getting that boy back on the right track because he's headed for a whole lot of trouble."

Papa sighed heavily and left the tree. "We'd better go in. I've gotta get an early start if I'm gonna get 'round to everybody."

"You're still set on going to Vicksburg?"

"I told you I was."

Mama laughed lightly in exasperation. "Sometimes, David Logan, I wonder why I didn't marry sweet, quiet Ronald Carter or nice, mild Harold Davis."

"Because, woman," Papa said, putting his arm around her, "you took one look at big, handsome me and no one else would do." Then they both laughed, and together moved slowly to the side of the house.

Seven families, including ours, still refused to shop at the Wallace store even with the threat of the chain gang. Mama said that the number was not significant enough to hurt the Wallaces, only enough to rile them, and she worried, afraid for Papa, Stacey, and Mr. Morrison to make the trip. But nothing she could say could change Papa's mind and they left as planned on Wednesday morning long before dawn.

On Thursday, when they were to return, it began to rain, a hard, swelling summer rain which brought a premature green darkness to the land and forced us to leave our hoeing of the cotton field and return to the house. As the thunder rumbled overhead, Mama peered out the window at the dark road. "Wonder what's keeping them," she said, more to herself than anyone else.

"Probably got held up someplace," said Big Ma. "Could've stopped to get out of this storm."

Mama turned from the window. "You're most likely right," she agreed, picking up a pair of Christopher-John's pants to mend.

As the evening fell into total darkness, we grew silent, the boys and I saying very little, Mama and Big Ma concentrating on their sewing, their brows furrowed. My throat grew tight, and without knowing why I was afraid, I was. "Mama," I said, "they all right, ain't they?"

Mama stared down at me. "Course they're all right. They're just late, that's all."

"But, Mama, you s'pose maybe somebody done—"

"I think you children better go on to bed," Mama said sharply without letting me finish.

"But I wanna wait up for Papa," objected Little Man.

"Me, too," said sleepy Christopher-John.

"You'll see him in the morning. Now get to bed!"

Since there was nothing we could do but obey, we went to bed. But I could not sleep. A cold fear crept up my body, churning my stomach and tightening its grip on my throat. Finally, when I felt that I was going to be sick from it, I rose and padded silently into Mama and Papa's room.

Mama was standing with her back to me, her arms folded, and Big Ma was still patching. Neither one of them heard the door swing open. I started to speak, but Mama was talking and I decided not to interrupt her. ". . . I've got a good mind to saddle Lady and go looking for them," she said.

"Now, Mary, what good would that do?" Big Ma questioned. "You runnin' 'round out there on that mare by yo'self in this darkness and rain?"

"But something's happened to them! I can feel it."

"It's just in yo' mind, child," Big Ma scoffed unconvincingly. "Them menfolks all right."

"No . . . no," said Mama shaking her head. "The Wallaces aren't just in my mind, they—" She stopped suddenly and stood very still.

"Mary—"

"Thought I heard something." The dogs started barking and she turned, half running, across the room. Pushing up the lock in a mad haste, she swung the door open and cried into the storm, "David! David!"

Unable to stay put, I dashed across the room. "Cassie, what you doin' up, girl?" asked Big Ma, swatting me as I passed her. But Mama, staring into the wet night, said nothing when I reached her side.

"Is it them?" I asked.

Out of the darkness a round light appeared, moving slowly across the drive, and Mr. Morrison's voice drifted softly to us. "Go on, Stacey," he said, "I got him." Then Stacey, a flashlight in his hand, came into sight, followed by Mr. Morrison carrying Papa.

"David!" Mama gasped, her voice a frightened whisper.

Big Ma standing behind me stepped back, pulling me with her. She stripped the bed to its sheets and ordered, "Put him right here, Mr. Morrison."

As Mr. Morrison climbed the stairs, we could see that Papa's left leg stuck straight out, immobilized by his shotgun strapped to it with a rope. His head was wrapped in a rag through which the dark redness of his blood had seeped. Mr. Morrison eased Papa through the doorway, careful not to hit the strapped leg, and laid him gently on the bed. Mama went immediately to the bed and took Papa's hand.

"Hey, baby . . ." Papa said faintly, "I'm . . . all right. Just got my leg broke, that's all. . . ."

"Wagon rolled over it," said Mr. Morrison, avoiding Mama's eyes. "We better get that leg set. Didn't have time on the road."

"But his head—" Mama said, her eyes questioning Mr. Morrison. But Mr. Morrison said nothing further and Mama turned to Stacey. "You all right, son?"

"Yes'm," Stacey said, his face strangely ashen, his eyes on Papa.

"Then get out of those wet things. Don't want you catching pneumonia. Cassie, you go to bed."

"I'll get a fire started," said Big Ma disappearing into the kitchen as Mama turned to the closet to find sheets for making a cast. But Stacey and I remained rooted, watching Papa, and did not move until Christopher-John and Little Man made a sleepy entrance.

"What's going on?" asked Little Man, frowning into the light.

"Go back to bed, children," Mama said, rushing to keep them from coming farther into the room, but before she could reach them Christopher-John spied Papa on the bed and shot past her. "Papa, you got back!"

Mr. Morrison swung him upward before he could jar the bed.

"Wh-what's the matter?" asked Christopher-John, wide awake now. "Papa, what's the matter? How come you got that thing on your head?"

"Your Papa's asleep," said Mama as Mr. Morrison set Christopher-John back down. "Stacey, take them back to bed . . . and get out of those clothes." None of us stirred. "Move when I tell you!" Mama hissed impatiently, her face more worried than angry.

Stacey herded us into the boys' room.

As soon as the door closed behind us, I asked, "Stacey, how bad Papa hurt?" Stacey felt around for the lamp, lit it, then plopped wearily on the side of the bed. We huddled around him. "Well?"

Stacey shook his head. "I dunno. His leg's busted up by the wagon . . . and he's shot."

"Shot!" Christopher-John and Little Man exclaimed fearfully, but I was silent, too afraid now to speak, to think.

"Mr. Morrison says he don't think the bullet hurt him much. Says he thinks it just hit his skin . . . here." Stacey ran his forefinger along his right temple. "And didn't sink in nowhere."

"But who'd shoot Papa?" asked Little Man, greatly agitated. "Can't nobody just shoot Papa!"

Stacey stood then and motioned Christopher-John and Little Man under the covers. "I've said too much already. Cassie, go on to bed."

I continued to sit, my mind unable to move.

"Cassie, go on now like Mama said."

"How the wagon roll over him? How he get shot?" I blurted out angrily, already plotting revenge against whoever had dared hurt my father.

"Cassie . . . you go on to bed!"

"Ain't moving till you tell me!"

"I'll call Mama," he threatened.

"She too busy," I said, folding my arms and feeling confident that he would tell the story.

He went to the door and opened it. Christopher-John, Little Man, and I watched him eagerly. But he soon closed the door and came back to the bed.

"What was they doing?" asked Little Man.

"Big Ma's tending Papa's head."

"Well, what happened out there?" I repeated.

Stacey sighed despairingly and sat down. "We was coming back from Vicksburg when the back wheels come off," he said, his voice a hollow whisper. "It was already dark and it was raining too, and Papa and Mr. Morrison, they thought somebody done messed with them wheels for both of them to come off at the same time like they did. Then when I told them I'd seen two boys near the wagon when we was in Vicksburg, Papa said we didn't have time to unhitch and unload the wagon like we should to put them wheels back on. He thought somebody was coming after us.

"So after we found the wheels and the bolts, Papa told me to hold the reins real tight on Jack to keep him still. . . . Jack, he was real skittish 'cause of the storm. Then Mr. Morrison went and lifted that wagon all by himself. And it was heavy too, but Mr. Morrison lifted it like it wasn't nothing. Then Papa slipped the first wheel on. . . . That's when he got shot—"

"But who—" I started.

"A truck come up the road and stopped behind us while we was trying to get that wheel on, but didn't none of us hear it coming 'cause of the rain and the thunder and all, and they didn't put their lights on till the truck stopped. Anyways, there was three men in that truck and soon as Papa seen 'em, he reached for his shotgun. That's when they shot him and he fell back with his left leg under the wagon. Then . . . then Jack reared up, scared by the shot, and I—I couldn't hold him . . . and . . . and the wagon rolled over Papa's leg." His voice cracked sharply, and he exploded guiltily, "It's m-my fault his leg's busted!"

I thought on what he had said and, laying my hand on his shoulder, I said, "Naw, it ain't. It's them men's."

Stacey did not speak for a while and I did not prod him to go on. Finally, he cleared his throat and continued huskily. "Soon's I could, I . . . I tied Jack to a tree and run back to Papa, but Papa told me not to move him and to get down in the gully. After them men shot Papa, they come down trying to get Mr. Morrison, but he was too fast and strong for 'em. I couldn't see everything that happened 'cause they didn't always stay in front of them headlights, but I did see Mr. Morrison pick up one of them men like he wasn't nothing but a sack of chicken feathers and fling him down on the ground so hard it must've broke his back. Ain't never seen nothin' like it before in my whole life. Then one of them other two that had a gun shot at Mr. Morrison, but he didn't hit him. Mr. Morrison, he ducked away from the headlights into the darkness and they went after him.

"Couldn't see nothin' then," he said, glancing toward the door where Papa lay. "Heard bones cracking. Heard somebody cursing and crying. Then I couldn't hear nothin' but the rain, and I was real scared. 'Fraid they'd killed Mr. Morrison."

"But they didn't," reminded Little Man, his eyes bright with excitement.

Stacey nodded. "Next thing I seen was a man coming real slow-like into the headlights and pick up the man lying in the middle of the road—the one Mr. Morrison thrown down. He got him into the truck, then come back and helped the other one. That one looked like he had a broke arm. It was hanging all crazy-like at his side. Then they turned the truck around and drove away."

"Then what?" Little Man inquired.

Stacey shrugged. "Nothin'. We put on the other wheel and come on home."

"Who was it?" I rasped, holding my breath.

Stacey looked at me and said flatly, "The Wallaces, I think."

There was a fearful moment's silence, then Christopher-John, tears in his dark eyes, asked, "Stacey, is . . . is Papa gonna die?"

"No! Course not!" denied Stacey too quickly.

"But he was so still—"

"I don't want Papa to die!" wailed Little Man.

"He was just sleeping—like Mama said. That's all."

"Well, when he gonna wake up?" cried Christopher-John, the tears escaping down his plump cheeks.

"In—in the morning," said Stacey, putting a comforting arm around both Christopher-John and Little Man. "Jus' you wait and see. He'll be jus' fine come morning."

Stacey, still in his wet, muddy clothes, said nothing else, and neither did the rest of us. All the questions had been answered, yet we feared, and we sat silently listening to the rain, soft now upon the roof, and watching the door behind which Papa lay, and wished for morning.

10

"How does it look?" asked Papa as I passed through the sitting room on my way out the side door. Over a week had passed since he had been injured, and this was his first morning up. He was seated by the cold fireplace, his head still bandaged, his broken leg resting on a wooden chair. His eyes were on Mama at her desk.

Mama put down her pencil and frowned at the open ledger before her. She glanced at me absently and waited until I had closed the screen door behind me, then she said, "David, do you think we should go into this now? You're still not well—"

"I'm well enough to know there's not much left. Now tell me."

I hopped down the steps and sat on the bottom one.

Mama was silent a moment before she answered him. "With Hammer's half of the mortgage money, we've got enough to meet the June payment. . . ."

"Nothing more?"

"A couple of dollars, but that's all."

They were both silent.

"You think we should write Hammer and borrow some money?" Mama asked.

Papa did not answer right away. "No . . ." he said finally. "I still don't want him to know 'bout this thing. If he knows I'm not on the railroad, he'll wanna know why not, and I don't wanna risk that temper of his when he finds out what the Wallaces done."

Mama sighed. "I guess you're right."

"I know I am," said Papa. "Things like they are, he come down here wild and angry, he'll get himself hung. Long as things don't get no worse, we can make it without him. We'll meet that June note with the money we got there." He paused a moment. "We'll probably have to sell a couple of the cows and their calves to make them July and August notes . . . maybe even that ole sow. But by the end of August we should have enough cotton to make that September payment. . . . Course we'll probably have to go all the way to Vicksburg to get it ginned. Can't hardly use Harlan Granger's gin this year."

There was silence again, then Mama said, "David, Mama's been talking about going into Strawberry to the market next—"

"No," Papa said, not letting her finish. "Too much bad feeling there."

"I told her that."

"I'll talk to her. . . . Anything we just gotta have before the first cotton come in?"

"Well . . . you picked up batteries and kerosene on that last trip . . . but what we're going to need more than anything is some insecticide to spray the cotton. The bugs are getting pretty bad. . . ."

"What 'bout food?"

"Our flour and sugar and baking powder and such are low, but we'll make out—we don't have to have biscuits and cornbread every day. We're out of pepper and there's not much salt, but we don't just have to have those either. And the coffee's all gone. . . . The garden's coming along nicely, though. There's no worry there."

"No worry," Papa muttered as both of them grew quiet. Then suddenly there was a sharp explosion as if something had been struck with an angry force. "If only this leg wasn't busted!"

"Don't let Stacey hear you saying that, David," Mama cautioned softly. "You know he blames himself about your leg."

"I told the boy it wasn't his fault. He just wasn't strong enough to hold Jack."

"I know that, but still he blames himself."

Papa laughed strangely. "Ain't this something? Them Wallaces aim a gun at my head and I get my leg broke, and my boy's blaming himself for it. Why, I feel like taking a bullwhip to all three of them Wallaces and not stopping till my arm get so tired I can't raise it one more time."

"You're sounding like Hammer."

"Am I? Well, a lot of times I feel like doing things Hammer's way. I think I'd get a powerful lot of satisfaction from whipping Kaleb Wallace and them brothers of his."

"Hammer's way would get you killed and you know it, so stop talking like that. Don't we already have enough to worry about? Besides, both Thurston and Dewberry Wallace are still laid up, so I hear. Some folks even say that Dewberry's back is broken. In any case, Mr. Morrison must have hurt them pretty bad."

"Where is he, by the way? I haven't seen him this morning."

There was an instant of silence before Mama answered. "Out looking for work again since dawn."

"He ain't gonna find nothing 'round here. I told him that."

"I know," agreed Mama. "But he says he's got to try. David . . ." Mama stopped, and when she spoke again her voice had grown faint, as if she hesitated to say what was on her mind. "David, don't you think he ought to go? I don't want him to, but after what he did to the Wallaces, I'm afraid for him."

"He knows what could happen, Mary, but he wants to stay—and, frankly, we need him here. Don't pester him about it."

"But, David, if—"

Before Mama finished, I spied Mr. Morrison coming west from Smellings Creek. I left the step and hurried to meet him.

"Hello, Mr. Morrison!" I shouted as Jack pulled the wagon up the drive.

"Hello, Cassie," Mr. Morrison greeted me. "Your papa awake?"

"Yessir. He's sitting out of bed this morning."

"Didn't I tell you nothin' could keep him down?"

"Yessir, you did."

He stepped from the wagon and walked toward the house.

"Mr. Morrison, you want me to unhitch Jack for ya?"

"No, Cassie, leave him be. I gotta talk to your papa then I'll be back."

"Hey, ole Jack," I said, patting the mule as I watched Mr. Morrison enter the side door. I thought of returning to my seat on the steps, but decided against it. Instead I remained with Jack, thoughtfully digesting all I had heard, until Mr. Morrison came from the house. He went into the barn, then reappeared with the planter, a plowlike tool with a small round container for dropping seeds attached to its middle. He put the planter into the back of the wagon.

"Where you going now, Mr. Morrison?"

"Down to Mr. Wiggins' place. I seen Mr. Wiggins this

morning and he asked to use your Papa's planter. He ain't got no wagon so I told him I'd ask your Papa and if it was all right, I'd bring it to him."

"Ain't it kinda late for seeding?"

"Well, not for what he got in mind. He thought he'd plant himself some summer corn. It'll be ready come September."

"Mr. Morrison, can I go with ya?" I asked as he climbed up on the wagon.

"Well, I'd be right pleased for your company, Cassie. But you'll have to ask your mama."

I ran back to the house. The boys were now in Mama and Papa's room, and when I asked if I could go up to Little Willie's with Mr. Morrison, Little Man and Christopher-John, of course, wanted to go too.

"Mr. Morrison said it'd be all right, Mama."

"Well, don't you get in his way. Stacey, you going?"

Stacey sat across from Papa looking despondently at the broken leg. "Go on, son," said Papa gently. "There's nothing to do here. Give you a chance to talk to Little Willie."

"You sure there ain't something I can do for you, Papa?"

"Just go and have yourself a good ride over to Little Willie's."

Since it had been my idea to ask to go, I claimed the seat beside Mr. Morrison, and the boys climbed in back. Little Willie's family lived on their own forty acres about two miles east of Great Faith. It was a fine morning for a ride and the six miles there sped by quickly with Mr. Morrison singing in his bassest of bass voices and Christopher-John, Little Man, and me joining in wherever we could as we passed cotton fields abloom in flowers of white and red and pink. Stacey being in one of his moods did not sing and we let him be.

We stayed less than an hour at the Wiggins farm, then headed home again. We had just passed Great Faith and were approaching the Jefferson Davis School Road when a ragged pickup came into view. Very quietly Mr. Morrison said, "Cassie, get in back."

"But why, Mr. Mor—"

"Do quick, Cassie, like I say." His voice was barely above a friendly whisper, but there was an urgency in it and I obeyed, scrambling over the seat to join the boys. "Y'all stay down now."

The truck braked noisily with a grating shriek of steel. We stopped. The boys and I peeped over the edge of the wagon. The truck had veered across the road, blocking us. The truck door swung open and Kaleb Wallace stepped out, pointing a long condemning finger at Mr. Morrison.

He swayed unspeaking for a long, terrible moment, then sputtered, "You big black nigger, I oughta cut your heart out for what you done! My brothers laid up like they is and you still runnin' 'round free as a white man. Downright sinful, that's what it is! Why, I oughta gun you down right where you sit—"

"You gonna move your truck?"

Kaleb Wallace gazed up at Mr. Morrison, then at the

truck as if trying to comprehend the connection between the two. "That truck in your way, boy?"

"You gonna move it?"

"I'll move it all right . . . when I get good and ready—" He stopped abruptly, his eyes bulging in a terrified stare as Mr. Morrison climbed down from the wagon. Mr. Morrison's long shadow fell over him and for a breathless second, Mr. Morrison towered dangerously near him. But as the fear grew white on Kaleb Wallace's face, Mr. Morrison turned without a word and peered into the truck.

"What's he looking for?" I whispered.

"Probably a gun," said Stacey.

Mr. Morrison circled the truck, studying it closely. Then he returned to its front and, bending at the knees with his back against the grill, he positioned his large hands beneath the bumper. Slowly, his muscles flexing tightly against his thin shirt and the sweat popping off his skin like oil on water, he lifted the truck in one fluid, powerful motion until the front was several inches off the ground and slowly walked it to the left of the road, where he set it down as gently as a sleeping child. Then he moved to the rear of the truck and repeated the feat.

Kaleb Wallace was mute. Christopher-John, Little Man, and I stared open-mouthed, and even Stacey, who had witnessed Mr. Morrison's phenomenal strength before, gazed in wonder.

It took Kaleb Wallace several minutes to regain his voice. We were far down the road, almost out of hearing, when his frenzied cry of hate reached us. "One of these nights, you watch, nigger! I'm gonna come get you for what you done! You just watch! One night real soon . . ."

When we reached home and told Mama and Papa and Big Ma what had happened, Mama said to Mr. Morrison, "I told you before I was afraid for you. And today, Kaleb Wallace could've hurt you . . . and the children."

Mr. Morrison looked squarely into Mama's eyes. "Miz Logan, Kaleb Wallace is one of them folks who can't do nothing by himself. He got to have a lot of other folks backing him up plus a loaded gun . . . and I knew there wasn't no gun, leastways not in the truck. I checked."

"But if you stay, he'll get somebody and they'll try to take you, like he said—"

"Miz Logan, don't ask me to go."

Mama reached out, laying a slender hand on Mr. Morrison's. "Mr. Morrison, you're a part of us now. I don't want you hurt because of us."

Mr. Morrison lowered his eyes and looked around the room until his gaze rested on the boys and me. "I ain't never had no children of my own. I think sometimes if I had, I'd've wanted a son and daughter just like you and Mr. Logan . . . and grandbabies like these babies of yours. . . ."

"But, Mr. Morrison, the Wallaces—"

"Mary," said Papa quietly, "let it be."

Mama looked at Papa, her lips still poised to speak. Then she said no more; but the worry lines remained creased upon her brow.

August dawned blue and hot. The heat swooped low over the land clinging like an invisible shroud, and through it people moved slowly, lethargically, as if under water. In the ripening fields the drying cotton and corn stretched tiredly skyward awaiting the coolness of a rain that occasionally threatened but did not come, and the land took on a baked, brown look.

To escape the heat, the boys and I often ambled into the coolness of the forest after the chores were done. There, while the cows and their calves grazed nearby, we sat on the banks of the pond, our backs propped against an old hickory or pine or walnut, our feet dangling lazily in the cool water, and waited for a watermelon brought from the garden to chill. Sometimes Jeremy joined us there, making his way through the deep forest land from his own farm over a mile away, but the meetings were never planned; none of our parents would have liked that.

"How's your papa?" he asked one day as he plopped down beside us.

"He's all right," said Stacey, " 'cepting his leg's bothering him in this heat. Itching a lot. But Mama says that's a sign it's getting well."

"That's good," murmured Jeremy. "Too bad he had to get hurt when he done so's he couldn't go back on the railroad."

Stacey stirred uneasily, looked at Christopher-John, Little Man, and me, reminding us with his eyes that we were not to speak about the Wallaces' part in Papa's injury, and said only, "Uh-huh."

Jeremy was silent a moment, then stuttered, "S-some folks sayin' they glad he got hurt. G-glad he can't go make that railroad money."

"Who said that?" I cried, jumping up from the bank. "Just tell me who said it and I'll ram—"

"Cassie! Sit down and be quiet," Stacey ordered. Reluctantly, I did as I was told, wishing that this business about the Wallaces and Papa's injuries were not so complex. It seemed to me that since the Wallaces had attacked Papa and Mr. Morrison, the simplest thing to do would be to tell the sheriff and have them put in jail, but Mama said things didn't work that way. She explained that as long as the Wallaces, embarrassed by their injuries at the hands of Mr. Morrison, did not make an official complaint about the incident, then we must remain silent also. If we did not, Mr. Morrison could be charged with attacking white men, which could possibly end in his being sentenced to the chain gang, or worse.

"I—I ain't the one said it, Cassie," stammered Jeremy by way of apology.

"Well, whoever saying it ought not be," I said huffily.

Jeremy nodded thoughtfully and changed the subject. "Y'all seen T.J. lately?"

Stacey frowned, considering whether or not he should answer. There had been much talk concerning T.J. and the Simms brothers, all of it bad. Moe Turner's father had told

Papa that T.J. had stopped by with the Simmses once, and after they had left he had discovered his watch missing; the Laniers had had the same experience with a locket. "That T.J. done turned real bad," Mr. Lanier had said, "and I don't want nothin' to do with no thief . . . 'specially no thief runnin' 'round with white boys."

Finally Stacey said, "Don't see him much no more."

Jeremy pulled at his lip. "I see him all the time."

"Too bad," I sympathized.

Stacey glanced reproachfully at me, then lay flat upon the ground, his head resting in the cushion of his hands clasped under his head. "It sure is beautiful up there," he said, pointedly changing the subject again.

The rest of us lay back too. Overhead, the branches of the walnut and hickory trees met like long green fans sheltering us. Several feet away the persistent sun made amber roads of shimmering sunlight upon the pond. A stillness hovered in the high air, soft, quiet, peaceful.

"I think when I grow up I'm gonna build me a house in some trees and jus' live there all the time," said Jeremy.

"How you gonna do that?" asked Little Man.

"Oh, I'll find me some real strong trees and just build. I figure I'll have the trunk of one tree in the bedroom and the other in the kitchen."

"How come you wanna live in a tree for?" Christopher-John inquired.

"It's so peaceful up there . . . and quiet. Cool, too," answered Jeremy. " 'Specially at night."

"How you know how cool it is at night?" I said.

Jeremy's face brightened. " 'Cause I got my bedroom up there."

We looked at him unbelieving.

"I-I do—really. Built it myself and I sleeps up there. Come these hot nights, I just climbs in my tree and it's like going into another world. Why, I can see and hear things up there that I betcha only the squirrels and the birds can see and hear. Sometimes I think I can even see all the way over to y'all's place."

"Ah, shoot, boy, you're a story," I said. "Your place too far away and you know it."

Jeremy's face dropped. "Well . . . maybe I can't see it, but that don't keep me from pretending I do." He was silent a second, then hopped up suddenly, his face bright again. "Hey, why don't y'all come on over and see it? My pa's gonna be gone all day and it'd be lots of fun and I could show y'all—"

"No," said Stacey quietly, his eyes still on the trees overhead.

Jeremy sat back down, deflated. "J-jus' wanted y'all to see it, that's all. . . ." For a while he looked hurt by Stacey's cold refusal; then, seeming to accept it as part of the things that were, he again took up his position and volunteered good-naturedly, "If y'all ever get a chance to build y'all-selves a tree house, just let me know and I'll help ya. It's just as cool . . ."

Papa sat on a bench in the barn, his broken leg stretched awkwardly before him, mending one of Jack's harnesses. He had been there since early morning, a frown line carved deep into his forehead, quietly mending those things which needed mending. Mama told us not to bother him and we stayed away from the barn as long as we could, but by late afternoon we drifted naturally to it and began our chores. Papa had disappeared within himself and he took no notice of us at first, but shortly afterward he looked up, watching us closely.

When the chores were almost finished, Mr. Morrison arrived from Strawberry, where he had gone to make the August mortgage payment. He entered the barn slowly and handed Papa an envelope. Papa glanced up questioningly, then ripped it open. As he read the letter, his jaw set tightly, and when he finished he smashed his fist so hard against the bench that the boys and I stopped what we were doing, aware that something was terribly wrong.

"They tell you?" he asked of Mr. Morrison, his voice curt, angry.

Mr. Morrison nodded. "I tried to get them to wait till after cotton picking, but they told me it was due and payable immediately. Them's they words."

"Harlan Granger," said Papa quietly. He reached for his cane and stood up. "You feel up to going back to Strawberry . . . tonight?"

"I can make it, but I don't know if this ole mule can."

"Then hitch Lady to it," he said motioning to the mare.

He turned then and went to the house. The boys and I followed, not quite sure of what was happening. Papa entered the kitchen; we stayed on the porch peering through the screen.

"David, something the matter, son?"

"The bank called up the note. I'm going to Strawberry."

"Called up the note?" echoed Big Ma. "Oh, Lord, not that too."

Mama stared at Papa, fear in her eyes. "You going now?"

"Now," he said, leaving the kitchen for their room.

Mama's voice trailed him. "David, it's too late. The bank's closed by now. You can't see anyone until morning. . . ."

We could not hear Papa's reply, but Mama's voice rose sharply. "You want to be out on that road again in the middle of the night after what happened? You want us worried to death about you?"

"Mary, don't you understand they're trying to take the land?" Papa said, his voice rising too so that we heard.

"Don't *you* understand I don't want you dead?"

We could hear nothing else. But a few minutes later Papa came out and told Mr. Morrison to unhitch Lady. They would go to Strawberry in the morning.

The next day Papa and Mr. Morrison were gone before I arose. When they returned in the late afternoon, Papa sat wearily down at the kitchen table with Mr. Morrison beside him. Rubbing his hand over his thick hair, he said, "I called Hammer."

"What did you tell him?" Mama asked.

"Just that the note's been called. He said he'd get the money."

"How?"

"He didn't say and I didn't ask. Just said he'd get it."

"And Mr. Higgins at the bank, David," said Big Ma. "What he have to say?"

"Said our credit's no good anymore."

"We aren't even hurting the Wallaces now," Mama said with acid anger. "Harlan Granger's got no need—"

"Baby, you know he's got a need," Papa said, pulling her to him. "He's got a need to show us where we stand in the scheme of things. He's got a powerful need to do that. Besides, he still wants this place."

"But son, that mortgage give us four more years."

Papa laughed dryly. "Mama, you want me to take it to court?"

Big Ma sighed and placed her hand on Papa's. "What if Hammer can't get the money?"

Papa did not look at her, but at Mr. Morrison instead. "Don't worry, Mama. We ain't gonna lose the land. . . . Trust me."

On the third Sunday of August the annual revival began. Revivals were always very serious, yet gay and long-planned-for, affairs which brought pots and pans from out-of-the-way shelves, mothball-packed dresses and creased pants from hidden chests, and all the people from the community and the neighboring communities up the winding red school road to Great Faith Church. The revival ran for seven days and it was an occasion everyone looked forward to, for it was more than just church services; it was the year's only planned social event, disrupting the humdrum of everyday country life. Teenagers courted openly, adults met with relatives and friends they had not seen since the previous year's "big meeting," and children ran almost free.

As far as I was concerned, the best part of the revival was the very first day. After the first of three services was dismissed, the mass of humanity which had squished its way into the sweltering interior of the small church poured onto the school grounds, and the women proudly set out their dinners in the backs of wagons and on the long tables circling the church.

Then it was a feast to remember.

Brimming bowls of turnip greens and black-eyed peas with ham hocks, thick slices of last winter's sugar-cured ham and strips of broiled ribs, crisply fried chicken and morsels of golden squirrel and rabbit, flaky buttermilk biscuits and crusty cornbread, fat slabs of sweet-potato pie and butter pound cakes, and so much more were all for the taking. No matter how low the pantry supplies, each family always managed to contribute something, and as the churchgoers made the rounds from table to table, hard times were forgotten at least for the day.

The boys and I had just loaded our plates for the first time and taken seats under an old walnut when Stacey put down his plate and stood up again. "What's the matter?" I asked, stuffing my mouth with cornbread.

Stacey frowned into the sun. "That man walking up the road . . ."

I took a moment to look up, then picked up my drumstick. "So?"

"He looks like . . . Uncle Hammer!" he cried and dashed away. I hesitated, watching him, reluctant to leave my plate unless it really was Uncle Hammer. When Stacey reached the man and hugged him, I put the plate down and ran across the lawn to the road. Christopher-John, with his plate still in hand, and Little Man ran after me.

"Uncle Hammer, where's your car?" Little Man asked after we all had hugged him.

"Sold it," he said.

"Sold it!" we cried in unison.

"B-but why?" asked Stacey.

"Needed the money," Uncle Hammer said flatly.

As we neared the church, Papa met us and embraced Uncle Hammer. "I wasn't expecting you to come all the way down here."

"You expecting me to send that much money by mail?"

"Could've wired it."

"Don't trust that either."

"How'd you get it?"

"Borrowed some of it, sold a few things," he said with a shrug. Then he nodded toward Papa's leg. "How'd you do that?"

Papa's eyes met Uncle Hammer's and he smiled faintly. "I was sort of hoping you wouldn't ask that."

"Uh-huh."

"Papa," I said, "Uncle Hammer sold the Packard."

Papa's smile faded. "I didn't mean for that to happen, Hammer."

Uncle Hammer put his arm around Papa. "What good's a car? It can't grow cotton. You can't build a home on it. And you can't raise four fine babies in it."

Papa nodded, understanding.

"Now, you gonna tell me 'bout that leg?"

Papa stared at the milling throng of people around the dinner tables. "Let's get you something to eat first," he said, "then I'll tell you. Maybe it'll set better with some of this good food in your stomach."

Because Uncle Hammer was leaving early Monday morning, the boys and I were allowed to stay up much later than usual to be with him. Long hours after we should have been in bed, we sat on the front porch lit only by the whiteness of the full moon and listened to the comforting sounds of Papa's and Uncle Hammer's voices mingling once again.

"We'll go up to Strawberry and make the payment first thing tomorrow," said Papa. "I don't think I'd better go all the way to Vicksburg with this leg, but Mr. Morrison'll take you there—see you to the train."

"He don't have to do that," replied Uncle Hammer. "I can make it to Vicksburg all right."

"But I'd rest easier if I *knew* you was on that train headed due north . . . not off getting yourself ready to do something foolish."

Uncle Hammer grunted. "There ain't a thing foolish to what I'd like to do to them Wallaces. . . . Harlan Granger either."

There was nothing to say to how he felt, and no one tried.

"What you plan to do for money?" Uncle Hammer asked after a while.

"The cotton looks good," said Papa. "We do well on it, we'll make out all right."

Uncle Hammer was quiet a moment before he observed, "Just tightening the belt some more, huh?"

When Papa did not answer, Uncle Hammer said, "Maybe I better stay."

"No," said Papa adamantly, "You do better in Chicago."

"May do better but I worry a lot." He paused, pulling at his ear. "Come through Strawberry with a fellow from up in Vicksburg. Things seemed worse than usual up there. It gets hot like this and folks get dissatisfied with life, they start looking 'round for somebody to take it out on. . . . I don't want it to be you."

"I don't think it will be . . ." said Papa, ". . . unless you stay."

In the morning after the men had gone, Big Ma said to Mama, "I sure wish Hammer could've stayed longer."

"It's better he went," said Mama.

Big Ma nodded. "I know. Things like they is, it don't take

but a little of nothin' to set things off, and Hammer with that temper he got could do it. Still," she murmured wistfully, "I sho' wish he could've stayed. . . ."

On the last night of the revival the sky took on a strange yellowish cast. The air felt close, suffocating, and no wind stirred.

"What do you think, David?" Mama asked as she and Papa stood on the front porch looking at the sky. "You think we should go?"

Papa leaned against his cane. "It's gonna storm all right . . . but it may not come till late on over in the night."

They decided we would go. Most other families had come to the same decision, for the church grounds were crowded with wagons when we arrived. "Brother Logan," one of the deacons called as Papa stepped awkwardly down from the wagon, "Reverend Gabson wants us to get the meeting started soon as we can so we can dismiss early and get on home 'fore this storm hits."

"All right," Papa said, directing us toward the church. But as we neared the building, we were stopped by the Laniers. As the grown-ups talked, Little Willie Wiggins and Moe Turner, standing with several other boys, motioned to Stacey from the road. Stacey wandered away to speak to them and Christopher-John, Little Man, and I went too.

"Guess who we seen?" said Little Willie as Stacey walked up. But before Stacey could venture a guess, Little Willie answered his own question. "T.J. and them Simms brothers."

"Where?" asked Stacey.

"Over there," Little Willie pointed. "They parked by the classrooms. Look, here they come."

All eyes followed the direction of Little Willie's finger. Through the settling dusk three figures ambled with assurance across the wide lawn, the two Simmses on the outside, T.J. in the middle.

"How come he bringin' them here?" asked Moe Turner angrily.

Stacey shrugged. "Dunno, but I guess we'll find out."

"He looks different," I remarked when I could see T.J. more distinctly. He was dressed in a pair of long, unpatched trousers and, as sticky hot as it was, he wore a suit coat and a tie, and a hat cocked jauntily to one side.

"I s'pose he do look different," murmured Moe bitterly. "I'd look different too, if I'd been busy stealin' other folkses' stuff."

"Well, well, well! What we got here?" exclaimed T.J. loudly as he approached. "Y'all gonna welcome us to y'all's revival services?"

"What you doing here, T.J.?" Stacey asked.

T.J. laughed. "I got a right to come to my own church, ain't I? See all my old friends?" His eyes wandered over the group, but no one showed signs of being glad to see him. His wide grin shrank a little, then spying me he patted my face with his moist hand. "Hey, Cassie girl, how you doin'?"

I slapped his hand away. "Don't you come messing with me, T.J.!" I warned.

Again he laughed, then said soberly, "Well, this is a fine how-do-you-do. I come all the way over here to introduce my friends, R.W. and Melvin, to y'all and y'all actin' like y'all ain't got no manners at all. Yeah, ole R.W. and Melvin," he said, rolling the Simmses' names slowly off his tongue to bring to our attention that he had not bothered to place a "Mister" before either, "they been mighty fine friends to me. Better than any of y'all. Look, see here what they give me." Proudly he tugged at the suit coat. "Pretty nice stuff, eh? Everything I want they give me 'cause they really likes me. I'm they best friend."

He turned to the Simmses. "Ain't that right, R.W. and Melvin?"

Melvin nodded, a condescending smirk on his face which was lost on T.J.

"Anything—just anything at all I want—they'll get it for me, including—" He hesitated as if he were unsure whether or not he was going too far, then plunged on. "Including that pearl-handled pistol in Barnett's Mercantile."

R.W. stepped forward and slapped a reassuring hand on T.J.'s shoulder. "That's right, T.J. You name it and you've got it."

T.J. grinned widely. Stacey turned away in disgust. "Come on," he said, "service is 'bout to start."

"Hey, what's the matter with y'all?" T.J. yelled as the group turned en masse and headed for the church. I glanced back at him. Was he really such a fool?

"All right, T.J.," said Melvin as we walked away, "we

come down here like you asked. Now you come on into Strawberry with us like you promised."

"It—it didn't even make no difference," muttered T.J.

"What?" said R.W. "You comin', ain't you? You still want that pearl-handled pistol, don't you?"

"Yeah, but—"

"Then come on," he ordered, turning with Melvin and heading for the pickup.

But T.J. did not follow immediately. He remained standing in the middle of the compound, his face puzzled and undecided. I had never seen him look more desolately alone, and for a fleeting second I felt almost sorry for him.

When I reached the church steps, I looked back again. T.J. was still there, an indistinct blur blending into the gathering dusk, and I began to think that perhaps he would not go with the Simmses. But then the rude squawk of the truck's horn blasted the quiet evening, and T.J. turned his back on us and fled across the field.

11

Roll of thunder
hear my cry
Over the water
bye and bye
Ole man comin'
down the line
Whip in hand to
beat me down
But I ain't
gonna let him
Turn me 'round

The night whispered of distant thunder. It was muggy, hot, a miserable night for sleeping. Twice I had awakened hoping that it was time to be up, but each time the night had been total blackness with no hint of a graying dawn. On the front porch Mr. Morrison sat singing soft and low into the long night, chanting to the approaching thunder. He had been there since the house had darkened after church, watching and waiting as he had done every night since Papa had been injured. No one had ever explained why he watched and waited, but I knew. It had to do with the Wallaces.

Mr. Morrison's song faded and I guessed he was on his way to the rear of the house. He would stay there for a while, walking on cat's feet through the quiet yard, then eventually return to the front porch again. Unable to sleep, I resigned myself to await his return by counting states. Miss Crocker had had a big thing about states, and I sometimes found that if I pretended that she was naming them off I could fall asleep. I decided to count the states geographically rather than alphabetically; that was more of a challenge. I had gotten as far west as the Dakotas when my silent recitation was disturbed by a tapping on the porch. I lay very still. Mr. Morrison never made sounds like that.

There it was again.

Cautiously, I climbed from the bed, careful not to awaken Big Ma, who was still snoring soundly, and crept to the door. I pressed my ear against the door and listened, then slipped the latch furiously and darted outside. "Boy, what you doing here?" I hissed.

"Hey, Cassie, wouldja keep it down?" whispered T.J., invisible in the darkness. Then he tapped lightly on the boys' door again, calling softly, "Hey, Stacey, come on and wake up, will ya? Let me in."

The door swung open and T.J. slipped inside. I pulled my own door closed and followed him. "I-I'm in trouble, Stacey," he said. "I mean I'm r-really in trouble."

"That ain't nothing new," I remarked.

"What you coming here for?" whispered Stacey icily. "Go get R.W. and Melvin to get you out of it."

In the darkness there was a low sob and T.J., hardly sounding like T.J., mumbled, "They the ones got me in it. Where's the bed? I gotta sit down."

In the darkness he groped for the bed, his feet dragging as if he could hardly lift them. "I ain't no bed!" I exclaimed as his hands fell on me.

There was a deep sigh. Stacey clicked on the flashlight and T.J. found the bed, sitting down slowly and holding his stomach as if he were hurt.

"What's the matter?" Stacey asked, his voice wary.

"R.W. and Melvin," whispered T.J., "they hurt me bad." He looked up, expecting sympathy. But our faces, grim behind the light Stacey held, showed no compassion. T.J.'s eyes dimmed, then, undoing the buttons to his shirt, he pulled the shirt open and stared down at his stomach.

I grimaced and shook my head at the sight. "Lord, T.J.!" Stacey exclaimed in a whisper. "What happened?"

T.J. did not answer at first, staring in horror at the deep

blue-black swelling of his stomach and chest. "I think something's busted," he gasped finally. "I hurt something awful."

"Why'd they do it?" asked Stacey.

T.J. looked up into the bright light. "Help me, Stacey. Help me get home. . . . I can't make it by myself."

"Tell me how come they did this to you."

" 'Cause . . . 'cause I said I was gonna tell what happened."

Stacey and I looked at each other, then together leaned closer to T.J. "Tell what?" we asked.

T.J. gulped and leaned over, his head between his legs. "I . . . I'm sick, Stacey. I gotta get home 'fore my daddy wake up. . . . He say I stay 'way from that house one more night, he gonna put me out, and he mean it, too. He put me out, I got no place to go. You gotta help me."

"Tell us what happened."

T.J. began to cry. "But they said they'd do worse than this if I ever told!"

"Well, I ain't about to go nowhere unless I know what happened," said Stacey with finality.

T.J. searched Stacey's face in the rim of ghostly light cast by the flashlight. Then he told his story.

After he and the Simmses left Great Faith, they went directly into Strawberry to get the pearl-handled pistol, but when they arrived the mercantile was already closed. The Simmses said that there was no sense in coming back for the pistol; they would simply go in and take it. T.J. was frightened at the thought, but the Simmses assured him that there was no danger. If they were caught, they would simply say that they needed the pistol that night but intended to pay for it on Monday.

In the storage room at the back of the store was a small open window through which a child or a person as thin as T.J. could wiggle. After waiting almost an hour after the lights had gone out in the Barnetts' living quarters on the second floor, T.J. slipped through the window and opened the door, and the Simmses entered, their faces masked with stockings and their hands gloved. T.J., now afraid that they had something else in mind, wanted to leave without the pistol, but R.W. had insisted that he have it. R.W. broke the lock of the gun case with an axe and gave T.J. the much-longed-for gun.

Then R.W. and Melvin went over to a wall cabinet and tried to break off the brass lock. After several unsuccessful minutes, R.W. swung the axe sharply against the lock and it gave. But as Melvin reached for the metal box inside, Mr. Barnett appeared on the stairs, a flashlight in his hand, his wife behind him.

For a long moment no one moved or said a word as Mr. Barnett shone the light directly on T.J., then on R.W. and Melvin, their faces darkened by the stockings. But when Mr. Barnett saw the cabinet lock busted, he flew into frenzied action, hopping madly down the stairs and trying to grab the metal box from Melvin. They struggled, with Mr. Barnett getting the better of Melvin, until R.W.

whopped Mr. Barnett solidly on the head from behind with the flat of the axe, and Mr. Barnett slumped into a heap upon the floor as if dead.

When Mrs. Barnett saw her husband fall, she dashed across the room and flailed into R.W., crying "You niggers done killed Jim Lee! You done killed him!" R.W., trying to escape her grasp, slapped at her and she fell back, hitting her head against one of the stoves, and did not move.

Once they were outside T.J. wanted to come straight home, but the Simmses said they had business to take care of and told him to wait in the back of the truck. When T.J. objected and said that he was going to tell everybody it was R.W. and Melvin who had hurt the Barnetts unless they took him home, the two of them lit into him, beating him with savage blows until he could not stand, then flung him into the back of the truck and went down the street to the pool hall. T.J. lay there for what he thought must have been an hour before crawling from the truck and starting home. About a mile outside of town, he got a ride with a farmer headed for Smellings Creek by way of Soldiers Road. Not wanting to walk past the Simmses' place for fear R.W. and Melvin had taken the Jackson Road home, he did not get out at the Jefferson Davis School Road intersection, but instead crossed Soldiers Bridge with the farmer and got out at the intersection beyond the bridge and walked around, coming from the west to our house.

"T.J., was . . . was them Barnetts dead?" asked Stacey when T.J. grew quiet.

T.J. shook his head. "I dunno. They sure looked dead. Stacey, anybody find out, you know what they'd do to me?" He stood up, his face grimacing with pain. "Stacey, help me get home," he pleaded. "I'm afraid to go there by myself. . . . R.W. and Melvin might be waitin'. . . ."

"You sure you ain't lying, T.J.?" I asked suspiciously.

"I swear everything I told y'all is the truth. I . . . I admit I lied 'bout tellin' on your mama, but I ain't lyin' now, I ain't!"

Stacey thought a moment. "Why don't you stay here tonight? Papa'll tell your daddy what happened and he won't put—"

"No!" cried T.J., his eyes big with terror. "Can't tell nobody! I gotta go!" He headed for the door, holding his side. But before he could reach it, his legs gave way and Stacey caught him and guided him back to the bed.

I studied T.J. closely under the light, sure that he was pulling another fast one. But then he coughed and blood spurted from his mouth; his eyes glazed, his face paled, and I knew that this time T.J. was not faking.

"You're bad hurt," Stacey said. "Let me get Big Ma— she'll know what to do."

T.J. shook his head weakly. "My mama . . . I'll just tell her them white boys beat me for no reason and she'll believe it . . . she'll take care of me. But you go wakin' your grandmama and your daddy'll be in it. Stacey, please! You my only friend . . . ain't never really had no true friend but you. . . ."

"Stacey?" I whispered, afraid of what he might do. As far back as I could remember, Stacey had felt a responsibility for T.J. I had never really understood why. Perhaps he felt that even a person as despicable as T.J. needed someone he could call "friend," or perhaps he sensed T.J.'s vulnerability better than T.J. did himself. "Stacey, you ain't going, are you?"

Stacey wet his lips, thinking. Then he looked at me. "You go on back to bed, Cassie. I'll be all right."

"Yeah, I know you gonna be all right 'cause I'm gonna tell Papa!" I cried, turning to dash for the other room. But Stacey reached into the darkness and caught me. "Look, Cassie, it won't take me but twenty-five or thirty minutes to run down there and back. Really, it's all right."

"You as big a fool as he is then," I accused frantically. "You don't owe him nothin', 'specially after what he done to Mama."

Stacey released me. "He's hurt bad, Cassie. I gotta get him home." He turned away from me and grabbed his pants.

I stared after him; then I said, "Well, you ain't going without me." If Stacey was going to be a fool and go running out into the night to take an even bigger fool home, the least I could do was make sure he got back in one piece.

"Cassie, you can't go—"

"Go where?" piped Little Man, sitting up. Christopher-John sat up too, yawning sleepily. "Is it morning? What y'all doing up?" Little Man questioned. He blinked into the light and rubbed his eyes. "T.J., that you? What you doing here? Where y'all going?"

"Nowhere. I'm just gonna walk T.J. home," Stacey said. "Now go on back to sleep."

Little Man jumped out of bed and pulled his clothes from the hanger where he had neatly hung them. "I'm going too," he squealed.

"Not me," said Christopher-John, lying back down again.

While Stacey attempted to put Little Man back to bed, I checked the porch to make sure that Mr. Morrison wasn't around, then slipped back to my own room to change. When I emerged again, the boys were on the porch and Christopher-John, his pants over his arm, was murmuring a strong protest against this middle-of-the-night stroll. Stacey attempted to persuade both him and Little Man back inside, but Little Man would not budge and Christopher-John, as much as he protested, would not be left behind. Finally Stacey gave up and with T.J. leaning heavily against him hurried across the lawn. The rest of us followed.

Once on the road, Christopher John struggled into his pants and we became part of the night. Quiet, frightened, and wishing just to dump T.J. on his front porch and get back to the safety of our own beds, we hastened along the invisible road, brightened only by the round of the flashlight.

The thunder was creeping closer now, rolling angrily over the forest depths and bringing the lightning with it, as we emerged from the path into the deserted Avery yard. "W-wait till I get inside, will ya?" requested T.J.

"Ain't nobody here," I said sourly. "What you need us to wait for?"

"Go on, T.J.," said Stacey. "We'll wait."

"Th-thanks, y'all," T.J. said, then he limped to the side of the house and slipped awkwardly into his room through an open window.

"Come on, let's get out of here," said Stacey, herding us back to the path. But as we neared the forest, Little Man turned. "Hey, y'all, look over yonder! What's that?"

Beyond the Avery house bright lights appeared far away on the road near the Granger mansion. For a breathless second they lingered there, then plunged suddenly downward toward the Averys'. The first set of lights was followed by a second, then a third, until there were half a dozen sets of headlights beaming over the trail.

"Wh-what's happening?" cried Christopher-John.

For what seemed an interminable wait, we stood watching those lights drawing nearer and nearer before Stacey clicked off the flashlight and ordered us into the forest. Silently, we slipped into the brush and fell flat to the ground. Two pickups and four cars rattled into the yard, their lights focused like spotlights on the Avery front porch. Noisy, angry men leaped from the cars and surrounded the house.

Kaleb Wallace and his brother Thurston, his left arm hanging akimbo at his side, pounded the front door with their rifle butts. "Y'all come on outa there!" called Kaleb. "We want that thieving, murdering nigger of y'all's."

"St-Stacey," I stammered, feeling the same nauseous fear

I had felt when the night men had passed and when Papa had come home shot and broken, "wh-what they gonna do?"

"I—I dunno," Stacey whispered as two more men joined the Wallaces at the door.

"Why, ain't . . . ain't that R.W. and Melvin?" I exclaimed. "What the devil they doing—"

Stacey quickly muffled me with the palm of his hand as Melvin thrust himself against the door in an attempt to break it open and R.W. smashed a window with his gun. At the side of the house, several men were climbing through the same window T.J. had entered only a few minutes before. Soon, the front door was flung open from the inside and Mr. and Mrs. Avery were dragged savagely by their feet from the house. The Avery girls were thrown through the open windows. The older girls, attempting to gather the younger children to them, were slapped back and spat upon. Then quiet, gentle Claude was hauled out, knocked to the ground and kicked.

"C-Claude!" whimpered Christopher-John, trying to rise. But Stacey hushed him and held him down.

"W-we gotta get help," Stacey rasped, but none of us could move. I watched the world from outside myself.

Then T.J. emerged, dragged from the house on his knees. His face was bloody and when he tried to speak he cried with pain, mumbling his words as if his jaw were broken. Mr. Avery tried to rise to get to him, but was knocked back.

"Look what we got here!" one of the men said, holding up a gun. "That pearl-handled pistol from Jim Lee's store."

"Oh, Lord," Stacey groaned. "Why didn't he get rid of that thing?"

T.J. mumbled something we could not hear and Kaleb Wallace thundered, "Stop lyin', boy, 'cause you in a whole lot of trouble. You was in there—Miz Barnett, when she come to and got help, said three black boys robbed their store and knocked out her and her husband. And R.W. and Melvin Simms seen you and them two other boys running from behind that store when they come in town to shoot some pool—"

"But it was R.W. and Melvin—" I started before Stacey clasped his hand over my mouth again.

"—Now who was them other two and where's that money y'all took?"

Whatever T.J.'s reply, it obviously was not what Kaleb Wallace wanted to hear, for he pulled his leg back and kicked T.J.'s swollen stomach with such force that T.J. emitted a cry of awful pain and fell prone upon the ground.

"Lord Jesus! Lord Jesus!" cried Mrs. Avery, wrenching herself free from the men who held her and rushing toward her son. "Don't let 'em hurt my baby no more! Kill me, Lord, but not my child!" But before she could reach T.J., she was caught by the arm and flung so ferociously against the house that she fell, dazed, and Mr. Avery, struggling to reach her, was helpless to save either her or T.J.

Christopher-John was sobbing distinctly now. "Cassie," Stacey whispered, "you take Little Man and Christopher-John and y'all—"

The headlights of two more cars appeared in the distance and Stacey immediately hushed. One of the cars halted on the Granger Road, its lights beaming aimlessly into the blackness of the cotton fields, but the lead car came crazy and fast along the rutted trail toward the Avery house, and before it had rolled to a complete stop Mr. Jamison leaped out. But once out of the car, he stood very still surveying the scene; then he stared at each of the men as if preparing to charge them in the courtroom and said softly, "Y'all decide to hold court out here tonight?"

There was an embarrassed silence. Then Kaleb Wallace spoke up. "Now look here, Mr. Jamison, don't you come messin' in this thing."

"You do," warned Thurston hotly, "we just likely to take care of ourselves a nigger lover too tonight."

An electric tenseness filled the air, but Mr. Jamison's placid face was unchanged by the threat. "Jim Lee Barnett and his wife are still alive. Y'all let the sheriff and me take the boy. Let the law decide whether or not he's guilty."

"Where's Hank?" someone asked. "I don't see no law."

"That's him up at Harlan Granger's," Mr. Jamison said with a wave of his hand over his shoulder. "He'll be down in a minute. Now leave the boy be."

"For my money, I say let's do it now," a voice cried. "Ain't no need to waste good time and money tryin' no thievin' nigger!"

A crescendo of ugly hate rose from the men as the second car approached. They grew momentarily quiet as the sheriff stepped out. The sheriff looked uneasily at the crowd as if he would rather not be here at all, then at Mr. Jamison.

"Where's Harlan?" asked Mr. Jamison.

The sheriff turned from Mr. Jamison to the crowd without answering him. Then he spoke to the men: "Mr. Granger sent word by me that he ain't gonna stand for no hanging on *his* place. He say y'all touch one hair on that boy's head while he on *this* land, he's gonna hold every man here responsible."

The men took the news in grim silence.

Then Kaleb Wallace cried: "Then why don't we go somewhere else? I say what we oughta do is take him on down the road and take care of that big black giant of a nigger at the same time!"

"And why not that boy he working for too?" yelled Thurston.

"Stacey!" I gasped.

"Hush!"

A welling affirmation rose from the men. "I got me three new ropes!" exclaimed Kaleb.

"New? How come you wanna waste a new rope on a nigger?" asked Melvin Simms.

"Big as that one nigger is, an old one might break!"

There was chilling laughter and the men moved toward their cars, dragging T.J. with them.

"No!" cried Mr. Jamison, rushing to shield T.J. with his own body.

"Cassie," Stacey whispered hoarsely, "Cassie, you gotta get Papa now. Tell him what happened. I don't think Mr. Jamison can hold them—"

"You come too."

"No, I'll wait here."

"I ain't going without you!" I declared, afraid that he would do something stupid like trying to rescue T.J. alone.

"Look, Cassie, go on, will ya please? Papa'll know what to do. Somebody's gotta stay here case they take T.J. off into the woods somewhere. I'll be all right."

"Well . . ."

"Please, Cassie? Trust me, will ya?"

I hesitated. "Y-you promise you won't go down there by yourself?"

"Yeah, I promise. Just get Papa and Mr. Morrison 'fore they—'fore they hurt them some more." He placed the unlit flashlight in my hand and pushed me up. Clutching Little Man's hand, I told him to grab Christopher-John's, and together the three of us picked our way along the black path, afraid to turn on the flashlight for fear of its light being seen.

Thunder crashed against the corners of the world and lightning split the sky as we reached the road, but we did not stop. We dared not. We had to reach Papa.

12

When we neared the house, the dull glow of a kerosene lamp was shining faintly from the boys' room. "Y-you s'pose they already know?" Christopher-John asked breathlessly as we ran up the lawn. "Dunno 'bout that," I said, "but they know we ain't where we s'pose to be."

We ran noisily up onto the porch and flung open the unlatched door. Mama and Big Ma, standing with Mr. Morrison near the foot of the bed, turned as we entered and Big Ma cried, "Lord, there they is!"

"Where have you been?" Mama demanded, her face strangely stricken. "What do you mean running around out there this time of night?"

Before we could answer either question, Papa appeared in the doorway, dressed, his wide leather strap in hand.

"Papa—" I began.

"Where's Stacey?"

"He-he down to T.J.'s. Papa—"

"That boy's gotten mighty grown," Papa said, clearly angry. "I'm gonna teach all of y'all 'bout traipsing off in the middle of the night . . . and especially Stacey. He should know better. If Mr. Morrison hadn't seen this door open, I suppose you would've thought you was getting away with something—like T.J. Well, y'all gonna learn right here and now there ain't gonna be no T.J.s in this house—"

"But, Papa, they h-hurt Claude!" Christopher-John cried, tears streaming down his cheeks for his injured friend.

"And T.J., too," echoed Little Man, trembling.

"What?" Papa asked, his eyes narrowing. "What y'all talking 'bout?"

"Papa, they hurt 'em real bad and . . . and . . ." I could not finish. Papa came to me and took my face in his hands. "What is it, Cassie girl? Tell me."

Everything. I poured out everything. About T.J.'s breaking into the mercantile with the Simmses, about his coming in the night fleeing the Simmses, about the coming of the men and what they had done to the Averys. About Mr. Jamison and the threat of the men to come to the house to get him and Mr. Morrison.

"And Stacey's still down there?" Papa asked when I had finished.

"Yessir. But he hid in the forest. They don't know he's there."

Papa spun around suddenly. "Gotta get him out of there," he said, moving quicker than I had thought possible with his bad leg. Mama followed him into their room, and the boys and I followed her. From over the bed Papa pulled his shotgun.

"David, not with the shotgun. You can't stop them like that."

"Got no other way," he said, stuffing a box of shells into his shirt pocket.

"You fire on them and they'll hang you for sure. They'd like nothing better."

"If I don't, they'll hang T.J. This thing's been coming a long time, baby, and T.J. just happened to be the one foolish enough to trigger it. But, fool or not, I can't just sit by and let them kill the boy. And if they find Stacey—"

"I know, David, I know. But there's got to be another way. Some way they won't kill you too!"

"Seems like they might be planning to do that anyway," Papa said, turning from her. "They come here, no telling what'll happen, and I'll use every bullet I got 'fore I let them hurt anybody in this house."

Mama grabbed his arm. "Get Harlan Granger to stop it. If he says so, they'll go on home."

Papa shook his head. "Them cars had to come right past his house to get to the Averys', and if he'd intended to stop them, he'd stop them without me telling him so."

"Then," said Mama, "force him to stop it."

"How?" asked Papa dryly. "Hold a gun to his head?" He left her then, going back into the boys' room. "You coming, Mr. Morrison?"

Mr. Morrison nodded and followed Papa onto the porch, a rifle in his hand. Like a cat Mama sprang after them and grabbed Papa again. "David, don't . . . don't use the gun."

Papa stared out as a bolt of lightning splintered the night into a dazzling brilliance. The wind was blowing softly, gently toward the east. "Perhaps . . ." he started, then was quiet.

"David?"

Papa touched Mama's face tenderly with the tips of his fingers and said, "I'll do what I have to do, Mary . . . and so will you." Then he turned from her, and with Mr. Morrison disappeared into the night.

Mama pushed us back into her room, where Big Ma fell upon her knees and prayed a powerful prayer. Afterward both Mama and Big Ma changed their clothes, then we sat, very quiet, as the heat crept sticky and wet through our clothing and the thunder banged menacingly overhead. Mama, her knuckles tight against her skin as she gripped the arms of her chair, looked down upon Christopher-John, Little Man, and me, our eyes wide awake with fear. "I don't suppose it would do any good to put you to bed," she said quietly. We looked up at her. She did not mean to have an answer; we gave none, and nothing else was said as the night minutes crept past and the waiting pressed as heavily upon us as the heat.

Then Mama stiffened. She sniffed the air and got up.

"What is it, child?" Big Ma asked.

"You smell smoke?" Mama said, going to the front door and opening it. Little Man, Christopher-John, and I followed, peeping around her in the doorway. From deep in the field where the land sloped upward toward the Granger forest, a fire billowed, carried eastward by the wind.

"Mama, the cotton!" I cried. "It's on fire!"

"Oh, good Lord!" Big Ma exclaimed, hurrying to join us. "That lightning done that!"

"If it reaches those trees, it'll burn everything from here to Strawberry," Mama said. She turned quickly and ran across the room to the side door. "Stay here," she ordered, opening the door and fleeing across the yard to the barn. "Mama, you'd better get some water!" she yelled over her shoulder.

Big Ma hurried into the kitchen with Christopher-John, Little Man, and me at her heels. "What we gonna do, Big Ma?" I asked.

Big Ma stepped onto the back porch and brought in the washtub and began filling it with water. "We gotta fight that fire and try and stop it 'fore it reach them trees. Stand back now out the way so y'all don't get wet."

In a few minutes Mama returned, her arms loaded with sacks of burlap. She quickly threw the sacks into the water and ran back out again. When she returned, she carried two shovels and several more sacks.

"Mama, what you gonna do with all that?" asked Little Man.

"It's for fighting the fire," she replied hastily.

"Oh," said Little Man, grabbing for one of the shovels as I started to take the other.

"No," Mama said. "You're going to stay here."

Big Ma straightened from where she was bent dunking the sacks into the water. "Mary, child, you don't think it'd be better to take them with us?"

Mama studied us closely and bit her lower lip. She was silent for several moments, then she shook her head. "Can't anyone get to the house from the Grangers' without our seeing them. I'd rather they stay here than risk them near the fire."

Then she charged each of us, a strange glint in her eyes. "Cassie, Christopher-John, Clayton Chester, hear me good. I don't want you near that fire. You set one foot from this house and I'm going to skin you alive . . . do you hear me now?"

We nodded solemnly. "Yes ma'am, Mama."

"And stay inside. That lightning's dangerous."

"B-but, Mama," cried Christopher-John, "y'all going out there in that lightning!"

"It can't be helped, baby," she said. "The fire's got to be stopped."

Then she and Big Ma laid the shovels across the top of

the tub and each took a handle of it. As they stepped out the back door, Mama looked back at us, her eyes uncertain, as if she did not want to leave us. "Y'all be sure to mind now," ordered Big Ma gruffly, and the two of them carrying the heavy tub crossed the yard toward the garden. From the garden they would cut through the south pasture and up to where the cotton blazed. We watched until they were swallowed by the blackness that lay between the house and the fire, then dashed back to the front porch where the view was clearer. There we gazed transfixed as the flames gobbled the cotton and crept dangerously near the forest edge.

"Th-that fire, Cassie," said Christopher-John, "it gonna burn us up?"

"No . . . it's going the other way. Toward the forest."

"Then it's gonna burn up the trees," said Christopher-John sadly.

Little Man tugged at my arm. "Papa and Stacey and Mr. Morrison, Cassie! They in them trees!" Then iron-willed Little Man began to cry. And Christopher-John too. And the three of us huddled together, all alone.

"Hey, y'all all right?"

I gazed out into the night, seeing nothing but the gray smoke and the red rim of the fire in the east. "Who's that?"

"It's me," said Jeremy Simms, running up the lawn.

"Jeremy, what you doing out this time of night?" I questioned, taken aback to see him.

"It ain't night no more, Cassie. It's near dawn."

"But what you doing here?" repeated Little Man with a sniffle.

"I was sleepin' up in my tree like I always do—"

"On a night like this?" I exclaimed. "Boy, you *are* crazy!"

Jeremy looked rather shamefaced, and shrugged. "Well, anyway, I was and I smelled smoke. I knew it was comin' from thisaway and I was 'fraid it was y'all's place, so I run in and told my pa, and him and me we come on up here over an hour ago."

"You mean you been out there fighting that fire?"

Jeremy nodded. "My pa, and R.W. and Melvin too."

"R.W. and Melvin?" Little Man, Christopher-John, and I exclaimed together.

"But they was—" I poked Christopher-John into silence.

"Yeah, they got there 'fore us. And there's a whole lot of men from the town out there too." He looked puzzled. "I wonder what they all was doin' out here?"

"How bad is it?" I asked, ignoring his wonderings. "It get much of the cotton?"

Jeremy nodded absently. "Funny thing. That fire come up from that lightning and struck one of them wooden fence posts, I reckon, and sparked that cotton. Must've burned a good quarter of it. . . . Y'all lucky it ain't headed this way."

"But the trees," said Christopher-John. "It gonna get the trees, ain't it?"

Jeremy looked out across the field, shielding his eyes

against the brilliance of the fire. "They tryin' like every-thing to stop it. Your papa and Mr. Granger, they got—"

"Papa? You seen Papa? He all right?" cried Christopher-John breathlessly.

Jeremy nodded, looking down at him strangely. "Yeah, he's fine—"

"And Stacey, you seen him?" inquired Little Man.

Again, Jeremy nodded. "Yeah, he out there too."

Little Man, Christopher-John, and I glanced at each other, relieved just a bit, and Jeremy went on, though eye-ing us somewhat suspiciously. "Your papa and Mr. Granger, they got them men diggin' a deep trench 'cross that slope and they say they gonna burn that pasture grass from the trench back to the cotton—"

"You think that'll stop it?" I asked.

Jeremy stared blankly at the fire and shook his head. "Dunno," he said finally. "Sure hope so, though." There was a violent clap of thunder, and lightning flooded the field. "One thing would sure help though is if that ole rain would only come on down."

All four of us looked up at the sky and waited a minute for the rain to fall. When nothing happened, Jeremy turned and sighed. "I better be gettin' back now. Miz Logan said she left y'all here so I just come to see 'bout ya." Then he ran down the slope, waving back at us as he went. When he got to the road, he stopped suddenly and stood very still; then he put out his hands, hesitated a moment, and spun around wildly as if he were mad.

"It's rainin', y'all!" he cried. "That ole rain a-comin' down!"

Little Man, Christopher-John, and I jumped from the porch and ran barefooted onto the lawn, feeling the rain fine and cool upon our faces. And we laughed, whooping joyously into the thundering night, forgetting for the moment that we still did not know what had happened to T.J.

When the dawn came peeping yellow-gray and sooted over the horizon, the fire was out and the thunderstorm had shifted eastward after an hour of heavy rain. I stood up stiffly, my eyes tearing from the acrid smoke, and looked out across the cotton to the slope, barely visible in the smoggish dawn. Near the slope where once cotton stalks had stood, their brown bolls popping with tiny puffs of cotton, the land was charred, desolate, black, still steaming from the night.

I wanted to go and take a closer look, but for once Christopher-John would not budge. "No!" he repeated over and over. "I ain't going!"

"But what Mama *meant* was that she didn't want us near the fire, and it's out now."

Christopher-John set his lips firmly together, folded his plump arms across his chest and was adamant. When I saw that he would not be persuaded, I gazed again at the field and decided that I could not wait any longer. "Okay, you stay here then. We'll be right back." Ignoring his protests, Little Man and I ran down to the wet road.

"He really ain't coming," said Little Man, amazed, looking back over his shoulder.

"I guess not," I said, searching for signs of the fire in the cotton. Farther up the road the stalks were singed, and the fine gray ash of the fire lay thick upon them and the road and the forest trees.

When we reached the burnt-out section of the field, we surveyed the destruction. As far as we could see, the fire line had extended midway up the slope, but had been stopped at the trench. The old oak was untouched. Moving across the field, slowly, mechanically, as if sleepwalking, was a flood of men and women dumping shovels of dirt on fire patches which refused to die. They wore wide handkerchiefs over their faces and many wore hats, making it difficult to identify who was who, but it was obvious that the ranks of the fire fighters had swelled from the two dozen townsmen to include nearby farmers. I recognized Mr. Lanier by his floppy blue hat working side by side with Mr. Simms, each oblivious of the other, and Papa near the slope waving orders to two of the townsmen. Mr. Granger, hammering down smoldering stalks with the flat of his shovel, was near the south pasture where Mr. Morrison and Mama were swatting the burning ground.

Nearer the fence a stocky man, masked like the others, searched the field in robot fashion for hidden fire under the charred skeletons of broken stalks. When he reached the fence, he leaned tiredly against it, taking off his handkerchief to wipe the sweat and soot from his face. He coughed and looked around blankly. His eyes fell on Little Man and me staring up at him. But Kaleb Wallace seemed not to recognize us, and after a moment he picked up his shovel and started back toward the slope without a word.

Then Little Man nudged me. "Look over there, Cassie. There go Mama and Big Ma!" I followed his pointing finger. Mama and Big Ma were headed home across the field.

"Come on," I said, sprinting back up the road.

When we reached the house, we dragged our feet across the wet lawn to clean them and rejoined Christopher-John on the porch. He looked a bit frightened sitting there all alone and was obviously glad we were back. "Y'all all right?" he asked.

"Course we're all right," I said, plopping on the porch and trying to catch my breath.

"What'd it look like?"

Before either Little Man or I could answer, Mama and Big Ma emerged from the field with Stacey, the sacks now blackened remnants in their hands. We ran to them eagerly.

"Stacey, you all right?" I cried. "What 'bout T.J.?"

"And C-Claude?" stammered Christopher-John.

And Little Man asked, "Papa and Mr. Morrison, ain't they coming?"

Mama held up her hand wearily. "Babies! Babies!" Then she put her arm around Christopher-John. "Claude's fine, honey. And," she said, looking down at Little Man, "Papa and Mr. Morrison, they'll be coming soon."

"But T.J., Mama," I persisted. "What 'bout T.J.?"

Mama sighed and sat down on the steps, laying the sacks on the ground. The boys and I sat beside her.

"I'm gonna go on in and change, Mary," Big Ma said, climbing the steps and opening our bedroom door. "Miz Fannie gonna need somebody."

Mama nodded. "Tell her I'll be down soon as I get the children to bed and things straightened out here." Then she turned and looked down at Little Man, Christopher-John, and me, eager to know what had happened. She smiled slightly, but there was no happiness in it. "T.J.'s all right. The sheriff and Mr. Jamison took him into Strawberry."

"But why, Mama?" asked Little Man. "He done something bad?"

"They think he did, baby. They think he did."

"Then—then they didn't hurt him no more?" I asked.

Stacey looked across at Mama to see if she intended to answer; then, his voice hollow and strained, he said, "Mr. Granger stopped them and sent them up to fight the fire."

I sensed that there was more, but before I could ask what, Chistopher-John piped, "And—and Papa and Mr. Morrison, they didn't have to fight them ole men? They didn't have to use the guns?"

"Thank the Lord, no," said Mama. "They didn't."

"The fire come up," said Stacey, "and Mr. Morrison come and got me and then them men come down here to fight the fire and didn't nobody have to fight nobody."

"Mr. Morrison come get you alone?" I asked, puzzled. "Where was Papa?"

Stacey again looked at Mama and for a moment they both were silent. Then Stacey said, "Y'all know he couldn't make that slope with that bad leg of his."

I looked at him suspiciously. I had seen Papa move on that leg. He could have made the slope if he wanted to.

"All right now," Mama said, rising. "It's been a long, tiring night and it's time you all were in bed."

I reached for her arm. "Mama, how bad is it really? I mean, is there enough cotton left to pay the taxes?"

Mama looked at me oddly. "Since when did you start worrying about taxes?" I shrugged, then leaned closer toward her, wanting an answer, yet afraid to hear it. "The taxes will get paid, don't you worry," was all the answer she gave. "Now, let's get to bed."

"But I wanna wait for Papa and Mr. Morrison!" protested Little Man.

"Me too!" yawned Christopher-John.

"Inside!"

All of us went in but Stacey, and Mama did not make him. But as soon as she had disappeared into the boys' room to make sure Little Man and Christopher-John got to bed, I returned to the porch and sat beside him. "I thought you went to bed," he said.

"I wanna know what happened over there."

"I told you, Mr. Granger—"

"I come and got Papa and Mr. Morrison like you asked," I reminded him. "Now I wanna know everything happened after I left."

Stacey sighed and rubbed his left temple absently, as if his head were hurting. "Ain't much happened 'cepting Mr. Jamison tried talking to them men some more, and after a bit they pushed him out the way and stuffed T.J. into one of their cars. But Mr. Jamison, he jumped into his car and lit out ahead of them and drove up to Mr. Granger's and swung his car smack across the road so couldn't nobody get past him. Then he starts laying on his horn.

"You go over there?"

He nodded. "By the time I got 'cross the field to where I could hear what was going on, Mr. Granger was standing on his porch and Mr. Jamison was telling him that the sheriff or nobody else was 'bout to stop a hanging on that flimsy message he'd sent up to the Averys'. But Mr. Granger, he just stood there on his porch looking sleepy and bored, and finally he told the sheriff, 'Hank, you take care of this. That's what folks elected you for.'

"Then Kaleb Wallace, he leaps out of his car and tries to grab Mr. Jamison's keys. But Mr. Jamison threw them keys right into Mrs. Granger's flower bed and couldn't nobody find them, so Melvin and R.W. come up and pushed Mr. Jamison's car off the road. Then them cars was 'bout to take off again when Mr. Granger comes running off the porch hollering like he's lost his mind. 'There's smoke coming from my forest yonder!' he yells. 'Dry as that timber is, a fire catch hold it won't stop burning for a week. Give that boy to Wade like he wants and get on up there!' And folks started running all over the place for shovels and things, then all of them cut back down the road to the Averys' and through them woods over to our place."

"And that's when Mr. Morrison come got you?"

Stacey nodded. "He found me when I followed them men back up to the woods."

I sat very still, listening to the soft sounds of the early morning, my eyes on the field. There was something which I still did not understand.

Stacey nodded toward the road. "Here come Papa and Mr. Morrison." They were walking with slow, exhausted steps toward the drive.

The two of us ran down the lawn, but before we reached the road a car approached and stopped directly behind them. Mr. Jamison was driving. Stacey and I stood curiously on the lawn, far enough away not to be noticed, but close enough to hear.

"David, I thought you should know . . ." said Mr. Jamison. "I just come from Strawberry to see the Averys—"

"How bad is it?"

Mr. Jamison stared straight out at the road. "Jim Lee Barnett . . . he died at four o'clock this morning."

Papa hit the roof of the car hard with his clenched fist and turned toward the field, his head bowed.

For a long, long minute, none of the men spoke; then Mr. Morrison said softly, "The boy, how is he?"

"Doc Crandon says he's got a couple of broken ribs and his jaw's broken, but he'll be all right . . . for now. I'm going to his folks to tell them and take them to town. Just thought I'd tell you first."

Papa said, "I'll go in with them."

Mr. Jamison pulled off his hat and ran his fingers through his hair, damp against his forehead. Then, squinting, he looked over his shoulder at the field. "Folks thinking," he said slowly, as if he did not want to say what he was about to say, "folks thinking that lightning struck that fence of yours and started the fire. . . ." He pulled at his ear. "It's better, I think, that you stay clear of this whole thing now, David, and don't give anybody cause to think about you at all, except that you got what was coming to you by losing a quarter of your cotton. . . ."

There was a cautious silence as he gazed up at Papa and Mr. Morrison, their faces set in grim, tired lines. ". . . Or somebody might just get to wondering about that fire. . . ."

"Stacey," I whispered, "what's he talking 'bout?"

"Hush, Cassie," Stacey said, his eyes intent on the men.

"But I wanna know—"

Stacey looked around at me sharply, his face drawn, his eyes anxious, and without even a murmur from him I suddenly did know. I knew why Mr. Morrison had come for him alone. Why Mr. Jamison was afraid for Papa to go into town. Papa had found a way, as Mama had asked, to make Mr. Granger stop the hanging: He had started the fire.

And it came to me that this was one of those known and unknown things, something never to be spoken, not even to each other. I glanced at Stacey, and he saw in my eyes that I knew, and understood the meaning of what I knew, and he said simply, "Mr. Jamison's going now."

Mr. Jamison turned around in the driveway and headed back toward the Averys'. Papa and Mr. Morrison watched him leave, then Mr. Morrison walked silently up the drive to do the morning chores and Papa, noticing us for the first time, stared down at us, his eyes bloodshot and unsmiling. "I thought y'all would've been in bed by now," he said.

"Papa," Stacey whispered hoarsely, "what's gonna happen to T.J. now?"

Papa looked out at the climbing sun, a round, red shadow behind the smoggish heat. He didn't answer immediately, and it seemed as if he were debating whether or not he should. Finally, very slowly, he looked down, first at me, then at Stacey. He said quietly, "He's in jail right now."

"And—and what then?" asked Stacey.

Papa studied us. "He could possibly go on the chain gang. . . ."

"Papa, could he . . . could he die?" asked Stacey, hardly breathing.

"Son—"

"Papa, could he?"

Papa put a strong hand on each of us and watched us closely. "I ain't never lied to y'all, y'all know that."

"Yessir."

He waited, his eyes on us. "Well, I . . . I wish I could lie to y'all now."

"No! Oh, Papa, no!" I cried. "They wouldn't do that to ole T.J.! He can talk his way outa just 'bout anything! Besides, he ain't done nothing *that* bad. It was them Simmses! Tell them that!"

Stacey, shaking his head, backed away, silent, not wanting to believe, but believing still. His eyes filled with heavy tears, then he turned and fled down the lawn and across the road into the shelter of the forest.

Papa stared after him, holding me tightly to him. "Oh, P-Papa, d-does it have to be?"

Papa tilted my chin and gazed softly down at me. "All I can say, Cassie girl . . . is that it shouldn't be." Then, glancing back toward the forest, he took my hand and led me to the house.

Mama was waiting for us as we climbed the steps, her face wan and strained. Little Man and Christopher-John were already in bed, and after Mama had felt my forehead and asked if I was all right she sent me to bed too. Big Ma had already gone to the Averys' and I climbed into bed alone. A few minutes later both Mama and Papa came to tuck me in, talking softly in fragile, gentle words that seemed about to break. Their presence softened the hurt and I did not cry. But after they had left and I saw Papa through the open window disappear into the forest after Stacey, the tears began to run fast and heavy down my cheeks.

In the afternoon when I awakened, or tomorrow or the next day, the boys and I would still be free to run the red road, to wander through the old forest and sprawl lazily on the banks of the pond. Come October, we would trudge to school as always, barefooted and grumbling, fighting the dust and the mud and the Jefferson Davis school bus. But T.J. never would again.

I had never liked T.J., but he had always been there, a part of me, a part of my life, just like the mud and the rain, and I had thought that he always would be. Yet the mud and the rain and the dust would all pass. I knew and understood that. What had happened to T.J. in the night I did not understand, but I knew that it would not pass. And I cried for those things which had happened in the night and would not pass.

I cried for T.J. For T.J. and the land.

ALSO BY
BEN MIKAELSEN:

JUNGLE
OF BONES

JUNGLE OF BONES

BEN MIKAELSEN

SCHOLASTIC INC.

ISBN 978-0-545-83761-3

12 11 10 9 8 7 6 5 4 3 2 1   15 16 17 18 19 20/0

Printed in the U.S.A.   40

First Scholastic paperback printing, January 2015

The text type was set in Sabon.
The display type was set in Ballers Delight.
Book design by Jeannine Riske

I want to dedicate *Jungle of Bones* to the young and courageous crews who manned the bombers during the Second World War. All citizens of our great country need to learn from these brave men that "freedom is never free."

PROLOGUE

Dylan slogged through the swamp toward the trees. He needed to find dry ground where he could spend the night again. Still he watched for snakes and crocodiles. The air reeked of rotting undergrowth. All day he had seen birds, rats, possums, and other animals to eat, but no way to catch them. The only critters Dylan could approach were snakes and crocodiles. He knew the snakes might be poisonous, and there was no way he was going to try to catch a crocodile, even a small one.

Before leaving the tall grasses, Dylan ate a few more grasshoppers, and then deliberately headed for a root-tangled path entering the jungle. Soon, the thick, matted screen of overhead vines and leaves muted any fading sunlight that made it through the clouds. For the next hour, Dylan stumbled along a trail, no longer looking down to pick his footing. He had to find some kind of refuge before dark, a place where he could be out in the open but on higher ground. He needed a space where he could lie down and still see wild animals approaching. Hopefully a place with fewer insects.

As the light faded, a brief shower of rain fell. Only a few drops penetrated the dense canopy overhead. Suddenly a sharp pain stabbed Dylan's ankle. He glanced down in time to see a dark brown snake recoil and slither across the trail and into the undergrowth. "Ouch," he muttered, crouching. He pulled up his right pant leg to find four small puncture wounds where the snake had sunk its fangs.

Without thinking, Dylan panicked and began running down the trail. But even as he ran, he realized it was probably the dumbest thing he could do after a snake bite. Still he kept running. If he stopped, he would just die here on some muddy overgrown trail in the jungles of Papua New Guinea. By morning, rats would have picked his bones clean. By next week, other critters would have his bones scattered through the forest like twigs and branches. The world would never even know what had happened to Dylan Barstow.

Dylan ran faster. He had to find protection or help.

Overhead the light had faded into darkness. Now the only light came from a hazy moon hanging in the sky like a dim lightbulb. At that very instant, Dylan broke into a clearing similar to the one where he had slept the night before. He walked out away from the darkness of the trees into the moonlight and froze in shock. Ahead were rocks, and next to the rocks stood a tall spiral tree that looked like a big screw. This was the same place he had left early this morning. Without a compass, he had walked all day in a huge circle, only to end up back where he had begun.

2

Dylan blinked his eyes, as if doing so might make the stupid tree disappear. He shook his head as a wave of despair washed over him, worse than any chill or fever. Dylan screamed, desperate and primal, his voice piercing the hush that had fallen over the clearing. As he finished, tears started down his cheeks, stopping to rest each time he hiccupped with grief. And then a different spasm flooded through his body, and his knees buckled. Dylan collapsed to the ground. The jungle spun in circles. He felt suddenly stiff and cold, as if his body were freezing in a blizzard.

And then there was nothing.

CHAPTER 1

"Remove your hat, son," the old man said, his voice matter-of-fact, his deep-set eyes intense.

"You're not my dad!" Dylan snapped. "Get out of my face."

The man glared at Dylan, hesitated, then turned back to keep watching the parade.

Dylan's mother, Natalie, turned to him. "Take your hat off," she said quietly.

When Dylan rolled his eyes, she reached out and grabbed his hat, motioning to the old people marching past. "Those men and women are the VFW, the Veterans of Foreign Wars. Remove your hat to show respect."

"Bunch of over-the-hill Boy Scouts with their dumb little hats," Dylan said, motioning. "I can leave my hat on if I want. It's a free country."

Frustration clouded Natalie's eyes as she tucked Dylan's hat into her purse.

"Give that back," Dylan demanded.

She ignored him and headed back toward the car.

"Hey, the parade's not over yet," Dylan said.

Natalie kept walking.

"What's the big deal?" Dylan muttered, following her.

━━━

When they arrived home, Dylan's mother worked around the house, giving him the silent treatment. Dylan knew he should feel lucky. Some parents yelled and shouted, or even hit their kids, when they were mad. His mom just clammed up. He could tell whenever she was angry because she quit talking. Dylan stomped up the stairs to his room, whistling for his dog, Zipper, to follow him. His black lab was the only sane thing in his life anymore. Zipper didn't care what anybody wore or said. He didn't care what time anybody went to bed or if they skipped school, as long as he could cuddle and get his ears scratched.

Dylan slammed the door to his room and flopped down on his bed. "C'mon up, boy," he said, coaxing Zipper onto the bed. That was something that bugged his mom; she said Zipper shed too much. But right now Dylan wanted the company. He lay back and stared at the ceiling. It wasn't like he had killed anybody or stolen anything. All he had done was not take his hat off. Since when was that a capital offense? Dylan looked around his room. He was too mad to play his computer games. Instead he took a tennis ball and bounced it repeatedly off the wall. That was something that *really* bugged Mom.

Most times Zipper would chase the ball around the room. Tonight, he curled on the bed, watching with lazy eyes.

"Are you giving me the silent treatment, too?" Dylan asked.

Zipper closed his eyes without even wagging his tail.

Natalie called up, "There's food in the refrigerator if you're hungry. I want you home tonight." Before Dylan could answer, the front door closed. Moments later, the car pulled from the driveway.

Dylan threw the tennis ball extra hard one last time. She hadn't made dinner for him, or said anything about bouncing the ball. What was the big deal not taking his hat off in front of a bunch of old geezers? But deep inside, Dylan knew it was much more than that.

Zipper shifted positions and plopped his nose on Dylan's lap.

Dylan's eyes grew glassy as he scratched behind the dog's ear.

———

It was after dark when Dylan's mother finally returned. He could hear her busying around downstairs for almost an hour. Before going to bed, she poked her head in Dylan's room to make sure he was home.

"What's wrong? Don't you trust me?" Dylan shouted as his mom closed the door. She retreated down the stairs without even saying hello.

Dylan's face flushed with anger. Why did she treat him like some little kid who needed babysitting? He would be in eighth grade this fall, yet she always acted like he was some screw-up who was about to set the house on fire. Dylan crossed the room. If she wanted a screw-up, he would really give her one. He eased his window open and crawled out onto the porch roof. He whispered back, "Zipper, stay!" Dylan could hear Zipper whining as he carefully tiptoed down the shingles and over to where a big maple tree grew near the gutter downspout. With practiced ease, he lowered himself to the ground.

He didn't know where he was going — he just began walking. When he reached the end of the block, an idea struck him. He quickened his pace and ran the next six blocks to the edge of town, where he squeezed under a wood-slatted fence that guarded the front of the local junkyard. Often, when he skipped school, he came out here to wander around the junked cars. He loved cars, any kind of car: antiques, hot rods, sports cars. He especially liked Corvettes — that had been Dad's favorite car. Dylan could tell just about every model that had ever been made. Not that there were any Corvettes in this junkyard, but there were other old cars that were pretty awesome.

Whenever Dylan wandered through this junkyard, the owner, a guy called Mantz Krogan, watched him as if he thought a crook were trying to steal something. To bug the owner, Dylan always walked extra slowly. During one of his visits, Dylan had noticed six or seven cars parked away from the others in a row beside the garage. He asked about them, and Mantz said they had been fixed up to run and were for sale. When Dylan looked inside the cars, he noticed keys in all the ignitions. That was something he remembered now as he crossed the darkened yard.

He walked straight to an old gray Plymouth in the middle of the row. A dim yard light cast eerie shadows from each car. Peering in, Dylan saw a key chain dangling from the car's ignition. He took a step back from the Plymouth and stood up straight. Maybe this wasn't such a good idea. He looked around at the empty and quiet lot. Most people were fast asleep by now, including his mom. If he just took the car for a quick ride and returned it, how would anyone know it was him? Dylan tried the driver's door. He expected it to be locked, but the handle clicked and the door swung open with a creak. Dylan took this as a sign and crawled inside.

Fumbling in the darkness, he stepped on the clutch, shifted it into neutral, and turned the key. The engine cranked several times before the old Plymouth growled to life. Dylan revved the engine. Grinning with nervousness, he slowly shifted the car into reverse and backed away from the building.

A freshly plowed field surrounded the junkyard, looking like a moonscape in the dim light. Dylan floored the gas pedal and popped the clutch, spinning the tires all the way down the gravel drive that circled the yard. When he reached the field, he twisted the steering wheel to the right and heard the twang of wire as the big car plowed through the fence.

Dylan left the lights off — the dim moon made the field look foreboding. Dylan imagined zombies appearing.

This far from the highway, on a dark night, Dylan doubted that anybody would even hear or see him. He shifted into second and floored the gas pedal again. The old Plymouth roared as it bounced across the deep furrows. Again and again the shock absorbers bottomed out, jarring the whole car. Dylan laughed aloud as he spun the wheel and began spinning circles. Dylan called it "cutting donuts."

Careening around in circles made the dry dirt kick up. Soon, a cloud of dust blocked even the half-moon from witnessing his joyride. In total darkness, Dylan kept the gas pedal pressed to the floor. His mom would be having a batch of kittens if she knew that her "little boy" was out spinning donuts in a farmer's field. Dylan closed his eyes and tilted his head back. Keeping the gas pedal floored, he smiled. Life was good!

It was nearly five minutes before Dylan opened his eyes again. He noticed a flicker of red through the thick cloud of dust and let up on the gas pedal. As the dust cleared, the moonlight returned, along with a set of headlights. Without the motor revving, Dylan could also hear a siren now. He straightened out the steering wheel and carefully drove out of the vanishing dust cloud.

Facing Dylan waited two patrol cars, red lights flashing, sirens wailing. "Stop the car and get out with your hands up!" an amplified voice shouted over a loudspeaker on top of one of the squad cars. "Get out *now!*"

Bright headlights blinded Dylan as he braked to a stop and shut off the engine. This was bad. His plan hadn't been to get caught. He panicked. Maybe he could jump out and run — in the darkness the officers probably couldn't catch him. But before Dylan could do anything, a deputy ran to the side of the old Plymouth. He jerked the door open and drew his pistol. "Get out with your hands up!" he shouted.

Dylan turned the ignition switch off and raised his hands. An eerie silence hung in the air, along with dust, as he crawled slowly from the car. "I-I was just having a little fun," he stammered, holding his hands above his head. He recognized the deputy.

"Put your hands on the hood and spread your legs!" the deputy demanded.

Now an officer from the other squad car ran up. He grabbed Dylan's hands, one at a time, and twisted them behind his back to snap on a pair of handcuffs. "You call this a little fun? Wrecking somebody's car, running down a fence, and ripping up somebody's planted field?"

"I'll pay for it," Dylan argued, his voice shaking. The handcuffs bit into his wrists.

"You bet you will," the deputy answered.

Dylan kicked at the dirt in frustration as the officer led him through clouds of dust to the back of the patrol car.

At the detention center, Dylan recognized the tall officer who processed him. He also recognized the small room with a big table where he sat across from the officer for questioning. This was where he had come several times before. Last time it had been for stealing candy bars. You would have thought he'd robbed Fort Knox.

The questioning seemed to last for hours. What was so different about this visit? They already had a file as thick as a phone book on him. Tonight the officer treated him like a real criminal, leaving the handcuffs on him and never cracking a smile. He acted as if he was interviewing a serial killer.

He said this was grand theft auto and would be treated as a felony.

Dylan slumped in his chair and tried not to look at the officer. It wasn't like he had really stolen a car. He just took an old junker for a little ride. What was so bad about that?

Finally the officer escorted Dylan to a bare white holding room where he flopped himself onto a thin mattress that covered a gray steel bed frame. The only other fixtures were a toilet, a small table, and a chair. A locked metal door guaranteed he wouldn't leave.

It was a good thing he didn't have to stay here long, Dylan thought. His mom would come get him out of the detention center soon. That was what she always did. Again, he would be given a warning, but nothing would come of it.

Nearly an hour passed before a lady in a uniform came to Dylan's holding room. She was a short, dumpy-looking woman with shoes that clopped when she walked. Her hair wrapped behind her head into a bun and she wore a dress that hung to the middle of her shins like a tent. She looked like some kid's grandmother — probably was. She smiled sweetly as if welcoming him to some fancy hotel. "Your mom won't be coming down to get you until sometime tomorrow, so make yourself comfortable."

"What do you mean, tomorrow?"

The lady spoke sincerely. "Well, that means she won't be coming tonight, because if she came tonight, that wouldn't be tomorrow. Tomorrow means she is coming on a whole different day, the one after today."

"I know what tomorrow is!" Dylan snapped.

"Oh," the woman said, placing a surprised hand over her mouth, "I could have sworn you asked me what I meant by tomorrow. Please accept my apology."

Dylan kept his cool, but wished he could throw something at this human antique as she left the room. He would love to wipe that smug look off her face. The noise of her key locking the door sounded like the cocking of a rifle.

Dylan walked in angry circles. Why was everyone so uptight? He wondered about his mom. She could have gotten dressed and come right down. Maybe he had pushed her too far. But so what? If this was the straw that broke the camel's back, maybe it would be fun having a dead camel lying around.

As Dylan stared at the gray metal door, a knot tightened in his stomach. He had a bad feeling about this whole thing.

By the time his mom showed up the next day, it was almost noon. A deputy unlocked the door and stood waiting as Natalie entered the holding cell. After a night locked up alone, Dylan wanted to unload on her with every name he could think of, but held back. He was smart enough to know he should act really sorry. At least for a couple of days.

Today his mom was quiet, a pained expression making her eyes look tired. She just stood in the doorway and stared at him.

"Aren't you going to ask me why I did it?" Dylan asked.

"Oh, I already know why you did it," she said.

"And why is that?"

"Because you think Dylan Barstow is the only person living on the planet who has feelings. Nobody else matters."

"Mom, I was just out having a little fun," Dylan explained.

"And why is it that every time Dylan Barstow has fun, somebody else pays or gets hurt? I'm getting really tired of your fun."

"The world is getting too uptight," Dylan said, standing up. "Let's get out of this hole."

"You're not coming home today. I came late this morning because I've spent the last two hours trying to convince Mr. Krogan not to press charges. Lucky for you, he agreed, but only if you're kept far away from his cars. I also called your uncle Todd. He'll be flying in tomorrow to take you back to Oregon. You're spending the rest of the summer with him."

Dylan glanced at the deputy blocking the door as his

thoughts raced. Uncle Todd was his rich uncle who lived near Portland, Oregon. He looked like a bulldog on two feet. His neck came straight down from his ears to his massive shoulders. The guy still ran, lifted weights, and shaved his head almost bald, the same as when he was in the Marines.

"Why did you call him?" Dylan demanded. "I'm not going to Oregon for the rest of the summer."

"It's that or get tried in juvenile court. Maybe you don't quite understand how much trouble you're in. You committed a felony last night. I can only imagine what your father would have thought of this."

"Well, I guess we'll never know!" Dylan said, raising his voice. "He was too busy getting himself killed over in Timbuktu!"

Dylan's mother spoke slowly and deliberately. "We've talked about this before. Your father was a war correspondent in Darfur, in Sudan. He was covering the genocide of tens of thousands of people when he was killed. He knew the risks, but if he could have, he —"

"If he knew the risks," Dylan interrupted, "he shouldn't have been there."

"Is that what you were thinking when you climbed out your window and went for a joyride last night?" She fumbled for something in her purse. "Or do your own rules not apply to you?"

When Dylan failed to answer, his mother shook her head. "I want to show you something I hadn't planned on showing you until you were older." She took an envelope from her purse and handed it to Dylan.

"What's this?"

"It's one of the last letters your father sent to me before he was killed."

Dylan opened the envelope with its weird stamp and funny markings. He wasn't a very good reader. Slowly he unfolded the letter and let his eyes take in the page.

My Dear Natalie,

If anything should ever happen to me, know that I love you and Dylan more than life. I'm working here in Darfur because life has given me this chance to be a part of something bigger than myself: helping to stop the genocide of a nation's people. If I should ever get killed, it will be so that others might live. What I am doing may not seem as noble as fighting in war as a soldier, but this is a battlefield, and I can contribute much. My weapons are my camera and my pen.

Please never let my devotion to this cause make you doubt my love for you and Dylan. I hope someday my son will understand the importance of sacrificing his own needs for the needs of another. I think of you both every morning when I wake and every night before I fall asleep. Hopefully I will be home soon.

All my love,

Sam

"He shouldn't have been there!" Dylan shouted, tossing the letter on the floor. He refused to make eye contact with his mother. He didn't want her to see his eyes tearing up.

Natalie stooped and picked it up. "You're not the center of the universe," she answered. "Sorry to be the one to tell you this. You're just not."

As Natalie turned to leave, Dylan raised his voice. "I'm not going to Oregon!"

She turned and shook her head. "You have no choice."

"I'll run away," Dylan shouted.

"Fine, then run away."

"You-you want me to?"

"No, I want you to be a decent human being. Somehow you think the world owes you something. Your father was the kindest person I've ever known, and you still have a mother who loves you more than anything. If you think that living on the streets will be better than spending the summer with your uncle, I can't stop you. I just don't want to be around when Todd finds you — and he will find you."

As his mother walked from the detention center, Dylan clenched his fists tightly. When his father died, it had hurt more than anybody could have known. Dad was the one person who understood. Mom tried, but Dad was the one who had liked his music, his skateboarding, and the writing that he never showed to anybody else, because they might laugh. He had never needed to protect his thoughts from Dad. He was like Zipper — he always listened. He never criticized.

But then he went and died.

Dylan didn't like feeling trapped, and right now he felt cornered. Having his mother afraid of what he might do had always been his ace in the hole. Now that card was disappearing and he didn't have any backup. He wasn't dumb enough to think that being on the streets would be any fun. Nor did he doubt his Uncle Todd would find him if he ran away. He would probably treat it like some high-tech mission with operatives and data searches. He'd probably use his connections to have the CIA or the FBI come after him. The man was a crazy war buff and still lived, talked, and dressed like he was in the military. Living with him would be like boot camp.

CHAPTER 2

Nobody called or stopped by the rest of the day. It wasn't until the following afternoon that a deputy came and released Dylan, leading him to the front office. "You have two people waiting for you," he said.

Dylan drew in a deep breath, bracing himself. He didn't like it when he wasn't in control. He shoved his hands deep into his pockets, pushing his jeans so far down that his shirt no longer covered his underwear. His mom hated when he wore his pants this way.

Dylan first spotted his mother and then Uncle Todd. The two sat patiently in a waiting room to the side of the reception desk. Seeing him, they stood and came out to greet him. Dylan purposely shuffled his feet and walked slowly to show his disdain. This wasn't cool, what they were doing.

Uncle Todd extended his hand. "Hi, Dylan," he said. At first Dylan didn't return the handshake, but Uncle Todd kept his hand extended with a patient stare until Dylan reluctantly shook his hand. Uncle Todd's grip was like a vice. "Good to see you, son. It's been too long."

"I'm not your son," Dylan muttered.

Uncle Todd motioned him through the front door leading outside. "Let's go home."

———

Dylan felt like a caged animal with his uncle in the house.

"We'll be flying back to Portland tomorrow," Uncle Todd said, as if commenting on the weather. He handed Dylan a piece of paper. "You need to bring the following items if you have them. If not, we'll go shopping in Portland."

Dylan glanced at the long list: compass, mosquito spray, suntan lotion, hiking boots, sunglasses, light jeans, T-shirts, athletic socks, toothbrushes, and about a hundred other things. "Where are we going? On an expedition?"

"Actually, we are. We are going to Papua New Guinea. But I'll fill you in on that while we're flying to Portland." He handed Dylan two white tablets. "Here, take these while I'm thinking of it."

"What are they?"

"Malaria pills. Starting now, we need to take them every week until we get back. Now take them."

Dylan stood and put out his palm. Pills in hand, he retreated to the kitchen. "I need some water," he called back. When he reached the kitchen, he pretended to swallow the pills, but instead threw them in the garbage. He wasn't going on any expedition, and he wasn't going to take any weird medications. After his dad died, the guidance counselor at school had recommended that Dylan take some kind of pills to help with his depression. They just made him feel numb and empty. After a couple months of this, Dylan refused to take them. Adults were always trying to fix or change him, instead of just leaving him alone.

"What if I don't want to go to this Pa Pa Guinea Pig place?" Dylan asked, returning to the living room.

Uncle Todd sat watching television. "It's not negotiable," he said, not even looking up. "And get used to the name Papua New Guinea. You'll be seeing that place in your dreams by the time we're done. It will be your home for the summer. If it's easier, some people call the place PNG."

"Where is it, and why are we going there?"

"Like I said, I'll explain it all tomorrow, but roughly, PNG is on the other side of the planet." He glanced at his watch. "We better get some sleep. You still need to pack your bags, and we need to be up at O-five hundred to catch our flight."

As Dylan started up the stairs, Uncle Todd called out, "Your mom told me about your climbing out the window. Tonight that would be a huge mistake. Good night and sleep well."

Dylan replied by whistling. Zipper shot up the stairs from his favorite spot near the couch. Dylan entered his room and slammed the door. Falling to his knees, Dylan hugged Zipper. "Uncle Todd probably put a land mine on the porch roof, or rigged a trip wire to a hand grenade," Dylan said. "What can I do?"

Zipper wagged his tail.

One thing Dylan did know about his uncle was he wasn't one to bluff. He meant every word he said. Dylan stood and paced back and forth in his room, holding his head in his hands. It felt like his brains were going to explode.

Dylan knew he had no choice right now, so he would go along with this stupid PNG thing. But when the time was right, he would bail out. He wasn't anybody's puppet. Hands shaking with anger and frustration, Dylan packed his suitcase. He paid no attention to the list Uncle Todd had given him, but he made sure to throw in his music headset. His headphones helped him to tune out the world, and right now the world really needed tuning out.

That night, Dylan's constant tossing and turning crowded Zipper off the bed. Dylan dreamed he was running across a desert with a demon chasing him. Ahead he spotted a root cellar with an open door. The demon had almost caught him when, at the very last second, Dylan dove into the darkness and slammed the door closed. He turned the lock and ran to the far corner. Crouched on the floor in the dark, he watched in terror as the demon attacked the door. Dylan covered his ears to muffle the demon's screams. With each charge, the door splintered and began ripping from its hinges. Finally, with one last charge, the door crashed to the ground.

. "Wakee wakee wakee," called the monster. "Get your butt out of bed. It's O-five hundred!"

Dylan woke with a start. Sitting up and breathing fast, he realized it was morning and Uncle Todd was standing in the doorway of his bedroom. "I'm awake," Dylan grumped, swinging his legs out of bed. It was still dark.

"Breakfast in ten minutes," Uncle Todd announced.

Dylan fumbled with his clothes, wishing he was back in the root cellar with the demon. By the time he dressed and dragged his suitcase downstairs, his mom had breakfast on the table. Uncle Todd sat sipping on a cup of hot coffee. "I'm not hungry," Dylan mumbled.

Uncle Todd motioned for him to sit. "This morning don't eat for yourself. It's not all about you."

"What are you talking about?"

"This morning you need to eat breakfast because your mother was kind enough to get up early and fix it for us."

Dylan looked to his mom but she avoided eye contact. For a moment he considered arguing, but Uncle Todd's intense gaze discouraged that. Grunting, Dylan slumped into a chair and began eating. He wouldn't have admitted it to his mother or Uncle Todd, but the scrambled eggs, hash browns, and bacon didn't taste half bad.

━━

As Dylan walked from the house that morning, he knelt and hugged Zipper good-bye. "I'm going to miss you, old boy," he whispered, blinking. A light rain fell, but that wasn't what made Dylan's eyes wet. With one last hug, he stood angrily and crawled into the car. He would have slammed the door but Uncle Todd was already holding it open for him, and closed it gently.

Nobody spoke much as they drove to the airport. Not until they pulled to a stop and climbed out did Natalie speak. "Dylan, I hope you have a good summer," she said, her voice wavering.

"You've already made sure that won't happen," Dylan snapped.

Suddenly his mother hugged him desperately. "Just know I love you."

Dylan stiffened, then pushed her away and pulled his suitcase from the trunk.

"Take good care of Zipper," he ordered, heading toward the terminal. He glanced back once and noticed that she was crying.

Uncle Todd caught up to Dylan as they approached the ticketing counter. "It doesn't take much of a man to be a jerk," he said.

Dylan ignored the comment, keeping to himself.

After clearing airport security and finding their gate, Uncle Todd finally turned to Dylan. "Okay, so here's what's happening. And the sooner you get aboard, the sooner this train leaves the station. Last winter, my father, your grandfather, Henry died. He had full-blown Alzheimer's disease. At the end, he had completely lost his memory and mind. During the Second World War, Henry was a B-17 bomber pilot and was shot down over Papua New Guinea. He never spoke of his war years. After Dad died, I was executor of his estate and in charge of cleaning out the old farmhouse down near Grants Pass. When I was cleaning, I found this in the attic."

Uncle Todd reached into his upper jacket pocket and pulled out a small leather-bound notebook. He handed it to Dylan. "This is a journal your grandfather kept during the months and weeks leading up to the day they were shot down. Five crew members survived the initial crash, but three died the first night. In the end, your grandfather was the only survivor. He was lost for two weeks in the jungle before being found by natives, badly dehydrated and burning up with fever from malaria and gangrene.

"The military searched for the wreckage but never found it. Jungles in PNG are so dense, thousands of planes crashed during the war and were never seen again."

"Why did so many planes crash?" Dylan asked.

"The air war against Japan to protect Australia was fought over Papua New Guinea. Most of the planes that crashed were shot down, but there was also bad weather, horrible maps with uncharted mountains, no radar or guidance systems, and a thousand other problems. It was hell. By the end of the war, more planes were lost in PNG than in any other country in the world. So many soldiers died that even today, after heavy rains, skeletons float up in the swamps."

"Cool," Dylan said, leafing through the handwritten journal. At a glance, it was all about missions, weather, bad living conditions, and missing home. He handed the journal back to his uncle.

"No, keep it. I want you to read every word," Uncle Todd said. "That journal actually survived the crash and your grandfather's two weeks in the jungle. I am convinced that somewhere in those pages we can find enough clues to help us finally find the wreckage. That's where we're going for the summer. We're going to join three other searchers. Our group will try to find your grandfather's B-17 bomber. The plane's name was *Second Ace*."

Dylan shrugged. "What can be so hard about finding some plane? We'll just get in a jeep and drive around looking for it."

Uncle Todd laughed aloud. "Papua New Guinea has everything from jungles and swamps to fourteen-thousand-foot peaks. It has some of the most unforgiving real estate on the planet. During the war, there were crews that crashed three miles from the airport. It took them more than a week to hack their way through the jungle with machetes to safety — and they knew where they were going. In some parts of the jungle, you can't see wreckage fifty feet away."

Dylan slumped down in his seat and put on his headphones. "This is really a dumb idea," he said, shutting his eyes and turning up the volume. The music hadn't even started when the headphones were pulled from his ears. He opened his eyes to find his uncle staring at him intensely.

"Hey, what did you do that for?" Dylan demanded.

"You need to read the journal so you can be part of the team. Every member has an obligation to every other member to be as knowledgeable as possible. It may save a life."

"I don't care if we find some dumb bomber."

Uncle Todd handed the headphones back. "You don't care much about anything."

"Okay, I'll read the journal, but I can still listen to music while I'm reading."

Uncle Todd shook his head. "You won't need your headphones anymore. You use them to tune out the world, and this summer is all about discovering the world."

Dylan hesitated, tempted to defy his uncle.

"Put them away, or I'll put them away for you," Uncle Todd said plainly.

Reluctantly Dylan opened the small leather journal and began to read, feeling the stare of his Uncle Todd.

June 21, 1942

Arrived in Papua New Guinea at the Jackson Airstrip at 0900 this morning. Was greeted by the commander with these words: "Welcome, gentlemen. This island is plagued with malaria, dengue fever, diarrhea, dysentery, and every other tropical disease known to man. If you are shot down and survive, do not start a fire unless you want to be caught. Always save one extra round of ammunition for yourself if you are captured by either the Japanese, cannibals, or headhunters. None will let you live. Headhunters will cut off your head. The Japanese will torture you and then kill you. And cannibals, just like in the movies, will roast you over

A FIRE ON A POLE AND EAT YOU. YOU TASTE A LITTLE LIKE CHICKEN.

"AVOIDING THE ENEMY IS THE LEAST OF YOUR PROBLEMS. WE HAVE TWO KINDS OF WEATHER, BAD AND WORSE. THERE ARE PLENTY OF SNAKES AND LIZARDS OVER TEN FEET IN LENGTH. BUGS ARE EVERYWHERE, SOME THE SIZE OF SMALL BIRDS THAT SUCK BODY FLUIDS FROM YOU WHILE YOU SLEEP. IF YOU DIE IN THE JUNGLE, RATS WILL PICK YOUR BONES CLEAN WITHIN DAYS. DON'T THINK WAR IS GLORIOUS. IT AIN'T.

"IF YOU MAKE IT OUT OF THE JUNGLE TO A RIVER, MOST RIVERS ARE THICK WITH CROCODILES. ONCE YOU GET TO THE OCEAN, THE SHARKS ARE JUST AS THICK. WAR IS SERIOUS BUSINESS AND IS NOT FOR NICE PEOPLE. YOU WILL NOT HAVE SECOND CHANCES.

"NOW, GET YOUR TRENCHES DUG QUICKLY. THE ENEMY ALREADY KNOWS YOU'RE HERE AND WE WILL BE UNDER FULL ATTACK IN TWO HOURS. ENJOY YOUR STAY!"

Dylan turned to Uncle Todd. "Do they still have cannibals in this New Guinea place?"

Uncle Todd nodded. "Twenty-seven of them were arrested just last week." He smirked. "Kind of brings new meaning to 'having a friend for dinner.'" Still chuckling, he added, "This summer, our biggest problem will be all the bugs and insects." He motioned to the loading gate. "It's time for us to board."

When they were settled on the plane, Dylan caught his

uncle watching him. Reluctantly he picked up the journal again. The next entry was written three days after the first.

JUNE 24, 1942

THIS IS AN UGLY PLACE. THE FIRST NIGHT WE ARRIVED, I THOUGHT THE FULL TROPICAL MOON WAS PRETTY. NOW I'M CUSSING IT. FULL MOONS ARE WHEN THE ENEMY BOMBERS COME. ALREADY WE HAVE BEEN UNDER TWO BOMBING ATTACKS AND HAVE NOT FLOWN A SINGLE MISSION. LAST NIGHT I SAW MY FIRST CASUALTY, A YOUNG SERGEANT BLOWN IN HALF BY ONE OF THE BOMBS THAT DROPPED. I HELPED CARRY HIS LEGS TO THE GRAVE WE DUG.

THE GREASE MONKEYS ARE STILL WORKING ON OUR PLANES. MAINTENANCE IS A JOKE. THERE ARE NO HANGARS, TOOLS, OR SPARE PARTS. WE HAVE WHAT WE LANDED WITH. AS OF RIGHT NOW, WE ARE LOSING THE WAR HERE. IF WE FAIL TO STOP THE JAPANESE, THEY WILL TAKE OVER ALL OF NEW GUINEA AND THE NORTHERN HALF OF AUSTRALIA. THE ENEMY IS ONLY SIX MILES UP THE TRAIL FROM US. A SNIPER IS PROBABLY WATCHING ME WRITE THIS ENTRY. OUR SHIPS LOAD AND UNLOAD AT NIGHT, HIDING AT SEA DURING THE DAY. WAR IS TOUGH.

Dylan read several more entries before realizing that Uncle Todd was still watching him. "What are you staring at?" Dylan asked.

"I'm trying to figure out how somebody who has had

everything handed to him on a silver platter could ever think the world owes him anything."

"I don't think that," Dylan said.

Uncle Todd shrugged. "Something else must be getting under your skin, then," he said. "You have a chip on your shoulder as big as a log."

To escape Uncle Todd's icy stare, Dylan looked back down at the journal.

July 1, 1942

Still have not flown a mission. Every day we try to make ourselves busy helping the grease monkeys work on our bombers or digging our trenches deeper. I went through my survival kit yesterday and added a few things. I now have a pistol and plenty of ammunition, a sharp knife, gas mask, first-aid kit, mirror, mosquito netting, fish hooks, and some extra rations and water to store in the cockpit in case we crash-land. This place is unlike any I have ever seen.

There are no buildings here at Jackson Airstrip except a small tower that is being built. Everything is done in the open, rain or shine, day or night, seven days a week. We are now officially in the boondocks.

Dylan's eyes had grown heavy and his head fell forward as he drifted into a deep sleep. Somewhere in the distance he thought he heard drum beats. He dreamed he had wings and was flying toward the sound. The drumming grew louder as he spotted smoke drifting upward like a ribbon of white from the jungle. Gliding closer, Dylan could see that the smoke billowed from a big fire. Tied to a pole and being roasted over the fire like a hotdog on a stick was a white-skinned boy named Dylan Barstow.

Dylan wasn't sure he liked the taste of chicken anymore.

CHAPTER 3

There wasn't much to talk about as the Boeing 737 took off. This was only Dylan's second ride in an airplane. His first had been when he was eight and his dad was still alive. They flew to Florida. While other kids enjoyed Disney World, his father, Sam, dragged him through mangrove swamps in the everglades looking for rare birds and alligators. And when they did go to an amusement park, it had to be Epcot, the more adult part of Disney World. At least they got to ride the Mission: SPACE flight simulator. Dylan had loved it. His mom screamed the whole ride and almost got sick from the G-force.

Dylan sat by the window and stared out at the shore of Lake Michigan passing under the wing. He fingered the journal as he stared out the window. He didn't like reading about waking up with spiders, being attacked by the Japanese, and keeping the crew's morale up, but finally, out of boredom, he opened the small leather journal to read more.

JULY 8, 1942

TODAY WE FLEW OUR FIRST MISSION. THE LANDING STRIP HERE AT JACKSON AIRSTRIP IS SCARY. IT'S LIKE LANDING AND

TAKING OFF FROM A POSTAGE STAMP. NOT A GOOD PLACE FOR AN OVERLOADED BOMBER WITH A FULL CREW. WE FLEW A BOMBING MISSION OVER LAE LOOKING FOR SHIPS AND ANTI-AIRCRAFT ARTILLERY SITES. WE BRIEFED OUR MISSION FOR 26,000 FEET WITH THREE OTHER B-17s. I THOUGHT THE HIGH-ALTITUDE COLD WOULD BE WELCOME, BUT IT WAS BITTER. MY OXYGEN MASK KEPT FREEZING UP. I FINALLY SWITCHED TO A PORTABLE FOR TEN MINUTES AFTER THE BOMB DROP. TWO JAPANESE ZEROS MADE A RUN ON US BUT WE HAD THE ADVANTAGE OF ALTITUDE AND THE SUN AT OUR BACKS. MY BALL TURRET GUNNER CLAIMED HE SAW SMOKE FROM ONE OF THE ZEROS BEFORE THEY TURNED TAIL TO RUN. SECOND ACE AND THE OTHER B-17s RETURNED WITHOUT DAMAGE. THINK WE KNOCKED OUT ONE OF THE AAA GUN SITES.

I UNDERSTAND NOW WHY THEY SAY, "NEVER PASS UP A MEAL, BECAUSE YOU DON'T KNOW WHEN OR IF THERE WILL BE A NEXT ONE."

Reading the journal made Dylan think about his dad. Had Dad ever written a journal like this? Mom showed him the one letter, but surely there were others. Suddenly Dylan wanted to know more about his father. What had it been like in Darfur? Dylan clenched his fists. If he was still in Wisconsin, he could have asked Mom about it. That was where he should be right now. Not stuck on some airplane with his uncle, flying to Oregon. What else would Uncle Todd think of to make life more miserable than it already was?

"Stupid," Dylan whispered under his breath, as Lake Michigan drifted away behind the wing.

They changed planes in Minneapolis and flew on to Portland. Uncle Todd had his car parked at the airport. Dylan hadn't known that his uncle drove a red Corvette. It was an antique 1962 Vette with the old-style rounded headlights and Stingray back. It had a hardtop that could come off in good weather. Dylan tried not to show his excitement.

Uncle Todd caught Dylan staring and smiled. "Back in high school, you could buy one of these in cherry condition for less than two thousand dollars," he said.

"How much do they cost now?" Dylan asked.

"I've seen them for way over fifty thousand."

"Must be nice having money," Dylan said.

"I'm surprised I still have a butt," Uncle Todd said.

"What do you mean?"

"I worked my butt off earning every penny I ever had. That's what makes it so great now. People who have things given to them never appreciate it." When Dylan didn't answer, Uncle Todd spoke again. "We won't be leaving for almost two weeks. Maybe you can drive this thing before we leave."

"No way — I don't have a license."

Uncle Todd grinned. "That didn't stop you before."

Dylan chuckled.

"I know where there's an abandoned parking lot south of here. That would be a good place."

"So how come you agreed to take me for the summer?" Dylan asked.

"Your dad, Sam, was my brother — it's what he would have wanted." Uncle Todd paused. "And I agree with your mom."

"Agree with what?"

"That you're a good person inside, if you ever take the time to find that person. Right now he's buried under a pile of anger. You're trying to prove something to yourself, and I haven't quite figured out yet what you're trying to prove."

"I'm not trying to prove anything," Dylan snapped. He hated being analyzed.

"Yes, you are. Just because Dylan Barstow says something with his mouth doesn't mean tiddly-dink as far as the truth. You should know that by now."

Dylan bit his tongue. His uncle was always so sure of himself. He had his own front he was keeping up for some reason. Why did he still live all alone and act like a drill sergeant?

They drove the rest of the way in silence. When Uncle Todd pulled up to his condo in Gresham, a town east of Portland, he revved the engine, then turned the key to OFF.

"Welcome to my world," he said. "We get a lot of rain here. Today it's sunny, so let's make use of it. Grab your stuff and I'll show you where your room is. Then we're going running."

"That's all right," Dylan said. "I don't like to run."

"Excuse me, did I say, 'Can we run?' Did I say, 'Would you like to take a little jog, Your Royal Highness?' Maybe we need to get something straight right up front. The reason you're here is because you've been making bad choices. This summer I make the choices. Is there anything about that program that you don't understand?" When Dylan didn't answer, Uncle Todd added, "Let's get you settled and then I'll meet you down here for a run in thirty minutes." Without waiting for an answer, Uncle Todd headed into the house, not even offering to carry Dylan's heavy suitcase.

━━━

The run turned out to be more than a jog. They ran five miles, as if it were the Boston Marathon. "Why do we have to run so fast?" Dylan complained, struggling to keep up.

"Because if we wanted to go slow, we'd have brought wheelchairs. I'm almost sixty years old. What are you — a fossil?"

Dylan didn't like being called a fossil. He ran out ahead of Uncle Todd until they returned home, where he collapsed on the grass. "Why do we have to go running?" Dylan gasped, breathing hard.

"When we get to Papua New Guinea, we'll be doing some serious hiking. We won't have time to get into shape then. You'll be thanking me for this when we get there. We have exactly two weeks to get you as strong as we can."

They headed inside and Dylan flopped onto the couch. He wouldn't be thanking Uncle Todd for anything. He was still trying to figure out how to get out of even going to this dumb PNG place. He had yet to figure out any plan. Just being here with Uncle Todd was Dylan's worst nightmare — his summer from hell!

"Go shower and get cleaned up. We're going out for pizza," Uncle Todd ordered.

"I'm not hungry," Dylan said.

"And I'm not a giraffe. But we're still going out for pizza. So, HOP! HOP!" Uncle Todd clapped his hands for emphasis.

Dylan wanted to scream as he shuffled slowly up the steps to his room.

———

He would never have admitted it to his uncle, but Dylan felt good for having run five miles, and he slept like a baby that night. He could have slept another five hours when he heard the dreaded "Wakee wakee wakee!" at six the next morning.

"We don't have any plane to catch," Dylan pleaded.

"No, but there is a new day out there waiting for us to get our butts out of bed. It's already light out. If you beat me this morning, I'll take you to Perkins for breakfast. I beat you, we come back here for some of my cooking. I suggest you try and beat me."

In ten minutes, they were running down the empty street.

"Let's jog to warm up," Uncle Todd said, "and then we'll see how fast Dylan Barstow can really run. Yesterday I took it easy on you."

Before they reached the end of the block, Uncle Todd reached over and nudged Dylan's arm. "Same route as yesterday, down around the park and then home." He shouted "Go!" and quickened his pace.

There was no way Dylan was going to let this arrogant old man beat him in a footrace. It didn't matter that he was a human bulldog. Knowing how he felt yesterday, running all out, Dylan paced himself, not even trying to get ahead of Uncle Todd. He could pass him anytime he wanted, but for now, let the old geezer think he was winning.

Soon they had rounded the park and were headed home. Dylan still hung back, waiting until he knew he could sprint to the finish. But as they neared home, Dylan realized he wouldn't be sprinting anywhere. Just keeping up with Uncle Todd had become a struggle. By the time they were a block from home, Dylan's legs felt like rubber. Still, he ran faster. Each pounding step felt like it was his last. At half a block he was even with his uncle. A hundred yards away, he was still even. Fifty feet away, they were running down the middle of the street. He closed his eyes and willed himself to run harder than he had ever run in his life. When he opened his eyes to angle up the drive, he was only inches ahead of Uncle Todd, but he was ahead!

Pumping his arms in the air, he collapsed on the grass. "I'm going to eat a whole cow at Perkins," Dylan panted.

Uncle Todd smiled, gasping for air himself. He bent at the waist, hands on his knees, as he struggled to catch his breath. "Now that's the Dylan I like and the Dylan I remember," he exclaimed. He caught several more breaths, and then continued. "You ran smart, pacing yourself. I thought you would run like a bonehead and try to be ahead of me from the beginning, but you didn't. And at the end, you had willpower. A lot of kids don't. You made me proud, and now you don't have to eat my cooking. You lucky stiff!"

For the moment, Dylan forgot his situation and grinned. He had just beaten Uncle Todd in an all-out footrace. He even got a compliment out of the old fart. His uncle extended his hand to help him up, and Dylan allowed himself to be pulled to his feet.

——

Sitting in Perkins waiting for their orders, Uncle Todd folded his cloth napkin back and forth. "By the way," he said. "If you want to call your mother, feel free any time."

"Why would I want to call her?" Dylan said. "She's the one that got me into this mess."

"No, you're the one that got you into this mess. Don't blame her."

"Whatever," Dylan said.

" 'Whatever' — you know what that means, don't you?"

"What?"

"That's code for 'screw you.' You're telling me my words aren't important."

"Is there anything I can do that isn't wrong?"

"It's not what you do, it's why you do it," Uncle Todd said. After a pause, he continued. "Look, you can live, dress, talk, do anything you want, if it's to be different. If you want to stand out, be comfortable, be noticed, be stylish, I'm okay with that. But from what I've seen, you don't blow your nose without attitude. Escaping with your headset, wearing your pants low, saying 'whatever' — you do all of those things to thumb your nose at people and be disrespectful.

"I dress and act a lot different than you, but nothing I say or do is meant to be disrespectful of you. I expect the same respect back. Maybe you got away treating your mom without respect. Now you're on a different planet."

"I don't do those things to be disrespectful," Dylan argued.

Uncle Todd shook his head and snickered.

"What's so funny?" Dylan asked.

"You," Uncle Todd said. "You think because your mouth says something, the whole world believes you. You're so angry that everything you do is to show your contempt. Treat me that way and we have a problem. Understand?" When Dylan didn't answer, Uncle Todd raised his voice and said,

"Do the respectful thing and answer my question. Do we understand each other?"

People in other booths were now staring over at them. Knowing there would be no escaping Uncle Todd, Dylan nodded. He wanted to say, "Whatever," but instead mumbled, "Yes."

CHAPTER 4

Each day with Uncle Todd became a bigger challenge. At home there had been a thousand ways that Dylan could get away with doing as he pleased. Here, he lived under a microscope. Every move, every word, every twitch of his muscles was analyzed. Dylan felt like a lab rat. And every morning they ran, even in the rain. Dylan made sure he beat Uncle Todd running. That was the single thing that brought him any satisfaction. But finally, even that lost its appeal.

One morning, a week after arriving in Oregon, Uncle Todd shouted "Go!" and sped up. Dylan didn't respond. Instead he kept trotting along slowly at the pace they had warmed up at. Uncle Todd looked back but then kept running. Dylan hadn't even reached the park when his uncle passed him, returning to the house. "See you at the house," he called. "I'm cooking this morning."

"Whatever," Dylan muttered. This was stupid, running in the rain.

———

By the time Dylan returned home, Uncle Todd had breakfast fixed. "Let's eat before we shower," he said. "Breakfast is ready."

Dylan slumped into a chair at the table, actually hungry.

"Here," Uncle Todd said, placing burned toast and a bowl of mystery mush in front of him. The mush was some kind of white slop that looked like oatmeal but was more grainy. "What is this?" Dylan asked.

"Those are grits," Uncle Todd announced proudly. "My favorite breakfast."

Dylan knew better than to refuse the meal, but he had to swallow each bite quickly to keep from puking. If this was someone's favorite breakfast, they were some kind of sick. Finally, swallowing the last gross mouthful of mush, Dylan stood. "I'm going up to shower."

"You can shower after telling me you appreciated me making breakfast, and after taking this." Uncle Todd handed Dylan another malaria pill.

Dylan lost it. "But I didn't like the breakfast," he snapped. "It tasted like crap!"

"Then say thank you out of respect. You don't have to like something to be respectful."

Feeling cornered, Dylan finally mumbled, "Thanks."

"Good," Uncle Todd said. "After we clean up, let's go drive the Corvette. If you're still up to it."

Dylan hid his excitement. "That would be okay," he said, shrugging. "Won't it be better if it's not raining?"

Uncle Todd shook his head. "With what we're doing this morning, rain is actually better for learning."

Bounding up the stairs, Dylan pumped his fists with excitement. He was getting to drive his first Corvette. Before showering, he flushed the malaria pill down the toilet.

As they drove back toward Portland, Uncle Todd explained their plan. "The place where we're going is a huge parking lot by a factory that has been closed down. Our car club has permission to go there. We'll use pylons to practice maneuvering. Ever heard of drifting?"

"As in like a snowdrift?"

"No, as in like controlled power sliding with a car."

Dylan shook his head.

Soon they pulled off the main highway and drove through an industrial subdivision for another mile. Finally they pulled up to a locked gate. Uncle Todd crawled from the red Corvette and unlocked the door.

"Is this legal?" Dylan ventured as Uncle Todd crawled back behind the wheel.

Uncle Todd nodded. "You don't mind doing something if it's legal, do you?"

"Just wondering."

Soon they circled behind a big building with almost a quarter mile of loading docks. Except for a few phone poles, the parking lot was a huge open expanse of concrete. Already highway cones marked a large course. "Okay, let me show you what we're going to do," Uncle Todd said. "Start out slow and then go faster."

"I'm not afraid to go fast," Dylan said.

"You should be — that's how people kill themselves," Uncle Todd said, downshifting. "There's no fools in this car, unless you know of one. First let me show you what happens if we do things wrong."

Uncle Todd sped up and headed out onto the small track created by the plastic pylons. As he steered into the first corner, Dylan knew they were going too fast to make the corner, especially on wet pavement. "You're going too fast," he said loudly.

As they entered the corner, the car spun out. The Corvette left the course, sliding backward until it came to a slow stop.

"I knew we were going too fast," Dylan bragged.

"We were going exactly thirty miles per hour — too fast for someone who doesn't know their butt from a banana. Now watch this." Uncle Todd shifted and drove around until he approached the corner again. "We're going thirty miles per hour again," he commented.

"And we're still going too fast," Dylan said.

"You would sure think so, wouldn't you?" Uncle Todd answered smugly.

Just as they entered the corner, Uncle Todd shifted down hard and hit the gas pedal as if to speed up. Was he crazy? The car began sliding, but this time Uncle Todd steered sharply in the opposite direction, away from the turn. As if held by a huge hand, the car drifted magically around the corner, turning at a sideways angle almost the whole way.

"This is drifting," Uncle Todd said. "A Corvette isn't the ideal car to use, but it's okay because it has rear-wheel drive. Racers use this technique all the time so they don't have to slow down for a corner."

"Can I try it?" Dylan exclaimed.

Uncle Todd nodded. "First I want you to practice a few things. We'll start by cutting donuts — you have experience with that."

"That's easy," Dylan said.

"We'll see," Uncle Todd said. "The night you broke into the junkyard, I'll bet this is how you cut your donuts." Uncle Todd floored the gas pedal and cranked the steering wheel to the left. Soon the car spun its tires on the wet pavement and rotated around in circles as if the front bumper was glued to a post. Uncle Todd leaned casually against the door and looked over at Dylan. As the Corvette continued to whip in circles, Uncle Todd said, "See, this is simple. Any knuckle-head can get a car to do this." He winked. "Even in a plowed field. But now let's make the donut bigger."

Instead of keeping the steering wheel cranked left into the turn, Uncle Todd turned the wheel to the right and let up slightly on the gas pedal. Slowly the car quit spinning around its front bumper and started to drift forward. "Okay, I'm going to keep the steering wheel just like this to the right, but

I'm going to control my drift and the size of our circle with only the gas pedal. Watch."

Dylan stared in amazement as the Corvette drifted in a bigger and bigger circle.

"Okay, I'm letting off on the power even more. Watch this." The car drifted into a bigger circle, but still to the left, nearly sideways. The steering wheel was cranked in the opposite direction. As if sitting comfortably in a lounge chair, Uncle Todd spoke casually. "I control everything with power, shifting, and steering. It's a fine balance that takes years of practice and skill. It's easier on wet pavement because you don't have to use as much power or speed. It doesn't wear the tires as much, and it's easier to practice. Are you ready to try?"

All of a sudden, Dylan wasn't so sure of himself. This wasn't as easy as he had thought. What if he screwed it up? What if he flipped the car? This was no longer a reckless joyride in a junked car. Swallowing his apprehension, Dylan traded seats and pulled his seat belt tight. "Okay, what do I do first?" he asked, his voice shaking.

"Get rid of your pride. Inside this car, no one is trying to show off, be cool, or prove anything. All you're doing today is learning. Drive around some, changing your speed and going through the gears to get used to the power. This isn't a junkyard now."

"Do you have to keep reminding me about that?" Dylan said.

"I hope you never forget. Now get used to the car."

Dylan obeyed. After a few minutes driving around and testing the controls and shift, he felt comfortable.

"Okay, now shift into first and go about ten miles per hour."

When Dylan was ready, Uncle Todd said, "Now crank the steering wheel all the way to the left and keep adding power until you're spinning donuts."

Dylan felt a huge lump in his throat. This car was no wreck from a junkyard. He was driving a fifty-thousand-dollar classic Corvette. If he wrecked this thing, it would really prove that he was a big screw-up. Carefully he cranked the wheel until the car began spinning in circles to the left.

"Add some power," Uncle Todd reminded him.

As Dylan added power, the car spun faster and faster, its front end holding to the inside.

"Okay, now crank your wheels all the way to the right. If you start to straighten out, don't let off the gas. Add power!"

Dylan sucked in a deep breath and cranked the wheel right. This went against everything his brain told him. You didn't add power and steer to the right to make bigger circles to the left. But that was exactly what he was doing, and as if by magic, the red Corvette started carving larger circles to the left on the wet pavement.

"Your power is overriding your steering," Uncle Todd said calmly, his voice as casual as if he were explaining where the milk was in the refrigerator. "Keep it just like this until you feel comfortable with what's happening."

After the car had made five or six big circles, Uncle Todd said, "Okay, now back off a little on the power and make an even bigger circle. If you have to, steer a little to keep from spinning or going straight."

Dylan obeyed, and soon found himself struggling to keep the high-powered Corvette under control.

"Okay, make the circle tighter again," Uncle Todd said.

Scrambling to think, Dylan slowly pushed on the gas pedal and felt the car start to drift more. He purposely oversteered as the car slowed and slid nearly sideways into a tighter turn.

"This is awesome!" Dylan exclaimed.

After half an hour of practicing, Dylan felt like he had run a marathon. Sweat dripped from every pore of his body, and his arm muscles cramped. This was way harder than spinning donuts in some farmer's field.

Finally, Uncle Todd said, "Okay, that's enough for today. Tomorrow, we'll practice this some more, and maybe practice entering a drift going faster."

Dylan was thankful the day's practice had ended. This hadn't been as easy as he had expected. Driving a powerful car this way was super hard. His body trembled as he stopped the Vette and let Uncle Todd back in the driver's seat.

"Thanks," he said.

"You did a good job," Uncle Todd said. "A few more years of practice and we'll have you driving sprint cars on some dirt track."

"Maybe I should stick to farmers' fields," Dylan said.

"I was hoping to get you away from that," Uncle Todd said, grinning. "Let's go get us some cheeseburgers."

As they drove off the big lot and out of the industrial complex, Dylan struggled with his feelings. On one hand he was still mad at his mom and Uncle Todd and at the stupid world. On the other hand, he wished all of the boys at school back home could have seen screw-up Dylan Barstow today drifting an expensive Corvette.

CHAPTER 5

The next morning, running in pouring rain, Dylan made sure to beat his uncle — he didn't ever want to eat burned toast and grits again. As they finished breakfast at Perkins, Uncle Todd informed Dylan, "I have someplace I want to take you today. We're driving up to Vancouver."

"What for?" Dylan asked.

"You'll see."

Uncle Todd's surprises made Dylan nervous. With the rain still heavy, they drove the Corvette north from Portland. Even when they pulled into a nursing home called Garden Acres, Dylan still didn't know what was happening.

"There's somebody I want you to meet. His name is Frank Bower. Frank flew twenty-five missions during the war."

"I've skipped school more times than that," Dylan bragged.

Uncle Todd gave Dylan one of his "you just said something stupid" looks. "During the war, the average number of missions flown before you were killed was seven," Uncle Todd said.

"Seven?" Dylan said. "That's suicide!"

Uncle Todd nodded. "Thousands of young men risked their lives so you and I could live as free people. Their regular missions were bad, and their bad missions were hell. Not many survived. Because of that, there aren't many of these old guys still living. I called up Frank and asked him if he would tell you about some of his missions, and he agreed. He was a waist gunner on a B-17 in Europe during the Second World War. Waist gunners shot machine guns out the sides of bombers at attacking fighters."

Dylan didn't really want to go hear some old guy talk about being in the war, but he knew he had no choice. He shrugged and almost said, "Whatever," but then bit his tongue and said nothing. Reluctantly he followed Uncle Todd into a nursing home filled with old people sitting in wheelchairs. Some wandered about with long-distance stares like zombies.

"This place freaks me out," Dylan mumbled.

"Someday we'll all be this age," Uncle Todd said. "Native Americans revered elders instead of throwing them away. Every person here has a story to tell. If you knew their past, you would want to talk to every one of them."

"Doubt that," Dylan said as he followed Uncle Todd.

Nobody was at the receptionist's desk, so they walked down the hallway to the nurses' station. A red-haired nurse greeted them and pointed them to the lounge, where they found an old man with a blue flannel shirt sitting near a window, staring out.

"Frank, how you doing?" Uncle Todd said loudly, announcing their arrival.

The old man turned his head and smiled. "I'm still breathing, if that tells you anything."

Dylan glanced around. He really didn't like being here. The old people made him feel like he was in some nuthouse. The smell in the air was like somebody had sprayed perfume in a bathroom after a bad fart.

Uncle Todd pulled up two chairs. "This is my nephew, Dylan. He's going with me to Papua New Guinea to help me look for that B-17, *Second Ace*, the one I told you about. I thought it would be great for him to hear right from the horse's mouth what it was like being a waist gunner during the war."

"You'll have to forgive me if sometimes I have a short circuit between my ears," Frank Bower said. The thin, silver-haired man laughed aloud at his wit, then explained. "I can tell you how many cows my dad milked during the blizzard of 1932, but sometimes I can't even remember my middle name. Time and war have scrambled my brain. I'll remember what I can. Did your uncle tell you I flew twenty-five missions?"

Dylan nodded. "He said most crews only lived through seven."

The old man nodded. "You already know more than most people. If you flew twenty-five missions, you got to go home. We called it the 'Lucky Bastards' Club.' Every crew member wanted to join that club, but most weren't lucky enough bastards." Again Frank laughed, then looked down at his lap. He twisted at his shirt with gnarly hands. His fingers had big knuckles. "You ever smelled death?" he asked Dylan, looking up suddenly.

Dylan really didn't like sitting here being questioned by this old codger, but the man's riveting glare couldn't be avoided. "Y-you mean like a dead cat?" Dylan stammered.

"I mean like your best friend drowning in his own blood as you hold him in your arms."

Dylan scuffed his shoes on the floor and looked out the window to avoid the old guy's stare.

"Most of my missions were in a B-17 called *Miss Audrey.* On my third mission over Germany, my ball turret gunner, Jamie, took a twenty-millimeter round through the stomach. It didn't kill him right away. His beating heart kept him conscious for about ten minutes, the longest ten minutes of my life. Bled all over everything.

"They could never wash away the blood, and I didn't like flying in *Miss Audrey* after that, 'cause she always had the smell of death. This wasn't a Hollywood movie. When you died, you really died." Frank stared out the window as if remembering, but then shook his head. "Uh, where was I?"

"You were talking about your crew members," Uncle Todd said.

"Yeah, well, our crew, we were a family. I still remember the boys like brothers. Big Sam, the pilot. Andy, the copilot.

Billy, the navigator. The bombardier, a farm boy called Luther. Mosley, the tail gunner. I was a waist gunner. The other waist gunner was Max. After Jamie died, we got another ball turret gunner. We called him Shorty, 'cause he was small enough to fit down in the ball turret. The top turret gunner was Sonny. Luke was the radio operator."

"Did you ever want to be a pilot?" Uncle Todd asked.

Frank shook his head. "If I'm going duck hunting, I don't want to row the boat." Frank laughed and coughed at his own joke. "What else do you want to know?"

"If it was so dangerous, why did you join the air force?" Dylan asked, his voice accusing.

"I guess I joined because I was patriotic, and at the beginning it was this great adventure, being flown across the Atlantic Ocean. We were stationed in England and drank warm beer in pubs with guys who talked with funny accents. We ate weird foods and drove on the wrong side of the road in fog as thick as soup. But the main reason we were there was to stop a madman called Hitler from taking over the world. After that mission when Jamie died in my arms, it wasn't patriotism anymore. It was revenge, and we were just trying to stay alive." Frank shifted in his wheelchair. "Let me explain something. I was twenty-two years old when I enlisted. Most of the boys were just kids, barely eighteen years old. But if you survived the war, you returned as a man who had been to hell and back."

When Frank quit talking again, Uncle Todd asked, "Did you know the other crews?"

"We didn't hang out much with the other crews, because your drinking buddy today would probably be the body bag you helped unload tomorrow. And the Japanese and Germans weren't our only enemies. The wretched weather killed a lot of us."

"Was that your worst mission, when Jamie got killed?" Uncle Todd asked.

Frank shook his head. "My worst mission was my last mission."

"Did you ever get hurt?" Dylan ventured.

"Sure did. But not as bad as Sonny and Mosley."

"What happened?"

"You don't want to hear that story."

"We do," Uncle Todd insisted.

Frank turned to Dylan. "You want to hear that story, too, kid?"

Dylan didn't like being called "kid," but he managed a nod. "I guess."

Frank took a deep breath, as if to prepare himself for something very difficult. "Like I said, my mind ain't so good anymore, but some things you never forget. Cold dark mornings getting up before a mission, looking back into the barracks wondering how many bunks would be empty by nightfall. Breakfast. Suiting up. Briefings. Jeep rides down the flight line to the bomber. The rumble of takeoff. Seeing hundreds of planes, all in formation. The shaking of the bomber as our fifty-caliber machine guns fought off fighters. Anti-aircraft flak thudding around us, thicker than fireworks at a Fourth of July party. The 'bombs away' call over the intercom. The quiet flight home wondering how many crews had died that day. The shot of whiskey the brass always gave us during debriefing to calm our nerves — I can tell you it was never enough to wash away the hurt of missing crews. Then we had to get ready for the next day's mission." Frank turned and stared out the window. "Yup, it was rough," he mumbled.

After several minutes, Uncle Todd prodded some. "What happened on that last mission?"

Frank shook his head as if clearing away cobwebs. "Well, the morning of that last mission, we were grounded for three hours by rain and fog that had the ducks walking. I had a bad feeling. We were flying with the Eighth Air Force out of England. We took off with almost three thousand gallons of gas, six thousand pounds of bombs, fully loaded with ammunition and all of our crew and equipment. We used the whole runway.

"Our wing of fifty-four bombers joined up with hundreds of others. We flew upper formation in the number two position at around twenty-eight thousand feet. Because our mission was to bomb the ball bearing factory in Schweinfurt, everybody wore their flak vests. It was one of those days — a day for flak vests, prayers, and good luck charms. Not sure any of them helped much."

"Flak was the name used for the exploding shells fired by the German anti-aircraft guns," Uncle Todd explained to Dylan.

"The Schweinfurt factory made bearings for Hitler's war machines," Frank continued. "His tanks, cannons, planes, you name it. The German Air Force, the Luftwaffe, knew we were coming that day and threw every fighter plane they had at us. Our own fighter planes kept us company partway. We called them our 'little friends.'" Frank paused. "You don't want to hear the rest," he said, his voice almost pleading.

Uncle Todd reached over and squeezed Frank's shoulder. "Only if you don't want to tell us."

Frank bunched his lips and swallowed hard. "What the hell," he said. "We crossed Belgium and had almost reached the German border when our 'little friends' waggled their wings to tell us they were running low on fuel and had to leave us. They had just left when the German Luftwaffe fighters jumped us. I heard the top turret gunner, Sonny, scream, 'Bandits ten o'clock high,' then 'thud, thud, thud, thud.'" Frank pounded his fist against his wheelchair. "Our plane lurched like a big boot had kicked us, then everybody on *Miss Audrey* started protecting their side of the plane. With all of the fifty-caliber machine guns firing, you never heard such noise. Some nights when there's thunder, I can still feel *Miss Audrey* shaking.

"For the next hour they hammered us, attacking from every direction. Parachutes floated everywhere, but we all fought well that day, never backing down. We didn't panic like in the movies. That was Hollywood. We all knew our jobs and we did our jobs well. I'm talking to you today because we did. We looked death in the face and handed the Germans some of their own medicine. There were many enemy pilots that day who died wishing they had left us alone. Everywhere I looked there were flames and exploding planes. I saw bodies and pieces of airplane falling like rain. God, it was bad!" Again Frank quit talking.

"What happened next?" Uncle Todd asked softly, as if taking a confession.

"A twenty-millimeter shell exploded near me and it felt like a baseball bat hitting my leg. Another shell hit the oxygen and messed up some control cables. I thought we had been lucky until another shell came through the upper turret position and exploded. Killed Sonny. Never even knew what hit him. The tail gunner, Mosley, also got hit and bled all over everything. The navigator, Billy, had flak crease his arm — not badly, but it got blood all over his charts. Big Sam took a bullet in his shoulder but he wouldn't quit flying. For forty-five minutes we lived in a madhouse of machine guns and explosions. I was up to my butt in empty shell casings, and we were getting hit hard." Frank paused. "You know, I didn't start out being much of a waist gunner — could barely hit the side of a barn with a stone. But when somebody shoots at you, your aim gets better really fast." He laughed, but the laugh was shallow.

"What happened next?" Uncle Todd asked.

"About five minutes before we dropped our bombs, we took some flak that knocked out one of our engines and blew a hole in the side of our plane. Now we had a new enemy. That high in the air it was minus forty degrees outside, and our plane wasn't pressurized. I felt a sting to my chest and looked down. Something had cut the front of my flight jacket open like a knife. Then I felt wet, like I had peed my pants. When I reached in to feel, my hand came out bloody.

"Didn't know how bad I was hurt because I was too busy firing my machine gun and taking care of everybody else. I do remember it hurt to breathe and my dumb right leg flopped around as I hopped back and forth. I must have been in some kind of shock because I don't remember much pain at the time. Finally we heard the beautiful words 'Bombs away,' and we headed for home. I tried to look down, but the black exploding flak was so thick, you could walk on it. I heard later the bombing run was a success. Parts of that ball bearing factory looked like a moonscape.

"By this time, another engine had been hit. With two engines out, a hole in the side of the plane, and the oxygen supply leaking, we had to leave the formation and descend. We were on our own. Our pilot, Sam, ordered us to jettison the ball turret that weighed half a ton. We needed the plane as light as possible to ever make it home.

"Sam called on the intercom for everybody to check in. That was when he found out that Sonny had cashed in his chips. He also found out that Mosley and Billy had been hit, but for some reason I didn't tell him I had taken flak, too. Maybe it was because he had getting home to worry about. I wasn't bleeding out. I hopped around on my one good leg, and with some help from Max, the other waist gunner, we got Sonny pulled out of his turret. I popped open his seat parachute and covered him up on the floor. He was sure a mess to look at." Frank grimaced as if in pain.

"Are you okay?" Uncle Todd asked.

Frank's eyes had become wet. "The only thing that saved us that day was the weather. With two engines out, we fell behind our formation and we were sitting ducks. We flew through every cloud we could find, cloud hopping all the way back across France, and finally the enemy fighters quit chasing us somewhere over Belgium. It was easy to find our way home that day; we just followed the trail of burning B-17s and fighters lying on the ground.

"We were barely holding altitude across the English Channel, plowing along at two thousand feet. We jettisoned our ammunition and anything else to lighten the load. We all had parachutes, but if we went down in the channel, we would die. The water would freeze us to death in half an hour. Lucky for us, none of us had to hit the silk that day."

Uncle Todd nudged Dylan and whispered, "That means using their parachutes."

Frank kept talking. "By now, Sam had radioed ahead that we had dead and wounded aboard. At the field, they shot up a red flare to tell the ground crews our bomber needed an ambulance. That day, they shot up a mess of other flares, too.

"We came in low over the trees, smoke pouring from the engines. The bump of the landing felt like more flak exploding. *Miss Audrey* rolled to a stop, smoldering. I rushed to help medics get Mosley and Billy out. Then I helped put Sonny in a body bag to remove him. I got to feeling woozy from losing blood myself, but I made sure I was the last one to crawl out that day. Before I got out, I sat down and cried. I didn't want the rest of the crew to see me cry. I was the 'old man' 'cause I was twenty-two years old, and I had to be strong for everyone else. I knew that day I was going to heaven."

"Why was that?" Uncle Todd asked.

" 'Cause I'd just made it back from hell." Frank coughed hard. "That was *Miss Audrey*'s last mission, too. She had more than three hundred bullet holes, two engines had taken direct hits and lost their oil pressure, and half of her tail was blown off. That sweet girl gave us all she had. After that she was salvaged for parts. But to those of us who made it back alive, she will always be the gallant lady that took us to the Promised Land. Home!

"That day we lost sixty bombers and over five hundred men. One of the saddest things I ever saw was the ground crews who stayed until after dark waiting for their crews to come home. The lonely ride back to their barracks when their planes and crews didn't come back, that broke my heart."

"I hope they gave you medals," Dylan blurted.

"I received two air medals of valor and some other tin during the war. But the best souvenir I have from the war is my Purple Heart — and these." Frank lifted his shirt to show a scar running the width of his chest. Then he bent forward and lifted his pant leg to show a twisted knee, distorted from operations. "I got these five hours before joining the Lucky Bastards' Club. Thought I had cheated the devil. Wasn't I lucky!"

Suddenly Frank broke down into tears. As he sobbed, he was trying to hum a tune.

"Frank, are you okay?" Uncle Todd asked.

Frank coughed hard into his fist, then kept humming, forcing out the tune until he finished. Then he looked over at Uncle Todd. "I'm fine," he said, his voice breaking, "That tune is part of the Air Corps' song. The words are 'We live in fame or we go down in flame.' "

Uncle Todd stood and placed a hand on Frank's shoulder. "You're a hero," he said. "A real hero."

Frank looked up, swiping at his wet eyes with the back of his bony hand. "It's all gone now," he said, his voice breaking. "It's all gone, and soon I'll be gone. The whole battle will be forgotten because there aren't battlefields to visit in the sky. No foxholes six miles up. You can't walk up a hill and say, 'Here is where Frank Bower fought.' The only people who looked up and saw the battle that day saw only para-chutes, explosions, smoke, and flaming planes. The machine guns, the flashes in the sky, the roaring engines, all of it's gone. It's quiet now. The rain washed the sky clean. People forget." Frank rubbed his eyes again. "I wish I could forget."

Then Frank turned and looked out the window, his eyes staring at another place in the universe, his thoughts as far away as the stars.

Dylan shifted uncomfortably in his chair. He wanted to leave. Uncle Todd stood and squeezed Frank's shoulder. "Take good care of yourself," he whispered.

As Dylan and Uncle Todd left the room, they heard Frank grunt loudly. They turned and found him with his arm raised to wave good-bye. "I was one of the lucky ones," Frank called.

CHAPTER 6

Because Dylan had no passport, Uncle Todd submitted an express application. While they waited, there were more shots and pills to take. Dylan couldn't avoid the shots, but whenever he could, he spit the pills into the toilet and flushed them. The pills still made him nervous, and when the doctor asked Dylan if he'd been experiencing any side effects, like nausea, vomiting, or diarrhea, he knew he'd made the right choice dumping them. He still had no intention of going to Papua New Guinea. It didn't make sense, going to some jungle on the other side of the planet to look for a bomber that probably didn't exist, searching for dead people who were skeletons by now. Dylan secretly hoped his passport wouldn't arrive on time.

His feelings became confused. Half of the time he hated Uncle Todd. But then there were afternoons when the Corvette was starting to drift at forty miles per hour and he could keep the car under perfect control by playing with the gas pedal or tweaking the steering wheel. At those times he caught his uncle's proud glances.

And he would never admit it, but sometimes he wished he was back with his mom. He still blamed her for sending him out to this place, but her cooking was sure better than Uncle Todd's. And talking to Uncle Todd was like trying to move a brick wall. Reluctantly Dylan admitted to himself that he shouldn't have pushed his mom so much. But it wasn't as if he had killed someone.

———

"We're leaving for PNG on Friday," Uncle Todd announced on a Monday morning after their run. He held up Dylan's blue passport. "And guess what arrived in the mail."

"Great," Dylan mumbled. He scrambled to think. How could he get out of going to this PNG place? Maybe running away would be best. Anything would be better than going with Uncle Todd over to some jungle.

"Have you finished reading Grandpa's journal?" Uncle Todd asked.

Dylan shook his head. He hadn't read a word since getting off the plane.

"You need to finish that before we get over to PNG," he said. "We only have this week to get ready. Once we get into the jungles, there won't be supermarkets or sporting goods stores. We'll be joining the other members of our search team in Port Moresby, the capital of Papua New Guinea, and then going into some of the most remote real estate on the planet. Nothing there is a joke. Be stupid and the place will kill you."

Uncle Todd wasn't one to lie, but with the cannibals and everything, Dylan wondered if he wasn't exaggerating as part of his "scare Dylan straight" rehab program.

He played along, packing everything on the list. But he also stashed away some candy bars and his headphones. A month was too long to go without music.

"Make sure you seal your hiking boots with this oil," Uncle Todd said, handing Dylan a small metal container.

After Uncle Todd left, Dylan tossed the container in the waste basket. He still had no plans on going to this Poopu Guinee place.

Like a clock ticking down on a bomb, each day was one less day Dylan had to get away from his uncle. Each night he lay awake in bed and puzzled over when and how he might escape before going to the airport. Finally, one night after midnight, he slipped out from under the covers and quietly pulled on his clothes. It was now or never. His bedroom was upstairs, like at home, but in the condo there was no porch roof to escape onto. Here he would have to sneak right past Uncle Todd's bedroom.

Carefully he eased open his door and tiptoed down the hallway. As he descended the steps, he froze each time his weight caused a creak. Finally he unlocked the front door and let himself out, leaving the door open. He paused beside the Corvette and glanced inside. It was too bad Uncle Todd hadn't left the keys in the ignition. The old Corvette would be the ultimate getaway car. Who knew what sort of tracking devices his uncle had in the car, though. He'd be better off on foot.

"Going somewhere?" a loud voice sounded.

Dylan spun, discovering Uncle Todd standing in the shadows of the doorway.

"Uh, ah, I c-couldn't sleep," Dylan stammered.

"Must not be getting enough exercise," Uncle Todd commented. "Go get your running shorts on. We'll take a little run."

"That's okay," Dylan said, walking reluctantly back toward the porch. "Maybe I can sleep now."

"Put on your shorts and tennis shoes. I'll meet you back here in two minutes."

"But it's the middle of the night," Dylan protested.

"And now you have only a minute and forty-five seconds. Get moving."

Uncle Todd's voice was absolute, with no allowance for discussion. Fists clenched tightly, Dylan returned through the front door. He turned sideways as he passed his uncle, making sure not to touch him, then he bounded up the steps. He seethed with anger as he changed into his running clothes.

With darkness casting haunting shadows across the street, Dylan and Uncle Todd began their run. "Keep up with me," Uncle Todd said.

Instead of the normal run down to the park and back, Uncle Todd headed down side streets, keeping a blistering pace. When it seemed like they should be returning, they turned instead toward the downtown section of Gresham. The deserted streets and misty rain gave the night an eerie feel. Their muted footsteps sounded like drum beats in the night.

After an hour of running, their pace slowed, but still Uncle Todd ran, not turning back toward home.

Finally Dylan panted, "Are we running all night?"

"We're going to run until you're tired enough to sleep."

Dylan's feet hurt and his legs were cramped by the time they finally returned to the condo. The dim light of dawn had softened the darkness.

"See if you can sleep now," Uncle Todd said, entering the condo. "If you can't, we'll take another run." He walked to his room without looking back.

Dylan limped up the stairs, his teeth clenched so hard his jaw hurt.

———

Uncle Todd never left Dylan's side during the last two days. "You want to join me in the bathroom?" Dylan asked when his uncle followed him into the backyard.

"Just keeping you honest," Uncle Todd said. "Stupid time is over. Now you need to get your head straight and join the team."

The night before they left, Dylan lay awake in the dark, scheming. Without warning, the door to his room opened and Uncle Todd's footsteps approached his bed. Dylan closed his eyes and pretended to be sleeping. The footsteps stopped, followed by a long pause, as if his uncle was thinking. Then Dylan felt the blanket being pulled up and tucked around his shoulders. Uncle Todd whispered, "There's a world waiting for you, son, when you're ready." Then the footsteps retreated from the room.

Dylan rolled over and stared intensely up at the dark ceiling. Outside, cars splashed through the rain in a steady rhythm. Dylan barely heard them. His eyes filled with tears and he rolled over and buried his head in the pillow.

———

Not until they had gone through the security screening and customs in Portland and boarded the jet did Dylan finally admit to himself that he couldn't avoid going on this trip after all. Maybe it would be okay. At least he wouldn't be treated like a child who needed babysitting anymore.

"We'll be flying most of the next two days until we reach Port Moresby in Papua New Guinea," Uncle Todd explained. "Then we'll have two days of travel until we reach the Sepik River on the northeast side of the island. Another day up the river, and then we'll be hiking our butts through swamps and jungles. I hope you're ready for an adventure. One week from now, you'll think you're on a different planet."

Dylan looked over at his uncle in his all-tan hiking outfit and giant floppy brown hat. "We already have an alien being," Dylan mumbled under his breath.

As they settled into their seats, Uncle Todd reached into the side pocket of Dylan's backpack and pulled out the small leather journal. "I want you to finish this before we land in Port Moresby." He tossed it onto Dylan's lap.

Reluctantly, Dylan opened the small journal and began reading where he had left off.

AUGUST 14, 1942

I AM NOT SURE WHICH IS WORSE, BEING BOMBED OR BOMBING SOMEONE ELSE. THIS WEEK WE LOST THREE SOLDIERS WHEN BOMBS HIT JACKSON AIRFIELD. WE ALSO LOST EIGHTEEN CREW MEMBERS WHEN TWO OF OUR B-17s WERE SHOT DOWN, ONE BY JAPANESE ZEROS, THE OTHER BY ANTI-AIRCRAFT FIRE. WE CALL THE ANTI-AIRCRAFT ARTILLERY "ACK-ACK," BECAUSE THAT IS WHAT IT SOUNDS LIKE. GETTING HIT BY ACK-ACK, I NOW KNOW, IS MUCH WORSE THAN HEARING THE SOUND. I HEARD THE DESPERATE CRIES OVER THE RADIO AS BOTH PLANES WENT DOWN. I WILL NOT SOON FORGET THOSE SOUNDS OF DEATH.

I AM LEARNING ONE LESSON VERY WELL: TO KEEP MY EYES OPEN. YOU SELDOM SEE THE ENEMY THAT KILLS YOU. BECAUSE OF THIS WEEK, I HAVE TAKEN A SMALL AMERICAN FLAG AND TUCKED IT IN THE MAP BOX BESIDE MY SEAT. I AM DETERMINED TO LEAVE IT THERE UNTIL I RETURN HOME TO REMIND ME ON EVERY MISSION THAT FREEDOM IS NEVER FREE. I BELIEVE NOW THAT FREEDOM'S WORST ENEMY IS INDIFFERENCE AND APATHY.

MY MISSION HERE IN THIS MOSQUITO-RIDDEN, GODFORSAKEN PLACE IS NOT TO SIMPLY DROP BOMBS BUT TO STOP THE

SPREAD OF TYRANNY. I DID NOT ASK FOR THIS DUTY, BUT I WILL NOT RUN FROM IT, EITHER. SOMEDAY MY CHILDREN AND THEIR CHILDREN WILL BE ABLE TO STAND PROUD WHEN THEY SEE OUR FLAG, AND MAYBE THEY WILL FIND IT IN THEIR HEART TO SAY, "MY DADDY, OR MY GRANDDADDY, FOUGHT TO PROTECT THIS FLAG."

Yawning hard, Dylan turned to the next entry.

AUGUST 19, 1942

THIS PLACE WOULD SEEM TO BE THE MOST BEAUTIFUL PLACE I HAVE EVER SEEN, WITH ITS SCENERY, EXOTIC BIRDS, PLANTS, AND WILDLIFE. BUT I QUESTION IF I WILL LIVE LONG ENOUGH TO ENJOY IT. IF I EVER GO DOWN IN THE JUNGLE, I DOUBT THERE WILL BE ANY SURVIVAL. THE FOLIAGE IS THICKER THAN YOU CAN IMAGINE. IT WOULD TAKE A HEALTHY MAN WITH A MACHETE A DAY TO GO A HUNDRED FEET IF HE LEFT THE BEATEN PATH. THE SWAMPS ARE EVEN WORSE, WITH WAIST-DEEP SLOP, BOGS, SLOUGHS, AND MUCKY TRAILS. THE MOUNTAINS ARE RUGGED PEAKS THAT CAN BE OVER TWO MILES HIGH AND HIDDEN WITH MIST AND RAIN. THEY SAY HERE THE CLOUDS ARE FILLED WITH ROCKS. IF THE ENEMY DOESN'T KILL YOU, THE LAND PROBABLY WILL. AND IF THE LAND DOESN'T KILL YOU, A THUNDERSTORM WILL PROBABLY RIP YOUR WINGS OFF.

I NOW AGREE WITH THIS ASSESSMENT.

By the time they changed planes in Los Angeles for the thirteen-hour flight to Australia, Dylan had read a dozen more entries that spoke of missions to bomb ships at Rabaul and other targets on New Britain, another island that was part of PNG. Dylan turned to his uncle. "All of Grandpa's missions so far were from Jackson Airstrip in Port Moresby out to New Britain. How did he crash way up by the Sepik River where we're going?"

Uncle Todd motioned. "Good question. Keep reading — you'll see."

Grunting his dismay, Dylan kept reading. Several hours later his mind was numb from stories of brutal weather and bad food. Dylan rubbed his tired eyes. They had been flying for almost six hours as he turned to the last two entries.

NOVEMBER 27, 1942

IT'S BEEN A HARD MONTH. I THINK WE'RE BEATING THE JAPANESE, BUT THEY'RE NOT GIVING UP EASILY. I'M HEADING OUT ON A BOMBING MISSION TOMORROW TO WEWAK ON THE NORTH COAST AND THE WEATHER FORECAST IS BAD. I SWEAR THE WEATHER AND TERRAIN KILL AS MANY OF US AS THE JAPANESE DO.

THEY CALL THIS WORLD WAR II. THEY SHOULD CALL IT "THE JUNGLE WAR." IF WE GO DOWN IN THE JUNGLE, OUR ENEMY BECOMES MALARIA, GANGRENE, DENGUE FEVER, BLACKWATER FEVER, DYSENTERY, AND DIARRHEA. DITCH IN THE WATER, AND OUR ENEMY BECOMES SHARKS. ON A NICE DAY,

THE MOUNTAINS MAY LOOK BEAUTIFUL FROM THE DISTANCE, LIKE SPIKES ON THE BACK OF SOME PREHISTORIC DRAGON. BUT CLOUDY DAYS LIKE TODAY, YOU CRASH INTO THEM, AND THEY KILL YOU.

I'M STARTING TO QUESTION WHY I'M HERE. EVERY MISSION, I TAKE OUT THE SMALL AMERICAN FLAG FROM MY MAP BOX TO REMIND ME OF WHY I AM RISKING MY LIFE.

Dylan continued to the last entry — now Uncle Todd could quit bugging him. The handwriting of the last entry was weird and hard to read, scribbled as if written by a child.

TWO DAYS AFTER WE CRASHED

HARD TO THINK. MAY BE MY LAST ENTRY. WEATHER TO THE EAST MADE US FOLLOW COAST NORTH BEFORE HEADING INLAND. ZEROS JUMPED US CROSSING THE MOUNTAINS TO WEWAK. WEATHER HAD US TOO LOW TO PARACHUTE AND THINGS WENT BAD FAST. LAST I REMEMBER, WE CROSSED THE SEPIK RIVER ABEAM CHAMBRI LAKE TO OUR RIGHT, SAME DISTANCE AWAY FROM MT. HAUK AT OUR ELEVEN O'CLOCK.

BELLIED INTO A SWAMP AREA WITH HEAVY TREES. PLANE DIDN'T BURN, BUT WE WRECKED BAD. FIVE OF US LIVED THROUGH THE CRASH, BUT THE FIRST NIGHT, THREE DIED. NOW ONLY GRAYSON, MY TAIL GUNNER, AND I ARE LEFT. WE WILL DIE IF WE STAY WITH THE PLANE. AM NOW BUSHWHACKING TOWARD THE SEPIK RIVER. I HAVE A BROKEN ARM AND AM WRITING THIS WITH MY LEFT HAND. GRAYSON HAS RIBS

HURTING HIM BAD AND IS THROWING UP BLOOD. DON'T KNOW
HOW LONG WE'LL LAST.

I FORGOT MY FLAG IN THE MAP BOX. IF ANYBODY
READS THIS JOURNAL, KNOW THAT I FOUGHT HARD AND I
LOVED MY COUNTRY.

Dylan closed the journal and handed it back to Uncle
Todd. "How long did it take Grandpa to make it out of the
jungle?"

"Almost two weeks. Natives found your grandfather hiking alone in the swamps, hallucinating and stricken with
malaria. He had infected cuts and scratches covering his
body, and thorns in his skin, and his body was caked with
mud. Looked pretty rough."

"What happened to Grayson?"

"He never made it. Your grandfather tried to bury him,
but that was hard in a swamp. Swamp rats probably ate him
the first night. But your grandfather was lucky. The villagers
who found him were friendly and able to take him through
the jungles and turn him over to some Australian soldiers,
who carried him to safety."

"If the military read this journal and couldn't find the
wreck, what makes you think we can?" Dylan asked.

Uncle Todd nodded his approval. "I like your questions.
Back then, this was hostile territory. Because of the Japanese,
headhunters, and cannibals, all the military could do at the
time was search from the sky, which they did. But that was

like looking for a needle in a haystack. With the dense jungle canopy over the top, you couldn't spot a whole army on the ground. When a plane went down, it was swallowed up by the trees and never seen again. The jungle was the perfect cover to hide from enemies, but the worst place for a search crew trying to find you."

"Why didn't the military look again later after the war?" Dylan asked.

Uncle Todd shrugged. "There were thousands of wrecks. The details in this journal were probably forgotten about when your grandfather came home. You can't live in the past, so he probably stored this journal away in the attic along with his other memories of the war. He never talked about his war years. Many veterans won't. But now that I found the journal, we can go in by land and ask local villagers if they know of any wreckages. That is how most of the wreck sites are being found."

"What happens if we find bodies?"

"All that would be left are teeth, some bones, and dog tags, if that. Maybe some watches, glasses, or buttons. If we find any remains, the military will come in with a team to do DNA studies and try to identify them. Those that can't be identified will be buried at Arlington National Cemetery in D.C."

"There's really that many planes still in the jungle?"

"Hundreds, maybe even thousands, are still hidden. Once in a while a new one is discovered. The wrecks are like swamp ghosts. Some villagers believe the planes are cursed by the spirits of the men who died. They believe that real ghosts protect the wrecks." He shrugged. "Who knows — many searchers have gone in and never come back."

"You're just trying to scare me," Dylan challenged. "What's the difference between cannibals and headhunters anyway?"

"Cannibals eat their enemies to steal their spirits. The headhunters, they hang the heads of enemies in their doorways to keep away bad spirits. Some native boys had to prove they had become adults by claiming the head of an enemy. This wasn't really that unusual. Some American soldiers kept the heads and other body parts of Japanese soldiers as trophies, even though the military had strict rules against that."

"That's gross," Dylan mumbled.

Uncle Todd shrugged. "When I traveled in Africa, young Maasai boys proved they had come of age by killing a lion. What's so different with taking the head of some enemy?"

"There's a bunch of heads I'd like to hang up."

Uncle Todd laughed. "I'm probably one of them. We don't do much of anything in our culture to show a boy has come of age. All we do is recognize those that don't grow up."

"How is that?" Dylan asked.

"We put them in juvenile detention centers and call up their uncles."

"Real funny," Dylan said. He stared out the window at the clouds passing lazily under the plane like pillows of white. His head hurt from thinking.

The flight attendants served a hot meal with chicken that tasted like rubber and a salad with dressing that tasted like turpentine. "Why can't they just serve a cheeseburger and fries?" Dylan complained.

"Then you would have to find something else to complain about," Uncle Todd said.

After eating, an announcement came over the intercom asking everybody to pull their window shades down. Tonight there would be little darkness because they were chasing the sun west the whole flight at about 500 miles per hour.

Uncle Todd picked up a book he had been reading and turned to a new page. He had a pair of reading glasses that he wore low on his nose. They had been in the air seven hours now since leaving LA, and Dylan was bored stiff. A movie showed on an overhead screen, but it was some love story. Dylan definitely wasn't feeling love. He didn't like how Uncle Todd always had to have the last word.

"You don't like me, do you?" Dylan blurted.

Uncle Todd glanced up from his reading and shrugged. "I like everybody on the planet. What I don't like is when people do dumb things for dumb reasons."

"So you think I do dumb things for dumb reasons?" Dylan asked.

Uncle Todd took off his reading glasses and studied Dylan. "I'm not sure what motivates you. For example, explain to me why you like wearing your pants halfway down your butt."

"Because I want to," Dylan said.

"So, if you want to do something, that makes it okay?"

"I guess. You wear anything you want," Dylan retorted.

"We already talked about this. I wear what I wear for a reason. To stay warm and because it's comfortable. What's your reason?" When Dylan didn't answer, Uncle Todd added, "I think you do it to thumb your nose at the world. The same as when you say 'whatever.' "

Dylan didn't like where this was going.

"You're bigger than that," Uncle Todd said. "I thought you were your own person."

"I am!" Dylan said, raising his voice.

"Do you deserve respect?" Uncle Todd asked, his eyes intense.

Dylan shrugged.

"Simple question," Uncle Todd repeated. "Do you deserve respect?"

"Yeah," Dylan answered.

"Well, you're never deserving of any more respect in life than you give. I don't see you showing the world much respect. Until you show the world respect, the world won't respect you, and neither will I."

Dylan folded his arms to hide his fists, which were clenched tightly. As usual, he regretted having started an argument with his uncle.

CHAPTER 9

Dylan hadn't realized a plane could stay in the air so long. Finally he needed to go to the bathroom. The movie had ended, so when he walked to the back of the plane, half the people stared up at him. The other half kept sleeping. The tiny bathroom was a joke, like pooping in a phone booth. It smelled horrible.

When Dylan returned to his seat, Uncle Todd had turned his overhead light off and was fast asleep. Dylan crawled over his legs and settled into his seat by the window. Bored, he pulled out the flight magazine from the seat pocket and paged through it. At the back he found maps showing where the airline flew, with lines to places all over the world. He saw the line from Los Angeles to Sydney, Australia.

Dylan tried to sleep but finally gave up and pulled up his shade to glance out the window. Below was nothing but the Pacific Ocean. They were just one of those lines in the flight magazine. One of the really long ones.

When Uncle Todd woke a couple of hours later, he looked over and found Dylan still awake. "You're going to be a tired puppy if you don't get some sleep," he commented.

"I'm already tired," Dylan answered. "But I can't sleep."

Uncle Todd reached under the seat to his carry-on bag and pulled out a map. He spread it out carefully on his fold-down tray table. "I want to show you how we narrowed down the search area."

Uncle Todd pointed to an inland lake on the map of Papua New Guinea. "This is Chambri Lake, and this is the Sepik River." He pulled out the journal and turned to the last entry. "Okay, so your grandfather first said the weather was bad so he had to follow the coast north from Port Moresby before heading inland." Uncle Todd traced his finger along the shoreline, and then pointed. "He doesn't say how far north, but let's say he went up to somewhere in here. Now let's draw a line between there and Wewak."

Already Uncle Todd had traced a line across the island to Wewak with a pencil.

"So, next the journal says, 'We crossed the Sepik River abeam Chambri Lake to our right.' He says Mount Hauk was about the same distance at his eleven o'clock." Uncle Todd pointed to a red circle he had drawn on the map. "This is the approximate location he would have been if he were flying a course across the island from the north coast, crossing the Sepik River, abeam Chambri Lake and at eleven o'clock from Mount Hauk."

Dylan wanted to say, "Whatever," but bit his tongue. "So, then, what's the big deal? It should be easy finding the bomber," he said.

Uncle Todd studied the map as if it were a puzzle. "It's all jungle and swamp," he said.

As Uncle Todd stared down, Dylan studied his uncle. Why did he want to go halfway around the world looking for a plane wreck? It wasn't like the wreck was filled with gold — then it might have been worth finding.

As much as Dylan hated to admit it, Uncle Todd was right about a few things. Wearing his pants way low was because other boys were doing it, and because it bugged the adults, especially his mom. Using the word "whatever" was a way of verbally flipping someone the finger and getting away with it. It told other people that their opinion was garbage. After his dad died, that's how Dylan felt about any adult's opinion. And like Uncle Todd had said, his headphones did let him tune out the world.

From the moment he'd found out about his dad's death, it seemed like every adult on the planet had an opinion about how Dylan should be handling it. They told him his dad was a hero and that he should be proud of him. They told Dylan he was depressed and he should take medication. They told him he should feel lucky he still had a mom that loved him so much. Eventually Dylan got sick of hearing about everything he should be doing or feeling. Sometimes the world really needed tuning out.

Especially Uncle Todd.

Dylan reclined his seat, trying to sleep, but his mind kept churning with thoughts, his butt hurt from sitting so long, and now two babies started crying in the seat behind them. Dylan would have given anything for his headphones.

He couldn't quit thinking about Uncle Todd. His mom had given up on complaining about the low pants, headphones, or saying "whatever," but Uncle Todd picked apart every little thing he did. Dylan wished that Uncle Todd would just back off. What was *his* weakness? What was the chink in his armor?

Numb with fatigue, Dylan rubbed his dry eyes. They felt like they had gravel smeared in them. He glanced over and found Uncle Todd asleep again, as if he were on the couch back home. He even snored a little.

When at last the flight crew announced the final approach into Sydney, Uncle Todd woke and nudged Dylan. "We have a three-hour layover before our flight to Port Moresby," he said. "Maybe we can get us a little bite to eat. You won't be getting many hamburgers and french fries in the jungle."

Dylan shrugged and stared out the window as they landed and taxied to the terminal. Half of this airport stuck out into a big bay like a peninsula, and the control tower looked like something out of a science fiction movie — everything was really modern. Papua New Guinea was only a hundred miles away. It was hard to imagine a place so close could be so different.

Leaving the plane, Dylan followed Uncle Todd through the crowded Sydney airport, stopping to get a burger. There were about a zillion people — families, sportsmen, tourists, and business people — all traveling through an airport Dylan hadn't even heard of a month ago. "I didn't realize Australia was so big," he commented. "I read in the flight magazine that it was just an island."

Uncle Todd chuckled. "A big island. Biggest in the world, almost as big as the lower forty-eight states of the United States, but just a fraction of the people. We'll have to come back to Australia sometime and go into the Outback. That's when you'll see big!"

"Not if I can help it," Dylan mumbled.

———

When they boarded the plane for Port Moresby in Papua New Guinea, it was a much smaller jet and a much shorter flight, mostly over water. Dylan stared out the window at the nothingness underneath. What in the world was he doing this far from home, headed for some jungle?

As they approached land, the mountains down the center of the distant island looked like the back of some green monster — sharp jagged splinters covered with trees. Clouds hung low on the peaks, with mist trailing down the slopes. As they landed, Dylan had an ominous feeling. He was stepping out of a world he recognized into a world he didn't even understand. Instead of seeing a boarding bridge connecting the plane to the terminal, Dylan looked out the window and saw two men pushing metal steps across the tarmac. The minute the door opened, a wall of hot muggy air flooded the plane like a sauna.

Uncle Todd turned and handed Dylan a small nylon pouch with a strong lanyard. "Put your passport, your tickets and anything else valuable from your pockets into this pouch. Wear it around your neck and tuck the pouch inside your pants. Then tighten your belt. When we leave the airport, this place will be a battle zone and thick with pickpockets. They would love to have you wear your pants halfway down. You'd be robbed blind in minutes. Stay close to me. We have a small van picking us up to take us to a hotel where we'll meet the rest of the team and stay overnight. Tomorrow, we all fly on to Wewak."

Dylan ignored the low pants comment. He wished his uncle would take a bath in a shark tank. As they descended the steel steps to the tarmac, Dylan glanced around. The terminal was a big white building. It felt like they had walked into an oven. By the time they reached the door going inside, Dylan was mopping sweat from his forehead.

"Corruption is what makes this place so dangerous," Uncle Todd explained. "People rob you at gunpoint tonight, and tomorrow when you report it at the police station, you might recognize the police officer as one of the men who robbed you the night before. Don't ever go walking by yourself, and keep an eye on everything you own."

The inside of the terminal was large and mostly empty, except for benches scattered around, one small vendor shop, an ATM where you could change currency, a plain check-in counter, and a big mural covering one wall. The bathrooms had old fixtures. Many floor tiles were ripped or missing, exposing the concrete. Worst was the smell. Urine had soaked into the floor and now made the warm air suffocating. Everything looked fifty years old. While they waited with their luggage to go through customs, Uncle Todd went over to the ATM and withdrew some kina, the PNG money. Dylan overheard one passenger explaining to another how the mural told the history of PNG and its people. Right now Dylan couldn't have cared less about the people of PNG. To him they were aliens from outer space.

It took almost an hour to clear customs, and Uncle Todd was right: When they exited the terminal building, a crowd of people hung outside the gate like a pack of wolves watching them with hungry eyes, pushing and shoving to peddle jewelry, sell drugs, even flag down a taxi for them. Anything to make money. Luckily, the hotel had sent a driver, who held a sign up with their name. Even as they followed him to a white van carrying their backpacks, a young boy ran up and tried to grab the lanyard around Dylan's neck. Fortunately Dylan had followed Uncle Todd's suggestion and tucked the pouch inside his pants. He tried to hit the kid, but the wiry boy was already running away.

The driver wagged his finger at Dylan. "Be careful," he said with a strong accent. "This place very dangerous. The rascals steal from you. Do not walk alone. Never walk out at night. Then rascals kill you."

They drove several miles to town in a white minibus, then wound their way through the streets of Port Moresby. Many of the intersections had roundabouts, which the driver treated like a race course. Dylan braced himself, staring in disbelief at the world he had entered. One beach they passed was covered with so much litter it lay vacant. Before leaving the bay, Dylan spotted a small village built on stilts out on the water. All of the nice homes or buildings were surrounded with razor wire like prisons.

By the time they reached the far edge of the city, the neighborhoods had turned into little more than shantytowns with run-down structures and tin-covered homes. The women wore simple handmade skirts and bright blouses; the men, dirty pants and shirts. The heavy smell of garbage hung in the air. In some places, garbage had been stacked for so long that weeds grew up around the piles. In many yards, smoky fires burned, bringing a sharp smell to the air. Almost every backyard had clothes hanging on lines. The hot choking smell of diesel and dust hung heavy, like a cloud. And there was another smell. Sewage.

Low dirt hills surrounded Port Moresby, covered with scrub brush. Even with the van's air conditioner, it was like being in an oven. The driver kept turning and explaining different things, taking his eyes off the road and then swerving whenever he looked forward again. His teeth and lips were red. From the back seat, Dylan could smell the strong body odor of the man — like he hadn't showered since he was born.

"How much farther to the hotel?" Dylan asked.

In reply, the driver swerved into the parking lot of a large pink building surrounded by tall razor fencing. "We are here," he announced.

Uncle Todd pointed at the stained red pavement as they crawled from the van. "That's from the betel nuts that everybody chews and spits. It's why the driver's teeth are red. Bad habit."

"We should have let the Japanese keep this place," Dylan said.

Uncle Todd gave Dylan a withering glance.

That night they met with the other members of the team: Allen Jackson, a thin man who had a tan but looked like a professor; Gene Cooper, a big man with a bald head who sweated even when they were sitting in the air-conditioned lobby of the hotel having dinner; and Gene Cooper's son, Quentin, a boy Dylan's age, but taller and skinnier. He wore large plastic-rimmed glasses that made him look nerdy. Definitely someone Dylan would have teased back home if they were classmates.

After introductions, they sat around eating and discussing the upcoming trip. "Did everybody take their malaria pills and get all their shots?" Gene Cooper asked.

Everybody nodded, including Dylan. Uncle Todd turned to Dylan. "I'm the organizer of this trip, but Gene is the military expert on planes. He's also our best medic and resident philosopher. Allen is our survival expert. He's been over here before and knows a lot about PNG and the jungles." Uncle Todd pointed. "Quentin is very analytical, and a walking encyclopedia. He's our go-to man for facts and history."

Dylan kicked the leg of the table. "And what am I?" he whispered. "The group's loser?"

Uncle Todd winked and whispered back, "That's totally up to you. I'm not sure you know who you are yet."

Quentin turned to Dylan. "Hey, did you know that the B-17 has a max speed of 207 miles per hour and a cruise speed of 182 miles per hour? Its range is over 2,000 miles depending on how heavy you load it. It has a service ceiling of over 35,000 feet. Its length is —"

"Quentin, give Dylan a break," Quentin's father, Gene, interrupted. "I'm sure Dylan already knows all that."

"I'll bet he doesn't," Quentin said.

Dylan glared at the skinny boy, but Quentin didn't even notice.

Allen Jackson handed each of them a manila envelope. "I've made a laminated map, a list of the survival gear you'll need if you get lost in the jungle, and a small laminated picture of the B-17 we're looking for. Her name is *Second Ace*. The wreckage probably won't be obvious after this long. She'll be grown over with vegetation. There may or may not be any nose art left to identify her. Carry that picture with you."

Everybody, including Dylan, tucked the picture into their pockets.

"Okay, let's all get a good night's sleep," Allen Jackson announced. "Tomorrow we fly to Wewak and then on to Ambunti. From there we'll be taking a dugout canoe five hours upstream to Swagup, and then we head in on foot. By then you'll all know why people call Papua New Guinea 'the land that time forgot.'"

As they stood from the table, Quentin turned to Dylan. "Did you know that after World War I, New Guinea's eastern half was controlled by Britain and Australia? The island's western half was controlled by the Netherlands — known as Dutch New Guinea. Hollandia was the capital then. But in World War II, because the island of New Guinea was in the center of the Pacific war zone, Japan invaded —"

"Quentin, stop! You're talking Dylan's ears off," Gene interrupted. "You'll have plenty of time to visit during the trip."

"We're not talking," Dylan snapped. "He's showing off!"

Reluctantly, Quentin shrugged, but then turned and blurted, "Did you know that New Guinea is barely a hundred miles away from Australia at the closest point?"

"Yes, I did know that," Dylan answered sharply, taking a deep breath, then adding, "Did you know I can drift a

Corvette at forty miles per hour?" Not waiting for an answer, he followed his uncle from the restaurant. Already the trip was getting long.

Before going to their room, Uncle Todd and Dylan walked outside to the fenced-in entrance to see what the weather was like. Dylan brushed away a mosquito. He remembered the journal Uncle Todd had given him describing PNG as "mosquito-ridden." They had mosquitoes a lot worse than this back in Wisconsin.

An armed guard with a rifle met them. Speaking in broken English, he said, "Do not go outside the fence. Even if you go around the building, I walk with you."

"We were just seeing what the weather was like," Uncle Todd said.

The man laughed. "We only have two weathers here. Hot and raining, or hot and not raining." He held his hand up as if to feel the air. "Now . . . it is hot and not raining." The man with the rifle was still laughing at his wit when Dylan and Uncle Todd returned inside.

Dylan stared in disbelief when they entered their room. It was plain and bare, except for two beds, a table, and some chairs. With a bug screen on the open window and no air conditioner, the room was hot and muggy. Roaches scrambled across the floor when the lights turned on. Dylan undressed and plopped himself on top of the sheets. When Uncle Todd turned off the light, Dylan lay sweating in the dark. "This room is worse than the holding cell at the detention center," he complained.

"This is a presidential palace compared to where we're going. Get used to it," Uncle Todd said. "Welcome to Papua New Guinea."

"Welcome to Timbuktu," Dylan muttered back.

CHAPTER 8

Any illusion Dylan had of the summer being easy or comfortable disappeared in the next two days. The small jet to Wewak had only about twenty people aboard, with cramped seats. Everything smelled rotted, moldy, or sweaty. Rough air kept the small plane bouncing and lurching all the way across the island. Dylan stared down at the miles and miles of jungle passing under the wings. How could there possibly be this much jungle anywhere on the planet? Suddenly the notion of finding a crashed bomber seemed absolutely ridiculous.

A lady two seats in front of Dylan kept puking her guts out into a barf bag. By the time they landed, Dylan was glad to get on the ground, feeling queasy himself. He looked to see if Quentin was sick, but the thin boy was laughing with his father.

The guard in Port Moresby was right. If the sun wasn't burning like a searing heat lamp in the sky, it rained. And not just a little. When they landed in Wewak, the rain came down hard in sheets, as if an ocean had spilled over. Passengers dashed from the plane to the terminal building holding plastic bags, newspapers, or anything they could over their heads. The hot humid air made it hard for Dylan to tell which had drenched him more: rain or sweat.

If Dylan had thought Port Moresby was remote, it was Disney World compared to Wewak. The terminal was a simple building with an overhang for passengers to stand out of the rain while a tractor and a flat trailer brought them their luggage. Instead of suitcases and backpacks, most of the luggage was carried in gunnysacks, plastic buckets, or any other container that could be used. The search team's backpacks were the fanciest luggage on the flight.

Most passengers picked up their luggage and then stood around waiting for the rain to stop so they could walk the several miles into town. Dylan waited with his group until the rain let up a little, then they hiked with their backpacks across the tarmac to a hangar, where they waited for their next flight.

"We'll be taking a private charter flight to Ambunti," Allen announced.

Dylan imagined a small exclusive Learjet picking them up.

He stared with his mouth open when, after they'd been waiting for almost two hours, a small high-winged Cessna landed. The frail craft looked like it was from an airplane junkyard, if there were such a thing. The faded paint looked like rust. The tires were bald, and the engine coughed and sputtered as it taxied up. The plane swung a sharp circle to stop next to the hangar.

"This was the only plane I could hire today," Allen Jackson explained as the pilot crawled out.

"Well, how are we all today?" asked the British pilot jovially, jumping to the tarmac. Holding his hand up to the downpour, he laughed. "This is just a drizzle. Wait until you see real rain. We should be able to get you to Ambunti today if we're lucky."

"And what if we aren't lucky?" Dylan grumped.

The pilot laughed. "Then welcome to life."

Gene Cooper nodded his agreement and added, "Sometimes you just have to go for it. Life doesn't provide guarantees."

"Now everybody's a philosopher," Dylan said.

Soon they were loaded. The plane's engine cranked over again and again before finally coughing to life. The pilot gunned the motor to keep it going, then taxied out and raced down the runway. Not until they reached the very end did the pilot finally pull back and coax the small overloaded craft into the sky.

Quentin hollered over at Dylan, "Did you know the air cools four degrees for every thousand feet we go up?"

Dylan frowned and yelled back, "That's why if you go to the moon, you freeze your butt off."

"No," Quentin shouted. "On the moon it's because there's no atmosphere. When bombers climb through the atmosphere to 35,000 feet, the actual air temperature is 140 degrees colder than on the ground. Even here it could be 40 degrees below zero."

Dylan tried to ignore Quentin, but that still didn't stop the tall, lanky boy.

"That's why B-17 crews were issued winterized fleece-lined flying suits even here in the hot jungle," Quentin hollered.

Dylan wished he had a coconut to stuff in Quentin's mouth. He would have given a million dollars to have his headphones on to tune Quentin out. They were in his back-pack only feet away in the baggage area, but they might just as well have been on a different planet.

The whole flight to Ambunti followed the Sepik River upstream. The river looked like a brown coiling snake under their wings — a boat would have had to travel three times the distance because of how the river twisted and turned. After barely a half hour, they banked sharply to land at a small, short strip on the edge of the Sepik River. For now, the rain had stopped.

As they taxied up, a rusted Toyota pickup pulled alongside the plane. The driver jumped out and shouted in broken English, "Welcome to Ambunti. Before we go to boat, I take you to market."

Soon they found themselves sitting sideways on planked bench seats in the back of the pickup with no seat belts, bouncing down a rough road beside the mighty Sepik River. On the way, Quentin pointed out every plant, tree, bird, or insect he recognized. He absolutely would not shut up. "Look, there's a yoli myrtle tree. Look, there's a tropical chestnut. Look, it's a rosewood. And there's a pencil pine and a kauri pine."

"Who cares?" Dylan said.

Quentin ignored the comment and pointed again. "Oh, look, there's a banyan tree."

"I knew that," Dylan interrupted forcefully. Wasn't there any way to shut Quentin's mouth? He looked desperately to Uncle Todd, who sat watching the countryside pass by. He caught Dylan's look of desperation and winked with a smile.

Suddenly Quentin changed subjects. "Hey, Dylan, did you know that crew members were issued whistles, and even winter boots with electric heated socks that could be plugged into the bomber's power? They also all got medical kits and gas masks. Some even got forty-five-caliber pistols." When Dylan didn't answer, Quentin changed subjects again. "Did you know that the first aerial bombing took place in 1849 over Venice, Italy, when the Austrian army dropped bombs from a hot air balloon?"

"I already knew that," Dylan said loudly, lying. He would do anything to shut this walking encyclopedia up.

"No, you didn't," Quentin challenged.

Dylan shrugged. "Whatever!" he said.

Uncle Todd glanced over and surprised Dylan with a smile.

Quentin continued. "If you know everything, what's the name of the trail used by the Japanese when they invaded from the north?"

"I don't care about any dumb trail," Dylan snapped. "I don't care if aliens used the trail to invade the planet Earth."

Allen Jackson interrupted the conversation. "Dylan, you need to know this. When the Allies arrived, we were losing the war here. If the Japanese weren't stopped, all of New Guinea and a lot of Australia would have been lost. To win the war, the Japanese had to come from Buna to the north and overrun Port Moresby to the south. But between these two points was the Owen Stanley mountain range, with some of the most rugged terrain on the planet Earth: ragged mountain peaks, raging rivers, cliffs, gorges, and thick jungles. Only one trail connected the two places, the Kokoda trail. But it was a primitive trail with slippery mud and rock. Troops sometimes crawled single file on their hands and knees, clinging to vines to keep from falling to their deaths. If the Japanese hadn't been stopped on the Kokoda trail you might not be sitting here talking as a free person."

"I wouldn't be sitting here talking if Uncle Todd hadn't brought me here," Dylan snapped. Ignoring his uncle's disapproving glance, Dylan turned away and stared at the endless greenery until they pulled to a stop at the marketplace.

For a half hour they explored local wares being sold beside the river. Instead of using stands, things were spread out on the ground on pieces of torn plastic sheets and woven rice bags that had been cut open. Again, Quentin acted like the tour guide. "Those are bilum bags full of betel nuts." He pointed out everything he could see, from dried fish to taro roots, shields and spears, sago starch and sweet potatoes.

Dylan picked up a banana. "This is a ba-na-na," he exclaimed.

Quentin picked up a papaya. "Do you know what this is?" he asked.

"Looks like your head," Dylan quipped.

Quentin ignored him and pointed excitedly at some fierce-looking masks. "Oh, look! Those are spirit masks."

Dylan looked around at all the plants and fruit he didn't recognize. "How do they know these things aren't poisonous?" Instantly he regretted his question.

"It's similar to our country," Quentin said. "All trial and error. With time, people have discovered the hard way what's good and what's bad. And if you —"

"Thank you, Quentin," Dylan said loudly, turning his back and walking away.

Women kept trying to hand Dylan items, repeating the memorized words, "Special price for you! Special price for you!" Several handed out sample slices of papaya and mango. Dylan refused to sample any fruits he didn't recognize. How did he know they weren't poisonous?

As they shopped, a small army of children followed them with curious stares. Most wore only dirty pants. Their little bellies stuck out like brown melons. As they had in Port Moresby, the women in the market wore colorful blouses and skirts. The men wore dusty pants and T-shirts. One had an

LA Lakers shirt. One shirt said BOB MARLEY. Another advertised Tide laundry soap. Dylan guessed the people didn't even know what their shirts said.

Most adults had mouths and teeth stained from chewing the betel nuts. "Why do they chew those things?" Dylan asked, being careful to direct the question to Allen Jackson.

"It's a socially ingrained habit. It's a sign of friendship to give or exchange betel nuts. The habit is an addiction but also part of their culture, the same as smoking, drinking, and drug use in our country. Maybe it's their way of escaping hunger and poverty. Who knows the whole reason?"

"He knows," Dylan whispered, pointing at Quentin. "He knows everything."

Allen smiled. "Let's get on the river. We want to be in the village of Swagup before dark."

—

Dylan stared in disbelief as they loaded their backpacks into a large dugout canoe almost forty feet long. The boat had been hollowed out of a single tree by hand. It had the carving of a crocodile on the front. "I feel like a cave man," Dylan said, settling into his spot for the five-hour ride. Every time someone moved, the dugout tipped dangerously.

Three local men, barefoot and wearing only blue jeans and T-shirts, accompanied them. "This certainly isn't Coast Guard–approved," Quentin's father, Gene, joked. "Riding eight people without life vests in a hollowed-out tree, up a river thick with poisonous snakes and crocodiles."

Dylan allowed a shallow laugh, swallowed hard, and looked into the water. This really was a stupid trip.

Uncle Todd cleared his throat. "From here on in, there are no more credit cards, banks, stores, electricity, nothing," he announced. "We're off the grid. Welcome to Papua New Guinea."

The dugout used a forty horsepower outboard engine on the back to plow through the water. They droned along, meandering past small villages or individual homes built along the high banked shore on poles. Most had thatched roofs and walls made of palm branches lashed together. Twisting smoke rose from many of the huts.

Allen Jackson pointed excitedly to an extra-large structure built high on the shoreline. It towered above the other buildings, with two floors and a thatched roof like some prehistoric church. "That's a Haus Tambaran, or Spirit House. Only men are allowed inside," Allen said. "It's like a church or spiritual place to house the good spirits, but some say they're haunted. Inside, they make elaborate wood carvings like we saw in the market to ward off bad spirits. It's where the men meet and socialize. It is also where the boys live for a month during initiation."

"How are they initiated?" Dylan asked, not sure he wanted to know.

Allen explained. "In this region, with razor blades. The crocodile is worshipped as the water spirit. Ornate rows of gashes are cut into their backs to make them look like crocodiles. They pack the gashes with mud to stop infection. Sometimes the boys die from the cuts. You might see some of these men in Swagup, although up there, villagers are known as the Insect People. Many of their rituals, ceremonies, and carvings center around insects."

"But why do they cut themselves?" Dylan asked.

"It's an initiation into manhood. A symbol of strength and power."

"It's a symbol of being crazy," Dylan said.

"That's what they say about our culture," Gene said.

Dylan noticed that Quentin was sitting quietly for the first time. The skinny know-it-all scratched at mosquito bites on his legs and stared nervously at the water. Dylan chuckled. "This is the wrong place to be if you don't like water," he said. "I'll bet they have piranhas."

"No, they don't," Quentin answered. "But they do have a similar fish with big teeth called a 'bolkata.' They call them that because of where they bite boys when they're swimming." Quentin kept eyeing the muddy river. "I can't swim," he added. "Is there any way to get to Swagup without going by boat?"

Allen shook his head. "This river is the backbone of the area, like an interstate. All commerce, travel, everything is centered on the river. There are no roads here."

"I hear bolkatas are really thick here," Dylan joked, staring at the water nervously himself.

———

The shoreline drifted past as they motored upstream, each curve in the wide river taking them farther into a strange world of thatched huts, women squatting beside the water to wash clothes, and men fishing the shoreline. Naked children swung from trees along the high bank to splash into the river. It puzzled Dylan — why weren't the children afraid of crocodiles or poisonous snakes? Gene was probably just trying to freak him out.

They passed other boats on the river. Some owners had no motors. They used only long, sharp paddles, standing up in their dugouts. Gradually, a steady beating of drums echoed above the outboard's engine. Their driver slowed the big dugout and motored near shore. On the bank, some kind of celebration was taking place. Villagers in costumes gyrated in circles, dancing.

"Sing sing," the driver said, pointing.

Allen explained that in PNG, celebrations were called *sing sings*.

The children nearest the shore turned and stared at the passing visitors as if they were aliens from a different universe. Dylan felt like one. "These people are so backward," he said.

"Or maybe more advanced," Gene Cooper commented.

"What do you mean?" Dylan said.

The big man scratched at his bald head as he talked. "Einstein once said, 'I do not know with what weapons World War III will be fought, but World War IV will be fought with sticks and stones.' If you think of humanity that way, perhaps cave-men were once the most advanced civilization to inhabit the planet. Maybe these people were once advanced millennia ahead of us."

Dylan held back a smart-aleck reply. Behind them, the sun fell low in the sky.

CHAPTER 9

Swagup was a dirty little village with no electricity or running water. The house they slept in that night was a private home up on poles. A thatched roof covered the structure, but it leaked even when a brief shower fell. For the first time, the mosquitoes swarmed thick. Quentin kept spraying mosquito repellent over his body. Dylan refused. He was tougher than some small bug. Quentin was such a wuss.

The owners served an evening meal of Sepik River catfish, some kind of yam, and funny-tasting rice. They also served thick pancakes of cooked sago starch that tasted gross and crumbled when Dylan tried a bite. Sitting with his back against the palm-bark wall of the hut, Dylan studied the locals. They were nice enough, but because they didn't speak English, they simply sat in the dim glow of a kerosene lamp and stole curious glances. Dylan felt like a sideshow.

At least a dozen other family members slept with them in the large single room that night, some of them snoring. Cooking in the kitchen drifted smoke throughout the hut, helping to keep the mosquitoes away until they went to bed. Like some backwoods hotel, the homeowner had six mats set up for visitors with mosquito nets over the top like tents. By the time they went to bed, Dylan itched all over because of all his mosquito bites. He tried not to scratch them except when nobody was looking. He was glad for the net over his sleeping pad. Maybe tomorrow he would put on a little spray when Quentin wasn't watching.

As Dylan lay awake in the dark, mosquitoes droned around the net, trying to find any small rip or opening. He wondered what other bugs were out there waiting to suck on his blood. Classmates back home would freak if they knew where he was tonight. This was something they couldn't even imagine. Was this what it was like in Darfur in Africa where his father had been killed? The thought haunted Dylan as he lay awake in the dark.

Newborn puppies under the home whimpered each time they wanted to nurse. The floor, made from palm-bark planks, bounced whenever somebody moved in the room. Half the night, Dylan lay wide awake listening to the sharp chorusing of bugs in the jungle. Quentin said they were called cicadas. Dylan didn't care if they were called "fart bugs" — he wished they would shut up.

The next morning the team rose early to begin hiking toward the foothills. This, Uncle Todd was convinced, was where they might find the B-17 *Second Ace*. They hired two men from the village to act as guides and to introduce them if they came to other small villages or camps. "Clans in each region are very territorial and don't like strangers trespassing," Allen explained.

It didn't make sense to Dylan. "How can you own the jungle?" he asked.

"In our country, Chief Seattle, a famous Native American leader and speaker, would have asked how anybody could own any part of the Earth," Allen said. "But just because you can't see property lines doesn't mean they're not there. Legal in any society is what you can enforce. Believe me, even with bows and arrows, these people can enforce plenty."

The guides were short wiry men with broad foreheads, big smiles, large wide noses, and black fuzzy hair. Their bare feet looked weathered like shoe leather, but they were agile, walking gingerly with a bit of a hopping motion, each step deliberate and sure. They spoke no English, except for what Allen called "pidgin English." Allen seemed to understand much of what they said, but Dylan could only understand a few of the words, like *humbug man* for *bad person*, *sit haus* for *toilet*, *sing sing* for *celebration*, *nat nat* for *mosquito*, *pis pis* — that one was obvious, and *bolkata* — that was obvious, too.

The trail they followed bordered the jungle to their left and a large swamp area to their right. Within a half hour of walking through the sweltering heat, Dylan was dripping with sweat. Unlike their guides, Dylan found himself tripping and stumbling if he didn't pay close attention.

As they walked, Allen lectured the group. "Make sure you keep the laminated picture of *Second Ace* on you at all times.

After half of a century in this hostile environment, the wreckage could just look like a twisted pile of undergrowth. The picture might be your only way of identifying the bomber. Finding *Second Ace* is like trying to find a needle in a haystack, but we do know she's here somewhere."

Allen paused, and then continued. "Do not, I repeat, do not eat or drink the water from a coconut you have found on the ground. After four or five hours in the sun, it can spoil and make you very sick. If you get a leech on you, do not pull it off. Wait and pour alcohol over its body — that makes it release. If you don't have alcohol, just leave them alone. When they fill up with blood, they just drop off. Always keep your compass with you — there is no other easy way of knowing directions in the jungle. Keep your whistle handy — you can be a hundred feet from the group and not know where you are. Use chlorine tablets in the water you drink. Use sunscreen lotion — the sun is deadly. Drink lots of water — sweating leaves you terribly dehydrated. Always use mosquito spray and keep taking your malaria pills — they do have malaria over here. Believe me, you do not want to get malaria. When you first get it, you're afraid you're going to die. When it gets worse, you're afraid you won't die. This place is beautiful, but it can and will kill you if you don't afford it respect."

This is just another stupid lecture, Dylan thought, *like not swimming in the river because there are poisonous snakes and crocodiles.* Lots of kids were swimming in the river. There probably wasn't that much malaria, either. The rules were dumb. It hadn't been hard keeping direction this morning. Even without guides, they just followed the trail. And what was the big deal with the whistle? Anybody could shout and be heard a long ways away.

This morning Dylan had put on some mosquito spray, but despite the spray, he found himself scratching at his old bites. He hated the bugs more than anything. They were everywhere, thousands of them: gnats, crickets, leeches, mosquitoes, and a zillion other little crawly things he had never seen before in his life. It did no good to swat or brush them away. It was like trying to wave smoke away. One time Dylan swatted his arm and killed ten mosquitoes with one slap. He kept spitting out bugs that flew into his mouth.

It was hard to watch where he stepped with so many new things to see. Clouds of waterbirds swarmed overhead. Parrots with green and red wings flashed past in bunches. Huge butterflies of every imaginable color dipped and darted about. Dylan saw several birds with really weird colors and long necks. One bird had a big black body, a white head, and a huge yellow beak. When it took off, its wings thumped loudly, like a chopper taking off.

"That's a hornbill," Quentin announced, pointing. "I was the first one to see it."

"Get a life," Dylan mumbled. Looking up, he noticed a single green parrot. It circled alone, away from the rest. Dylan knew how it felt. It had probably been kicked out of the flock for being different, or for being too green. Or maybe it was just watching the strange white-skinned people wandering through the swamps below. The parrot was probably laughing at them — if a parrot could laugh.

"Look, Dylan!" Quentin exclaimed, pointing at two colorful birds perched in a nearby tree. "Birds of paradise."

"I knew what they were," Dylan lied, flicking a wormlike insect off his arm. A lizard dashed across the trail, vanishing under a rock.

———

All morning they had been walking out in the hot sun. By midday, the swamp felt like a steam bath. Dylan's clothes dripped with sweat and clung to his body as if he had been swimming. Allen kept pointing out poisonous plants or insects. Soon, Dylan was afraid of what he could touch and not touch, where he should step and not step.

In some places the trail passed through swampy meadows of tall *kunai* grass with sharp edges that cut at their arms like little knives. Dylan's boots grew soggy and filled with ooze. With each step, his feet squished. He wished he had taken Uncle Todd's suggestion of coating the boots with oil. Sitting in a cozy dry condo in Oregon, he never really thought he would end up in this weird place. Now, Dylan wanted to stop and dry his feet. "How much farther are we going today?" he complained.

"We have another four hours of hiking to a small village called Balo, where we'll stay tonight," Uncle Todd said. "From there we begin asking locals if they know of any wrecks."

Dylan was thankful when the trail finally angled into the jungle. The intense sun disappeared, but the foliage became dense and thick. This wasn't a jungle where Tarzan could swing from tree to tree. If you left the trail some places, you couldn't crawl on your hands and knees. It was a solid wall of vegetation from the ground up. Ferns and palms grew everywhere in the moist, steamy air. The only way to leave the trail here was with a machete. Decaying moss and rotting foliage left the air ripe and pungent.

Sago palms had thorns that ripped at Dylan's arms, but he had to walk with his arms out in front to protect his face from the twisted vines. They curved everywhere, like the intestines of some huge monster that had swallowed him. Now other new things appeared: frogs as big as his boot, little swift birds that darted here and there catching insects, and plenty of slithering salamanders, lizards, and snakes.

"Be careful," Allen warned. "The more colorful a critter is, the better chance that it's poisonous."

"Look!" Quentin exclaimed, pointing to where a huge fifteen-foot python lay stretched across a fallen log.

"We ain't in Kansas no more, Toto," Dylan mumbled. That had been his father's favorite saying.

CHAPTER 10

When they finally reached the clearing that exposed the small village of Balo, Dylan was spent. "Where's the Holiday Inn?" he asked.

"Welcome to the municipality of Balo," Allen announced, as if he were the head of the Balo Chamber of Commerce.

"This is going to get old, sleeping in these things," Dylan said, pointing at the dozen small thatched pole huts standing high off the ground.

"Would you rather sleep in the jungle?" Uncle Todd said.

Barking dogs announced their arrival, and quickly villagers peered out from behind trees, huts, and doorways. Smoke from the cooking fires curled upward but hung like a fog around the village in the heavy heat. Under each hut, pigs squealed, chickens clucked, children played, and the women cooked over smoldering fires. The air smelled burnt.

Villagers turned to watch the visitors walking among the huts. Some of the women had no front teeth. They smiled with big toothless grins, their mouths stained red from chewing betel nuts. Some had necklaces made from dogs' teeth.

Dylan's shoulders felt as if they were floating when he removed his backpack. Exhausted, he slumped to the ground. He didn't feel very good. His whole body ached, and he was sweating more than the others. The rest of the group, including Quentin, waited eagerly to be shown around the small village. "You coming along, Dylan?" asked Gene. The big bald-headed man spoke the least of anybody in the group.

Before Dylan could answer, Uncle Todd motioned. "Come along. I want us to stay together."

Reluctantly Dylan struggled to his feet. What could there possibly be to see?

It was obvious the village didn't get many visitors. A cluster of curious children followed behind the group. All were barefoot. Allen pulled out his picture of the B-17 *Second Ace*, and tried to explain to the elders that this plane had crashed near here and that they were looking for it. The two elders spoke excitedly between themselves, motioning and gesturing with their arms, but finally shook their heads. They hadn't seen any plane wreckage.

Allen explained, "They say they haven't seen *Second Ace*, but that may not be true. Sometimes the wreckages have become forbidden places because of the dead. Sometimes local chiefs have performed ceremonies to appease the spirits of the swamps. Once a chief told me he hadn't seen anything but was actually wearing a GI's dog tag for a necklace." Allen shrugged. "We just keep asking. We'll find something."

Because of the jungle, it was hard to tell the sun had gone down, but nightfall came on quickly, leaving them rushing to grab their backpacks. Motioning, an elder led them to their hut for the night. There were no dogs barking under this hut, but Dylan heard pigs squealing, rutting, and grunting. He also heard chickens scratching and clucking, their chicks making peeping squeaks as they scurried about. Under the hut hung the quarters of a pig that had been killed. The smell made Dylan dizzy and sick to his stomach. He fought the urge to throw up.

"You pay for atmosphere," Uncle Todd joked, climbing up into the hut. The ladder was no more than a single log leaned at an angle with notches cut for steps. Carefully Dylan followed. He felt faint.

With no mosquito nettings provided, each of them dug into their backpacks to pull out mosquito tents they had brought along themselves. Dylan struggled to hold the flashlight as he fumbled with the thin netting. He had barely spread it out on the floor when Quentin stood and announced, "Mine's up!"

"You probably practiced that at home," Dylan said sarcastically.

"Actually, I did," Quentin said seriously. "In better light, I can do it in less than two minutes."

When all of their mosquito nets were up, Allen gathered everybody together. "I want you to each look through your survival kits tonight to remind yourself of what's in there.

Here, it may save your life." He rubbed his chin. "Don't go anywhere without your backpack and survival kit. It's your only defense against a jungle that is profoundly beautiful but can easily kill you. From now on, your survival kit should be part of your body."

Obediently, everybody sorted through their kits.

Dylan rummaged through his pack. He pulled out canned ham and eggs, plus bacon, Spam, hash, and stew. There were several dry powders for making milk and orange juice, and some matches — as if he was going to need them in this heat.

The candy bars he had smuggled along had melted all over the bottom of the back pack and onto many of his clothes. Already ants had discovered the chocolate. Dylan grunted with frustration and tried to ignore the mess, stuffing everything back on top. Uncle Todd would love to chew him out for doing something else stupid.

Dylan had thought the food was bad in Swagup, but tonight they ate some kind of rat and more pads of cooked sago starch. It didn't matter because Dylan had lost his appetite. It could have been pizza and he still wouldn't have been hungry. Lying awake in the dark, listening to the monotonous wailing of insects, Dylan felt chilled. Loud, vicious grunts sounded from deep in the jungle. Dylan looked over and could make out Quentin sound asleep under his mosquito net, his breaths deep and regular.

The next morning the group rose early again, this time hiking mostly among the trees. Huge roots poked out of the ground like big tentacles trying to trip them. Branches, vines, palms, and grasses swiped at their faces and arms.

"What was that grunting sound last night?" Dylan asked.

"Those were feral pigs," Quentin said. "They're wild, but they were once tame. Somehow they escaped or got lost, so now they're considered feral. That's what feral means; they were tame to begin with, but now they're wild. If they had always been wild, the —"

"Okay, okay!" Dylan said. "I get it!"

Quentin frowned, his feelings hurt.

A big cobweb snared Dylan's face and arm as he passed. He swiped madly at it, as if at some invisible monster, only to trip on a gnarly root and sprawl headfirst onto the ground. The heavy cloud of mosquitoes swarmed over Dylan like a haze, always biting.

Quentin moved to help him up, but Dylan grunted and waved him away. He stood slowly on his own.

"I don't need your help," he snapped. "And I don't need you explaining everything to me like I'm a kid."

"I'm just trying to be nice," Quentin said.

"No, you're just trying to show off. I get it, Quentin. Everybody gets it. You're the Einstein and I'm the screw-up. Go brag to someone else. I'm not interested."

"I don't think —"

"Yes, you do!" Dylan shouted. He jabbed his finger at Quentin's chest. "You all do. I know Uncle Todd told you all why I'm here. I'm the dumb nephew who got in trouble. I'm the bad kid he has to scare straight with a hike through the jungle. Well if Uncle Todd thought this was going to fix me, he was wrong. This whole trip is a stupid idea."

Dylan stomped off, leaving Quentin behind. For some reason he felt like he was about to cry, and there was no way he'd let Quentin see that.

Because of the thick canopy of trees, nobody noticed the dark, ominous clouds gathering over the jungle. It was mid-afternoon before they broke into a small opening and could look up and see the angry sky churning above them. Allen called a stop. "Everybody take a little break. Let's see what this weather is up to."

Uncle Todd approached Dylan. "Stay close," he ordered quietly.

"You're not my babysitter," Dylan shot back.

"Actually, I am," Uncle Todd replied. "Don't make me sit on you."

Dylan waited until Uncle Todd turned away, and then mouthed, "Whatever!"

He had to go to the bathroom like everybody else, but before walking away from the group to relieve himself, Dylan reached into his backpack and pulled out his headphones. He didn't need his backpack, because he was just going to the bathroom, but he was going to have a few moments of sanity alone.

Dylan walked until the jungle hid the group from his sight, and then put on the headphones and cranked up the volume. The blast of heavy metal music carried him instantly away from where he was. After relieving himself, Dylan deliberately walked farther from the group. They would be mad if they knew what he was doing, but he didn't feel good, and he was angry and tired. He really didn't want to talk to Quentin anymore. Especially not after admitting he was a screw-up.

The trees where Dylan walked were dense, with several small paths branching off. He looked down and could see his footprints clearly in the soft ground. It would be simple to follow the tracks back to the group. He kept walking, each step a deliberate act of defiance against the stupid adults who thought they knew what was best for him. His loud music kept Dylan from hearing the whistles and shouts from the group — already they were trying to locate him.

Dylan decided he didn't care what anybody thought anymore. If the group wanted to play Boy Scouts, that was okay. But he didn't have to. He swayed and bobbed to the beat of his music, walking aimlessly down the twisting trail. He pushed his pants down some. He felt big drops of rain hit his arms but ignored them — every day it rained a little in the jungle. Not until the drops became heavier did Dylan take notice and finally turn around to head back. Suddenly, a sharp clap of thunder sounded over the music in his ears. At the same instant the sky burst open and dumped water, as if a swimming pool had been turned upside down.

At first Dylan walked slowly back toward the group, enjoying the cool drenching relief. Rain wouldn't hurt him. But then he looked down and discovered his prints had disappeared, washed away by a small stream now covering the path. Dylan quickened his pace, but the first intersection he came to looked strange and unfamiliar. He turned and looked back, no longer sure which path had taken him away from the group — he hadn't been paying attention. He pulled off the headphones and began to shout, but his voice was totally washed out by the drenching downpour and the deafening claps of thunder that echoed back and forth across the sky.

Dylan tried to stay calm. He couldn't be very far from the group. Stumbling, he began running down the trail, dodging the branches and tangled vines that hung over the narrow path. The rain stung his eyes. An exposed root tripped him, and he sprawled on the muddy trail. Picking himself up, he rubbed a bruised elbow and kept running. Where was the group?

It had begun with nervousness and then grown into a nagging fear. Now blind panic gripped Dylan. He screamed desperately and kept plunging ahead into the downpour, searching frantically for anything that might look familiar.

How long he ran he couldn't even guess. Soon his lungs burned, and he sucked in hard to catch his breath. The wind and rain continued. The streams down the paths became small rivers, and with each step, Dylan's feet sank deeper and deeper into the water and muck. Still, nothing looked familiar.

Lightning flashed above the thick tree cover like madness in the sky, and the deafening thunder sounded almost constantly. Dylan gasped for air as he kept running. He stumbled wildly through the trees until the path disappeared and he found himself standing deep in the jungle, up to his ankles in water. Then, as suddenly as the rain started, it stopped.

Dylan stood trembling. He screamed again, but for the first time he realized how many other noises there were in the jungle. These weren't the noises he was used to back home: children screaming, doors slamming, lawn mowers running. Here there were weird, scary sounds, strange grunts and rustles in the undergrowth, the screeching and screaming of birds in the canopy overhead, and the ear-piercing chorusing of the insects.

Probably nobody in the world could hear his puny, insignificant voice screaming. For the first time in his life, Dylan felt so very small. His cheeks had dried from the sweat and rain, but now they became wet again with desperate tears.

CHAPTER 11

At first, Dylan thought this whole thing was just a bad dream. A tiny mistake. A little screw-up. Anytime now, one of the guides would come running down the path calling out his name. They would find him and take him back to the rest of the group — that was their job. Allen Jackson would give him a lecture on survival. Uncle Todd would get mad in his typical drill sergeant way. And everybody would say, "We told you so."

But that wasn't happening. Each long minute that passed, the knot in Dylan's stomach tightened. If only he had just stopped running when the rain first started. Now he could be miles from the group. What should he do? Even as he stood debating, mosquitoes swarmed around his head and arms, biting. Rain and sweat had washed off any repellant he had put on that morning. Walking might help a little, but what if he was walking farther away from the group? While he was standing still, however, the mosquitoes kept chowing down.

Dylan looked around desperately for anything that looked familiar. Where was the big swamp they had walked along? Where was the long log where they had seen the python?

What direction was the village of Balo? Or some other village? Any village! There had to be people somewhere.

This was all Uncle Todd's fault. It was his idea to come on this trip. Who did he think he was, some stupid explorer?

But Dylan knew the truth. He had been a bonehead. If only he had taken his pack when he went to the bathroom — that was what everyone else had done. And it would have been so easy to stay near the group. Allen had warned all of them how dangerous the jungle could be. Already Dylan knew he was a big screw-up, but would this be his last mistake?

To make things worse, Dylan felt the same nausea he had felt earlier, in the village. And his chills had grown worse. Something wasn't right — it had to be almost 100 degrees out. After the rain, the jungle had become a steam bath, so why was he so cold? He shivered as if he were standing naked in a snowstorm. Dylan buttoned up his shirt all the way to the top, but it didn't help.

Again and again Dylan waved at the mosquitoes, but it was wasted motion. Instantly the hungry little vampires returned, attacking his face and neck. Dylan tried pulling the shirt up over his head, but then the blood suckers feasted on his back and stomach. Dylan turned and kept going — he couldn't just stand there. If he walked fast, surely he would come to someone or someplace soon.

Overhead, clouds hid the sun. Dylan realized that even if he could see the sun, he hadn't made a mental note of where it was earlier when they were walking. That was the guides' job — to keep them from getting lost. With blind determination, Dylan plunged deeper into the jungle, searching for anything familiar. But everything looked the same. Overhead, trees formed a solid canopy of jumbled, twisted branches. Now he couldn't even see the sky.

Still Dylan continued walking.

For the first time he really noticed the strange world in which he was lost. Heavy beards of some kind of moss hung from the branches and vines. Flowers with blazing colors and strange shapes blossomed among the deadfall. Everywhere new growth sprouted, green buds, things alive and fresh, shoots and vines beginning life. But there were also decay and rot, things dead or dying. With the heat and moisture, trees probably decayed in weeks. That was the cycle of life. What bothered Dylan was the thought that he might soon be part of the dead-or-dying segment of the cycle.

For Dylan, time disappeared. How long had it been since the rainstorm when he became lost? Two hours? Ten hours? Had he walked one mile or five miles? He existed in a daze, simply here at this moment, chilled and nauseated, mouth as dry as dust and muck up to his shins. He could barely even feel his feet.

When Dylan's chills ended, he began to sweat. He imagined Quentin's voice back in the group. "Why didn't Dylan listen? Why didn't Dylan think? What was dumb Dylan thinking?"

Dylan envied Quentin right now. Himself, he didn't know a single plant or bird. He had no idea what he could touch or eat. Every noise was weird and new. Strange and scary sounds came from the underbrush, sometimes moving away as if scared, but sometimes coming closer — those sounds raised the hair on his neck. Dylan had no choice but to keep going. For the next few hours he trudged down narrow paths, no longer looking for something familiar, no longer waving the mosquitoes away. Just moving.

Finally he had to stop. Dylan touched his cheeks, puffy from all the mosquito bites. His mouth had become chalk-dry but he dared not drink water from the puddles all around him — the murky fluid smelled stagnant and putrid. Dylan tried to swallow, but his tongue was dry and swollen, like a big rock in his mouth. He looked for a coconut tree but couldn't find one. There had been dozens of coconut trees near Balo and Swagup. Allen had said something about them being planted by villagers.

Somehow Dylan knew he had to find fluid. Finally he came across a single coconut tree. Dylan tried to climb the thin tree but gave up — his body could barely stand. Reluctantly he picked a coconut off the ground that looked fresh and examined it. It wasn't like the ones in the market. This one still had a tough husk covering the shell. In any case, it couldn't be too old. Allen Jackson had said something to the group about not drinking from a coconut on the ground, but what choice did he have? Allen was probably talking about coconuts that had fallen a while ago. This one looked fresh — probably just fell off the tree today.

Dylan began ripping at the husk. If only he had his knife from his survival kit. Even after much ripping, most of the husk clung stubbornly to the shell. Finally, Dylan gave up and began striking the husk against a sharp edge of a rock until a small crack appeared in the shell. He held the coconut up and sipped the wet juice leaking from the crack. The coconut water ran down the sides of his cheeks as he drank. When the shell was empty, Dylan picked up another and ripped at the husk again. Once more he gave up and pounded the shell on the rock. It took great effort for the small amount of coconut water he was able to drink. It tasted gross but was wet.

Finally able to swallow again, Dylan looked down. His ripped and muddy shirt hung open, and clinging to his stomach like small sausages were three big leeches, their black bodies stark against his white skin. Dylan freaked, raising his hands up and jumping around in circles. In desperation, he reached down and one by one he ripped them off, throwing them into the jungle like tiny grenades.

Dylan examined his stomach. Each leech had left a welt that now leaked blood from the center. It was at that moment that Dylan remembered Allen Jackson saying, "If you don't have alcohol, simply leave leeches alone. Once they're full of blood, they just fall off. Don't pull them off!"

Dylan wanted to scream. He knew what he should have done, but he had already ripped them off. Why did he always have to do things without thinking? He believed that everything and everybody in the world was stupid except him. But maybe that was all a big lie. Everything that had happened at home — stealing, fights, skipping school, breaking into the junkyard — it had all been his fault. And here — thinking mosquito spray was for wimps, wandering away from the group without his survival kit, pulling off the leeches — that had all been his fault, too. He was the stupid one.

Dylan stared down into a smelly pool of water and saw his reflection. He hardly recognized the dirty ghost he saw. He spit angrily at the puddle and kept walking. He had no idea what to do or where to go, but he had to keep moving. That meant he was still alive. Walking made a moving target for the mosquitoes. But walking had become hard. His wet boots rubbed on his heels, causing big blisters that burned with every step and made him limp. His legs felt like rubber posts. His mud-caked boots felt like big anchors on his feet. Dylan had the haunting feeling that if he stopped too long, he would die.

Finally, Dylan stopped again. He could ignore the stinging of his leech wounds and the painful hurt from his blisters, but the itching of mosquito bites made his skin feel like it was on fire. He reached down and cupped handfuls of mud in his hand and smeared them over his face and body to ward off the vicious small insects that kept attacking him. Then he continued limping down the trail.

Sometime later, he glanced up, fearing it would soon be getting dark. And then what? How could he survive a night in the jungle? There were probably animals that came out at night that would like nothing better than to eat a bonehead boy from Wisconsin.

Suddenly, Dylan's stomach began cramping. He stopped and bent over until the big knot relaxed. Then again he walked and again he cramped. This time the pain felt like a knife stabbing him in the belly. The third time he bent over, he couldn't stand again. Falling to his knees, he started throwing up. Again and again, he heaved up the food he had eaten that morning. Then what came up was bile that stung his throat and tasted like battery acid.

Finally, weak and unable to throw up anything more, Dylan stood. Loud growls sounded from his bowels and stomach. Before he could start down the trail, diarrhea began. Almost too late, he pulled his pants down and sprayed the ground. When he thought he was finished, his stomach cramped again. The stabs of pain left him nauseous, sweating, and chilled all at once. Then he gagged up more bile.

For the next hour, Dylan kept moving, taking a few steps and then stopping with diarrhea or more retching. Without toilet paper, he used leaves, which left his bottom more raw with each new bout. One big leaf left a stinging rash. Dylan screamed in anger. Whatever was happening to him was no joke. But being angry didn't help. A swamp didn't care about blame or anger. This was real. The world was trying to kill him.

Once again Dylan hobbled down the trail. The sky had begun to darken with nightfall when he broke out into a small opening where an outcropping of rocks had kept trees from growing, all except for a single brown tree beside the rocks that had twisted upward in a giant spiral. The weird tree looked like a big screw piercing the sky. Dylan walked over to the base and looked up for a few minutes. This would be where he would try to spend the night. But how did one prepare for a night in a jungle? Whatever he did, it had to be quick.

With a survival kit, he could have started a fire. That alone would have been a comfort, driving away the mosquitoes and keeping wild animals at a distance. But that wasn't a choice. Dylan had no idea how to make a fire without matches. He also needed something to protect him from the mosquitoes and someplace for shelter in case it rained again. And he needed food.

The only thing he could think of for shelter was to gather a pile of the bearded moss that hung from the trees. He would have given anything to have Zipper here by his side, cuddling close and growling if anything approached. Why had he ever complained about sleeping overnight in Balo? Tonight he would have loved to smell smoke and hear people snore. It wouldn't bother him to hear pigs snort, dogs bark, and chickens scratch.

Armful after armful, Dylan pulled down the clammy moss and piled it next to the big screw tree. Hopefully the pile would allow him some protection. Feeling the chills coming on again and with darkness fully settled over the jungle,

Dylan pulled off his boots, hung up his socks and crawled under the moss. The pungent wet smell threatened to suffocate him, but still Dylan gathered the musty green vegetation closer to his body to ward off the mosquitoes.

As he lay on the hard ground, nausea swept over his body again like a wave trying to drown him. The shivering returned, and a pounding headache made his head throb. Dylan felt hot and confused. His joints ached and he couldn't sleep. For long hours into the night he suffered through hot flashes, shivers, and sweating. All the while, haunting new sounds echoed from the jungle, vicious and evil. High-pitched screaming, shrieking, and growling. Dylan was totally alone. Never in his life had he craved companionship so much. Even Quentin would have been great. Talking!

While chills and sweats wracked Dylan's body, his teeth chattered until his jaw hurt. Maybe the diarrhea and throwing up were from eating the coconuts, but the chills and fever had to be something worse. Could they possibly be from malaria? If so, Dylan felt like the biggest fool in the world. Why hadn't he taken the malaria pills? They were just little tiny white pills. It would have been no effort to swallow them. In fact, it had taken more effort to remove them from his mouth and throw them away.

During the long night, breathing became painful. Dylan took breaths carefully, as if sucking through a straw, so it wouldn't hurt. Big beads of sweat stung his eyes. Each time the fever disappeared, chills returned and left Dylan exhausted and short-winded.

Finally, too tired to stay awake, he fell into a troubled sleep. His dreams became nightmares. He dreamed that everybody he had ever known in the world was in the bleachers of a gym laughing at him. Then he dreamed rats were fighting over the last bits of his body here in the jungle. That's all he was good for, rat food! Before he woke up, he dreamed he was being eaten by cannibals. At least somebody could say something good about him. He tasted a little like chicken.

CHAPTER 12

Dylan woke with fire burning his skin. He screamed and rolled over, opening his eyes. Where were the flames? The only light he found came from the dawn breaking dimly over the small clearing in the jungle. Clawing away the moss covering his body, Dylan rolled to his knees and discovered ants, hundreds of them, swarming over his body. The small red insects attacked him like bees. Dylan leaped to his feet. He ripped off every piece of clothing he wore and ran naked away from the moss pile, slapping and brushing at the infernal little monsters.

When he was finally free of ants, Dylan returned to the tree and examined his body. Dozens of tiny welts blistered his skin. He shook his clothes until the last ant fell to the ground, and then pulled on the damp rags. His soggy boots were still coated with muck. Dylan was preparing to pull on a boot when something moved inside. He knocked the boot against a log, and out fell a big scorpion.

"Cripes!" he muttered, examining the insides of both boots more carefully. Then, grunting with pain, he pried a foot into each boot. The idea of walking another day made him want to cry.

By the time he was ready to leave, dawn had brought a warm glow to the sky. At least the mosquitoes and other insects hadn't started swarming yet. Dylan tried to think clearly, but even a simple thought proved difficult. He needed to find food of some kind today. And he needed to find something to drink. If he didn't find food and water, he would die. He didn't want to die. That thought kept repeating in his mind.

Small animal trails angled out of the clearing away from the screw tree. Dylan stood, trying to decide which one to follow. As he weighed his choices, he noticed a single human footprint close to the big tree on the side of a trail where rain had not washed it away. The small barefoot imprint looked to be that of a young child. If there had been a child here, this clearing couldn't be that far from some kind of civilization. Dylan looked around the clearing, trying to guess which trail might have brought that footprint here. He picked what appeared to be the path most used and began walking.

Never in his life had Dylan hurt this much. Nausea churned his stomach, fever and chills swept through his body, blisters pained his feet, his rash from the diarrhea burned, and the leech bites looked puss-filled and swollen. And now the ant bites left little welts that stung.

Still, only one thing really mattered.

Food.

Dylan would have given anything for the canned and powdered food in his survival kit. Now the catfish, sago starch, and cooked rat didn't seem so bad. He stumbled down the trail, searching for anything he could eat. The jungle had plenty of berries and plants and weird fruit-looking things hanging on the trees, but Allen had warned that many were poisonous. And yet, how ironic would it be if searchers found him starved to death, lying beside some plant that he could have eaten. The epitaph on his gravestone would read, "Here rests a boy who was too stupid to live!"

As Dylan plodded down the trail, the dense jungle thinned. By mid-morning he had broken out of the trees into a swamp, but this swamp looked different from the one they hiked past when they were leaving Balo. The sky had clouded over, but not with the angry churning clouds that brought the downpour yesterday. These clouds brought relief from the relentless sun.

Dylan collapsed on a log. His blisters bled and hurt so badly he had no choice but to remove his boots and carry them over his shoulder. Barefoot, he continued. It felt wonderful to take off the soggy anchors that had pained his feet, but now every step had to be careful and deliberate. This was hard in places where his feet sank into the muck up to his shins, or where the water rose above his waist. By mid-afternoon, Dylan still hadn't found anything to eat. His body began to grow weak. He was a car running out of gas.

The swamp was quieter than the jungle, and Dylan tried shouting. His puny voice didn't even echo. It sounded no louder than a cricket across the endless fields of swamp grass. At home, he had always thought he was so important, the center of attention one way or another — usually it was another. But here, he was insignificant, a pebble tossed into a huge ocean. This place didn't care about him. He could die in this jungle and it would be no different than a rat dying. Realizing he was so small terrified him.

Looking around at the swampy marshland, Dylan puzzled. There had to be something to eat. Besides the mosquitoes, there were tons of other insects and bugs. Even as Dylan brushed a grasshopper from his pants leg, other grasshoppers bounced about, thick in the tall grasses. Dylan paused, struggling to recall a vague memory he had of somebody eating chocolate covered ants. Or was it grasshoppers? Ants wouldn't be very filling but grasshoppers might be okay. Hesitantly, Dylan cupped his hand over a grasshopper and crushed it. Before chickening out, he stuffed the springy little bug into his mouth. The legs and shell crunched as he chewed, and a black ink squirted out from its tail. When Dylan wiped his lips, black fluid smeared the back of his hand.

It didn't matter what the grasshopper tasted like, Dylan knew only that he needed to eat more or die. He would find out really quickly if these grasshoppers were poisonous. Dropping to his knees, he crawled through the marsh, grabbing frantically at the bouncing insects and stuffing the unlucky ones into his mouth as fast as he could. They kicked at his tongue as he chewed them.

Dylan captured and ate grasshoppers until his hands and knees bled from crawling around on the spongy, prickly ground. This satisfied his need for food, but where could he find water? He remembered one thing from school; the human body could live for a month without food, but only three days without water. Not having water would kill him, especially dehydrated as he was from sweating and diarrhea.

Thunder sounded overhead and a light breeze picked up. By now Dylan's lips were swollen. When he opened his mouth, his lips cracked. It would have hurt terribly to smile. Besides, today there was nothing to smile about. Even as it began raining again, Dylan had no idea how he could collect the water that fell. He tilted his head back and painfully opened his mouth, but only a few drops hit his tongue. Here he was with thousands of gallons of fresh water dumping from the sky and he could barely capture a single drop. Then an idea struck him.

Dylan pulled off his shirt and spread it out on top of the chest-tall grass, letting the muddy ripped material soak up the rain. In minutes, water dripped from the cloth. Dylan rolled up the wet shirt and held it up so that when he wrung it out, the water drained into his mouth. Brown water squeezed from the muddy shirt, but it worked. Again, Dylan stretched the ragged cloth out, and again he wrung the water into his mouth. Knowing that when the rain stopped, his water supply would end, Dylan kept drinking. Even after he felt full, he gulped and gulped more. Water was the single thing he needed most to stay alive.

As quickly as the light shower started, it ended. For the first time, Dylan knew he had done something smart. For once he had done the right thing, and he felt proud.

For a few brief minutes the mosquitoes had disappeared during the rain, but now they returned, along with swarms of other insects, some big enough to suck serious blood. Dylan kept walking, constantly waving the pests away from his face. He carefully picked each step as he slogged through the rotting and stinking swamp. There had to be a village somewhere.

Some places in the swamp, Dylan had to wade through water up to his chest. He inched forward, eyeing snakes that glided past. One was green, another brown. Two were bright orange. But what else was in the water? Were there water monsters waiting for Dylan's next step? He watched for crocodiles, but were there flesh-eating bolkatas this far from the river? Dylan waded, swishing one hand in front to guard himself. What else was out there that he didn't even know about?

Something big brushed against his leg, big enough to stir the water when it swam away. Dylan fought the urge to go crazy, splashing and convulsing and screaming in sheer panic.

Instead he reached his foot forward hesitantly, consciously breathing slower. His heart beat like a drum in his chest.

Deliberately, Dylan waded into shallower water where the grasses grew.

Though reeds sliced at his arms and legs, he decided this was safer. By late afternoon, blood seeped from long cuts crisscrossing his body. His pants looked like shredded rags. Again Dylan risked wading into deeper water. He spotted more snakes, and angled toward a part of the bog where large stones dotted the surface.

Twenty feet from the stones, Dylan suddenly realized they had eyes. What he had thought were rounded rocks was actually a group of small crocodiles watching him, lying motionless, mostly submerged. Being in the same water with them really freaked Dylan out. It reminded him of the anti-aircraft fire Grandpa mentioned in his journal. When the shells exploded, the puff of black and the exploding bomb fragments were called *flak*. One of the journal entries had said that it was never the flak you saw that killed you — it was the flak you didn't see. Maybe that was how it was with crocodiles and snakes, too.

Holding his breath, a lump clogging his throat, Dylan moved slowly away from the group of beady eyes. He didn't know which was better, wading through smelly black water with snakes and crocodiles, stumbling through the wet marshland with grass reeds cutting him up like knives, or hiking deep in the jungle where nobody could see him twenty feet away? An extra-big green snake that swam past within feet of him made Dylan decide to find higher ground.

As he waded toward distant trees, a dull droning of an aircraft sounded far away. At first, Dylan ignored the faint sound, but slowly it grew louder and louder. Dylan stopped and searched the empty sky, waiting. No aircraft had flown anywhere close since he became lost. Now the droning became a roar. In a blinding flash, a blue and silver plane screamed past overhead, so low and fast that Dylan didn't even have time to wave his arms or shout. As quickly, the droning of the engine faded.

Then it disappeared and silence returned.

Dylan stood all alone in the middle of the grassy swamp looking up, blinking back tears. The plane probably carried tourists from Wewak or Ambunti who were being shown the beautiful swamps and jungles of Papua New Guinea — the same beautiful place where a boy from Wisconsin was lost. The same beautiful place that was slowly killing Dylan Barstow. "Please come back," Dylan cried out, his voice just one more insignificant animal sound in the great expanse of nothingness. He turned and kept wading toward the trees. Down here it wasn't so beautiful.

The setting sun worried Dylan. He had been able to find food and water, but could he survive another night in the jungle? Or was he just postponing his death with everything he now did? Maybe he was going to die anyway in two or three days after a lot of wasted suffering. Maybe it would be better to just lie down here in the swamp and give up — let the snakes, crocodiles, and rats have a free lunch. Who said he only thought of himself!

But then Dylan thought of his grandfather. Uncle Todd had said that Grandpa had survived for two weeks in these jungles — and that was while wounded after crashing in a bomber. The very notion shamed Dylan and filled him with deep respect. He wouldn't have lived even this long if Uncle Todd hadn't made him run to get in shape. If Grandpa had survived for two weeks, Dylan knew he had to make it at least one more day. If he couldn't, he deserved to die. Dylan clenched his teeth. He wasn't ready to die yet.

He struggled to concentrate as random images bombarded his mind: the old waist gunner from the nursing home, the VFW marching past in the parade, the police car waiting for him to quit spinning circles in the junkyard, shoplifting, all the trips to the principal's office, the many fights he had picked, arguing with his mom, drifting Uncle Todd's Corvette. Everything seemed to be part of some big pattern. Dylan's thoughts became clouded and confused as he walked.

Dylan slogged through the swamp toward the trees. He needed to find dry ground where he could spend the night again. Still he watched for snakes and crocodiles. The air reeked of rotting undergrowth. All day he had seen birds, rats, possums, and other animals to eat, but no way to catch them. The only critters Dylan could approach were snakes and crocodiles.

He knew the snakes might be poisonous, and there was no way he was going to try to catch a crocodile, even a small one.

Before leaving the tall grasses, Dylan ate a few more grasshoppers, and then deliberately headed for a root-tangled path entering the jungle. Soon, the thick, matted screen of overhead vines and leaves muted any fading sunlight that made it through the clouds. For the next hour, Dylan stumbled along a trail, no longer looking down to pick his footing. He had to find some kind of refuge before dark, a place where he could be out in the open but on higher ground. He needed a space where he could lie down and still see wild animals approaching. Hopefully a place with fewer insects.

As the light faded, a brief shower of rain fell. Only a few drops penetrated the dense canopy. Suddenly a sharp pain stabbed Dylan's ankle. He glanced down in time to see a dark brown snake recoil and slither across the trail and into the undergrowth. "Ouch," he muttered, crouching. He pulled up his right pant leg to find four small puncture wounds where the snake had sunk its fangs.

Without thinking, Dylan panicked and began running down the trail. But even as he ran, he realized it was probably the dumbest thing he could do after a snake bite. Still he kept running. If he stopped, he would just die here on some muddy overgrown trail in the jungles of Papua New Guinea. By morning, rats would have picked his bones clean. By next week, other critters would have his bones scattered through the forest like twigs and branches. The world would never even know what had happened to Dylan Barstow.

Dylan ran faster. He had to find protection or help.

Overhead the light had faded into darkness. Now the only light came from a hazy moon hanging in the sky like a dim lightbulb. At that very instant, Dylan broke into a clearing similar to the one where he had slept the night before. He walked out away from the darkness of the trees into the moonlight and froze in shock. Ahead were rocks, and next to the rocks stood a tall spiral tree that looked like a big screw. This was the same place he had left early this morning. Without a compass, he had walked all day in a huge circle, only to end up back where he had begun.

Dylan blinked his eyes, as if doing so might make the stupid tree disappear. He shook his head as a wave of despair washed over him, worse than any chill or fever. Dylan screamed, desperate and primal, his voice piercing the hush that had fallen over the clearing. As he finished, tears started down his cheeks, stopping to rest each time he hiccupped with grief. And then a different spasm flooded through his body, and his knees buckled. Dylan collapsed to the ground. The jungle spun in circles. He felt suddenly stiff and cold, as if his body were freezing in a blizzard.

And then there was nothing.

CHAPTER 13

When Dylan lost consciousness, time disappeared. He remembered little of that night. His body jerked and sweated and shook with chills. His dreams became violent nightmares with terrible ghoulish creatures skulking around his body with toothy snarls and hungry yellow eyes. Other sounds were evil: shrieking, barking, and hissing. When Dylan tried to open his eyes, shadows hunkered over him. He dug his fingers into the soil to try and cling to sanity.

He never knew when night became day. He woke to the feeling of something eating his leg. He jerked and sat up. Nothing made sense. He expected a monster, or maybe a wild pig or rat. Instead he found a small girl wearing only a grass skirt and a T-shirt. She backed away from him when she saw him become conscious. Her curious eyes showed no fear. She was short and stocky, with brown skin, curly hair, skinny legs, and a small potbelly. Her weathered bare feet were rough and worn like leather. Blood smeared her cheeks and lips. Deliriously, Dylan thought of a child eating a big ice-cream cone. An ice-cream cone made of Dylan's blood.

He looked down at his leg and found the skin ripped from the girl biting on his ankle. Blood was everywhere, even in the grass. "Get away from me!" he shouted. "You cannibal!"

She remained crouched, eyeing him. Hesitantly she raised her small hand and pointed at his ankle.

Dylan felt dizzy. "You're crazy!" he challenged again. "That's my foot. You were trying to eat me."

The girl held a bag in her left hand made of bark strips. She edged toward his foot, and Dylan pulled back. "I said, stay away from me!" he shouted.

The girl cocked her head sideways, as if trying to figure out a puzzle. She motioned again at his ankle. "You're talking stupid. You have a snake bite," she said in plain English.

Dylan stared at the young native girl. "You speak English?"

"So do you," she quipped back.

Dylan grimaced. The girl's English sounded nothing like the awkward broken sentences he'd heard other natives use. She pulled a paste from her bag. "This might help," she said, smearing the greenish paste on Dylan's ankle.

It hurt, but Dylan was too weak to argue. Still he didn't trust this girl — her English was too perfect. Where had she come from? "What's your name?" Dylan asked.

"Kanzi," she said. "And what's yours?"

"Dylan."

"Deeeeloooon," she said, playing with his name.

Dylan looked at his ankle and at the mangled skin. "How come you were chewing on my ankle?" he demanded.

"I had to make the skin bleed. A snake with poison bit you."

"I knew that," Dylan said.

"Then why didn't you make the bite bleed?" Her tone of voice was slow and deliberate, as if she were talking to a child.

Even as she spoke, Dylan clenched his teeth and grimaced to ward off the waves of chills that coursed through his body. He examined the small girl skeptically. "Where do you live?"

Kanzi motioned over her shoulder with her chin. "In Maswa — far away." Then she pointed at Dylan. "Where do you live?"

"In Wisconsin — far away, too," Dylan said. "What are you doing here?"

The impish girl lowered her head in shame. "This place and this tree, it's one of my secret places." She looked at him, her brow wrinkled with concern. "You're sick. Why are you here?"

Dylan lay back on the ground. "Because I was stupid and because I walked in circles."

The air had warmed, and the mosquitoes and flies swarmed thick around them. Kanzi reached down and pulled on Dylan's hand. "Get up," she said, motioning to the shade across the clearing. "Don't sit in the sun."

Kanzi held Dylan's elbow as he stood. It took all of his strength to hobble into the shade, where he collapsed again to the ground. The shade felt better, but the insects still attacked him. "I wish we had a fire," he stammered, shivering in spite of the heat.

Kanzi reached into her bag and pulled out a stick, a small block of wood and some dry wood shavings. Her fingers moved swiftly as she bent over and braced the block of wood against her chest and rolled the stick back and forth between her palms.

Dylan grimaced. No way would she start a fire by just twirling a stick back and forth between her palms.

Still Kanzi kept rolling the stick with quick, sharp movements. She stopped once to gather the shavings closer, and then kept working, determination bunching her lips.

"That won't start a fire," Dylan mumbled at almost the same instant that a wisp of smoke curled upward.

Kanzi bent forward and blew gently until a faint glow appeared. Carefully she added more bark shavings and blew again. Soon smoke billowed upward, and in seconds the whole pile of shavings burst into flames.

Dylan watched with amazement as the young girl coaxed the flames higher by adding more shavings. Soon a crackling flame warmed the air. Kanzi gathered damp moss to feed the fire so the smoke would keep insects away. She smiled, then pointed at the smoke and announced, "No more nat nats!"

Dylan felt embarrassed for having doubted the young girl. He wanted to hug her. "No more nat nats!" he allowed. Dylan looked at the girl, so alone but so confident. Who was she really? "My mom would freak if she knew I was out here alone," he said.

A sad look crossed Kanzi's face. "You're very lucky if you have a mother — that must make you happy. I have only parents who are not parents."

"What do you mean?" Dylan asked.

"My parents died in a flood when I was young. In Maswa, relatives take care of children who lose their parents. My grandmother took care of me but she has grown very old. My uncle who takes care of me now is a humbug man and does bad things. That's why I have special places where I go by myself. Everyone else is scared of the special places." She puffed up her chest. "Kanzi isn't scared."

With the fire going, Kanzi reached into her bark bag and pulled out chunks of dried fish and pads of cooked sago starch wrapped in banana leaves. She also had some kind of bird meat that definitely was not chicken. Three days ago, this food would have grossed Dylan out. Now, he ate it eagerly. He had little appetite, but this food meant life.

Kanzi pointed at him. "You're sick — go home."

Dylan shook his head. "I live too far away to go home."

She gave him a puzzled look. "Nobody is ever too far away to go home. The place you said, Wisconsin . . . is it near Ambunti or Wewak?"

Dylan shook his head. "Wisconsin." He spread his arms like an airplane. "I came from the other side of the world."

"Alone?"

"I was with four other people but I walked away from them, and it started raining. Now I'm lost."

Kanzi stared in disbelief. "You don't know where you are right now?"

"Everything looks the same," Dylan argued.

Kanzi shook her head. "No, every place is very different. The jungles and swamps always tell me where I am by how they look." She frowned. "You walked away from friends in a place where you could get lost? Why did you do that? That was stupid."

Dylan frowned at Kanzi. "Why don't you just say what you think?"

"Here in the jungle, many white people die because they're stupid," Kanzi said. She paused. "Stay here so you don't get lost again. I'll bring more food for the little lost white boy."

Dylan didn't argue but he didn't like how she treated him like a child. She was even younger than he was.

It seemed only minutes before Kanzi returned with a possum and some kind of tree rat, both freshly killed. Dylan was too weak and tired to care how she killed them. Hearing her talk and watching the young girl in her grass skirt, moving deliberately about, deft and light on her feet, he remembered an episode of *Star Trek*, that old TV show his mom loved. The crew of the starship *Enterprise* returned in a time warp

146

to Earth and remembered their primitive beginnings when humans still used money and had to earn their livings and pay taxes.

Maybe there was nothing dumb or simple about Kanzi. Maybe she knew more about how to survive in the world than every kid in Dylan's school combined. Maybe the latest clothes he wore from the mall, his smartphone and computer games, maybe those weren't the right measure of how intelligent and educated people were. Around this young, mouthy native girl, he felt really stupid.

Suddenly, Dylan had a thought. It took all his strength, but he reached into his back pocket and removed the laminated picture of the bomber *Second Ace*. "Have you ever seen this?" he asked, handing the picture to Kanzi.

She took the photograph and glanced at it with idle curiosity, but then her eyes grew big and she brought the picture closer to her face as if she were looking at a ghost.

"Have you ever seen that plane?" Dylan asked again.

She looked at Dylan and nodded, her eyes still wide. "It's one of my secret places." She studied Dylan. "Why did you come to my country?"

Dylan felt weak, but he began at the beginning and told everything, even how he was arrested at the junkyard and about not taking his malaria pills.

Kanzi listened carefully and watched him, like a judge preparing a verdict. At first her stare was almost fierce. As Dylan told his story, her gaze softened, becoming concerned.

"Now we want to find *Second Ace* and return the remains of the crew to their families so they can be buried," Dylan concluded.

Kanzi shook her head. "Stay away from *Second Ace*," she said.

"Why?" Dylan asked.

She lowered her voice as if telling Dylan a secret. "It has bad spirits. There are bones," she said. "Many bones."

CHAPTER 14

Dylan considered his situation as he struggled to think straight. This girl, Kanzi, knew where *Second Ace* was. Physically, he had neared the end of his rope. Kanzi said her village, Maswa, wasn't near. He was still separated from Uncle Todd, Quentin, Gene, and Allen — it was anybody's guess where they were now. So, how could he survive and try to find them?

"How far is your village from here?" Dylan asked.

"You're sick — Maswa is too far for you," she said.

"How far away is the bomber?"

She looked over her shoulder and shrugged. "Not far. For me, only a little ways. For you —" She shrugged again.

"It's too far to go to your village. I can't stay here. You have to take me to the bomber and let me stay there while you find my group."

Kanzi shook her head. "Kanzi doesn't have to do anything!" she said resolutely.

Politely, Dylan asked, "Will you please take me to the bomber and help me find my group?"

"There's bad spirits. Already white people have died trying to find that plane."

"I don't believe in bad spirits," Dylan said.

Kanzi smirked. "There are many things that white people don't believe. And what they do believe makes them fat and sick and weak. They always think they're smart, but when they come to our village, they have to be led around like pet monkeys. They must be told everything: not to stand in the sun, not to eat bad fruit, not to touch snakes. Even a frog knows these things. Many white people won't carry the heavy bags they bring. Do they have broken arms? Are they too weak? They know only their language, not ours. They talk as if we're dumb, and they come here to my country to steal from us. They burn our forests. They dig mines and make our rivers dirty."

"Do they know that you speak English?"

Kanzi shook her head. "No, and they don't ask. I never say anything because I like to hear the stupid things they say when they think we don't understand."

Dylan spoke carefully — he didn't want to make this girl mad. She was his only chance of getting out of here. But she was also being a jerk. "I didn't come to hurt your country," he said. "If you go and find help, where can I stay that's safe?"

Kanzi wrinkled her forehead in thought. "I can find your friends, but we're too far from my village to take you there. You can't stay here alone — it's lucky you didn't die yesterday." Now Kanzi ballooned her cheeks and stuck her bottom lip out in thought. Then, with a simple shrug, she said, "Yes, the big airplane is best. I hope you like bad spirits."

Dylan grimaced. He wished he didn't have to walk — every movement hurt.

Kanzi motioned for him to stand. "Let's go. You need medicine, and staying here doesn't make you stronger."

Painfully, Dylan stood and followed Kanzi away from the clearing. Trying not to stumble as he walked, he watched the odd little girl ahead of him. She was like a graceful cat, not tripping or touching branches, passing like a shadow through the undergrowth. The nimble, barefooted girl hopped from stump to stump, scampering across fallen logs wet with moss, dodging around ferns and vines and undergrowth, and finding trails where Dylan saw none.

Dylan kept falling behind. "What's the hurry?" he called.

Kanzi turned. "The sun and the moon don't wait for Deeeeloooon."

"No, but I need to catch my breath," Dylan complained.

"Does that make the darkness come later?" she asked.

Dylan pushed ahead through a thorny stand of palms, slipping on a muddy log. "This place sucks!" he said.

Kanzi ignored him, continuing down the root-tangled path, moving effortlessly and with confidence. Every few minutes she stopped and waited for Dylan to catch up, her dark hooded eyes showing impatience.

"I'm glad a crocodile isn't chasing us," Dylan commented, breathing hard to catch his breath.

Kanzi shrugged. "It would be okay, because he would catch you first."

"Real funny," Dylan said, gasping for air, his mouth dry as dirt. Hot spells and chills kept sweeping through his body in waves. A blade of tall grass sliced open his left hand like a knife, and the air reeked of the rotting undergrowth. His diarrhea had ended, but the bad rash left him limping.

Suffocating heat rose like steam in the jungle. Kanzi angled to the left of the faint path, hiking out of the trees into waist-deep swamp. "This way is shorter," she said, refusing to slow down.

"Why do you even live in a place like this?"

"Why does a fish live in water? Why does a bird fly in the air? Kanzi lives here!" she said, swinging a hand that purposely splashed Dylan with swamp muck.

When they finally waded up out of the deep black soup, Dylan collapsed beside the trail. "This place sucks!"

Kanzi turned and walked back to where he rested beside the trail. She stared at him with her big curious eyes. "Why are you this way?" she asked.

"What way?" Dylan muttered.

She shrugged. "You're not part of the world. You don't think. You don't listen to the sounds that come to your ears. You don't take time to look at the world. You are never thankful. You don't respect the world. You don't feel when the world touches you, or smile when it's funny. You don't cry when the world is sad. All you do is complain. You think the world was made only for Deeeeloooon."

"Whatever," Dylan grumped. "How much farther do we have to go?"

Kanzi looked down the trail as if calculating, then shrugged. "Maybe we'll get there when we get there." She laughed aloud at her own wit. "Or maybe you think we'll get there before we get there."

"You're not funny," Dylan snapped, struggling to his feet. He kept following Kanzi along the side of a huge swamp.

It was late afternoon before Kanzi pointed to a stand of trees nearby. "There's the airplane that's in your picture."

At first, Dylan saw nothing except dense vegetation. Had Kanzi not pointed, he would have noticed nothing.

But then he spotted the wreckage.

It looked like the huge bomber had tried to land in the marsh, but overshot and collided with the trees. Only the side of the fuselage was visible until they walked closer. One wing had been torn off, but the tail section remained intact. Trees must have been mowed down like grass when the bomber crashed, but now new trees had grown back around the wreck, making it look as if the plane had been set in place with a crane. Two of the engines had ripped off and rested like moss-covered boulders in the marsh grass. From the twisted wreckage, it was hard to believe that anyone had lived through such a crash.

As they approached the wreckage, Kanzi motioned. "Come over here."

Dylan walked around the front of the mangled fuselage. One side of the nose was totally destroyed, but on the other side somebody, probably Kanzi, had rubbed away the dirt. Faintly, but without any question, was painted a large red ace of hearts. Arched over the top, big letters read SECOND ACE. Dylan pulled the laminated photograph from his pocket and stared in stunned silence. This was it. After sixty years, it was like looking at a ghost. "I thought Uncle Todd was just dreaming," he whispered.

CHAPTER 15

"Come." Kanzi motioned. "I'll show you how to get inside." She led Dylan around through the tall grass. At one point they had to crawl on their hands and knees on spongy moss until they were almost under the tail, where Kanzi had found a ragged hole big enough to squeeze through. "The edges are sharp," she warned, pulling herself through the twisted opening. "And don't touch the bones. That is wrong."

Dylan squirmed up through the opening. "I won't touch the bones 'cause it gives me the creeps," he said, stopping to let his eyes adjust to the dim light. Every movement had to be careful because of the ragged metal edges left from the crash.

Kanzi crawled forward in the plane, swinging her small bag back and forth to knock down the spiderwebs that criss-crossed the open spaces.

Dylan stared quietly at the inside of the giant bomber. He could only imagine what it must have been like the day this mammoth machine went down, the injured crew yelling and screaming for help, the massive radial engines roaring and then suddenly going quiet, hissing and steaming in the swamp. How did his grandfather ever live through this wreck? For the first time it all became real to Dylan. These were real people, real planes, real crashes, and real war.

As his eyes adjusted to the darkness, Dylan stood upright, mouth open, stunned. There were bones, dozens of them, some chewed on, strewn around as if somebody had tossed them there. Probably rats and other animals had eaten all the flesh. Rodent droppings covered the muddy floor. But there was also a pair of glasses, boots, and a flak helmet with a human skull inside. A ring still hung from one skeleton's hand.

Over the years, storms and winds had washed mud through every opening. But some things looked untouched. Carefully, Dylan worked his way forward in the fuselage, climbing over the ball turret and stopping at the waist gunner's position. The two old fifty-caliber machine guns still rested in their cradles. Except for all the cobwebs, they might still work.

Continuing forward, Dylan crouched as he balanced on the narrow walkway that crossed the bomb bays. Somehow the top of the fuselage had been compressed downward and the top ball turret position had been totally wiped out. Maybe the plane had cartwheeled during the wreck. The cockpit looked like something out of a time warp, with all of its old controls and instruments. Dylan spit on his finger and rubbed one of the gauges. The dust and mud smeared off the glass to show numbers and calibration.

Kanzi refused to follow Dylan forward. She pulled the last of the food she had from her bag. "Come," she called. "I'll show you what you need to know if you're going to stay here tonight."

"Just a second," Dylan answered, searching around the cockpit, looking for the map box. He remembered his grandfather's journal talking about the flag he had stored to remind him why he was fighting. Almost ready to give up, he spotted a square container alongside and to the rear of the left seat. He had to pry at the cover to force it open, but stored in the box, with only a little dust, was a folded American flag.

"Hurry," called Kanzi. "I have to leave to get you help."

Dylan crawled back across the bomb bay, the flag tucked under his arm. Every movement took great effort. "Are you leaving right now?" he asked.

She shrugged. "Is it better if I leave next week?"

"No, I just thought with night —"

Kanzi held her index finger to her lips. "You talk too much for somebody who is foolish," she said.

Dylan collapsed on the floor and leaned against the side of the fuselage, too tired to argue with this smart-alecky young girl who was his only hope of living.

Kanzi squatted beside him. She handed him a big stick. "When rats come in, sit very still until they're close, then use this to kill him. They will make good food until your friends find you."

"You're coming back with them, aren't you?" Dylan asked.

Kanzi ignored his question. "Tell me what your friends look like."

Feeling as if he were going to pass out, Dylan kept pinching his eyes closed as he tried to describe each person. He ended by saying, "The boy that is my age is taller and thinner than me, and is called Quentin. He wears glasses and never quits talking."

"He's like you," Kanzi said. Then she corrected herself. "No, you don't wear glasses."

Before Kanzi left, she brought some big, soft leaves inside and showed them to Dylan. "Use these when you go poo poo. Other leaves can hurt you."

"Now you tell me," Dylan muttered.

"If you go outside, always stay where you can see the plane," she said. "If you're stupid again, Kanzi will let you die. The world doesn't need more foolish people." She turned and gave him a handful of marshmallow-sized betel nuts. "Chewing on these might help your pain, but spit out the juice." She pointed to a place where the twisted aluminum formed a trough halfway down the side of the bomber. "When it rains, good water drips here. Drink all you can. If it doesn't rain, you can drink the blood from rats."

As an afterthought, before crawling out the bottom of the fuselage, Kanzi turned and said, "Crocodiles and snakes don't come in here because of the rats. People don't come in here because there's bad spirits. So what are you, a rat?"

Dylan took one of the betel nuts and threw it at Kanzi but missed. "Looks like you've been here a couple of times, too," he said.

She giggled as she squirmed out the bottom of the fuselage. Dylan peeked out through a rip in the metal and saw her disappear like a shadow into the trees. Once more an eerie silence blanketed the bomber.

Dylan examined his new home. Even with the cobwebs, bones, rat droppings, and mud, it was still better than another night in the open jungle. He used his boots to clear a space on the floor between the two waist gunners' positions where he could lie down. This was way better than sleeping out in the open in the clearing beside the twisted tree. At least here he was somewhat protected. The bones gave him the creeps, and the rat smell made him want to throw up. But for the moment he was safe, and now somebody on the planet knew where he was — a small smart-alecky jungle girl who treated him like a child.

After Kanzi left, an overwhelming weariness came over Dylan. He had a sense that he would never leave this place walking. He would be carried out on a stretcher, either dead or alive. All day he fought sweats and chills and had horrible and bizarre hallucinations of falling off cliffs, being eaten very slowly by crocodiles, and running and running to get away from a bad spirit — he could never see the spirit's face. Dylan stared at the twisted metal and closed his eyes. Nothing mattered anymore — he would either live or die now. That was okay.

As dusk turned to night, the sky darkened and became inky black. The swamp awoke with a new sound in the distance, a yapping like wild dogs. Waves of chills came over Dylan, and without thinking, he unfolded the small American flag and pulled it over his chest. As he lay on his back, he stared at the openings in the wreck where faint hints of moonlight leaked in. He felt exhausted, but tonight it didn't matter if he had chills or sweats. It didn't matter if the thorns in his heel hurt, if he was hungry or thirsty, if his rash bled, or if his many insect bites itched or hurt. Nothing mattered anymore because somebody now knew where he was!

Sometime during the night it began to rain. The heavy drops beating on the fuselage sounded like the steady tattoo of a drum. Tossing back and forth in tortured sleep, Dylan imagined the loud hacking of a 50-caliber machine gun firing out the side of the bomber at an attacking fighter. The sound grew louder, and Dylan's nightmare continued. A sergeant woke him up. "Mission's on!" the man yelled, running toward the next barracks. Dylan knew his job. He was a waist gunner on a big B-17 bomber called *Night Rider*.

Today's mission was over Berlin. Almost seven hundred bombers were taking part. Dylan heard the rumble of the engines in the early-morning air, and he smelled the smoky exhaust of the big radial engines starting. He saw crew members praying fearfully. Others threw up behind the tires of their bombers before crawling aboard. They would be at high altitude, so everyone wore heavy flight suits, thick jackets, and pants made from leather lined with wool. Dylan felt the rough lumbering takeoff of the fully loaded bomber. As they approached enemy territory, the bomber climbed to 25,000 feet and Dylan put on his oxygen mask.

In the swamp, the rain beat harder on the outside of *Second Ace*, but what Dylan heard was the beginning of an attack. He heard the rapid firing of machine guns and the nose gunner's voice screaming over the intercom, "Bandits coming in at nine o'clock!"

Dylan rolled back and forth on the dirty floor of the wrecked *Second Ace*, mumbling "No, no, no." In his hallucinations he swung his 50-caliber machine gun around and began firing. His tracers squirted out of the barrel, carving long arching streaks across the sky. An enemy fighter flew directly at him, firing. Dylan fired back. Still the fighter kept coming, its guns blazing, ripping up the bomber. Dylan kept firing, but nothing stopped the fighter.

Lightning and thunder struck over the swamp, but all Dylan heard was explosions. He heard screaming and the vibration of other machine guns firing. Water from the storm leaked into the fuselage of the wrecked *Second Ace*, dripping on Dylan's legs where he was lying. Dylan felt the wet and looked down. An enemy round had exploded near him, leaving his legs numb and wet with blood.

Rats squeaked and squealed, scurrying from the swamp into the fuselage to escape the pouring rain that dripped through the openings, drenching the floor. All Dylan heard was the faint cries for help from other crew members who were also injured, dripping so much blood that the floor glistened. The bombardier yelled, "Bombs away!" and the B-17 banked to head for home.

The rain and lightning let up over the jungle, but Dylan's hallucination continued. With only one of the main gear down and two engines out, the B-17 limped home, then ground-looped on landing, bursting into flames as it slid down the runway. Somehow Dylan crawled from the burning wreck, and then sat in the grass and watched their B-17, *Night Rider*, erupt in flames. All of his friends and fellow crew members tried to escape, but the flames were too hot. All Dylan could do with his injured legs was sit beside the runway and watch his friends burn to death.

Was all of this worth the price? Had they helped to stop Hitler? The questions were like the clouds of smoke billowing out from the plane. They surrounded Dylan, choking his throat and tearing his eyes. He couldn't get his brain around them.

Dylan's nightmare continued in flashes of pain and emotion. An operation to remove his mangled legs. The grim satisfaction of learning to use a wheelchair.

Finally being sent home on the Fourth of July.

The mayor invited him to be in a parade. What a bittersweet honor, being pushed down Main Street in his wheelchair, an American flag draped over his missing legs. At least people would recognize his sacrifice.

Waving to the crowds, Dylan noticed that nobody was cheering or waving back. People were already laughing at the clown that traipsed along behind Dylan, blowing up skinny balloons. Children scrambled along the curbs to gather candy that had been thrown. A group of boys sitting on a brick wall in front of the library shouted and taunted Dylan.

"Hey, you old fossil, find a coffin that fits you!"

"Hey, gimp, why didn't you duck!"

Dylan wanted to run over to the boys and chew them out. He wanted to lecture them on respect, but he didn't even have legs to stand on. He couldn't even scratch his butt.

CHAPTER 16

As dawn broke, Dylan opened his eyes but couldn't remember where he was or what he was doing. All night, his hallucinations had been so real. Even as he sat up, he looked around, searching for the crew members and all the blood. What was real and what wasn't? He still wasn't sure. Nothing that had happened in the last week seemed real.

His muscles ached and cramped as he struggled to stand. Stumbling around, he stuffed some of the withered leaves Kanzi had given him for toilet paper into his pocket, then worked his way to the back of the fuselage. He squeezed carefully through the jagged opening in the tail. Bending at the waist like an old man, he hobbled away from the bomber to go to the bathroom.

Dylan squatted with his pants down and tried to relieve himself. For the first time, crouched in this awkward position, he had a chance to look around at the landscape outside *Second Ace*. This place was trying to kill him, but it also held a harsh beauty: giant gray clouds hanging like huge bellies from the sky as morning crept over the jungle; the tangled pattern of thick, woody vines overhead; heavy beards of moss and lichen hanging from branches; and the flaming colors and weird shapes of the flowers. Two feet away, a dragonfly landed on a leaf, its translucent wings and brilliant body shimmering in the light.

Thankfully, Dylan's diarrhea had cleared up, but the rash kept making him cry out in pain. The leaves had blood on them after he used them. It took every ounce of his strength to return to the bomber and crawl back inside. To keep conscious, Dylan picked up the American flag that had been his blanket. First he counted the stars again and again. Then he concentrated on folding it, making sure each crease was exact. It probably wasn't very respectful, but now, lying on the hard floor, surrounded by human bones and rat droppings, he used the folded flag as a pillow.

Dylan breathed deeply to stay conscious. Each time he fell asleep, it was harder to wake up. Soon he would simply fade away. Blinking his eyes forcefully, he stared up at the compressed top of the fuselage. What had the crash been like? How much had the crew suffered? The journal said that five crew members had lived through the actual crash, but three died during the first night. Dylan reached out and picked up one of the bones and stared at it hard. It would have been easy to ignore the bones if they were from some animal, but each one came from somebody's father or son. Did those crew members ever think they would end up as rat food in some jungle on the other side of the planet?

Other questions forced their way into Dylan's thoughts.

Had the families of these men, especially the children, ever imagined what their fathers had sacrificed? That they gave their lives so that others could be free? Growing up without fathers, what had the children thought? Did they blame their fathers for leaving home?

As his chills returned, a deep shame came over Dylan. He rolled the bone back and forth in his hands. It had been easy blaming his father for being away, saving somebody else's kids. Dylan realized now that he was wrong. His dad had known that freedom wasn't free. That was why he was reporting on the slaughter and genocide of innocent people in Darfur. It didn't have anything to do with how much he loved his family. Maybe, in a twisted way, it showed his love more. Maybe as he watched those poor people being butchered, it was his own wife and son that he saw. Maybe he couldn't just let their deaths go ignored.

Dylan carefully set the bone back on the floor as big, watery tears flooded his eyes. Why was he so stupid? Why did he have to be half dead, lying in a crashed bomber in the middle of some jungle, to realize this? Now it was probably too late. Even as he cried, Dylan felt himself drifting unconscious again. Try as he might, he couldn't keep the huge wave of numbness from pulling him under.

Once again his hallucinations returned, but this time it wasn't gruesome or terrifying. This time he dreamed a silly children's story of a little rabbit that left home and got lost. He got lost for so long that when he found home, it wasn't home anymore. He had grown so big and changed so much that he wasn't the same rabbit. Nobody even recognized him.

Dylan woke suddenly. A big rat had crawled up on his chest and sat watching him, its nose and whiskers twitching. Convulsing, Dylan swung his arm, sending the rat scurrying away.

Dylan's chills had morphed into profuse sweating. With the sun higher in the sky, the bomber had heated up like an oven. Dylan's sweaty shirt clung to his skin. The last image he remembered from his dream as he woke was the lost rabbit looking in a mirror. The image in the mirror had been his own, Dylan Barstow. What did that mean? Had he also changed? Dylan no longer knew who he was, but deep inside he felt different. Here he had energy and time for only one simple focus: survival.

As he lay flat on his back, his head resting on the folded American flag, Dylan drifted in and out of consciousness. Sweaty heat flashes and chills wracked his body. He could no longer stop the violent shaking. He looked down at his stomach and discovered two big black sausages hanging from the side of his stomach. It took several minutes to comprehend that he was looking at two new leeches. Somewhere in the swamp they had hitched a ride and clung to him, sucking his blood.

He wanted to brush them away but hesitated. In a stupor, Dylan stared at the leeches for a long while. Something deep inside kept him from trying to remove the bloodsucking sausages. Maybe he was too sick. Maybe he was tired of fighting the world. It didn't matter anymore. Nothing mattered anymore. Doing everything his way had almost killed him. Deliberately he turned his head and stared to the side.

Now Dylan felt as if he were swimming through the universe. First he passed too close to the sun and started burning up; then he shivered in the black empty cold of outer space. Next, he entered a black hole, the pressure so great it crushed his skull and vaporized every atom of his body. He became part of the universe, instead of being Dylan Barstow, major screw-up from Wisconsin.

Slowly at first, but then louder and louder, sounds echoed. How weird. There weren't supposed to be any sounds in outer space. Dylan heard shouting and screaming, and then movement, bumping and lifting and being rolled over. Then grunting.

"Hold him steady!"

"Move him slowly down."

"What's his temperature?"

"He's burning up."

"Okay, I have him."

"What's his pulse?"

"We have to move quickly."

"Keep him level!"

"Okay, Dylan, can you hear us? Dylan, wake up. Can you hear me?"

Dylan felt rain on his face but that wasn't right — there wasn't rain in outer space, and surely not in a black hole. Something pried his eyes open and held his head up to put fluid in his mouth. He coughed and choked on the fluid. Now his clothes were being removed. But if he was in space, that would be his space suit. Taking his space suit off would kill him, so Dylan tried to swing his arms and fight back. He couldn't let anybody take his space suit off.

Strong hands held him still. Something was being pried from his fingers. He couldn't fight against all the hands that gripped him. Why were they trying to kill him? What were they doing taking off his space suit? Then more voices sounded.

"Make sure his airway is clear."

"Hold his arm. We have to get some medication onboard for his malaria."

"How could he have gotten malaria?"

"Keep giving him fluids — he's dehydrated."

"Looks like a snake bit his ankle."

"What ripped the skin up so bad?"

"Looks like the jungle tried to kill him."

"Okay, somebody cover him with bug spray and suntan lotion — we need to get moving."

Then Dylan felt jostling motion. He wanted everything to be still again. He wanted to float again through space. Instead it was as if he were being dragged down a bumpy dirt road. He felt powerless, and every movement hurt. He tried to shout, but a huge hand pinched his throat. Another strong hand kept him from sitting up. He tried to open his eyes but they felt glued closed. Finally Dylan gave up and clenched his teeth to ward off the pounding pain. If this was what it felt like to die, he wanted to get it over with. But the end refused to come.

—

It seemed forever before the bumping and jostling finally subsided into stillness. Dylan lay unconscious in a pole house in Balo, never seeing the villagers' eyes peeking in at him during his heavy slumber. Ghostly voices whispered in the distance — different voices than those that whispered across the room.

Dylan woke once during the night, long enough to wonder where he was and what had happened. A slight breeze blew through the palm planks covering the walls.

Not until morning could he finally open his eyes and stare up at a ring of concerned faces: Uncle Todd, Quentin, Allen Jackson, Gene Cooper, a young, tired-looking woman from the village, and an odd old man. They all stood looking down at him. Dylan eyed the old man. His skin was wrinkled as a prune. His whole body had been rubbed with coals from a fire, making him all black except for his face, which was painted white. Painted with the shapes of a skull. A necklace of shells, dogs' teeth, and feathers hung from his neck. Bones hung from his stretched earlobes. Only a breechcloth of leaves covered his lower body, like a skirt, swishing each time he moved. Dylan stared at the strange man.

"Hey, how are you doing, trooper?" Uncle Todd asked, reaching down and placing the folded American flag on Dylan's chest. "We found you hugging this in the bomber."

Dylan ran his hand over the soft cloth. "Thanks," he said, his voice scratchy. "That was the flag Grandpa talked about in his journal."

"Hey, Dylan. We were worried about you," Quentin said.

Dylan wanted to close his eyes to escape the stares. "I screwed up," he mumbled.

"How you feeling?" Allen asked.

"Like a truck hit me," Dylan said.

The old man with the painted black body smiled at Dylan. "I must leave now," he said. He stooped and touched Dylan's forehead gently, then he walked to the ladder and began crawling down. Before his head disappeared, he called, "Good-bye, Deeeeloooon."

Dylan jerked his head up to look, but the man had disappeared. "Who was that guy? A witch doctor?" he blurted.

"He saved your life," Uncle Todd said. "He came and told our group where you were. Told us how he helped you find the bomber. Not sure we would have believed him except he knew the name *Second Ace* and he described you and the clothes you wore."

"I didn't meet that old man," Dylan said. "I've never seen him before."

Uncle Todd shook his head. "You must have. Maybe you were delirious. He said his name was Kanzi."

Dylan stared, wide-eyed, and shook his head. "No, no, no," he stammered. "Kanzi was a young girl, younger than me. She said she was from a village called Maswa."

Uncle Todd shook his head. "Kanzi was definitely that old man. He said he started a fire for you, fed you, and led you to *Second Ace*."

The young village woman put her hand on Uncle Todd's arm. She spoke quietly, with broken English. "No village called Maswa. *Maswa* means *dreams*. Kanzi, he be who he needs to be."

"What do you mean?" Gene Cooper asked.

"Many people come here for bad reason. Some look for airplanes to steal engines or take money from dead people. Kanzi sometimes kills people with bad reasons. Kanzi knows you come for good reasons. That is why he lets you live." She looked at Dylan. "Kanzi knows you have good heart."

Dylan shook his head. "I wasn't crazy. Kanzi was just a young girl. She bit on my ankle and made it bleed because of the snake poison. She started a fire and brought me food. I know she was real."

The young woman nodded, toying with the reed bag she carried. "Kanzi is a girl for you because you need a girl to help you."

Dylan bit his tongue — he didn't need any girl to help him! But even as the thought came to him, he knew he had needed Kanzi desperately. Maybe someone younger, with an innocent face and a sharp tongue to make him feel humble. That was exactly what he had needed.

The bashful woman turned to Gene Cooper. "You needed old man painted with black to help you believe." She raised her hands upward. "Maybe everything is real. Maybe nothing is real. Real is what we believe. We all believe different. I think today Kanzi comes to say good-bye to all of you."

Gene Cooper turned and stared at the pole ladder Kanzi had climbed down, then he turned back and spoke to Dylan. "Right now, you need a hospital. You were in rough shape last evening when we found you inside *Second Ace*, so we brought you here to Balo. If you're up for it, we'll carry you to Swagup today. Then we have a dugout canoe ready to take us back to Ambunti."

Uncle Todd stood nearby, unable to hide his worry and stress. When he spoke, his voice sounded angry. "If you're still alive, a plane will take you to Port Moresby, where we'll get you into a hospital until you can travel back to the US. We're not going to rush things. You've been through a lot."

Dylan looked up. "Thanks, everybody, for helping me," he said.

"While we get ready, you get more sleep," Gene said, motioning for the rest to leave.

Dylan panicked. "Somebody stay here," he pleaded.

"I'll stay," Quentin said.

"Is that okay?" Gene asked.

Dylan nodded. "I don't want to be alone."

As everybody left, Quentin sat down beside Dylan's pad on the hard floor. He adjusted the mosquito netting. "Man, we looked all over for you," he said. When Dylan didn't answer, Quentin kept talking. "Our guides had three villages searching. It was like you disappeared into nowhere. One second you were there, the next second you evaporated. I thought you had died or maybe some critter had gotten you. I was thinking that if you had —" Suddenly Quentin stopped. "I shouldn't be talking so much, should I? You need to sleep."

Dylan reached his hand toward Quentin until it touched the netting. "I don't ever want to be alone again in my life. Please keep talking," he said.

CHAPTER 17

When Dylan woke next, he was being lowered down the notched pole ladder, the same ladder the old man who had claimed to be Kanzi had crawled down. Dylan's body ached, and he felt drained of all energy. Carefully, Uncle Todd and Allen placed him on a rough stretcher they had fashioned from two poles and some canvas. Two men from the village had been hired to guide them and to help carry Dylan through the jungle and swamp to Swagup.

As they left, Dylan clenched his teeth against the constant jarring. It had rained most of the night, and each time one of the carriers brushed against a bush or a tree, a shower of water drenched the stretcher. Everybody took turns helping to carry Dylan, even Quentin. In the suffocating heat, sometimes they traded turns every hundred yards.

Dylan tried to take his mind off the jarring pain by looking up at the steaming jungle. He smelled the trees, the palms, the mosses, and the heavy, pungent odor of decay. For the first time, he noticed how the smells were stronger after rain. And he heard sounds in a way he had never noticed, the rustling in the underbrush, wind blowing through the jungle canopy, and birds and insects chorusing with a piercing harmony. The sounds were beautiful.

Suddenly, Dylan felt sick to his stomach and he turned sideways and threw up. He had never felt so rough in his life. Allen had put alcohol on the leeches to remove them, but the hot and cold flashes persisted. Dylan's insect bites and sunburn covered his body with boils and welts. The thorns in his heels had infected and oozed pus. His arms ached from gripping the stretcher poles. Worst was his ankle, which was still swollen from the snake bite. He could no longer put weight on that foot. Even lying on the stretcher, it ached.

Struggling to carry Dylan across a deep stretch of swamp, Allen Jackson lost his balance. Dylan found himself suddenly swimming to keep his head up. Uncle Todd helped Dylan back onto the stretcher. "Hang in there," he said, his words sounding more like a command than encouragement.

When Quentin took his next turn carrying the stretcher, he asked Dylan, "Why did you walk away from everybody?"

Dylan didn't want to think. "I was mad," he mumbled.

"Because of me?"

"No. Because of a lot of things, most of which had nothing to do with you. I didn't want to be here anymore."

Quentin breathed heavily. "Lots of times I don't get what I want, but I don't walk away into a jungle," he said.

"I was just being stupid," Dylan admitted.

Quentin was quiet for a moment. "Well, you found *Second Ace*," he said finally. "And you survived. I don't know what I would have done if I'd gotten lost. Freaked, probably. But you aren't a screw-up. At least I don't think so."

"Thanks," Dylan said, his voice shaking. He closed his eyes tightly. He felt hot and wet. "That means a lot, Quentin."

———

To keep Dylan from falling off, Uncle Todd and Gene Cooper wrapped a rope around the stretcher, tying Dylan to it. Each time the team traded turns carrying him, they took a short rest. During one rest, Dylan asked in a coarse whisper, "Did you guys get what you needed at the bomber?"

Gene shrugged. "We couldn't spend as much time at the wreckage as we would have liked, because we had to get you out of there. We were able to establish coordinates for finding it again. Quentin found two sets of dog tags, and we took a number of pictures that will help with recovery."

"What happens now?" Dylan asked.

"You get rest," Gene suggested.

"I won't rest until I get off this stretcher," Dylan said. "What happens now with *Second Ace?*"

"A U.S. Marines recovery team will come in. That team will be made up of forensic anthropologists, a communications officer, explosive disposal officers in case there are live bombs, and a whole slew of other experts."

"What happens to the bones?" Dylan asked.

"Everything they find will be taken to Hawaii for identification. Individual remains will be returned to their families. A separate memorial service will be held at the Tomb of the

Unknown Soldier in Arlington National Cemetery out in D.C. for the remains that can't be identified. That ceremony will honor and recognize the whole crew."

"It's too bad this didn't happen years ago," Dylan remarked. "Grandpa could have been there."

"It's hard finding wrecks in the jungle," Gene said. "The PNG government doesn't want them removed, saying they're a part of their country's history and could bring tourist money to the region. Local chieftains often think they're sacred because of the dead. For some crew members, the memories are too hard. And —" He shrugged. "Some people just don't care anymore." He looked at Dylan, who was still clutching the folded American flag. "Do you want me to put that flag in my backpack?"

"No," Dylan replied. "I'm going to be the one who takes it home. It belonged to Grandpa."

"What are you going to do with it?" Gene asked.

"Haven't decided yet," Dylan said.

"Whatever you do, I'm sure it would have made your grandfather proud."

Dylan grew silent. He hadn't made anybody proud with anything he had done. "There's so much stuff I didn't know," he said.

Gene gave him a curious look, allowed a guarded smile, and then nodded. "Okay, everybody, let's hit the trail again. Swagup isn't getting any closer."

By the time they reached Swagup, the setting sun cast long shadows. Everybody had reached the end of their endurance. Even holding the flag was now a struggle for Dylan. When they helped him from the stretcher, his leg gave out and he fell hard to the ground. His swollen ankle had doubled in size and pained him terribly. Huge beads of sweat dripped from Dylan's face, and his body burned with fever.

"You're in a bad way!" Gene exclaimed. "Let's get you lying down where I can check you over."

"I'll help," Quentin volunteered. He and his father helped Dylan up and carried him to the pole hut where they would all sleep that night. It took everybody to lift Dylan up the steep ladder to the main floor. Carefully Gene took Dylan's blood pressure and temperature, then examined every inch of his body.

Dylan rested, listening to everyone talk. Hearing voices again was sweet music. There were times in the jungle when he had thought he would never again hear another human voice. For a short time, Dylan passed out. When he awoke, he found the team gathered in one corner of the small hut, whispering to each other.

Dylan called out, "Hey, what's the big secret?"

"It's nothing," Allen said, turning. "Just planning tomorrow."

Dylan watched the family who owned the pole hut as they prepared the evening meal. He realized how kind and giving the villages of Papua New Guinea could be. He had come over here afraid of cannibals and headhunters, thinking everybody was backward and uncivilized. What he had found was kindness. They didn't have to help a stupid teenager from America. His life meant nothing to them. But again and again complete strangers had helped their team. During the last week, Dylan had come to feel that he was the one who was uncivilized. He was the one whose world was all screwed up.

Quentin interrupted Dylan's thoughts, bringing food. "Here, eat something," he pleaded. "You need to do everything you can to help your body recover."

"I'm already better," Dylan said.

"No you're not!" Quentin said forcefully, as if he knew something that Dylan didn't.

Reluctantly, Dylan forced down some cooked sago and salted fish. The rain water he drank in the jungle was better than the water here. This stuff had iodine from pills Allen Jackson added to kill germs and bacteria.

Villagers kept crawling up the ladder to peek at the white boy who almost died in the jungle — the one who had met Kanzi. By bedtime, Dylan felt really rough. The infection in his leg had grown worse. It hurt to even touch his ankle.

Before going to sleep, the team gathered around Dylan. He could tell from their faces that serious news was coming.

"Dylan, I'm sorry to have to tell you this, but you have bad gangrene in your leg," Gene said bluntly. "That means your cells are dying, and bacteria have begun to grow in the tissue. The hospital may have to amputate, or it could kill you."

"You mean cut my leg off?" Dylan exclaimed.

Gene nodded. "It all depends on how fast we can get you to Australia. Sydney will be your best chance now. Not Port Moresby."

"That's what you guys were whispering about," Dylan said.

Uncle Todd nodded, his expression grim.

Dylan's chest felt suddenly tight. The small hut seemed to press inward. He couldn't believe this. His eyes grew hot, and it took all his strength to hold back his tears. "This wouldn't have happened if Mom hadn't sent me to your place. It's all her fault!" he blurted.

Uncle Todd spoke sharply. "Don't you dare blame your mom or me or anyone else for what happened. You will never know how hard it was for your mother to call me for help. You're the one who pulled this dumb stunt in the jungle that almost killed you."

Dylan felt a sudden shame. This was the first time he had seen his uncle show real anger. He knew Uncle Todd was right, but he had wanted desperately to blame someone else. Being mad had always been easier than looking in the mirror. "I'm sorry," he said. "I didn't mean it that way."

Uncle Todd hesitated as if wanting to say something. Then he turned to leave. "We leave early to take a dugout down the Sepik to Ambunti. Get some sleep — you'll need it. Hopefully we can fly you direct from Ambunti to Port Moresby instead of going through Wewak. Your leg may depend on it."

Quentin remained beside Dylan's mosquito netting after the rest left. When the gas lantern was turned off, Quentin sat down on the floor. "Are you mad at me?" he whispered in the dark.

"No," Dylan whispered back. "What makes you think that?"

"I don't have any friends back home. Dad tells me I talk too much, and that I always act like I know everything. It's not like I know everything, but I do know a lot of stuff. Once a guy stopped me in a store and —"

"Your talking didn't give me gangrene in my leg," Dylan interrupted. "Not yet."

"A person couldn't get gangrene in their leg from talking unless you sat on that leg. Maybe then the leg could lose circulation and —"

"I was just joking," Dylan said. "Go get some sleep."

Quentin allowed a shallow laugh. "Uh, oh yeah, you were just joking." He stood and paused awkwardly in the dark. "I really hope you don't lose your leg."

"Thanks. I'll be okay." As Quentin turned to leave, Dylan whispered, "You helped save my life. Nobody would do that except a friend."

Dylan thought he heard a sniffle in the dark. "That's cool," Quentin said, disappearing into the darkness with a small flashlight he had turned on.

Dylan reached down and felt his ankle. It was hot, swollen, and numb as a post. He had a sick feeling inside as he stared up into the darkness. Already somebody snored loudly.

Dylan slept little all night, tossing back and forth, grimacing. Each time he rolled over, his ankle made him cry out with pain. Between the nausea, pain, fever, and chills, the dark night became a living hell.

When the team rose before daylight, Dylan felt numb with exhaustion. Once again he was lowered down the ladder and carried the short distance to the shore of the Sepik River. Gene insisted that he eat some fruit and cold fish left from the night before. They placed Dylan in the middle of a large dugout canoe, stretched out on the bottom where there would be the least movement. In minutes the outboard engine fired up and Dylan felt the boat being shoved out from shore.

Riding down the river was much easier than being carried on a stretcher. Occasionally they plowed across the wake of another boat, but mostly it was calm

"It's a race against time," Uncle Todd shouted to Dylan above the engine's steady drone. "We hired the fastest boat and paid him extra to keep her at full speed. We won't find out until we arrive in Ambunti if they were able to arrange a plane direct to Port Moresby. Pray they can!"

Dylan clenched his teeth against the constant pain and wondered if the ride would ever end. Every half hour, Uncle Todd leaned over and gave him water. After a time, Dylan lost the ability to focus on what was happening around him. Now he endured each second, holding on to his sanity as if clinging to the edge of a cliff. How much longer could he hold on? What would happen if he couldn't? What choice did he have?

When Dylan was certain the trip would never end, the boat slowed and motored ashore in Ambunti. Already, Allen Jackson was calling to somebody on the riverbank to check on the airplane. Dylan heard other voices, then Allen shouted, "Great. We'll have him there in fifteen minutes."

Again, the movement made Dylan grimace with pain, and once more, he threw up, this time mostly fluids. Uncle Todd stretched a mat out on the floor of a small van but it didn't soften the jarring as they bounced down the rough road, headed for the airport beside the river. All Dylan could do was pinch his eyes closed and moan. He knew everyone was trying to help him, but it was killing him. Why couldn't they just leave him alone to die? At least then the pain would end.

Gene spoke loudly to Dylan as they rushed toward the airport. "I'll get on the phone and see if I can arrange some pain meds in Port Moresby while you wait for the flight to Sydney."

Dylan answered with another grimace.

The ride was short. Soon, Dylan felt hands all over him, pulling and shoving and lifting to move him somewhere else. "This is going to be a bit uncomfortable," Allen Jackson said, helping to lift Dylan into a small Cessna aircraft. "There won't be room to lie down. You might be able to stretch your leg out some. See you in Sydney."

When the small plane took off, there was only room for the pilot, Uncle Todd, and Dylan. "We might make it over the top of the peaks today if this weather decides to hold," the Aussie pilot shouted at them as he banked the plane to the southwest.

Dylan opened his eyes to look out, but then bent forward, hugging his leg to drive away the pain and keep from throwing up.

"If you upchuck, you best be doing it into this bag," the pilot informed Dylan, handing him a barf bag.

Dylan wished he had been handed a body bag instead.

CHAPTER 18

Dylan remembered only portions of the next eight hours: bad turbulence flying over the Owen Stanley Mountains on the way to Port Moresby, clenching his teeth so hard his gums hurt, someone giving him a shot to ease the pain. There was another endless chartered flight to Sydney, followed by an ambulance ride with sirens and flashing lights. Dylan was carried into a hospital, where several nurses and a doctor examined him, then gave him another shot.

Then nothing again.

The next thing Dylan remembered, he woke up feeling drugged and fuzzy in a sunny, air-conditioned hospital room. All he had known for days was heat, mosquitoes, jungle, and pain. Now a television on the wall was broadcasting world news from CNN. He rested in a big, white, padded bed. All his pain had disappeared, and beside the bed sat Uncle Todd, looking tired and unshaven, with a grim stare.

"What happened?" Dylan asked.

"They operated last night," Uncle Todd said hoarsely.

Dylan looked down at his legs but couldn't tell if his leg was missing because of the bunched-up covers.

"What happened?" Dylan asked.

"They saved your life," Uncle Todd said, not offering to explain.

Dylan didn't like the tone of his uncle's voice. He looked down again and tried to wiggle his right foot but still couldn't feel movement. "Did they have to take my leg off?" he asked.

Uncle Todd hesitated. "They said you were very lucky. If it had been one day later, they would have amputated. The way it was, they had to remove a lot of dead tissue. You'll have a few scars and some recovery."

Dylan looked down and found the folded American flag from *Second Ace* still lying by his side. "Thanks for bringing that along," Dylan said.

"Don't thank me," Uncle Todd said. "You had a death grip on that thing until they put you under for surgery. What's so important about that flag?"

Dylan reached down and ran his fingers over the colored cloth, then shrugged. "Not sure — maybe because it was Grandpa's. I never even met him except at family reunions when I was really small. He was just this weird old man. I never dreamed of all the stuff he went through."

"That's the way all old people are," Uncle Todd said. "Someday, you'll be old and some young punk will look at you and think you're just an old fossil and it's darn sure going to burn your butt eight ways from Sunday. But you know what?"

Dylan hesitated, then mumbled weakly, "What?"

"You're going to be so old you won't be able to do anything about it except whiz in your pants because the nurse didn't get to you in time." Uncle Todd shrugged. "There's really only one thing you can do about the whole thing now."

"What's that?" Dylan asked.

"Treat old people with respect. Pay it forward. Then maybe, just maybe, someday when you're too old to hold back a fart, some young kid will respect you for who you are."

Big tears flooded Dylan's eyes. "I'm just a screw-up," he said, his voice close to breaking.

Uncle Todd smirked. "If life ended today, I'd probably agree with you. But it hasn't ended yet. For you, life is just beginning. Maybe this trip will screw your head on straight."

"It's too late. I'll be in eighth grade next year. You were probably at the top of your class and an Eagle Scout by my age."

Uncle Todd allowed a thin smile. "See, there you go again, feeling sorry for yourself and judging people without knowing the truth." He pointed at the wrinkles on his own neck. "These aren't wrinkles from growing old," he said. "These are stretch marks left from getting my own head screwed on straight. By the time I graduated from high school, I had a rap sheet twice as long as yours. Your grandfather had the judge give me a choice — either go to jail or join the military. That's when I joined the Marines."

"You didn't join 'cause you were patriotic?" Dylan asked.

Uncle Todd laughed. "I couldn't have cared less about this country. Everything was a joke, until Vietnam. I still have questions about that war, but I will tell you this: When you see death, you grow up real quick and start to think. When I came back from Vietnam, I felt like the whole country was in a fishbowl and I was the only one on the outside. No matter what I had done, no matter how many lives I had saved, no matter how brave I was or how many medals I'd earned, the country ignored me. They ignored me and all the other soldiers who fought."

Dylan twisted at a corner of the bedsheet. "Does Mom know what happened to me?"

"She had to give her permission for the operation. She's plenty worried, but knows there wasn't an amputation. She was . . ." Uncle Todd's face took on a pained expression. "She said she was going to fly out here immediately. I had to practically order her not to. You'll be here in the hospital a few more days, and then it's time to go home. When you're up to it, you need to call her."

"What can I tell her? That I screwed up again?"

"Tell her whatever you want. I do know this — she's never given up on you. You're the one I'm worried about. You've already given up on yourself."

———

Three times a day, nurses changed the dressing on Dylan's ankle. Twice a day, he took antibiotics, and this time he didn't spit out the medications. By the second night, he quit having hot and cold flashes. Slowly his insect bites faded. What the hospital couldn't treat were his troubled thoughts. Dylan hated closing his eyes, fearing he would wake up back in the jungle.

Gene, Allen, and Quentin stopped in when they arrived back in Sydney. They had little to say as they surrounded the hospital bed. Dylan felt like he had let everyone down. The whole month's trip had been changed now because of him. "I'm sorry for everything," he kept saying.

"Hey, you found *Second Ace*," Quentin reminded him again.

"You get well and let us know how you're doing," Allen Jackson said after being there only a few minutes.

"I'll call all of you," Dylan promised.

And then they left. The three planned on touring Australia for several weeks and returning to the US on their scheduled flight. By then, Dylan would be back in Wisconsin with his mother. Uncle Todd would be back in Oregon, no longer having to deal with his pain-in-the-butt nephew.

"Did you call your mom yet?" Uncle Todd asked each morning and evening when he visited the hospital.

"I'll call her soon," Dylan kept promising, still not knowing what to say.

Finally he summoned the courage. He made the call one evening with Uncle Todd sitting nearby and staring at him intently.

"Hello?" the distant voice answered.

"Hello, Mom, this is Dylan."

"How are you?" she asked, her voice guarded.

Dylan found it hard to talk. "I'm good," he said. "I can't wait to get home."

"The hospital says you'll be out in a couple of days, and then Todd said he's buying you a ticket home on Wednesday."

"I kind of screwed things up over here," Dylan said meekly.

There was deafening silence on the phone.

"I'm done being stupid," Dylan said.

"You always say that," she said.

"This time I mean it. I can't wait to tell you everything that happened."

"I'm sure you'll have quite a story," she said.

Dylan could tell from her voice that she still didn't believe him. What could he possibly do to convince her that he had changed?

"Mom," he said. "I know that Dad leaving wasn't because he didn't love us."

"He never quit loving us," she said. "But you've never believed that. Now I feel as if I've lost you both."

"You haven't lost me," Dylan said. "Not anymore."

She hesitated. "Listen, we'll talk when you get back." She spoke as if she wanted to end the phone call.

"Okay," Dylan said. "I'll see you." Suddenly, tears flooded his eyes. He took a deep breath. "And, Mom . . . I love y —"

Dylan heard a dial tone. Already she had hung up.

He slowly hung up as Uncle Todd eyed him closely.

"Mom said you're getting me a ticket home on Wednesday," Dylan choked.

Uncle Todd nodded.

"What are you going to do when we get back?" Dylan asked.

"I think I'll head back to Gresham the same day. I've got things to get done. I'll fly as far as Los Angeles with you."

"I know it costs extra, but can I go back to Oregon with you before going home? I'll earn the money and pay you back."

"Why?"

"I want to see Frank Bower again."

"What for?"

"I want to give him this flag." Dylan held up the American flag that he still kept by his side on the bed.

"I'll give that to him for you," Uncle Todd said.

Dylan shook his head. "No, I have to give it to him myself. It won't be the same otherwise."

Uncle Todd studied Dylan before answering. "Why you?"

"I'm done being stupid," Dylan insisted.

Uncle Todd turned in his chair to face Dylan. "You know, I almost thought you were sorry before, too. When you first met Frank and he told you his story, for half a second I thought you had learned something. But then you were right back to complaining, feeling sorry for yourself, and thinking you were the center of the universe."

Dylan blinked back his tears. "I think Mom still thinks the same thing. So what do I do? How can I change if you guys don't give me the chance?"

"You've had a hundred chances. Maybe you should start by being honest. Not just with other people, but with yourself."

"And how will you ever know if I have?" Dylan blurted.

Uncle Todd leaned back in his chair and gave Dylan a long, hard stare.

Dylan met his stare, but not with attitude. He just wanted Uncle Todd to know he was a man and didn't have to look down.

Suddenly Uncle Todd slapped the arm of the chair and stood. "Okay, I'll bite one more time. I'll make the ticket so you fly into Portland overnight before going home. Please don't make me sorry I trusted you."

———

Using crutches, Dylan left the hospital to spend their last night in Sydney at the hotel with Uncle Todd. Hobbling everywhere they went, Dylan looked around town a little, then they went out later for a big cheeseburger, fries, and a chocolate shake. Every bite made Dylan remember the grasshoppers he had eaten just to stay alive. Never in his life had a cheeseburger tasted so good. Uncle Todd let him order seconds. He ate until he was absolutely stuffed.

"What are you going to do with the rest of your summer?" Uncle Todd asked.

Dylan answered without hesitation. "I'm going to do whatever I can to help Mom out. She doesn't earn a lot, and I know she usually spends any extra money on me instead of herself." Dylan paused and added, "And I will pay you back the extra flight cost of stopping in Oregon."

Uncle Todd laughed. "Well, you're not even in eighth grade, so don't expect to be pulling in the big bucks mowing lawns. Don't worry, I'll take care of the extra airfare. Helping your mom sounds real good, but words are cheap. Let's see if it actually happens."

"It's as good as done," Dylan promised.

———

Dylan packed his backpack early the next morning. He was still taking his antibiotics and malaria medication, and would need to for some time. By mid-morning they had cleared customs and were in the air flying home. They flew on a Boeing 747, and the plane was huge. Dylan tried several times to start conversations, but Uncle Todd kept to himself, answering Dylan's questions with only "Yup" or "Nope."

No matter what Uncle Todd had said about one more chance, it was obvious he had already written Dylan off as a loser. "Will you go back to see *Second Ace* sometime?" Dylan asked, trying one more time to break the ice.

Uncle Todd just shrugged and said, "Who knows."

Dylan turned and stared out the window. "Who knows" was as bad as "whatever."

For Dylan, this trip to Papua New Guinea was like something out of a science fiction story. Less than two weeks ago, he had been flying from the United States, angry at the world, and never having met Allen, Gene, or Quentin. He hadn't cared about a B-17 bomber called *Second Ace*, and he had resented being with his uncle.

Now it felt as if he had been through some kind of time warp. All of his experiences in the jungles of PNG already seemed like a dream or an experience from another lifetime. Had it all been real? What puzzled Dylan most was when he looked in the mirror. Who was that baby-faced punk kid he was looking at? Was he just looking at someone who would go back to being angry and doing stupid things, blaming everything on everybody else?

Even Dylan didn't know that answer for sure.

CHAPTER 19

During the flight, Dylan's ankle ached. He swallowed the pills the doctor had given him to curb the pain, but they made him sleepy. He slept most of the way across the Pacific. When they landed in Los Angeles, he felt like a zombie. They had a two-hour layover before flying on to Portland. Still Uncle Todd gave Dylan the silent treatment, as if he were a criminal. Maybe going to Oregon before returning home was a mistake.

By the time they arrived in Portland, they had been flying most of the last twenty-four hours. Uncle Todd opened the front door to his condo in Gresham. It was almost dark. "When do you want to stop by the nursing home to see Frank Bower?" Uncle Todd asked. "Tonight? Or tomorrow before I take you to the airport?"

Dylan yawned hard. "After we get some sleep."

"Whatever you want," Uncle Todd said. "That's what you usually do."

Dylan knew his Uncle Todd had every reason in the world for not trusting him, but he wanted to explain that he had changed, and not just a little. He really did feel differently now about the world, and himself. But starting a conversation now would be like trying to light a match to look inside a powder keg. "How about tomorrow morning?" Dylan suggested.

"I said whatever you want," Uncle Todd repeated, heading for his room. "As long as it's early enough to get you to the airport."

Still carrying his backpack and using his crutches, Dylan hobbled up the stairs to his room. As much as he had hated Uncle Todd's constant lectures before they left, now it bugged him even worse to get the silent treatment.

Dylan lay on the bed with clean sheets and no mosquitoes, listening to the many noises from the street. A car drove past with a radio blasting. Dylan didn't like loud sounds anymore, but he understood them. Each sound he heard tonight he could place in his brain neatly and explain it. But then he remembered the jungle, lying under the damp moss, mosquitoes so thick he choked on them, suffering through sweats and chills, and hearing strange growls and screeches in the underbrush. Alone.

Dylan felt as if he had a stranger's brain in his head. Who was it that was really lying here awake in the guest room of Uncle Todd's small yellow condo? Before leaving the US, Dylan had needed to be in control. The angrier he became, the more he blamed others. The bigger the chip on his shoulder, the more attitude he projected. The more other people tried to help him, the more he laughed in their faces. But in the jungle, that control had disappeared. The more attitude he displayed, the more the world slammed him and tried to kill him.

So now who was Dylan Barstow? What did he want to do? How would he act tomorrow morning when the sun came up? There had been something safe about carrying an attitude around. Dylan had loved the disgusted looks from adults when he wore his pants low. He felt in control when he thumbed his nose in someone's face. Whenever he dismissed someone's thoughts with a "whatever," it did mean he didn't care how people felt or what people did. If he was always angry, he didn't have to look in the mirror and take responsibility. He had always been the center of the universe. Dylan Barstow's universe.

But now he felt like a fish that had been dumped from its fishbowl. Suddenly Dylan had discovered a world that wasn't so simple — so small. No longer did things look so wonderful back inside the little protected world he had created for himself in Wisconsin. Dylan wondered what would happen if he quit thinking only of himself? What if he quit blaming his father for dying? What if he were to be respectful? Take the risk of being hurt again? Give up his attitude? Give up control? Then what?

It would be like a fighter exposing his bare chest. People could make fun of him because he cared. People could hurt him. Friends might tease him. Not that he had any real friends — just other kids protecting themselves.

Dylan clenched his fists under the covers. Dad had shown him many pictures of villagers crowding around the trucks where aid workers were handing out food. To Dylan, the people had seemed like animals, climbing over each other's backs, shoving and pushing, fighting for little scraps of anything. He had blamed them and everybody else in the whole world for taking his father away. Dad's death had hurt so very much.

But now Dylan remembered crawling through grass in the swamps on his hands and knees, stuffing grasshoppers in his mouth and squeezing muddy water out of his shirt to drink. It was no different, except in the swamps there had been nobody to even offer help. Dylan also knew that the people who crowded the trucks in Darfur were victims. They had been born in Sudan. They didn't deserve the cruel genocide that was killing them. They hadn't done anything to cause their starvation. It hadn't been their fault!

That's what made Dylan ashamed now. He hadn't caused Dad's death. But neither had everybody else he blamed. It had been an accident. Still he had blamed Dad for dying. He had used that as an excuse for breaking into the junkyard and skipping school. He had picked fights at school and stolen things. He was the one who spit out the malaria pills and walked away from the safety of their group in the jungle. Everything had been his fault. He could blame others, but that would be lying to himself.

One feeling overwhelmed Dylan. It was the same feeling

he had felt lying half dead under the screw tree covered with moss in the middle of the jungle. Overwhelming loneliness. Nobody knew his feelings. And nobody probably cared anymore. Dylan's eyes watered. He wanted to run downstairs and wake Uncle Todd up and say, "Hey, look at all the things I'm thinking. I'm not stupid. I'm really sorry. I don't always have to protect myself with attitude. Please, give me just one more chance."

But even as he swung his feet to the floor, he heard his uncle's muffled snoring downstairs. Dylan crawled back under the covers.

▬

A heavy drizzle fell as Dylan woke and heard his uncle moving around downstairs. It took a couple of seconds to remember where he was. He would never have admitted it, but he missed his uncle's "Wakee wakee wakee!"

Dylan sat up and slowly unwrapped the gauze from his ankle. The doctor had said if there wasn't any infection or drainage, it would be okay to remove the bandages after getting home. He said it would be better for the skin to get air.

Dylan dressed and used only one of his crutches to get down the stairs. His ankle felt much better. "Good morning," he said, trying to sound cheery as he entered the kitchen.

"Good morning," Uncle Todd said, picking up a newspaper to start reading. "There's food in the refrigerator if you want breakfast." His voice was matter-of-fact.

"Do you want some, too?" Dylan asked.

"I've already eaten," Uncle Todd said and kept reading.

Dylan fried himself a couple of eggs, not because he was hungry, but because he wanted to prove to Uncle Todd that he wasn't this spoiled punk kid who couldn't do anything for himself. But it didn't make any difference. Uncle Todd never said a single word or looked up once from his newspaper.

When Dylan finished eating, he hurried upstairs to get his luggage and to get the flag, then came back down and asked, "Can we go see Frank Bower now on the way to the airport?"

"You might want to call him first," Uncle Todd commented.

"I want to surprise him."

"*Whatever* you want," Uncle Todd said.

Dylan *wanted* to scream. It was as if Uncle Todd had totally written him off. "You don't even care if I give this flag to Frank Bower, do you?" Dylan said, his voice accusing.

Uncle Todd turned to face Dylan. "I care. I just don't like doing anything on this planet that wastes my time," he said. "Babysitting a spoiled kid who can't take a crap without thinking the world owes him toilet paper is wasting my time."

———

The drizzle had turned to rain as they drove to the Garden Acres Rest Home. It wasn't much fun riding in the '62 Corvette with Uncle Todd in a bad mood, not speaking.

"You want me to wait in the car?" Uncle Todd asked, pulling to a stop outside the sprawling brick rest home.

"Can you come in with me?" Dylan asked.

"Whatever you want," Uncle Todd said, crawling out.

Dylan stood in the rain, holding the American flag from *Second Ace*. He looked across the top of the Corvette at his uncle. "Why don't you just say 'whatever'?!" he shouted. "That's what you mean. Now you're the one saying 'screw you'! You're the one telling me my words don't count! You're the one not showing me respect."

"Maybe because I'm still not sure you deserve respect!" Uncle Todd shot back.

"You'll never know!" yelled Dylan. "Not if you don't give me another chance." When Uncle Todd didn't answer, Dylan shouted again, "Is that it, then? I'm a screw-up, so good-bye and don't ever come back? Adios!"

Uncle Todd looked back at Dylan. Ignoring the rain that had become a downpour, he pointed his finger at Dylan and shouted, "Do you know what it would have been like to call my brother's widow and say, 'I'm sorry, but I got your son killed!'? I never slept one minute until we found you. You were my responsibility, and I failed! I won't be making that mistake again. Go kill yourself on your own time!"

Thunder rumbled across the sky.

Dylan glared back at his uncle and saw a deep hurt in his eyes. He realized how much Uncle Todd must have cared. But now it was too late. Fighting back his tears, Dylan turned and limped without crutches across the parking lot through the deluge of rain. He tried to protect the flag under his arm.

Uncle Todd followed.

"You sure picked a rainy day to visit," said the receptionist as they entered the front door, drenched.

"Can you tell me where to find Frank Bower?" Dylan asked.

The receptionist pointed down the hall. "Go ask at the nurses' station. I'm new and can't keep the patients straight."

With Uncle Todd following, Dylan limped down the hallway, stepping around several old people with walkers or in wheelchairs. He recognized the red-haired nurse at the nurse's station. "We came to see Frank Bower again," Dylan announced. "Can you tell me where he's at?"

The nurse recognized them, too, and hesitated. "Are you family?"

"No, I just wanted to give him this." Dylan held up the flag.

The nurse looked at Dylan and at the flag. "I probably shouldn't be telling you this if you're not family, but Frank died last Thursday. He had a heart attack. Died in his sleep."

Dylan stood, stunned. "Died?" he said. "I just talked with him two weeks ago."

The nurse nodded. "He was quite a guy."

Dylan spoke, almost frantically. "Did you know he was a waist gunner during the war? He flew twenty-five missions and belonged to the Lucky Bast —"

"I'm sorry to interrupt you," said the nurse, coming from behind the counter. "But we're two aides short this morning so I'm alone on the floor. Is there anything else I can help you with?" She started down the hallway, not waiting for an answer.

Dylan shook his head as he watched her disappear. "No," he whispered. "You can't help me. Nobody can anymore."

CHAPTER 20

Dylan hung his head for a moment. Frank Bower being dead was the last straw. Somehow holding on to the American flag and bringing it back to the US for Frank had been a mission of sorts. Dylan knew he had screwed up everything else, but that was the one single thing he had planned on doing that was right. And now he couldn't even do that.

"Are you satisfied now?" Uncle Todd asked.

Dylan grew suddenly angry. "No, I'm not satisfied," he shot back. "This isn't about me being satisfied. You can be mad at me, and you have every reason to be. But now you're being a jerk. I thought that was my job."

For a moment, Uncle Todd looked like he was going to blow up. His face twitched and a vein stood out on his neck. But then he motioned and started toward the front door. "Let's get out of here."

Dylan was turning to follow when he heard a loud grunt from a side hallway. "Help, please help!" cried a weak voice.

Without thinking, Dylan ran down the hall. Again the desperate voice sounded. Dylan discovered an old man with silver hair lying on the floor inside his room beside the toilet, his pants still down. His wheelchair lay beside him. It looked like he'd been trying to go to the bathroom and had fallen while swinging himself onto the toilet. He grimaced.

Dylan ran to his side. "Are you okay?" he asked.

"No, dang it, I'm not okay. My wheelchair got away from me. I have my pants down and I'm lying on the floor. A person ain't okay when they're like that."

Dylan set the folded flag on the dresser and grabbed the man under his arms. His frail body felt like a skeleton as Dylan lifted him onto the toilet.

"I'm already done crapping," the man scolded. "I need to get back in my wheelchair."

Obediently, Dylan set the wheelchair upright. Once more he lifted the old man and swung him into his chair. With each move, it felt like the old man's bones would break. "Are you okay now?" Dylan asked.

"You're never okay when you're my age," the man said. "But I'm as good as it gets."

"Need anything else?" Dylan asked.

"Yeah, a young body like yours and a cuter nurse."

Dylan smiled. "Well, I gotta go." He was turning to leave when he spotted a small medal pin on the headrest of the old man's wheelchair. It was a VFW pin. "Were you in the military?" Dylan asked.

"Guess I was," the old man said. "Ever heard of the Bataan Death March?"

Dylan shook his head.

The old man pointed a finger at Dylan. "I have some family coming to see me this morning, but come back this afternoon and I'll tell you what I went through. Compared to the Death March, going to hell would have been a vacation."

"I have to go to the airport," Dylan explained. He looked at the man in his wheelchair and then picked up the folded flag off the dresser. "But can I give you this?"

The old man reached out his bony hand. His fingers trembled as he ran them across the red, white and blue cloth. A pained expression crossed his face. "A lot of soldiers went through hell to protect that old flag."

"Can I give it to you?" Dylan asked again. "I found it in a B-17 bomber in Papua New Guinea. My grandfather had it."

The old man pulled his hand back from the flag, then shook his head sadly. "No," he said. "That flag don't need to be in no skunk-hole place like this sitting on some old fossil's dresser. You find a better place."

"You're not an old fossil," Dylan blurted. He had come to hate that word.

"If you say so," the old man said.

"I say so," Dylan said. "What's your name?"

"John Taylor. And what's yours?"

"Dylan Barstow."

The old man nodded and extended his hand. "Glad to meet you, Dylan Barstow. You sure are a fine young man. I'll bet your parents are proud of you."

Dylan shook the old man's hand but ignored the comment. "I'm glad to meet you, too, John Taylor. I might not know anything about this Death March, but I do know one thing I learned getting that flag."

"What was that, son?"

"Freedom is never free."

John Taylor trembled as he spoke. "No, it sure ain't, son. It's never free."

Dylan turned and discovered Uncle Todd standing in the doorway watching all that had gone on. "Maybe you should come back this afternoon and hear about the Bataan Death March," Uncle Todd said.

"I have to catch the plane," Dylan said.

Uncle Todd shrugged. "Your mom might understand if you wanted to stay one more day, but that's up to you," he said. "You think about it."

"But I thought you were mad at me."

"I am. But maybe this is more important."

Dylan allowed a smile. "I would love to hear about the Death March," he told John Taylor. "I'll call Mom and tell her why I'm staying one more day. I do need to get home — I'm missing her."

"Ready to go?" Uncle Todd asked, his voice softer.

Dylan nodded. "I guess."

Without speaking, they ran through the pouring rain to the parking lot, rushing to crawl into the Corvette. Dylan gripped the folded flag and looked out the side window in silence. Big raindrops ran down the glass like tears. Dylan blinked, but the raindrops continued.

Again, neither of them spoke as Uncle Todd drove from the parking lot. They were halfway home when suddenly Uncle Todd pulled the Corvette over to the side of the road.

"Is something wrong?" Dylan asked.

The rain had let up, but a light drizzle still misted the air as Uncle Todd eyed Dylan. "That's what I'm trying to decide." He continued staring. Finally a soft smile melted his intense expression. He looked out at the gray, drizzly sky. "It's a great day for drifting a Corvette. Do you think you can do it at fifty miles per hour?"

"But you think I'm a screw-up."

Uncle Todd shook his head. "I would never let a screw-up even touch my Corvette!"

THE END

EPILOGUE

Five months after the discovery of the B-17 bomber *Second Ace*, a Marine task force completed its investigation and recovery of remains from the wreckage. Because many remains could not be identified, an official full-dress ceremony was held at the Tomb of the Unknown Soldier in Arlington National Cemetery. As the individual who officially discovered the wreckage, Dylan Barstow was invited to present a wreath at the tomb.

On a blustery winter's day, an honor guard gave a twenty-one-gun salute. The ceremony was witnessed by relatives of the lost crew. Also among the small group stood one very proud mother, as well as the other members of the search team, Gene and Quentin Cooper, Todd Barstow, and Allen Jackson. They all watched as Dylan Barstow walked solemnly to an easel placed in front of the tomb. There he hung a green spruce wreath woven with nine roses — the number of crew members who perished on a stormy day back in 1943 in a swamp in Papua New Guinea.

When the wreath had been hung, Dylan reached inside his jacket and removed a folded American flag. He paused for a moment to touch the cloth one last time and to remember how the flag had come into his possession. Then he rested the flag gently on the wreath. "Thanks, Grandpa," he whispered. "Thanks, Dad," he added. He paused one more time. "And thanks, Kanzi, whoever you are."

Before leaving the grave, Dylan knelt and placed a simple note on the marble tomb. The note was written in the messy handwriting of a young teenager. It said simply,

Freedom is never free!

For the record, not that it mattered anymore, but Dylan Barstow's pants hung down a little bit that day only because it was more comfortable.

AUTHOR'S NOTE

I must say that during the writing of each of my novels, it is not me who creates and changes the story as much as it is the story that changes me. I was well aware of many of the historical facts of the Second World War, but after hearing the personal accounts of bravery during my research for *Jungle of Bones*, I was humbled to tears. The adage that "freedom is never free" became more than simple words. Those words became very real and not only imprinted themselves on my mind but are now chiseled like stone in my heart.

Ben Mikaelsen

ABOUT THE AUTHOR

Ben Mikaelsen is the winner of the International Reading Association Award and the Western Writer's Golden Spur Award. His novels have been nominated for and have won many state Readers' Choice awards. These novels include *Rescue Josh McGuire*, *Sparrow Hawk Red*, *Stranded*, *Countdown*, *Petey*, *Touching Spirit Bear*, *Red Midnight*, *Tree Girl*, and *Ghost of Spirit Bear*. Ben is known for his in-depth research and the magical worlds he creates. This research has taken him around the world from the North Pole to Africa. He has made over 1,000 parachute jumps, boated the length of the Mississippi, cycled in nearly every state, lived with the homeless in Mexico, raced sled dogs, and ridden a horse from Minnesota to Oregon. Ben lives in a log cabin near Bozeman, Montana, with his wife, Connie. For twenty-six years he raised a 750-pound black bear, Buffy, that he saved from a research facility. Visit Ben online at www.benmikaelsen.com.